Tiger Lilies

Also by Judith Glover:

The Stallion Man
Sisters and Brothers
The Imagination of the Heart

TIGER LILIES

Judith Glover

St. Martin's Press
New York

Library of Congress Cataloging-in-Publication Data

Glover, Judith.
    Tiger lilies / Judith Glover.
        p.   cm.
    ISBN 0-312-05977-9
    I. Title.
PR6057.L64T5   1991
823'.914—dc20   90-27885
                                                              CIP

First published in Great Britain by Hodder and Stoughton.

First U.S. Edition: June 1991
10 9 8 7 6 5 4 3 2 1

When two mouths, thirsty each for each, find slaking,
And agony's forgot, and hushed the crying
Of credulous hearts, in heaven – such are but taking
Their own poor dreams within their arms, and lying
Each in his lonely night, each with a ghost.

Rupert Brooke
from 'Love'

Tiger Lilies

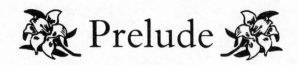 Prelude

Flora would always remember the first time she set eyes on Roseen O'Connor. It was 1905, and she was ten years old, and her father had taken her out for an afternoon drive in the trap. Usually they would go somewhere in the country around Wolverhampton; but on this occasion Papa drove right into town to an area Flora had never visited before, a poor area full of shabby little terrace houses and narrow back alleys darkened by the spilled shadows of factory chimneys.

He stopped the trap at the end of somewhere called Raby Street, and telling Flora he'd only be gone a minute went in at the door of a house opposite. While she waited she noticed a child was watching her from the open upper window, leaning forward with arms folded on the sill: a girl of about her own age, with red-gold hair falling in corkscrew curls about the tiny shoulders, and a small face that would have been pretty if its expression were not so sullenly hostile.

They stared at one another.

Remembering her manners, Flora offered a polite smile, to which the other responded instantly by crossing her eyes and poking out her tongue.

Then Papa came out from the house again, wiping his mouth on his handkerchief, and as he climbed into the trap he looked up at the window and waved. The child there waved back to him, all trace of hostility transformed into a sudden dazzling flash of eagerness and pleasure as she hung forward over the sill.

"Who's that little girl?" Flora had wanted to know when they were driving off.

7

"Oh – one of the tenants' young 'uns," her father replied. Then, somewhat oddly, "You won't mention any o' this to your mother, will you, our Flora. She doesn't like me doing the rent-collecting myself. Not now I employ a man to do it for me. She thinks it's lowering."

It was the first time he had asked her to keep something secret from her Mama, and because she was a dutiful child she obeyed; but when later at tea he'd said in a casual fashion, "We enjoyed that little drive out in the country, didn't we, love," she had felt uncomfortable, as though caught telling a lie.

And because the girl with the red-gold hair lived at the house where Papa had called, she too became part of the deceit.

*

George Dennison was a self-made man. Twenty years ago an uncle had left him a small grocery shop at Bradmore on the outskirts of the Midlands town of Wolverhampton. He'd had the enterprise and ambition to work hard, and the foresight to marry into money, and now there were some half a dozen Dennison's Stores patronised by the more discerning class of customer, and a fine house at Stockwell End in a part of town much favoured by the gentry.

The fact that he was Trade intruding himself into this rarefied social stratum had worried George Dennison not a bit. He was a man who, as he put it, held 'no truck' with those who looked down their noses at his background when they had, some of them, hardly two ha'pennies of their own to rub together; and it was a matter of some personal pride to him that his accent was Black Country not county, and his prosperity a reflection of his own business worth and application.

Indeed he could afford his pride: his house was the show-piece of the neighbourhood, his wife and daughter most handsomely turned out, and his domestic staff a byword for civility and smartness.

There was only one cloud to blight the horizon. After the birth of young Flora in 1895 his wife had been unable to bear him further children, thus denying Mr Dennison a son to

8

inherit his business. Not only that, but her barrenness had denied him his conjugal rights too, since Maud saw no purpose in their continuing to share the same bed when his physical attentions were so patently a waste of time and effort.

As a consequence of this, Mr Dennison had perforce sought elsewhere for his satisfaction, and for the past four years had been keeping a mistress in one of the properties he owned in the central area of Wolverhampton.

He'd first made the acquaintance of 'Connie' O'Connor early in 1901. It was the week of old Queen Victoria's funeral and a cold, raw January day with an ice-honed wind cutting to the flesh. He'd been up to Raby Street to collect the rents from his tenants, and fancying a brandy to chase away the chill, called in at the White Rose public house before driving back to Stockwell End.

A handsome, red-haired woman was leaning against the bar-room piano, humming a tune to the player who was doing his best to pick it out on the keys. She was tall and well-built with a good bosom set off by a tightly-corseted waistline, emphasising her fashionable hour-glass figure; and something in the way she stood, one hand on her hip and her head tilted a little sideways, made George Dennison look at her twice.

She caught his eye, and seeing his interest, gave a slight smile which seemed to ask, 'Hello, who are you?' and leaving the pianist, sauntered across to the counter. Without glancing again at Mr Dennison she'd said to the barman, "Give us another port and lemon, Jack."

"Perhaps I can buy it for you?" He had already decided she wasn't the type of woman who would take offence at his invitation.

Resting an elbow on the counter she turned to look at him and smiled again, her heavy-lidded eyes holding an indolent expression. "Sure, but 'tis kind of you to offer." The voice was throaty and warm, laced with an Irish brogue.

"A port and lemon, was it?"

"It was."

Mr Dennison gave the barman the order, with another brandy for himself.

"We've not met before," the woman said, her glance sliding

9

from the neatly-clipped moustache and well-groomed hair to the Chesterfield overcoat, unbuttoned to reveal the swag of a gold watch-chain. "D'you not come in here often?"

"No, not often."

"Ah." She took up her glass and raised it. "Well – here's luck to you, sir."

"And to you." His own glass saluted her in turn. "Happy days."

There was a pause while she drank, then, "D'you have a name I might call you?"

He rolled the brandy round his tongue and swallowed it. "George."

"George. And is that all?"

"George will do."

It was plain she didn't know him from Adam, but even so, best to play safe. He didn't want her connecting him with Dennison's Stores.

"George it is, then." She took another sip of her port and lemon, and put the glass aside on the counter. "I'm Connie. That's what they call me – on account o' being an O'Connor, d'you see. 'Twas my late husband's name, God rest him."

A sideways look accompanied this pinch of information to see whether the fact of her husband's death had been registered.

It had.

"You're a widow, then?"

"Aye. I am that."

George Dennison tossed back the rest of his brandy.

"Well, Connie. Perhaps you'll be here if I call by again next week?"

"I might be."

She watched him button his overcoat, her expression betraying a touch of pique that he was going so soon.

"Good. I'll buy you another drink, then, when I see you."

He had left things at that, not sure whether he'd go back to the White Rose or not. There were women like Connie in almost every public house in the town, looking for company, accepting the familiarity of strangers; only a step or two away from selling themselves on the streets.

Something about her, though, some promise of sensuality in the sway of her hips and the sidelong glance of those heavy-lidded eyes, had kept her there in his thoughts; and about a fortnight later he had stopped by again and treated her to the drink he'd promised – several of them – and learned some of the details of her history. It was the usual story. The late Mr O'Connor had been a drunkard and a wastrel and had left her virtually penniless when he'd inconsiderately fallen headlong under a tramcar the year before.

Thrown out of their lodgings, she had gone to stay at various addresses while she looked for work around the town; but things hadn't been easy on account of the child.

The revelation that there was a child in the background had tended to cool George Dennison's interest, and he didn't bother going back again for almost another two months after that.

Then, driving by the White Rose one afternoon in March, he'd passed Connie leaning against the wall in the sunlight with a little girl at her side; and the sight of that child had turned his heart over.

She was about the same age as his own daughter Flora, but daintier and more finely-boned, and with a face that would have charmed the angels out of heaven. Pretty – ! In all his life he'd never seen prettiness to match it. And her hair – well, what could one say about hair like that. Not a coarse, russet-red like her mother's, but shining golden-copper set in a halo of curls round the delicate features.

He had pulled up a moment to speak, and then driven on, thinking of Flora, well-nourished and warm at Stockwell End, wrapped safe and secure in the comfortable luxury of a privileged childhood; and he compared that with the life facing this little mite, the poverty and the ignorance and the cheap, paltry standards which stripped away so much of human dignity.

Mr Dennison was by no stretch of the imagination a philanthropist, but he'd experienced a feeling of pity at the senseless waste of it all; and with the pity, too, a kind of protective benevolence as though some voice at his ear were saying, 'Look, you've got the money, George, you could do a lot for this little 'un, keep an eye on her, give her a good start, see she gets the chance to make some'at worthwhile of her life.'

The child's mother was only a secondary consideration. But as things turned out the proposition he'd put to Connie over a drink some days later in the White Rose had proved a beneficial arrangement for both of them. Within a week she was given the tenancy of one of his properties in Raby Street – nothing fancy, a two-up and two-down terrace house with communal lavatory, but rent-free and furnished – and by the summer of that year their sexual intimacy had developed into a permanent relationship of lover and kept mistress.

★

All that was four years ago.

Time passed.

By 1905 Connie had started drinking more. Not much; but being able to afford the gin she'd soon acquired a taste for it, a taste which was slipping ever so surely towards an addiction. She herself blamed her 'little weakness' on boredom and loneliness. George Dennison visited her as a rule twice a week, and always during the day (only once had he stopped overnight at Raby Street, and that was when his wife Maud had taken Flora to a relative's funeral in Newbury).

Left so much to her own devices in the evenings, Connie found a glass or two of gin helped to pass the time. Mr Dennison didn't like her going out by herself at night, especially to her old haunts round the local public houses. Now that she'd got him to look after her, he wanted her to keep herself to herself more, he said, and not go swanning about quite so much. Besides – and here he'd really put his foot down – he didn't want young Roseen being left alone in the house.

So Connie stayed in with a bottle of gin for company, prinking herself in the gaslight in front of the kitchen mirror while the evening hours stretched slowly towards a solitary bedtime.

For Roseen life had changed even more. A child of strong passions, she utterly adored her 'Uncle George' who treated her like a little princess and was for ever bringing her presents – she was the best-dressed youngster in Raby Street, and the

12

most popular too, with so many toys to share. The settled domestic background of the past four years had done a good deal to banish the insecurity of her earlier infancy, a period now only vaguely remembered as full of strange voices and faces and rooms, and cold, dark streets, and hunger.

Since her sixth birthday she'd been a pupil at the Roman Catholic school of St Mary and St John just down the road. She enjoyed it there, and was good at her lessons. Her only grievance was that her mother was seldom up early enough of a Sunday to take her to Mass, so that she had to go with the Kavanaghs across the way, who had snotty noses and wet their drawers; and her only sorrow, that her Uncle George had not been present to see her make her First Communion.

Roseen was not a religious child, but she relished being the centre of attention, and never more so than in church where the nuns ooh'd and ah'd over her and said what a darling little angel she looked. And indeed she *had* looked an angel that day. It was June 25th, 1905 and she wore a new white frock with satin trimmings, white net gloves, white kid-leather boots, and a circlet of silk lilies of the valley with a white lace veil covering her hair to her shoulders.

Kneeling at the altar rail to receive her First Communion wafer from Father Doran, she had composed her face into its sweetest expression, placed her hands together palm to palm, and closed her eyes. This was how she imagined God wished her to look – very beautiful and holy – and she wanted everyone in the church to notice her, especially Uncle George.

Her temper when she discovered his absence was truly fearsome. She had wept tears of rage all the way back to Raby Street, and once in the house, sat in the middle of the kitchen floor and screamed until she was sick down her white Communion frock. It was no use Connie telling her Uncle George couldn't come because it was his own little girl's birthday tea-party that afternoon, and anyway, he wasn't a Catholic. Roseen hated him. *Hated* him. She would never *ever* speak to him again. And she hoped his little girl would get pox scabs all over her face, like Tommy Kavanagh.

The rage had soon blown itself out. Roseen's tantrums, though violent, seldom lasted. True, she was inclined to be distant with Mr Dennison when he called next day; but the sight of the gift he'd brought to make up for his absence – a French china-headed doll which cried 'Mama' when tilted and had glass eyes which opened and shut – had brought instant forgiveness and reconciliation.

★

He had purchased an identical doll as a birthday present for young Flora; which, in its way, said much about his attitude towards these two children, one his own flesh and blood, the other the daughter of his Irish mistress. Perhaps the reason he loved them both equally, though differently, was that they were so entirely unalike: Flora very quiet and grave, a chubby, plain, sweet-natured little girl; Roseen impetuous, passionate, high-spirited, full of life and vivacity, always demanding attention. Like negative and positive, black and white, they were the complete antithesis of one another.

This dissimilarity was reflected likewise in his attitude and conduct towards their mothers: with Maud, always perfectly proper, considerate and accommodating of her interests; with Connie, somewhat less the gentleman, more relaxed, more selfish of his own appetites.

How much Maud had guessed about Raby Street and Connie he had no idea. Possibly she was aware there was someone, but she never referred to the subject, never asked for details; not wishing to know. She was a fastidiously proud woman of good family background, and very dignified. The words 'mistress' and 'kept woman' were not in her vocabulary.

George Dennison loved his wife. He would never do anything to hurt her or cause her distress. The fact that she could give him no more children was scarcely her fault. He was responsible for her well-being and security just as he was now responsible for Connie's. They both depended upon him, to a greater or lesser degree, as he upon them: the one for his domestic comfort and social appearance, the other for his basic natural requirements as a man. But they were kept strictly apart, segregated by morality and class, occupying entirely separate areas of his life.

His two little families.

It was a comfortable arrangement.

What he did not realise was that by taking young Flora to Raby Street that day in 1905, when she'd first been made aware of Roseen's existence, he had allowed these two separate worlds to meet; and from that meeting would flow attitudes and actions and events which were to colour the rest of their lives.

 1

Dusty rays of sunlight spilled through the lace curtains drawn across the window, filling the room with a soft, diffused glow. The bed was unmade still, rumpled sheets thrown back over the brass footrail, the bolster pillow impressed with the hollow left by Connie's head; and clinging to everything was that smell, warm and close and intimate, a mixture of cheap, scented face-powder and tuberose perfume and stale body odour. Connie's smell.

Young Roseen wrinkled her nose and went and pushed up the window sash to let in some of the morning's freshness. The lace curtains began stirring idly in the slight current of air. Sounds of voices raised in argument carried from across the street; somewhere a baby was crying, a dog barked, and children were playing a sing-song skipping game, their high-pitched breathless chant keeping time with the rhythmic slap of the rope on the pavement.

She leaned over the cluttered top of her mother's toilette stand and used her sleeve to wipe away the dust which filmed the sunlit surface of the mirror, then rested forward on her elbows, chin cupped in her hands, staring at herself.

She was beautiful. Everybody said so. Uncle George. Her teacher, Miss Doyle. The fat, red-faced policeman. Mr Thompson from the corner shop. Her mother (of course). All of them said how beautiful she was. Only this last week one of the bigger boys at school had caught hold of her in the playground and tried to kiss her on the mouth. She might have let him, too, if he hadn't been so rough.

The argument going on across the way grew suddenly

more heated as the noisy exchange of abuse turned into shouts and screams. There was a crash of breaking glass.

Roseen pursed her lips into a pout and kissed the space in front of her reflection, watching herself to see what kissing looked like. The green eyes, flecked with hazel, held a rapt expression. She was twelve years old and had an avid curiosity about this sort of thing. Why did people do it? What was nice about it? Did it feel different, depending on whom you did it with? Her mother had told her she'd find out all in good time when she was older. Well, she was older now; she'd had her first monthly show (what Connie called the bleedin' nuisance) and her figure was starting to develop. None of the other girls in her class was anywhere near as fast growing up. But she still hadn't found out what she wanted to know.

She half-closed her eyes and looked at herself intently. Down in the street a door slammed shut with a bang, silencing the racket, and in the sudden quiet came the sound of a pair of hob-nailed boots clattering on the cobbles in the direction of the White Rose.

Removing one hand from under her chin, she took the lid from a small white pot among the disarray in front of her, and poked a fingertip into its contents. The finger came out carmined red with soft waxy lip-rouge. Pursing her lips again, she wiped the rouge inexpertly round and round and then examined the result, smiling at her jammy-mouthed image in an artificially bright manner, as she'd seen her mother do. Not satisfied with this she opened another pot, containing a fine sooty powder, and spitting on the same finger to moisten it, applied the resulting mess to her eyelashes.

"Roseen – ? Are you up there?"

Her mother's voice shouting to her from the foot of the stairs made the young girl give a quick, guilty start. Connie must have come in by the back alley; that's why she'd never heard the front door go.

"Roseen!"

"I'm just coming, Mam." She looked round hastily for something to wipe her face on. "I won't be a minute – "

The nearest thing to hand was a cotton chemise hanging on the back of the toilette stand. Roseen snatched it up and rubbed it vigorously over her mouth and eyes, then stuffed it away out of sight under the bed.

"*Roseen!*"

"I'm coming – "

She scrambled across the room and out on to the small dark box-landing. Her mother's head was poked round the open door below, shadowed by the light from the kitchen behind her.

"What're you doing there in my room?"

"Nothing. Just looking out the window." Roseen jumped down two steps at a time, until she was level with the feather in her mother's black straw hat. "The Handleys have been having a row."

"Aye. I heard it, as did half the street. And what's that you have all over your face?"

Connie grabbed her daughter by the arm and hauled her out from the staircase into the kitchen, for a better inspection. Two black-smudged eyes looked back at her in feigned innocence.

"What's what all over my face, Mam?"

"Don't come that with me, you little madam. I can see plain enough what you've been doing. You've been up there among my pots again, have you not. Just look at the sight o' you! Your Uncle George would go mad if he knew, so he would."

As always when she was angered, Connie's Dublin brogue grew more exaggerated. Keeping a firm grip on Roseen, she hauled her along behind her into the scullery and ran some water into the brownstone sink.

"You're a wicked, bad girl, Roseen, and I'll tell Father Doran of you, so I will, if I catch you at my face-pots again. 'Tis forbidden, d'you hear, and I'll not have it!"

Seizing the child by the hair, she jerked back her head and commenced scrubbing at the smears with a piece of coal-tar soap; then, splashing off the sudsy mess, dried her roughly on a length of towelling hanging on a nail beside the sink.

"The soap's in my eye – " Roseen wailed petulantly.

"Serve you right."

Connie went through again to the kitchen. She'd been out to the market to do her Saturday shopping and was in an irritable temper from lugging two heavy bags up the long slope of Snow Hill. Pulling off her hat, she patted her hair back into place out of habit, with a quick glance in the mirror above the range, and without looking again at her daughter emptied the two bags on to the kitchen table and started removing the contents from their newspaper wrappings.

Suddenly she stopped, and bending down, began searching frantically through the paper just discarded on the floor.

"Oh – *no* – !"

Rising to her feet again, she declared in vexation, "Well, would you believe it. I bought two pig's sweetbreads, and what have I done but left them there at the butcher's. 'Twas that Mrs Dwyer made me forget, so it was. Her and her blether! You'll have to go down and fetch them, Roseen, or he'll be selling them to somebody else, the old divil."

"Oh, but Mam – "

"Do as you're told!" The cry of complaint was cut short. Connie tossed a sharp look over her shoulder; and seeing the obstinacy in her daughter's expression, tried softening her tone to a more wheedling note.

"Sure, but I can't be going all that long way myself. If you're good and be quick now, there'll be a ginger beer for you."

Roseen knew what this meant. She'd find her mother round at the White Rose by the time she got back from her errand.

"I'll go if I can have threepence to spend."

"You! D'you think I'm made o' money?"

But already Connie's mind was on the drink she'd been promising herself all the way home from the market.

Five minutes later, clutching a silver threepenny-bit, Roseen was skipping along Powlett Street towards Snow Hill. She'd put on her woollen tam o'shanter, but the spring morning was warm enough for her not to need a shawl over the frilled white pinafore covering her cotton frock; and with a breeze to carry away the pungent sourness of the nearby brewery, the air smelt of that dusty freshness which follows overnight rain.

Once on Snow Hill itself a sense of adventure seized her. She was a town child, used to the streets, and knew her way round the area as well as any adult. Instead of making directly for the market, a ten-minute walk at most, she cut across into George Street and through to St John's Square with its imposing old church and walled graveyard overlooked by handsome Georgian town-houses.

This was one of her favourite places. The trees deadened the noise of traffic from the surrounding streets, and in the stillness the sound of birdsong filled the square, coming from the melodious throats of caged linnets and canaries trilling at open windows, and echoed by the whistle of thrushes among the leafy branches.

She jumped up on the wall and sat there swinging the heels of her boots against the brickwork. At the opposite corner next to the church a baker's delivery van had stopped, and the blinkered horse stood quietly between the shafts, its head down in an attitude of stoic resignation. Apart from the horse and the birds and Roseen, the only other living thing in St John's Square this morning was a housemaid over beyond the other side of the graveyard, polishing a brass nameplate beside a front door.

The child sat for a few minutes drinking in the peace and enjoying the warmth of the sun on her upturned face, and thinking as always how grand it must be to live somewhere as posh as this, where the neighbours never brawled in the street, and never came home maudlin drunk of a Saturday night. From what he'd told her, she imagined her Uncle George had his house in an area much like this one; only *his* had a big garden right round and stables at the back, and if you looked out of the upstairs windows you could see all the way into the country.

She loved her Uncle George. She wished she could go to live with him instead of staying in Raby Street, but her mother said his wife wouldn't like that. Roseen knew why, of course; or thought she did. His wife didn't know that her mother and Uncle George were 'friends'. It was a secret. And as he'd explained, if she *did* know, she'd cause no end of a fuss and he'd have to stop coming to visit.

Roseen hated his wife. And she hated too that stuck-up, prim-faced little Flora. If it wasn't for that pair her mother could marry Uncle George and then they'd move to live at Stockwell End and be happy ever after.

Suddenly impatient to be on her errand again, she jumped down from the wall and went running out of the square, not stopping until she reached the busy, noisy bustle of Victoria Street. Ahead, at the top of the hill, was another of her favourite places – the Empire Palace theatre. It had been built only nine years ago, in 1898, and really was like a palace inside, with its red-plush seating and potted palms and gilt stucco work, and the enormous ceiling which Roseen always thought was like an Arabian magic carpet suspended above her. She came here often with her mother and they'd sit high up among the wooden tiers of the 'gods' looking down on the circle and stalls bathed in the soft, golden glow of concealed gaslights.

The most exciting moment of her life had happened here. A wild animal act was on stage, and one of the animals – a lion – had been sitting on an upturned barrel when it suddenly leapt with a roar and attacked its trainer, knocking the man to the floor and seizing him in its jaws. Everyone in the theatre had jumped from their seats screaming, and for a while absolute pandemonium reigned as the pit orchestra tumbled over itself trying to get out of the way. Finally a group of stage hands armed with broomheads and a net had managed to trap the lion inside a cage, and the trainer had been carted off on a trestle, covered in blood and mauled almost to death, the *Express and Star* said afterwards.

The poor lion had been shot on a patch of waste ground behind the theatre.

Dodging the horse traffic in Queen Square, Roseen crossed over into the street leading down to the market hall. She knew which butcher her mother used, and once inside the vast, cavernous building with its elaborate cast-iron pillars and glass roof, pushed her way confidently along the crowded aisles to Mr Whitehouse's stall.

Turning from serving a customer, Harry Whitehouse recognised the strikingly pretty child with the mass of copper-coloured curls beneath her tam o'shanter. Without pausing from his conversation, he wiped his hands on the gore-smeared front of his blue-and-white-striped apron and reached under the counter to produce the sweetbreads which her mother had left behind. After being all this time in the same piece of newspaper the meat had started seeping through, and before handing it to Roseen he re-wrapped it in a couple of fresh sheets.

" 'Ere y'are, bab," he interrupted himself to tell her, leaning over. "Yo' tell Connie 'er'll lose 'er 'ead one o' these days!"

She smiled at the wink which accompanied this good-humoured observation; then, turning away with the packet, retraced her steps back along the aisle, in the direction this time of a stall selling ribbons and laces and buttons and all sorts of other general haberdashery goods. Already the choice had been made upon what to spend her threepenny-bit. Roseen liked sweets; but her Uncle George brought her sweets enough every week, and today she'd set her mind on a new green ribbon for her hair.

Struggling to get through the mill of market shoppers blocking the way with their baskets and pushcarts, she felt herself suddenly caught by the arm, and looking round, found a thin-faced man in a greasy bowler right behind her.

"Here, I haven't done anything!" she exclaimed indignantly, squirming to try and free herself. "Let me go!"

His grip tightened. "Lost your Ma, have you?" he said, bending his face towards hers and smiling in a way that she didn't like.

"No, I haven't. Let go!"

"Where is she, then?"

"She's at home."

"You're here all by yourself are you, little girl?"

The 'little girl' annoyed her even more than having him holding her so hard by the arm.

"What's that to you? I'm old enough. If you don't let go of me I'll scream."

"I'll give you sixpence," he said quickly, the smile going and a sudden curious intentness showing in his pale eyes. "Sixpence, all to yourself."

Roseen stopped her squirming and looked up at him warily. "For doing what?" Her mother had warned her never to speak to strangers; but she'd not said anything about taking money from them.

The man smiled again, spittle gathering at the corners of his mouth. "Come along wi' me and I'll show you."

23

"Come where? What have I got to do?" She pulled back as he tried to shove her in front of him across the crowded aisle.

"Just over there, that's all. Just round by that door."

"But our Mam's expecting me home – " The meat in its newspaper wrapping was shown as evidence.

"It won't take more'n a minute. Come on."

He urged the child with his body towards the door; and reaching it, pushed her inside and shut it fast behind them both. They were at the top of an ill-lit stone stairway leading down into darkness, and the cramped area stank of rotten vegetables and urine.

After a sharp glance round, Roseen decided she should get herself out of here again as fast as possible.

"Well – ?" she demanded, raising her small chin aggressively. "Where's the sixpence you promised?"

The man's expression wore a look of feverish excitement. He fumbled in his waistcoat pocket.

"Here – "

As she accepted the coin from him he grabbed her by the wrist, and pulling her against him, said hoarsely, "Now you be a good little girl and drop your drawers for me, eh?"

She shrank back from the leering, spittle-flecked lips so close to her face. There was something here that she didn't understand, and it disgusted her. There was no fear in her reaction, though; only an anger and revulsion which manifested itself as instant temper.

"I won't hurt. Just let me feel you – " he went on. But that was as far as he got before Roseen's sharp little teeth fastened themselves into the fleshy base of his thumb.

The next moment the man's yell of pain rose even higher as she kicked at his legs, the toe-cap of her boot catching him across the shin. Tearing herself away, she flew to the door and was through in a flash, leaving him there cursing impotently after her; and without staying to look back, she went darting off into the market crowd, not satisfied until she'd put a good distance between herself and that end of the hall.

★

24

Crossing back over Queen Square into the safety of Dudley Street, Roseen's headlong progress was checked from a run to a walk by the sheer volume of traffic and people about. She kept looking over her shoulder to see whether or not she was followed, ready to scream at the top of her voice if her molester came anywhere in view. It wasn't that she was frightened of him – nothing frightened Roseen O'Connor – but the thought of his pale, wet mouth and his hands feeling under her skirt made her skin crawl.

She paused for a minute to get her breath in front of Hyam's the Outfitters, and catching sight of herself mirrored in one of the tall plate-glass windows, made a rapid inspection of her appearance. The meat had seeped through a bit and marked the front of her pinafore where she'd been clutching it against her, and her wrist was still red from being gripped so hard; but apart from that, there was no damage done that she could see.

Straightening her tam o'shanter, the child smirked at her reflection, recalling the way she'd stood up for herself – then in an oddly mature manner, tossed back her head and suddenly laughed out loud. She wouldn't tell her mother about her adventure. She'd only get walloped for talking to strangers; and anyway, what was there to tell? All she had done was to go behind a door with a man and get sixpence off him for nothing.

She laughed again; and passers-by turned to look at the pretty little girl with the lovely red-gold curls, such a delightful picture of innocence.

2

"I think – " said George Dennison, laying aside the table napkin on which he'd just wiped his mouth, "I think it wouldn't be a bad idea if we had some sort of a Christmas party this year. What d'you think, Maud? A party for all our employees' kiddies."

His wife glanced up at him from the other side of the dining-table, but being still engaged in eating made no immediate response. Only a slight creasing of the white, smooth skin of her brow indicated that she would have preferred not to hear the word 'kiddies' used in front of Flora.

"Yes, and we could have the tenants' young 'uns, as well," Mr Dennison went on. "No need for them to be left out."

"Oh, not the children from Raby Street, surely." Maud, having now emptied her mouth of the final morsel of treacle suet pudding, permitted herself to speak, and the way in which she said Raby Street with a slightly acidic emphasis was indication enough of her opinion.

"Why not? They're as much a part of our big happy family as those I employ in Dennison's Stores."

His wife shot a pained look towards Flora, sitting quietly between them at the table, hands folded in her lap, spoon placed at the correct angle in her pudding-dish.

"I do wish that you would not refer to your employees as family, George. They are not family. They are people you pay to work for you. Please remember what I have so often said before, that as owner of this business you have a position to maintain, and over-familiarity with inferiors in whatever capacity they are employed, can only breed contempt."

George Dennison smoothed a forefinger over his clipped grey moustache. He knew his wife's views. He had heard them so often they no longer irritated him, but fell upon ears now deafened to the predictability of their argument. He liked to think of himself as the Guv'nor, the paternal benefactor of all those men and women whose livelihood was his responsibility – and that included dependants and children as well. With more than a hundred people drawing wages, it was a burdensome commitment but one which he relished shouldering in his role as their employer.

He motioned to the spotlessly-dressed young housemaid standing behind his chair.

"Thank you, Tilly. You can clear the dishes now."

And when she had gone from the room with her laden tray, "I've asked you not to pass that sort o' comment in front of the staff, Maud."

The rebuke was uttered mildly; but Maud, who had an inbred middle-class belief in the invisibility of servants, took umbrage at it.

"I hope that I may be allowed to speak as I wish beneath my own roof?" Her words held just a touch of frostiness, and served to underline the silent but always present reminder that it was her money which had enabled George Dennison to purchase the house in which they were living.

When the two of them had first made each other's acquaintance – introduced at the Staffordshire County Horticultural Show in 1889 – Mr Dennison had only recently set his foot on the ladder of commercial success and had little more than ambition and good looks to recommend him. Maud Kemp was a shrewd young woman, however, as well as a practical one, and felt assured that his faith in himself was not misplaced. Somewhat against her father's wishes she had married; and had brought sufficient money of her own to give the Dennison grocery business the impetus to grow and to prosper. And if it should irk her that, under cover of the clatter of china teacups, her Stockwell End neighbours sniffily referred to her as the Grocer's Wife, at least she had the satisfaction of seeing her dowry earning its interest in bricks and mortar up and down the high streets of the Black Country.

She pushed back her chair and rose from the table, a slim, straight figure in grey silk evening dress.

"Come, Flora. It is time for you to go upstairs. Say goodnight to Papa."

Obediently the young girl got up from her seat and went round the table to kiss her father. As she leaned against him, her hand on his shoulder, he caught her round the waist in a hug and returned her kiss on the cheek with hearty affection.

"You'll give us a hand with this Christmas party, won't you, our Flora. There'll be a lot to organise – presents for all of the kiddies, games to keep them amused, that sort of thing. I'll need a list making out as soon as I know how many we've got coming, so put your thinking cap on."

He hugged her again and she smiled, a shy, loving smile that lit up her serious features.

"Right. Off to bed with you." He tapped her on the nose, then, to his wife, "I don't think I'll bother with coffee, Maud. I'll have a brandy and soda in the office instead. Will you tell young Tilly to bring one through?"

★

Flora left her parents together in the dining-room and went upstairs. A coal fire had been lit in her bedroom grate against the dank October night's chill and she undressed herself on the hearth in front of it, folding her clothes neatly ready for Agnes or one of the other maids to put away. At thirteen she was too old now for a nurserymaid, and personal needs such as her wardrobe were seen to by whichever of the domestic staff was on duty, or else by her mother's own lady's maid, Agnes Reid.

Pulling her white flannel nightgown over her head, Flora knelt on the hearthrug and stretched her hands to the flames, warming herself thoroughly before she had to make a dash along the landing corridor to the icy, white-tiled arctic of the bathroom. She recalled wistfully the time when hot water was brought in a jug for her to wash herself in cosy comfort by the fire, but that was before Papa had had the new bathroom installed, replacing one of the guest-rooms.

The firelight shone between her hands, outlining each finger in a rosy glow. Except for the rustle of the flames and the companionable tick of the mantel clock, there wasn't a sound to be heard. She tucked her legs beneath her and stared into the incandescent coal-caverns of the grate, watching the heat-shimmer play on their surface, the glitter of spark-patterns blaze for a moment and die again.

She loved to sit like this, quiet and alone, seeing pictures in the fire, drifting away from the world into a make-believe place of fantasy, of fairy princesses and dragons and witches and many-towered castles wrapped in enchantment. Almost since she first began reading her vivid imagination had been fuelled by story-books, especially those of Andrew Lang with their re-telling of magical tales from faraway lands and their eerie, other-worldly, dreamlike illustrations. She read them again and again, begging new volumes for Christmas and birthdays to add to her growing collection.

Mama said it wasn't healthy to spend so much time with her nose in a book, stuffing her head with fairy stories; but Papa said no, let her be, where was the harm in it; it showed the child had an inventive mind.

Thinking of her father now and the party he proposed giving, Flora wondered whether the girl from Raby Street would be included in the invitation. She had learnt a little about her from the chance remark – that her name was Roseen O'Connor; her school and her birthdate. Exactly why she should have this interest in a perfect stranger, Flora didn't know; but since first seeing her three years ago she'd never been able to rid herself of the vision of that girl leaning from the window to wave to her Papa, so full of fearless impudence and laughter and self-confidence, so startlingly pretty . . . everything which she herself was not.

There was something else too which she'd never been rid of; something darker, half-forgotten, that seemed to cling to the edge of her memory like a burr, refusing to let go. A feeling of complicity in some sort of deceit.

She gave a deep, unconscious sigh; then remembered the bathroom, and with an expression of chagrin got up from the hearth and glanced at herself in the mirror. Oh, what would it be like to be Roseen O'Connor for just one day, instead of Flora Dennison, too plump, too plain, too shy, too ordinary ever to be noticed.

★

In the end there were more than fifty children invited to the Christmas party, and Dennison's Stores hired a church hall in Wolverhampton to accommodate them all. Thank goodness the weather was fine; cold, but with a brittle, bright December sun pouring in at the windows to add its illusion of warmth to the two Dutch stoves burning cheerfully at either end of the hall.

The sober drabness of the place, redolent of soup-kitchen evangelism, had been entirely transformed by the gaiety of festive decorations. Swags of paper chains festooned the wooden rafters, filling the space overhead with a kaleidoscope of colour; there were bunches of holly looped with red ribbon against the plainness of the walls; and best of all, a splendid Christmas tree bedecked with glittering tinsel and shining glass baubles, and hung from the lower boughs with presents, each of which bore the name of one of the young guests here this afternoon.

The wrapping and labelling of the presents had been Flora's responsibility.

First of all, while everyone was settling down and to get them into the right, jolly mood, a sing-song was conducted by one of the store managers dressed as a clown. The programme contained a medley of nursery rhymes and carols and favourite seasonal tunes and – most popular by far – the patter-songs of music hall turns, learned at home from parents; but after a while of this, small throats began to get thirsty and heads to turn longingly towards the trestle tables laid out ready at the other end of the hall.

One of Flora's suggestions for this party was that every child should be given a number as he or she came in, matching a corresponding one on the table settings. She had even gone as far as cutting out coloured circles of cardboard with the numbers boldly crayoned on, to be affixed to the recipient's garment with a safety-pin. George Dennison had thought this a capital method of avoiding what he called 'a free-for-all bunfight at teatime' and praised his young daughter accordingly; and it gave Flora a glow of achievement now to look round the noisy, crowded hall at this mixed assembly of children, all sporting one of her numbered circles like a badge of identity.

Her eyes stopped at a girl in an ivory-coloured muslin frock with deep lace collar and satin sash, standing against the wall at the back. Expecting to see her here, she knew at once who it was; but even so the sight of Roseen O'Connor made Flora catch her breath with sudden sharpness, as though startled. She stared at her, watched her joining in the singing, animated and confident, hands on hips, tapping time with one foot; and wondered whether they'd be seated near one another at tea, close enough to speak. And then, later, she didn't know whether to feel relieved or disappointed when she found herself sitting directly opposite the girl, but at a separate table.

Roseen had obviously recognised her too. From time to time she glanced across from her place, unsmiling, something almost spiteful in the way her expression narrowed slightly. Then she would turn away again to her neighbour, a nice-looking boy who kept catching Flora's eye and winking; and the laughter would spring back into Roseen's face and the sunny exuberance of her manner spill over everyone round her.

Her attractiveness fascinated Flora. Spellbound her. It conjured up in her mind instant images of the enchanted damsels of Mr Lang's fairy tales. The heroines with whom she filled her adolescent dreams were beautiful and lithe and noble, with hair of just that shade of Roseen's copper-gold, rippling in waves about their shoulders. She was reminded of Fair Olwen, and Imogen, and the Countess of the Fountains. What a pity the two of them could not be chums! Why did the girl appear so to dislike her? Perhaps she should ask, and find out . . . if only she weren't so ridiculously shy.

As a matter of fact it was Roseen herself who broke the ice and – typically – was first to sound an overture of friendship. Her mother Connie had threatened her to be on her best behaviour at the Dennison's Stores party; no showing-off, no pushing and shoving for food, no fighting, and most of all, *no* mentioning Uncle George. She'd have to pretend she didn't know him hardly. Never mind why. Just do as she was told if she knew what was good for her.

Knowing what was good for her was something Roseen had learnt early in life, and so she had paid no attention to her Uncle George this afternoon, apart from saying hallo and smiling when he'd winked. She was inclined not to pay any attention to his daughter either, no matter how much the silly, fat thing gawped and goggled every time she looked in her direction. But a little voice of native cunning whispered she'd do better for herself to make friends with Flora Dennison than keep on ignoring her. What had she to lose, after all? It could work out to her advantage – her Uncle George would be pleased, she was sure. She might even get an invitation to stay at Stockwell End with them.

And so she'd put on her sweetest and most beguiling smile and gone across the hall to speak to Flora.

After tea was ended and the tables cleared away, and those who wished or needed to had visited the lavatory outside, the young guests were entertained by a professional magician complete with silk top hat, magic wand and a black cloak big enough to wrap round him twice. He began with a few simple tricks, plucking fans of cards seemingly out of thin air, and then, to the ohs and crikeys of his enraptured audience, went on to produce an astonishing number of different objects from various parts of his person. Coloured handkerchiefs appeared from his wax-mustachio'd mouth, drawn out in an endless line, all knotted together like naval flags on a halyard; white mice ran from a coat sleeve shown to be empty of everything except its owner's arm; rabbits popped from the hat he'd just swept from his head in a bow; and the cloak revealed all kinds of wonders, from torn-out patterns to real live pigeons which flew up with a clap of wings and settled themselves among the decorated rafters.

"I've seen him before," Roseen said, coming and leaning on the back of Flora's chair. "He was at the Empire Palace."

The other girl turned and looked up; and when she saw who it was there, a blush of confusion spread across her cheeks in a quick stain of colour. For some silly reason, to find herself suddenly so close to Roseen O'Connor made her bashful, and to her mortification all she could answer was,

"Oh . . . his name is Mr Williams, but he calls himself Maurice the Magnifico."

"He was billed as something else when I saw him," Roseen said, kneeling down at Flora's side and resting her arm in the most natural way on the other's knee. "He's good, though. He sawed a woman completely in half, right through her middle."

"Right through her – ?" Flora was horrified. "Heavens, but didn't that hurt her?"

"Go on, it was only a trick!"

What a juggins, Roseen told herself; fancy believing a thing like that. Aloud she went on, stroking the soft material of Flora's party frock, "I do like this you're wearing. It's ever so pretty. Your Dad buy it you, did he?"

"Well – actually – my mother's dressmaker made it specially." A shy smile pressed dimples into Flora's cheeks. "Yours is pretty too."

"This old thing? No it in't. I hate it."

Roseen pulled her hand of friendship away and a sullen little pout threatened to betray the quick resentment. It wasn't fair. Herself, she'd had to make do with a frock bought off the landlady of the White Rose, whose daughter had outgrown it. There'd been quite a shindy at home. She didn't want anybody else's second-hand stuff! Uncle George would buy her a frock for the party if she asked him. But Connie had put her foot down. She wasn't to expect Uncle George to go reaching in his pocket for every blessed thing she wanted. Folk didn't like being taken for granted. About time she learned that.

"Your name's Roseen, isn't it," Flora said above the sound of applause for Maurice the Magnifico. "I'm Flora – Flora Dennison. We've seen each other before, if you remember."

"Have we?"

"Yes. A long time ago, though. My Papa brought me to Raby Street once, and called at your house."

Roseen tossed the ringlets from her shoulders and made no answer, pretending to give her attention to the magician's next trick.

"You were looking out from an upstairs window. You waved goodbye as he left."

There was a half-shrug. She recalled the occasion very well.

33

She also recalled feeling bitterly jealous of the well-dressed child queening it below in Uncle George's pony trap.

"No, I don't remember," she said. Then, suddenly, distracted by something and switching again to her most winning manner, "Here, are all those presents on the Christmas tree for us lot?"

"The presents – ? Oh, yes. Yes, they are. They're to be given out at the end of the party, just before everyone leaves."

A happy thought struck Flora, and she went on in a quick rush, "I say, you wouldn't like to help, would you? I'm supposed to be the one giving the presents, you see, and . . . well . . . it would be jolly nice if you'd lend me a hand."

Jolly nice. Roseen squirmed inside with laughter.

" 'Course I'll help, if you want," she answered, leaning herself back once more and resting her head against the other's arm as though in a spontaneous gesture of girlish affection.

Her hair in its bandeau of cream satin ribbon brushed Flora's hand. She longed to reach out and stroke the red-gold softness. Shyly she said instead, "I'd like you to be my friend, Roseen. Will you? Please?"

She couldn't see the bitter-sweet expression, half triumph, half contempt, which touched those smiling lips.

3

From the beginning it was a somewhat incongruous friendship – incongruous because so unlikely. On the surface to all appearances an attraction of opposites; certainly on Roseen's side a means to an end.

Roseen O'Connor was a manipulator. She was only thirteen, yet already she knew instinctively how to use the gifts of winsome charm and picture-postcard prettiness to sway people to her. She could not be described in any way as hard or vicious – such traits were never to show in her character – but she was shaped by nature and breeding to be entirely self-centred, and this inherent attitude was so woven into the very fibre of her personality that it coloured every thought and action, making her view life's offerings always from the angle of greatest advantage to herself.

Once she'd made up her mind to a thing, for as long as it suited her purpose she pursued it with singular tenacity, throwing heart and soul into achieving what she wanted; and it suited her now to accept Flora Dennison's friendship, however little in common there might seem to be between the shyly-mannered, middle-class English girl and this self-assertive street child of Irish working-class background.

In her own quiet way, though, Flora too could be equally persistent. Knowing that her mother would refuse to countenance social intimacy with anyone from Raby Street, she approached her father instead to ask if she could invite Roseen to spend a Saturday afternoon at Stockwell End.

Many men would have thought it unethical to bring their mistress's child into their house, but not George Dennison.

Secretly he was rather pleased that the two girls should have formed an acquaintance 'off their own bat' so to speak. He'd known young Roseen since she was four, and felt a genuine deep affection for her; and now that she was old enough to appreciate something of the situation at home and could be trusted (he hoped) to keep her mouth shut, he saw no reason why Flora shouldn't have her as a friend. In his opinion it would do the pair of them a power of good. Flora was far too cosseted by the artificial atmosphere of the private school she attended – about time she started mixing company a bit; and Roseen, well, as he said to his wife, with kiddies like that the boot was on the other foot; kiddies like that, they had too many chances taken away and not enough given.

Had he suggested introducing cholera into the house Maud Dennison could not have been more aghast. Never mind that the wages of their domestic staff came from the rents of their tenants, Raby Street to her was synonymous with poverty, drunken violence, dirt and illiteracy, and she could not believe her ears that her husband was seriously wishing to encourage a friendship between their daughter and some child from that area; a child who was, moreover, Irish and Catholic!

Mr Dennison understood her alarm and regretted it. Coming from a working-class background himself, he disliked prejudice and particularly when it was directed against those born without the silver spoon of privilege. To please his wife he could have sold his properties in Raby Street years ago; but that would have been betraying his own roots, and therefore he chose to continue as landlord, to please himself.

Roseen was invited to Stockwell End.

*

Contrary to Maud Dennison's most dreaded expectations, the girl appeared clean, well dressed, perfectly mannered; and most disarmingly appreciative of the Dennisons' hospitality. The only fault to be found was with her accent, which, while not unattractive, combined the cadence and flattened vowels of the Midlands with a subtle Irish intonation. Mrs Dennison sincerely hoped that Flora's own speech (made faultless by elocution training) would not be affected; but otherwise there seemed little to justify fears of her daughter's contamination by contact with this young person.

The February afternoon had been a cold and wet one, and the girls were permitted after tea to go up to play in the attic lumber-room until it was time for Roseen to go. So far during this first visit there'd been a certain amount of awkwardness between them both, the result of Flora's natural shyness and Roseen's guarded watch on herself to make sure she didn't blot her copybook; but here among the trunks of discarded out-of-fashion clothing a genuine link of affinity was quite suddenly and unexpectedly forged as the two discovered they shared a mutual passion for dressing-up and play-acting.

In the weeks that followed they might spend their Saturday afternoons together doing other things (playing croquet, which Roseen thought a stupid game and refused to learn, or bicycle-riding, which she quickly mastered and loved) but inevitably the pair of them would be off upstairs after tea, to pursue their favourite game.

In this one thing they were perfect foils for one another. Roseen liked to dress up simply because she loved the feel of fine materials against her skin, because she revelled in the drama of looking beautiful and being the object of admiring attention; whereas Flora enjoyed it because, imaginative as she was, dressing-up became an escape into fantasy and allowed her the pretence of a totally different identity. All her schoolfriends had been useless, with their giggling and sniggering and silly remarks, refusing to be serious and play the game properly; but Roseen was perfect; Roseen *adored* being a queen or a flower fairy or a Viking maiden, as long as she could deck herself in Mrs Dennison's old furs and evening gowns in front of the cracked cheval-glass.

Whatever role was suggested, Roseen didn't seem to mind at all, not one bit, and Flora, in her naïve infatuation, thought she was wonderful.

*

Someone *did* mind, however. Roseen's mother, Connie. Connie thought the whole thing a most peculiar affair. From the start she hadn't felt happy about her child swanning off on a Saturday to Stockwell End to be entertained to tea at her

37

lover's table. It seemed all cock-eyed somehow, making friends with his daughter like that. What if something should come out, about him and her? What then? As soon as his wife got wind of the business, depend on it, that'd be the last they'd see of Mr George Dennison.

She had been his mistress for all of eight years, and just lately their relationship had started going wrong. He wasn't calling to see her as often as before, and when he did, half the time he'd simply sit and talk and wasn't interested in taking her to bed. Oh, there were others who'd guessed what was going on between them – you couldn't keep a secret long in Raby Street – but knowing *they* knew wasn't what was keeping him away.

She was losing her looks. That was the truth of it. Her mirror told her. She was starting to get puffy-faced from the drink, bloated; and not so clean either as she'd once been. The nights spent sitting against the kitchen-range fire with a bottle of gin for company had left large purple blotches mottling the skin of her thighs, and her hair, her glorious, thick red hair that men used so to admire, was coming away in handfuls and its colour turning the pepper-and-salt of an old woman's.

Dear Mother of God, she was thirty-eight years old, and staring middle-age in the face. No wonder George Dennison didn't fancy her in bed the way he had. It only needed one word spoken out of turn from young Roseen, and they may as well pack their bags, for they'd be out on their heels from Raby Street, the pair of them.

In this, though, Connie was wrong. George Dennison had wearied of her, true; wearied of her drunken, blowsy body and her maudlin tears; but he would never discard her. No matter that he no longer wanted her for his mistress, he would still continue to keep her. She was Roseen's mother. Roseen was her security against the future.

★

The Dennisons always went away to Aberystwyth for a week's holiday at Whitsuntide. Mr Dennison enjoyed the bracing sea air and the long, invigorating walks offered by the hills around; while his wife preferred to find a seat along the Marine Terrace where she could sit sheltered from the elements with a blanket for her knees, taking in the view.

For some years now Flora had been allowed to bring along a schoolfriend as holiday companion, but her choice had not always proved successful since the type of girl she asked grew bored or homesick, and the week would end on a fretful, bickering note.

This year, of course, 1909, it was Roseen O'Connor she invited. Apart from a couple of day trips into the country with the nuns from St Mary's and St John's, Roseen had never been on a holiday before, let alone seen the sea, and the prospect of travelling by steam train to spend six whole nights in some smart hotel was the closest thing she could conceive of to heaven.

Connie didn't go to the station to see her daughter off. She went to the White Rose instead, and cried, and got drunk. Roseen had never left her before, and it was a terrible thing; but she daren't have said no. The girl was growing more and more wilful and headstrong, with a fierce, quick temper which Connie had tried to curb with threats but couldn't; and of late she found it easier to seek the consolation of alcohol than cope with a child she could no longer manage.

"Ta-ra, Mam. I'll bring you something back for the mantelpiece," Roseen called out up the stairs; and then she'd gone running from the house with her bag of things, holding her hat to her head, away off down to the station and the Dennisons waiting for her at the platform barrier.

The journey to Aberystwyth was an adventure in itself. It was like being in a foreign country, going into Wales, with the queer-looking place-names, and the sheep-dotted hills rising green and gaunt against a milky-blue sky, occasionally unfolding to give tantalising views of the coastlands beyond.

Roseen's first glimpse of Cardigan Bay had her jumping from her seat in excitement, her face pressed to the carriage window, hardly able to believe that anything could be so vast, all that heaving grey water stretching on and on with nothing to contain it. What astonished her most was that the water actually *moved*. She'd always supposed the sea to be still, like a lake, and for the final stage of the journey stared mesmerised at the dirty white froth of waves rippling in a never-ending cascade towards the shore.

Her pleasures continued to pile themselves one upon another. The hotel bedroom she shared with Flora looked out across the promenade directly on to the beach, and though she could scarcely keep her eyes open for tiredness that first night, she would never forget the wonderful experience of lying between clean-smelling sheets, listening in the darkness to the drawn-out sigh of the sea exhausting itself on the shingle; and awakening in the moth-light of dawn to the raucous cries of gulls beyond the window.

After breakfast in the hotel dining-room (Roseen carefully watching what Flora did in order to copy her: the sideboard buffet of dishes presented an unfamiliar hazard) it was decided that the two girls could explore the castle ruins for an hour while Mrs Dennison chose herself some books in the lending library. The ruins lay quite close to the pier pavilion and were not considered at all dangerous.

"When the weather's really fine," said Flora, awkwardly scrambling up to perch with Roseen on one of the crumbled, creeper-clad walls of the castle, "you can see right across the bay as far as Bardsey Island at the tip of Caernarvonshire."

Her companion appeared unimpressed.

"Papa told me so," Flora added, screwing up her eyes against the glitter of the sea in the hazy morning sunshine.

They sat for a few minutes side by side in silence, the salty breeze blowing their loose hair about their faces; then Roseen exclaimed peremptorily, "Well, come on – let's find something to do, shall we? Are there any shops or anything round here?"

"Shops – ? Yes, I think so. Why?"

"To see what they're selling, of course."

"You mean souvenirs, that kind of thing?"

There was a shrug.

"Mama will take us tomorrow, if you wish," Flora said helpfully. "I'll ask her at luncheon."

"But we can go by ourselves, can't we? Why do we need your Mam?"

"Because I expect she'll want to accompany us."

40

"But *why*? Haven't you ever been in a shop by yourself before?"

"Actually, no. Have you?"

Roseen gave her a startled look. "You mean you've never been down Wolverhampton market?"

Flora shook her head, brushing the straight brown fringe of hair away from her eyes.

"Blimey." The other limited her disbelief to a single exclamation, one of many she was careful not to use in front of Mr and Mrs Dennison.

There was another silence. Below them, beyond the limpet-covered rocks of the foreshore, a fisherman was bringing his boat into the shallows.

"You got any money to spend?" Roseen said casually after a while.

"Money? No. Why should I?" Flora's attention was fixed on the fisherman. "If I want anything, I ask for it. Don't you?"

The response to this was a cynical laugh. "Asking in't the same as getting. Do they give you *everything* you want?"

"Well . . . really, I don't want very much."

"What, not lots of nice clothes, and jewellery, and all that?"

"I'm too young to wear jewellery, Mama says. Besides, I like books better. If I do ask for anything it's usually a new book."

"You're daft." Roseen jumped from the wall and tugged at her short, navy-braided jacket. It was worn every day to school, but having no other she was obliged to make do with it for holiday best as well. "You need your head looking at, you do. Come on – "

She held out a hand to Flora, to pull her down.

"Let's go and look round for a bit. See what we can find."

Caught between obedience to her parents and the desire to please her friend, the other hesitated.

"Come *on*!"

Without even waiting to see whether she followed, Roseen went running off ahead across the grass.

A short distance from the castle, behind a warren of terraced boarding-houses, the two of them came into the town's main thoroughfare, a wide street with rows of shops on either side.

As well as being a seaside resort and the social centre for the surrounding area, Aberystwyth was the site of the University College of Wales, opened in 1872, and consequently there was an air of bustling activity about the place, with almost as many motor-carriages and bicycles to be seen as in Wolverhampton.

"Coo, look at these – aren't they pretty!"

Roseen had stopped on the pavement outside one of the shops, and catching Flora's arm, pointed to a window display of decorated sea-shells. At the back of the window, pinned to a felt-covered board, hung a variety of necklaces, bracelets and ear-drops all made from mother of pearl.

She pressed her nose flat to the glass, her eyes hurrying greedily from one piece to another.

"I like that there – that bracelet in the middle. See it? With the bits of coral in between? I wonder how much they want for it."

Flora looked, not terribly impressed by the gaudy cheapness of the souvenir jewellery.

"Let's go in, shall we?" Impulsively, Roseen caught her by the arm again and started pulling her into the shop's entrance.

"But we haven't any money – "

"That don't matter! They won't charge us for having a squint round."

There was a small, thin, middle-aged woman behind the counter, serving a couple and a child as they went inside.

"I'll be with you in a minute, dears," she called across to them in Welsh; then, seeing their blank response, repeated herself in English, adding, "Is there anything special you want to see?"

"Can we look at the jewellery, please?" Roseen switched on her best polite manner, and indicated a similar display board to that in the window, propped on a shelf amongst a good deal of clutter at the back of the narrow shop. "I've got three bob to spend on a present for our Mam."

She gave Flora a sly wink; and leaving her there beneath the single gaslight which was all the place seemed to have for illumination, went over to the board and started examining each piece of shell-ware in turn.

"Don't take them off their pins, there's a good girl," the shopkeeper called, seeing her removing a bracelet. "Those bits are only for show, look you. If there's something you like, I have the same here at the counter."

As Roseen half-turned to acknowledge this, the braid on her jacket cuff must have caught on one of the pins; and she couldn't quite manage to prevent the board toppling forward off the shelf, shedding its display.

"Oh – I'm ever so sorry!"

Before the shopkeeper, exclaiming in vexation, could move from behind the counter, she'd knelt down at once, out of sight, to start putting right the damage, trying to hang the jewellery back on the board.

"No, no, leave that. *Dyna gawl.* I'll see to it myself," the woman said.

Roseen got to her feet again. "I said I'm sorry . . . Anyway, there wasn't really anything there our Mam would like. But thanks for letting me look."

With a quick, apologetic smile she went back to Flora and almost pushed her over in her sudden haste to get the two of them out of the door and on to the pavement.

"*Lletchwith* – !" the woman threw after them.

"Come on, quick – let's clear off out of here in case she finds something missing."

Roseen seized Flora by the hand and started running down the street, towing the other along in her wake.

"Missing – ?" Flora's plump legs, encumbered by her long skirt, had trouble keeping up. "What do you mean?"

"I'll tell you in a mo'."

Roseen steered them both round a corner at the junction of four ways and carried on running. Up ahead on the right was a grey-brick church. Dodging round a delivery cart, she increased her speed and swerved across towards it.

"Thank God for that – it's one of ours!" she whooped, seeing the legend 'Our Lady of the Angels' in large gold letters on the board outside.

She took the steps two at a time, with Flora stumbling behind, and shot in at the open doorway, reaching automatically for the holy water stoup as she passed. Splashing drops

43

of water down herself in a hurried sign of the cross, she pushed ajar the inner door and went through.

In the dimness of the empty church the red candle-flame of the sanctuary lamp at the far end burned like a single watchful eye amid the shadows of the altar.

Catching her breath, Flora shook off Roseen's hand.

"I shouldn't be here," she whispered nervously, casting a look round at the Italianate symbols of Catholic devotion, the painted statues of saints above their votive candle stands, the Stations of the Cross upon the walls; everything made yet more disturbingly unfamiliar by the closeness and silence of the incense-fragrant atmosphere.

"Don't talk daft. If a priest comes in, just start crossing yourself and he won't know any different."

Roseen tugged at her arm and pulled her down beside her on to the nearest pew. Digging into her jacket pocket, she produced something which she held up for Flora to see, and there was a smile almost of malicious satisfaction on her face.

"What d'you reckon, eh? And the old biddy never even noticed."

Flora's blue eyes widened as she recognised the mother of pearl and coral bracelet from the souvenir shop.

"*Roseen!* How did you get that?"

"Pinched it, of course." There wasn't the slightest trace of embarrassment in this admission. "Here – put it on for me." She offered her wrist, pushing back the braided cuff.

Flora huddled away as though stung.

"What's the matter? Oh – don't tell me – " the tone became swiftly sarcastic, "I suppose you're going to say it's wrong to take things."

"It *is* wrong to take things!"

"Pooh. I've done it lots of times. So there."

Roseen continued to dangle the bracelet in the air.

"You ought to go straight away and give it back," Flora told her, keeping her voice low, not knowing whether to be angry at such blatant dishonesty, or frightened. She had thought it strange when her friend made that remark in the shop, about having three shillings to spend, when it was a fact that she had no money at all. To discover now that the wonderful, the beautiful Roseen O'Connor was not only a

44

liar but a thief was one of the most unpleasantly hurtful things ever to happen.

The other shot her a narrow-eyed look, and tossing the corkscrew ringlets from her shoulders retorted, "Take it back be blowed! It's mine now."

"It's stolen."

The look froze into something holding a glint of warning. "Are you going to tell on me? 'Cos if so – " Flora's arm was given a painfully sharp little pinch which made her cry out. "If so, you won't be my friend any more. Now then – "

The aggression was gone as quickly as it had shown itself, and Roseen's features broke into the sudden beaming warmth of a smile. She held out her wrist once more.

"Put the bracelet on for me, and we'll go and show it your Mam and Dad."

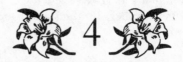

4

Discovering her friend to be an unrepentant thief cast the first specks of blight upon Flora's infatuated attachment to her. As though sensing this, Roseen hit back by starting to make unkind and sarcastic remarks which hurt, and the magic was even further tarnished.

It wasn't long after their return from the holiday at Aberystwyth that Roseen smugly announced she'd got herself a boyfriend – one of the senior monitors at school – and this too had a cooling effect upon the two's association. Flora knew nothing of boys. The private school she attended was for girls only, and her experiences of the opposite sex so far had been limited to social occasions such as birthday tea-parties. Roseen's luridly boastful accounts of her boyfriend's behaviour, and the liberties she allowed him, quite appalled the innocent Flora. A kiss on the cheek she could understand (her story-book heroines were kissed there often enough), but how could Roseen let a big boy of almost fifteen kiss her on the mouth; and worse, how could she *possibly* let him lift up her skirt and petticoat and put his hand where he shouldn't.

It was . . . well, very common; and it upset Flora to think that the girl she'd loved as best friend could demean herself in such a cheap and nasty way.

She was beginning to realise that Roseen O'Connor was not as nice a person as at first she'd blindly imagined; that her well-mannered behaviour was only put on for show, to impress grown-ups; that her sweetness soon soured to temper if she didn't get all she wanted; and that she often played quite deliberately upon her prettiness, in fact could be spiteful and greedy and selfish.

It was a sad awakening for Flora as one by one the scales of adolescent worship fell from her eyes, for although she'd had 'crushes' on other girls, her artless affection had never been given so warmly, nor her confiding nature entrusted so completely. 'I write my name upon this page,' she had penned in Roseen's autograph-book, 'for though our paths may sever, true friendship is a heritage which will last for ever.' But by the winter of 1909 when both were fourteen, that year-old friendship was virtually over, and other interests, other companions were found to fill its place.

*

At the end of the Christmas term that year, Roseen left school to start work at Dennison's Stores, earning three shillings and sixpence a week as a junior shop-girl at the branch in Wolverhampton's Dudley Street.

George Dennison himself had given her the job, with a warning not to make capital of the fact. Normally it was his store managers who interviewed and took on employees, and if she went about flaunting the Guv'nor's favour she'd be getting herself off to a bad start with the other assistants. They tended to resent anyone they thought had pushed their way in through influence 'over the counter', as it were.

If there *was* any resentment against Roseen it was from the younger, plainer females at Dennison's, who objected to the amount of admiring attention she received. Her figure was starting to fill out noticeably into feminine curves, set off by the uniform of dark blue blouse and crisply starched white apron; and a little coronet of frilled linen pinned on top of her upswept red-gold curls complemented the pertly vivacious appeal of her features. She was growing into what the men called 'a right little bobby-dazzler'; and she knew it, and made the most of that knowledge.

Young Arthur Evans, in charge of the bacon and cooked meats counter, was particularly smitten.

"You doing anything tonight, Roseen?" he asked boldly, managing to waylay her in the passage from the stock-room when she'd been at Dennison's hardly more than a fortnight.

47

She looked him up and down, equally bold. "What's it to you what I'm doing tonight?"

"I thought I might take you out somewhere."

"Is that a fact now."

She made to move past him, but Arthur leaned his arm against the wall. "How about going to the flickers? They're showing *Dr Jekyll and Mr Hyde* at the picture-house in Bilston Street."

"And what makes you think I've time to waste with you in a flea-pit like that?"

Before he could answer, she dodged smartly under the outstretched arm and made her escape through the passage door into the shop, smirking to herself at the response she'd given his invitation. She liked Arthur Evans well enough, but she recognised him for the type he was, self-assured and cocky. He'd have to go down on his knees and *beg* her for an evening out before she'd consider saying yes.

"Come on, look quick about it! You'll have Mr Sims after you."

One of the other girls on the tea counter where Roseen worked hissed her a warning as she reappeared, giving a jerk of the head in the direction of a gentleman in morning suit standing in the doorway of the manager's office.

Roseen sketched a shrug in reply and got on with serving a customer waiting her attention; but as soon as she was free again she said offhandedly, "It was that Arthur Evans held me up. He wanted to take me to the picture-house," and watched with inner satisfaction the dark flush of jealousy colour the other girl's face.

"I suppose you told him yes?"

"Not bloomin' likely! If I want to go to the flickers I can find myself better company than Arthur Evans, thank you."

"You mean you turned him down?"

There was a note of incredulity in the question. Not only was young Evans the best-looking chap in the shop, he was the most popular one with the girls, and the idea that anyone in their right mind would say no to spending an evening out with him was unbelievable.

Roseen turned to attend to another customer's order,

measuring out four ounces of best Ceylon tea from a black-lacquered container into the brass scoop of the scales. Receiving half a crown in payment, she put the money and chit into a cylinder and, reaching up, attached it to the pulley whose overhead wires ran like tramlines across the shop to the cashier's office, elevated behind a glass window half-way up the wall at the back.

Waiting for the change to be returned, she gave the girl an indifferent look. " 'Course I turned him down. He hasn't got a motor-car."

"Blimey, you're choosy, aren't you?"

The conversation ended there, and it was another ten minutes or so before there was a chance for any further exchange between them as the queue of customers started thinning.

"Eh, watch it – " Moving closer to Roseen, the girl gave her a quick nudge in the ribs. "He's back again, your Mr Bennet. What's the betting he's come for some more of his usual?"

Roseen glanced towards the street door. A stocky, bald-headed man had just come through within, wearing a check suit with a yellow silk bow-tie, and buttoned felt spats. He was one of Dennison's 'regulars' and it was becoming something of a joke among the assistants that he'd begun making an almost daily visit to the tea counter, and always waited to be served by the new shop-girl.

"Good morning, Mr Bennet." She gave him one of her special smiles as he approached. "And how are you today?"

He was years older than her – old enough to be her father, easily – but Roseen's sharp eyes had already picked out the social indications of wealth, the diamond neck-pin, the heavy gold watch-chain, the crested signet ring on the little finger; and money had a way of making the years disappear.

"I'm top-hole, thank you, Roseen." His answer was invariably the same. "All the better for seeing you."

"And what can I get you, sir."

"Well now, let me think." Not once did his eyes leave her face as he pretended to give his attention to the matter of deciding which sort of tea he would purchase today. "What was that you sold me on Tuesday, can you remember?"

Since she always sold him Indian, this presented no problem.

"It was the Assam, sir," she said with another of her smiles, keeping half a watch on Mr Sims the manager, still standing in his doorway. She'd already been warned about showing too much familiarity to customers.

"Then I'll have another quarter-pound of that," Mr Bennet responded, leaning forward just a little across the mahogany counter as if he couldn't have enough of the sight of her.

"Thank you, sir."

As she was weighing it out, he went on in a casual tone, "I hope a pretty young girl like you has someone to see her safely home after work? I wouldn't like to think of you walking the streets alone of a night, not with the riff-raff there is around these days."

"Oh, I'm all right, Mr Bennet. I don't live very far."

She took his money; and as she did so, he cast a quick look round to see that the other assistants were out of earshot, and lowered his voice.

"It'd be no trouble to see you home myself, dear. I run a motor-car, you know."

The green eyes opened wide. "What, *really* – ?"

A nod. "A Sunbeam. Would you like a ride in it?"

"Coo-er, not half!"

"Is everything to your satisfaction here, sir?" The cool, clipped tones of the manager's voice interrupted at Mr Bennet's shoulder, and one eyebrow was raised in a frosty glance towards Roseen. "Is Miss O'Connor attending to your order?"

Mr Bennet turned, thumbs stuck into his waistcoat pockets in a manner which smacked of the superiority of rank and customer privilege. "Thank you, Mr Sims, I'm being looked after very well. If I may say, it's a pleasure to be served by Miss O'Connor, and I wish some of your other assistants were half as obliging."

With that, he accepted his packet of tea with a friendly nod for Roseen, and sauntered off towards the confectionery counter.

"You'll have to watch yourself with old Sims," the other

girl said once the manager had gone again. "He'll be giving you the sack."

"What for? Serving his bloomin' customers? He wouldn't dare!"

"Oh, wouldn't he, just."

It was on the tip of Roseen's tongue to start boasting her connection with her 'Uncle George' Dennison; but she thought wiser of it, and said instead, smugly, "What d'you think? Mr Bennet wants to give me a ride in his motor-car. I told you I could find myself something better than that stupid Arthur Evans."

★

The car was waiting at the bottom of Dudley Street, its polished black coachwork sleeked with rain and glistening in the light of the gas lamps. Recognising the man's outline in the driving seat, Roseen's breath caught on a heart-skipping tingle of excitement. All afternoon she'd been thinking about his invitation, wondering if he meant it. She didn't care a hoot that Mr Bennet was bald and in his forties, with a wife at home an invalid cripple; the fact that he was rich and owned a motor-car absolved him of all that.

She ducked aside into a shop doorway to shake the rain from her boater-style hat (it was a new one, decorated with ruched loops), setting it on again at a saucier angle; then stepped back on to the pavement and started walking slowly until she'd passed the driver's door.

When it didn't open at once, she paused to glance over her shoulder, the street lamp's misty halo reflecting the oval of her face, for one awful minute thinking he hadn't recognised her. Then she saw a movement, and the windscreen flap was lifted.

"Roseen – ?"

She smiled.

"Where do you live?" Mr Bennet asked once she was inside and he'd secured the passenger door and cranked the engine into noisy, coughing life.

"Raby Street."

"Raby Street. That's somewhere at the top of Snow Hill, isn't it?"

"Yes." The cowhide upholstery of the seats had a lovely expensive smell. "Off Powlett Street, past the White Rose."

He did something to a lever and suddenly they were moving away. It was the strangest sensation, with no horse there in front to pull them along. Roseen was so tense with excitement she thought she was going to burst.

"Tell you what, dear – " He shifted another lever and they started going faster, the yellow beams of the headlamps picking out the needle-strokes of drizzle. "It's only a few minutes away, your house. What do you say to a quick drive round first. Just down Cleveland Street and back up into Queen Square."

"Oh – " Her mother Connie would be waiting with her tea cooked and ready. "Oh, all right. Thanks, Mr Bennet, that'd be ever so nice. I've never been in a motor-car before."

She stroked the backs of her fingers across the seat, loving the smooth comfortable warmth of its leather.

He reached out his hand and gave the fingers a little squeeze. "No, I didn't think you had," he said.

When they came into Queen Square he let her put on the brake lever as the Sunbeam stopped to give way to a horse-drawn brewery dray, watching her face as she laughed in pleasurable, childlike delight at the rapid noise of castanet clicks the lever ratchet made.

"Would you like to have a go sitting behind the wheel, Roseen?"

She glanced at him quickly, the laughter still in her eyes.

"I'll pull in for a second over there – " He gave a nod towards the unlit side-street running off the square to the rear of the Empire Palace theatre, and turned the car; and when it was halted in the rainswept shadows, its engine still running, he moved across from the driving seat so that the young girl could take his place.

"They'll never believe me at Dennison's when I tell them!" she crowed, pretending to 'drive' the steering wheel, hardly able to believe it herself. Blimey, this was better than the swing-boats at the fair!

Mr Bennet leaned over and put his arm round her small strong shoulders. "Well now, Roseen, how about saying thank you before I take you home?"

Something in his voice and in the way he touched her told her what it was he expected. She took her hands from the wheel and turned her face to his, trying to keep a straight expression, responding innocently, "Thank you, Mr Bennet. I appreciate your kindness, I really do."

"A little kiss won't hurt, then, will it." His grip tightened on her shoulder and he pulled her closer, his bald head catching the reflection of gaslight from the square.

His lips were surprisingly warm and soft, and his kiss not a bit like the ones she'd had from the boys at school. Roseen closed her eyes, feeling the excitement of this whole adventure heightening to a wonderful head-whirling exhilaration as Mr Bennet's lips stayed pressed against hers, trembling ever so slightly with what she supposed must be uncontrollable passion.

This was the first time she'd been kissed properly by a man. She was really enjoying it.

"Ooh, kiss me again, Mr Bennet," she whispered breathlessly when he released her. And he did, drawing her tighter into his arms, the clean-soaped smell of his skin mingling with the warm, expensive smell of his motor-car.

Afterwards he drove her home to Raby Street in silence; and just as she was getting out at the corner, he said, "Let's keep this a secret, eh? Don't tell them at Dennison's I kissed you, there's a good girl."

"Will you give me a ride in your car again, then?"

In the darkness she couldn't see his expression, but he pressed her hand and nodded. "If you keep quiet about it."

"I will, Mr Bennet. I promise."

She watched him reverse the Sunbeam and go driving off, back along Powlett Street; and when the last sounds of the engine had faded she turned and ran down the entry, home.

"You're late coming in – where is it you've been?" Connie demanded, her voice slurred, a glass of gin half-way to her mouth.

Roseen took off her hat.

"It's raining hard. I had to shelter for a bit. What's for tea, Mam, I'm hungry."

5

Sidney Hathaway leaned forward, elbows resting on the gallery balustrade, his attention claimed by the young woman standing below in the college entrance hall. She was one of the new students who had recently started the two-year course to gain their Elementary School Teacher's Certificate, and Sidney, now in his fourth term at Moseley College, had several times noticed her particularly.

He couldn't say what it was about her that attracted him. She seemed very quiet and dreamy, almost shy of contact; and her manner of dress was plain, though neat, usually a white tuckered blouse and dark tailored skirt worn to the ankle; and with her brown hair swept back into a bun at the nape of the neck she looked exactly what she was: a student-teacher. There was nothing at all about her looks to catch the eye, and yet she had something – a gentleness in the gravity of her expression, a sweetness in the timidity of her smile – which Sidney found undeniably appealing. Even her name (discovered from the notice board) had a demure attraction for him: Flora.

He wondered whether she was waiting there below for someone. As ever when he saw her, she had her nose buried in a book, reading in a most absorbed fashion as though nothing else existed but the images of prose and poetry conjured from the printed page. He was in half a mind to go down and speak to her, introduce himself; but just as he was straightening, some other fellow equally immersed in reading matter came striding out of the main corridor into the hall, and not looking where he was going, collided with the young woman and sent the book flying from her hand.

"That's one way to effect an acquaintance, I suppose," Sidney thought wryly, and leaned forward once more on the balustrade, to observe the consequences.

★

"I say – I *am* sorry!"

Flora's arm was caught in a firm grip.

"I haven't damaged you, I hope?"

She found she was being scrutinised by a pair of warm brown eyes whose expression held both friendliness and genuine concern; and recovering herself, managed to shake her head.

"No, it's quite all right. I shouldn't have been standing in the way."

"And *I* should be more careful where I'm walking."

The young man released her arm and bent to retrieve the book he'd knocked to the floor. As he handed it back, he glanced at its title and exclaimed with a quick smile, "Aha – Swinburne! So you're a fellow-devotee?"

"Oh . . . oh, yes. I admire him enormously. And . . . and you?"

"*Rather*! His poetry's a triumph of pure, glittering genius."

He moved aside to let a group of people by, and as he did so his smile turned to one of mock chagrin. "I say, do please forgive my ill manners. I should introduce myself. My name's Robert Wells."

Flora felt her face start to colour up, and inwardly cursed the shyness which even now, at the age of seventeen, made her blush so furiously. A little awkwardly she shook the hand he offered.

"I'm Flora Dennison. One of the new students."

"I thought I hadn't seen you before."

She wondered whether he too was a student. He looked older than the others, about twenty-five, she thought.

As though reading her mind, Robert Wells went on disarmingly, "Yes, I'm studying for the Certificate as well – I'm in my final year – but I must confess I feel quite the doyen of the college amongst all you young ones." He glanced at her

55

book again. "Perhaps one day when you've time, we can discuss Algernon Charles together."

The blush deepened in Flora's round cheeks. She lowered her eyes. "Yes . . . yes, I'd like that, Mr Wells."

"Good! We'll meet again, then."

And with that he was gone, his quick stride swallowing him into the stream of young men and women flowing along the corridor.

She stood where she was for several moments composing herself, then turned towards the stairs to get her notes ready for the afternoon's lecture. As she was going up to the first floor one of the students coming down stood aside to let her pass. He was one she had noticed earlier leaning on the gallery balustrade, and as she passed him she wondered why he should look at her so very earnestly; then chided herself for imagining things, and promptly dismissed him from her mind.

★

Moseley College for the Training of School Teachers was situated in a pleasant residential area of Birmingham, and stood in its own grounds along a wide, tree-lined road which ran south from the suburbs towards the Warwickshire countryside. It was administered by the city education authorities, and was one of a number of similar colleges which had opened in recent years following the Education Act of 1902.

Flora had decided at the age of fifteen that she wanted to take up teaching as a profession. With a father as wealthy as George Dennison she had no need to work at all; indeed, had she been born into the middle classes a generation earlier, the idea would have been frowned upon as a nonsense. But times were changing. Victorian conceptions and social attitudes were no longer adhered to as rigidly as once they had been, and the accession of George V in 1910 had seemed to herald a new era of emancipation from the past.

During her final term at private school Flora had sent off for details of several Midlands colleges. Liking Moseley best, she'd visited the place with her parents and in due course applied for admission and was accepted. Apart from its most immediate benefits, Moseley had the advantage of taking both male and female students: having thus far spent her education entirely amongst members of her own sex, Flora thought the experience of a mixed establishment might help her overcome her crippling reticence in the presence of young men.

The college had one further advantage too, in that it was not far distant from home, and yet far enough to justify her wish to become a weekly boarder, thus gaining for herself a measure of independence. Shy she might be, but she was also developing a sensible and practical nature, a side of her character which those who didn't know her well tended not to appreciate, having only the outward impression of a studiously dreamy, rather withdrawn young woman.

She'd settled into the routine of college life easily enough after the first few testing weeks – weeks of great adjustment, during which Flora found she must adapt not only to attending to herself in shared accommodation with three other girls, but also to being integrated into a community of fellow-students representing an entire cross-section of British class and society.

Two of her room-mates, Jessy Craig and Winifred Unsworth, soon made friends with her; the other, May Prothero, tended to keep herself a little aloof, preferring to find her friends among the older students. Ironically, in view of this lack of chumminess, it was May who effected the introduction of Sidney Hathaway into Flora's life and thus acted as an agent of Fate in what was to follow.

The end of her first college term in December 1912 coincided with the start of the festive season, and the talk was of nothing but the Christmas dance and who would be partnering whom. Winifred and Jessy had already been spoken for, which left Flora the only one without an escort.

"As a matter of fact," May Prothero said casually, coming into the conversation as she sat buffing her nails in their room, "someone asked only this morning whether or not I knew if you had a partner."

"Oh – ?" Flora looked nonplussed. "Who?"

"Sidney Hathaway. One of the second-year students."

"What's this, Flora – some dark horse you've been keeping secret from us?" Winifred teased her.

"No – honestly! I've never even heard of him."

"Well, he seems to know about you," May said over her shoulder. "In fact he wondered if he could ask you to the dance himself."

"Oh-ho," came in Jessy with a broad wink, "do I smell romance in the air? What's he look like, this Sidney who's-it?"

May shrugged. "Nothing especially wonderful. No background to speak of. Rather mundane, actually."

"Which tells us a fat lot about his appearance, I must say. Come on, May – is he tall, short, dark, fair – what?"

"Oh, I don't know." Another bored shrug. "Brownish hair, ordinary face, medium height. I told you, nothing especially wonderful."

Meeting Sidney Hathaway for herself a few days later, Flora was inclined to agree. May introduced them in the college tea-room, and at first sight the only thing to strike Flora was the young man's teeth, which looked as though they could have done with a jolly good brushing. He had a pleasing enough manner, however, and blue eyes attractively deep-set under straight, dark brows; and what was probably most important, a way of making Flora feel quite at ease with him, so that within fifteen minutes of their meeting she was laughing as naturally at his dry humour as if she'd known him for years.

Afterwards he asked if she would walk with him in the College grounds for a while before dinner.

"And if you say no, I warn you, I shall throw myself into the lily pond."

"But the lily pond's hardly more than a foot deep."

"So? Did I mention anything about suicide?"

The winter light of late afternoon held a softness which seemed to mist the trees and lawns, and beyond the naked branches the sky was full of swathes of dove-grey cloud edged with the pink of approaching sunset.

"I know where I've seen you before," Flora said bravely as they descended the terrace steps together. "You were in the entrance hall gallery one day, leaning on the rail. I remember noticing you."

"You remember noticing me." Sidney repeated her words in the drollest manner. "I shall write that in my memoirs. 'She was kind enough to acknowledge that she remembered noticing me.' "

"But it was only because someone walked into me and almost knocked me over," she added at once, hastily, not wishing to give the wrong impression.

"Ah." He pulled a face and kicked at the leaves lying fallen in drifts on the flagstones. "For a moment you raised my hopes. I thought at last here was someone who found my physiognomy unforgettable."

Not knowing quite how to answer this, Flora smiled shyly and pretended to give her attention to a group of students engaged in a lively discussion of a book one of them was holding.

"And have you met him again since?" Sidney asked when the group had gone by.

"I'm sorry – ?"

"That fellow you collided with in the hall. Have you met him since?"

"Oh, you mean Robert Wells. No, no, actually I haven't." She hesitated a second, then added, "Do you know him at all?"

"Robert Wells? Only slightly. He's very cerebral – you know, one of these intellectual chaps. A fount of poetic philosophy. Not really my sort."

He took her elbow to steer her round a puddle.

"As a matter of fact, I can't say I recall seeing him lately. Usually he's stuck in the library swotting away at his lecture notes."

"Perhaps he's been unwell," she answered, trying to sound indifferent. "There's quite a lot of influenza about at the moment. Shall we . . . shall we turn back now?"

Since being literally almost swept off her feet by Robert Wells that day in the college hall, Flora had been waiting for him to keep his promise to discuss the poems of Swinburne. So far she'd waited in vain. If it were not for the fact that he'd been so sincerely attentive she would have dismissed him from her mind; but her mind refused to forget him, and hardly a day went by when she'd not glanced round the

59

dining hall or scanned the stairs and corridors, hoping for a second meeting, even allowing herself the dream that he might ask her to the Christmas dance.

In the event, however, it was Sidney Hathaway who did that.

★

This dance was the first major social event of Flora's adult life, and her father had generously footed the bill for an evening gown to match the importance of the occasion. The fittings had to be done at weekends when she was at home, interrupting what little time she had for leisure, but the result was worth it: a high-waisted gown in peach crêpe de Chine which suited Flora's plumpish figure beautifully and made her seem taller, especially with her hair set into curls and worn up on the crown.

Viewing herself in the cheval-glass, she felt she was beholding a stranger.

The dance was held in the assembly hall of Moseley College, with a band called Danny James and his Jolly Boys who eschewed the usual black tie and evening jacket in favour of flannels, striped blazers and straw boater hats. Syncopated dance music was beginning to be all the rage, and mixed in amongst the waltzes and military two-steps on the evening's programme Flora discovered the Turkey Trot, the Bunny Hug and the Grizzly Bear.

"How on earth does one dance to those?" she enquired of Sidney in alarm. Such bizarre gyrations had hardly been a feature of her dancing lessons at Stockwell End.

"That I shall demonstrate in due course," he promised, rising to hold out a hand in invitation to take the floor for a comparatively safe waltz *à trois temps*.

The hall was crowded with students and made a wonderfully colourful scene; but the press of bodies prevented anyone doing more than steer their partners sedately round the floor, a restriction which Sidney found irksome, since he considered himself in his own words 'nifty on his pins' and wanted to impress Flora with his expertise.

His chance to do so came at last with the Turkey Trot.

"Come on, old thing – " he shouted above the hubbub of noise and laughter, "this is our chance to shine!"

Gripping her tightly round the waist, he launched them both on to the floor and commenced a most ungainly step-routine, a half-running, half-bouncing series of movements in which Flora was jerked violently back and forth, one moment crushed against him and the next thrust away at arm's length, so that she felt (as she wrote in her diary afterwards) like a rag doll on the end of a piece of string.

By the time this performance was finished she was thoroughly out of breath and only too glad to sit down again, refusing Sidney's invitation to stay on the floor for the next dance.

"We seem fated to bump into one another, don't we," said a voice at her shoulder. "You almost sent me flying there."

Not recognising who'd spoken, Flora turned quickly in her seat.

"Oh – " Her hand went to her mouth in startled surprise. "Oh, it's *you*!"

Robert Wells smiled. "Yes, it's me. May I – ?" He indicated Sidney's empty chair beside her, and seated himself. "What's happened to your energetic partner?"

She answered abstractedly. "He's – er, gone outside. He'll be back in a moment." And then in the same breath, "I didn't really send you flying just now, did I?"

"Almost. I managed to hop out of your path in time. That's a very frisky dance you were doing."

Flora looked down, unable to meet the good-humoured warmth of his gaze. "Actually, I felt terribly stupid. I hope people weren't laughing too much."

"Not at all! They were probably thinking the same as I was – what a jolly good sport you were. It takes pluck, you know, to do something like that in public."

There was a teasing note in Robert's voice, and glancing up at him again she saw the smile was still there; and realised in the self-same instant what a very attractive face he had and how glad she was that they'd met again.

Sidney Hathaway was making his way back between the dancers. Quickly, impulsively, she said, "You haven't forgotten we were going to discuss Swinburne?"

"I haven't forgotten. We will next term, I promise. I've had to spend the last few weeks – "

He stopped as Sidney joined them, and stood up to relinquish his chair.

"Yes, we know one another, of course," he said, putting out a hand in greeting.

"Yes." Sidney's blue eyes held a slightly chilly look, Flora thought.

"I was just explaining," Robert continued, giving her his attention once more, "I've had to spend part of this term away from college. Illness in the family, I'm afraid."

"Oh, I'm sorry to hear that. Nothing serious?"

"Measles. Both the children went down with it together, and my wife couldn't possibly cope with them single-handed."

Robert pulled a doleful face; then his expression at once warmed again into humour as he added, "Well, I'll leave you two to enjoy yourselves. I only came in here for half an hour as a token gesture of sociability."

And with a nod and a smile for Flora, he walked away, leaving her with the strangest, saddest feeling; as though the revelation that he was a married man had taken something from her dreams.

 6

The previous year of 1912 had not been a lucky one.

In February a national strike of coal miners had paralysed the country. In April the White Star liner SS *Titanic* struck an iceberg in the Atlantic and sank with the dreadful loss of over one thousand five hundred lives. In August the simmering tension in the Balkan States erupted into conflict when Montenegro declared war on Turkey. In November, as a tragic outcome of the British South Pole Expedition, a search party found the frozen bodies of Captain Scott and his companions. And to show that misfortune affected commoners and kings alike, the Emperor of Japan and the King of Denmark both died.

"People at college are saying this business in the Balkans is bound to cause trouble closer to home," Flora told her father in conversation a few days before the start of the new year's term. "What's your opinion, Papa?"

"As long as Germany keeps out of things, it shouldn't amount to much. A bit of sabre-rattling, that's all."

"And if Germany becomes involved – ?"

George Dennison shook his head in resigned fashion.

"It wouldn't mean a war, would it?" she pressed him anxiously.

"God help us if it did! France and Belgium and the rest, they're balanced like a line of dominoes at present. It only needs a shove from the Kaiser and the whole damn' lot might go toppling one after t'other."

He patted her hand.

"But don't fret yourself, our Flora. He wouldn't be that daft. There's too much at stake."

She repeated her father's words to Robert Wells when the two of them met again in January. A note to her had said he had a free college period the following week, and if it was convenient, would she care to join him for a pot of tea and slice of cake at Velma's Tea Shop. This was a popular venue of students in Moseley's old 'village' around the parish church, and Flora had been there several times already with her room-mates Winifred and Jessy. She had hesitated a little before accepting. Now that she knew Robert had a wife and children it didn't seem quite right that he should issue social invitations to unattached young women; but as Jessy Craig pointed out in her customary forthright manner, what possible scandal could come from sitting in Velma's in full public view, warbling on about Swinburne over a few cups of tea? Hardly the scene for seduction, my dear!

And so here they were, the two of them, sharing a check-clothed table by the window in the generous warmth of the room's Dutch stove, enjoying slices of rich cherry cake and watching the flurries of snow scudding past the lighted shopfronts opposite as they discussed the situation in the Balkans.

"Yes, I'm inclined to agree with your father," Robert said, taking a sip of hot, sweet tea. "His simile of a stacked row of dominoes for European politics sums up the position rather well. There are so many obligations between one country and another, to honour this treaty or that. A disturbance in the Balkans might seem a pretty minor affair to us here, but its effects in the long run could well prove extremely serious."

He put his cup down in the saucer and looked at Flora. The warmth of the stove had brought a flush of colour to her cheeks that was nothing to do with her usual shyness, and her expression held a wide-eyed, vulnerable innocence.

"So there *will* be a war in Europe, as everyone thinks?"

"Well, I'm no expert." The way she was gazing at him made Robert feel very mature and very clever. He leaned back in his chair. "It needs a crystal ball to predict the course of events over the next few years. We'll just have to keep our

64

fingers crossed and hope this Peace Conference in London can settle the Balkan question amicably without too much loss of face on either side."

Flora nodded, and looked down at her plate.

"Come on – let's change the subject," he went on suddenly, watching her. "Let's talk about you, shall we?"

Startled, she looked up again.

"About *me* – ?"

"Mm. Your name is Flora Dennison. You come from Wolverhampton. You want to be a schoolteacher. You admire Swinburne. That much I know already. What else is there?"

She made a little gesture, a half-shrug of confusion, and picked up the last of her cherry cake from the plate. "Nothing, really."

"Now I won't believe that! What about brothers or sisters? Do you have any?"

"No. There's only me."

"Friends?"

"A few. Those I've made here at college."

"But no one in particular – no one from your schooldays, for instance?"

Flora remembered Roseen O'Connor. Since their friendship ended three years ago, her only news of Roseen was that the girl was now working for Dennison's. In all that time she'd seen her just once, one evening early last summer, sitting inside a motor-car in Dudley Street looking very grown-up in a cheap and tarty way and (Flora was sure) wearing lip-rouge on her mouth.

After a moment, when she'd swallowed the cake, she shook her head in response to Robert's question. "No. There's no one in particular."

"Not even . . ." He teased her slyly. "Not even Sidney Hathaway?"

This time the rush of colour in her cheeks was of pure embarrassment, and before she could speak he'd got in again quickly, "Look, I say, I'm sorry. That's none of my business. Shall we have another change of topic? And *you* ask the questions this time."

"Very well." Flora marvelled at her sudden nerve in taking

up his invitation. "Tell me – tell me about your children. What are their names? How old are they?"

"They're my stepchildren, actually. Margaret and Jack. Aged six and four."

He took another sip of his tea while she assimilated this information.

"I can see what you're thinking. That my wife can't have wasted much time between husbands."

There was something almost self-defensive in the way he said this, and without waiting for her response, he leaned the leather-patched elbows of his jacket on the table and went on, "I've known Helen – that's my wife – since childhood. We grew up in the same place. She married a second cousin of mine who worked as an engineer in Southampton. And when he was killed, very tragically, in an accident at the docks, well – " Robert looked directly into Flora's eyes, "I took on the responsibility of looking after her and the two little ones. I have, perhaps unfortunately, a great sense of moral duty."

"Why do you say that?" she enquired. "What's unfortunate about a sense of duty?"

He laced his fingers together and glanced down at them while considering his answer. The light from the tea-room's gaselier was reflected in the gloss of thick, dark wavy hair falling forward over his forehead. Flora watched his face, unconscious of the wistful expression upon her own, which, to anyone observing, revealed far more of her feelings than she herself was probably aware of.

He raised his head again, and now the gravity had gone, replaced by the old smile she was growing to know so well.

"No, there's nothing wrong with a sense of duty. I've never regretted my decision to marry Helen. She's a marvellous woman." Then, as if he felt he owed some explanation, "It's just that I was very young when it happened, and perhaps I could have done with rather more experience of life before making such a serious commitment."

Outside the window the snow flurries were starting to give way to a sleety rain, and although it wasn't long after four o'clock, already the pewter-grey murk of a January dusk had darkened the street, making Velma's Tea Shop a haven of cosy warmth and light.

"Shall we order another pot of tea?" Flora suggested tentatively, not wanting to seem too curious about his private life.

"Let's – what a good idea." Robert straightened himself in his chair and turned to wave to the waitress over by the counter. "And some more of that cherry cake, as well."

"Oh, not for me – "

"Nonsense! An extra slice will fortify you against the wintry blast." He eyed her in mock-severe fashion. "I hope you're not one of those modern misses who think a good appetite ruins the figure. You're perfect just as you are, Flora."

Suddenly shy again, she ducked her head at the compliment and smiled. May Prothero had said cattily only the other day that she ought to eat less; but Flora was naturally plump – not fleshy or large-boned, but of that comfortably rounded softness which men have always found so attractively feminine.

While they waited for their order Robert took something from his jacket pocket and leaned over to put it down in front of her.

"What's this?" she asked him with a questioning look.

"A book."

"I can see it's a book. I mean, what is it about?"

"Why not open it and find out."

She obeyed, turning the hand-tooled leather cover of the slim volume. On the title page she read, '*The Flowerless Fields of Heaven*, being the collected poems of Charles Anthony la Motte.'

"You'll recognise that title, of course," Robert said.

"*The Flowerless Fields of Heaven*?" Flora thought a moment. Then she clapped her hands in sudden recognition. "Oh, yes – of course! It's from the opening lines of Mr Swinburne's *Atalanta in Calydon*. 'Maiden, and mistress of the months and stars now folded in the flowerless fields of heaven . . .' "

She stopped, biting her lip in embarrassment, not because she'd remembered the quotation, but because the young couple at the next table had paused in their conversation to look across at her.

"Who is Charles Anthony la Motte?" she asked quickly, to cover her confusion.

"One of our latter-day men of letters." Robert held out his cup and saucer. "And a genius, in my opinion. I worked for him for several years in the capacity of secretary and general dogsbody."

Filling the cup from the fresh pot of tea, Flora passed it back again. She hardly liked to say that she'd never heard of the gentleman in case it should reveal her own ignorance. Instead she observed, "That must have been wonderfully interesting! How did you make his acquaintance?"

"He lives at Osborne on the Isle of Wight." With a nod of thanks, Robert added a spoonful of sugar to his tea and stirred it. "My parents were both in service there, at Osborne House, and knew his father, Sir Edward la Motte. Perhaps I ought to explain, before I start sounding very grand, that Sir Edward was an equerry to the old Queen, and my parents were employed on the domestic staff. I was born at Osborne House, as a matter of fact," he helped himself to another slice of the cherry cake, "but on the wrong side of the baize door, I'm afraid."

Flora's slate-blue eyes widened. Imagine it, *actually born in a royal residence*! This was the stuff of fairy-tale romance on which her imagination had enriched itself since infancy.

"Did you – did you ever see the Queen?" she asked a little breathlessly.

"Never inside the house, no, because the servants' quarters were in quite a separate part. But every now and again I'd see her in the grounds, usually driving in her carriage." There was a pause while he took a bite; then, with his mouth half-full, "She spoke to me once, one day when I was with my father."

Flora leaned forward, chin in hand, enraptured.

"She tapped me on the cheek and said what a healthy child I looked." The mouthful was swallowed. "I remember being very sad when she died, because although she *was* the Queen, to me she'd always seemed just a very stout and rather amiable old lady."

Robert draped one elbow over the back of his seat, enjoying the expression of childlike wonderment on his companion's face. The couple at the next table got up to go, with a scraping of chairs on the wood-block floor and a 'Thank you, goodbye,' to the waitress.

Her gaze half-following them, Flora asked, "And your parents – they've remained at Osborne?"

He finished off his cake and gave a nod. "They have a small cottage in the grounds, a grace and favour residence. The house itself is still occupied, of course. Since King Edward presented it to the nation, part of it has become a convalescent home for officers, though I understand there are plans afoot to use it as a Royal Naval college."

"Oh."

There was a short silence.

Opening the book of poems again she began leafing through its tissue-thin pages, stopping here and there to read a line. "Please don't think me inquisitive," she said awkwardly, without looking up, "but . . . well, what made you leave Mr la Motte's employment? The work must have given you a lot of pleasure, surely?"

"It did!"

For a moment it seemed that would be all the answer he'd give; but then, with a slight shrug of the shoulder, Robert went on, "It was immensely rewarding and I enjoyed it. Loved it, in fact. However, once Helen and I were married I found I wasn't earning sufficient to support a wife and family."

There was a note in his voice which might have been anger, except that his face carried a look of wry detachment.

"For a time I worked in Southampton as a clerk. Dull stuff – routine pen-pushing – nothing to exercise the mind at all. But I stuck at it until I'd managed to save enough money for us to scrape along while I studied for my Teacher's Certificate here at Moseley."

Flora nodded. "Why did you choose Moseley, though? It's a long way from home."

As though her questioning had become a sudden irritation, Robert Wells picked up his cup to drain the rest of his tea, and taking out his pocket-watch to consult it, said briskly, "Good Lord, it's time we were thinking about going! I hadn't realised how late it was, your company's been so enjoyable."

He started to get up from his seat. "Will you excuse me – I'll just settle our bill."

When they came out of Velma's Tea Shop dusk had given way to darkness and the gas lamps were being lit along the street, reflecting a hazy light on the wet pavement. Flora huddled inside her Ulster overcoat, collar turned up against the cold sleety wind, grateful that she'd had the sense to bring a large, black silk umbrella which belonged to Winifred.

"I say – " Robert held on to his Homburg hat with one hand and ducked beneath the brolly. "Do you think I could share this with you?"

He was not wearing any top-coat – a fact which surprised Flora – and the shoulders of his jacket were already glistening from the rain. She raised the umbrella in invitation, and offered it to him to hold since he was so much taller; and as he took it, he slipped his arm through hers in friendly fashion so that they fell into step side by side.

"We never did discuss Swinburne, did we," he said.

She could feel the warmth of his body through the sleeve of her coat. "No . . . no, we didn't."

"Tell you what, Flora, read *The Flowerless Fields of Heaven*, and when I next take you out to tea you can let me have your opinion. I'd value it. *Then* we can indulge ourselves in Swinburne."

He looked down at her and smiled and gave her arm a companionable little squeeze.

She had asked him why he'd chosen to study at Moseley, so far away from home. Perhaps the answer lay here, in the cold and the dark and the wet of a January evening. The freedom to come and go. The freedom to share his mind. The freedom of his youth and youth's experience before responsibility and duty stole it from him.

Robert Wells loved his wife, and loved his stepchildren. But he was only twenty-six, and sometimes a man needed to dream a little before the demands and burdens of life made him forget what things there were to dream about.

7

Even though it was a beautifully warm and sunny day outside, Connie had a fire lit in the kitchen range and was sitting slumped by it in a chair, her face unwashed and glistening with perspiration.

George Dennison ran a finger round the neck of his collar.

"Why d'you need a fire in weather like this? It's a blasted oven in here."

She lolled her head against her shoulder and squinted up at him. The blouse she was wearing was none too clean and had a couple of buttons missing from the bodice, and on her feet – none too clean, either – just a pair of scuffed old slippers. The kitchen stank unpleasantly of sour milk and stale cooking.

He looked round him in disgust.

"When was the last time you took a broom to this place?" he asked her. "Look at it – ! I wouldn't keep a pig in here, the state it's in." His critical glance took in the sagging net at the window, dirty with grease, the clothes flung anyhow across a chair, the stained tablecloth, the broken gas-mantle, the empty bottles.

"What's the mater with you, Connie? Eh? Can't you see for yourself what a muck-heap it is?"

She blew out her lips in the exaggerated fashion of someone more drunk than was apparent, and made a vague gesture of the free hand not clutching a glass to her breast.

" 'S all right. Jus' needs a bit o' tidying. Bit o' tidying, tha's all. Roseen'll do it."

"No. *You'll* do it." George Dennison took a step across the hearth and seized her by the arm. "Come on, Connie – stir yourself and clean this mess up. You can't expect young Roseen to do it. She's at work all day."

"Leggo o' me!" Connie's wail had the self-pitying sound of drunken resentment. "You're not to be maulin' me when I'm feelin' so bad."

"You're only bad because you drink yourself sodden." He let her arm drop, seeing the futility of argument. The stifling heat in the room and the rancid smell were making him feel a bit queasy.

"Have you looked at yourself lately? You used to be a handsome woman when first I met you," he went on, turning away. "Now you're not worth a penny of any man's time. Where's your pride? Don't you care any more?"

" 'Course I care." Tears started gathering in Connie's puffy eyes. Unsteadily she put her glass to her mouth and gulped off the contents. " 'S *you* wha's not carin' any more. Leavin' me all alone by m'self week after week wi' never the sight o' you – "

"Oh, don't start about that again. We've had it out already. You and me, we reached the parting of the ways years ago, and you should count yourself damn' lucky you've still got a free roof over your head. If it wasn't for Roseen – "

George Dennison finished his sentence by pulling out his handkerchief to wipe the sweat trickling down his forehead. Blast it, he could do without coming here, he told himself. It was the same performance every time – maudlin tears that ended in shouting matches. His doctor had warned him, he wasn't to let himself get worked up; after that slight heart attack last month, he'd got to learn to take things easier.

Connie hauled herself from her chair and stumbled over to the table to refill her glass from among the clutter of bottles. He glanced at her dispassionately, at the hair hanging in greasy strands from its pins, the lardy-white, fat-dimpled flesh of her arms.

The back door slammed.

"Mam – ?" That was Roseen's voice calling.

She came into the kitchen bringing with her a breath of fresh air and sunshine from the street, and at sight of George Dennison her young face broke into a cheeky smile.

72

"Well, fancy finding you here, Uncle George! I thought you'd lost our address."

"There – even the child says it herself, the way you're neglectin' us," her mother chimed in, clutching at the edge of the table for support.

"Oh, shut up, Mam, and sit down, you're drunk," Roseen told her. "Have you offered Uncle George a cup of tea?"

"No, I won't have anything, thanks," he replied for himself. "I only called by on the chance of finding you here, Roseen, seeing it's Sunday."

"Tha's nice – didn't even come t' see *me*," Connie interrupted again, preparing for argument now that she had another full glass of gin in her hand.

"Mam, *sit down*," Roseen said loudly, not even looking at her. Then, "What d'you want me about, Uncle George? It's nothing to do with the shop, is it? Mr Sims hasn't been complaining, has he?"

"Not complaining exactly, no." George Dennison glanced from the girl to her mother. Connie had shuffled back to her chair and was now slumped forward gazing morosely into the fire. "He's had a word with me about Mr Bennet."

Roseen's chin went up a fraction. "Oh? Mr Bennet?"

"He thought I ought to know." They exchanged looks. "Since it was me as put you into the shop in the first place."

"Well he's got a nerve, I must say – "

"It's Sims's job to keep an eye on the staff, Roseen, and mine to know exactly what's going on among my employees. That's the way I run my business."

"So – ?" She gave a shrug and started taking off her straw summer hat, her face set in a mask of defiance. "Mr Bennet's given me rides in his motor-car, what's wrong with that?"

"Nothing. If rides is all it's been."

"Who's this Mr Bennet? I never heard o' the man," Connie joined in again.

She was ignored.

"What's Mr Sims been saying about me – I've got a right to hear. He's had it in for me ever since I started at the shop." Roseen threw the hat aside. "I've done nothing I shouldn't. A couple of times in Mr Bennet's motor-car, that's all."

"It's been more than a couple of times," George Dennison reminded her. "And Bennet's a married man."

"I know. He told me. There's no law against it."

"Look, Roseen. I'm only pointing this out to you for your own good. You're hardly more than a kiddie – "

"I'm old enough to take care of myself, Uncle George." The defiance was openly mirrored now in her attitude, lower lip set stubbornly under its scarlet rouge, green eyes narrowed. She looked like a cat about to spit, he thought.

"You're seventeen, that's all. I don't want to see you being taken advantage of."

"Ha!" She tossed back her head in derision. "Did you hear that, Mam? That's rich that is, coming from you, Uncle George."

"What d'you mean?"

"You know what I mean. You're a married man yourself. But my name isn't Connie O'Connor, and no man takes advantage of *me*."

He stared at her for a long moment as the import of her words struck home. Of course she wasn't a child. She'd known for years what was going on between him and her mother. But, paradoxically, that was why he wanted to protect her from someone like Bennet who'd only abuse her young body for self-satisfaction, and probably ruin her chances of a decent social future.

"Wha's that you're sayin', Roseen. Wha's that you're sayin' now t' your Uncle George." Connie's gin-slurred question held a note of angry bewilderment. "You mind how you speak t' him, d'you hear!"

"Yes, Mam, I'm sorry." The flash of sudden temper died as Roseen realised she might have said too much. After all, Uncle George had been keeping her in food and clothes and home for most of her life, and both she and her mother relied on him still for money.

"I'm sorry," she said again, looking at him. "Anyway, there's no cause to worry about Mr Bennet. I've got myself a regular young man now, see, and me and our Billy – well, we're courting, like. So I shan't be taking any more rides in motor-cars."

"I'm relieved to hear that." George Dennison took up his

bowler from the end of the table and dabbed at his temples with his handkerchief. He'd be glad to get out and back into the sweet fresh air. "Is he a local lad you're seeing?"

"Billy's a good Cat'lic boy," said Connie indistinctly, tilting the glass to her mouth.

Roseen started moving around the kitchen, picking things up, making the place look tidier. "He comes from off the Willenhall Road. I met him in church."

"And how old's the young fellow?"

"Eighteen. He's got a good job, an' all." Roseen glanced across at her Uncle George and smiled suddenly, the fetchingly pretty face softening with happiness. "I love him *ever* so much. He's golden to me, he is. In fact . . . in fact I think he wants to marry me."

★

To be honest, Billy Kelly hadn't actually *said* anything about wanting to get married – come to that, he wasn't the sort who said much anyway – but his amorous attentions left Roseen in no doubt what was at the back of his mind. They'd met at St Mary's and St John's as she said, except that the circumstances weren't quite as pious as she'd made them sound to George Dennison.

What happened was that she'd gone into the church to pull her garters up after getting out of Mr Bennet's motor-car on Snow Hill; and while sitting in a side-pew to do this, she realised too late there was scaffolding rigged along one wall, and a couple of workmen up there distempering the plaster.

"Blimey, now I've seen it all!" one of them said loudly, nudging his mate in the ribs. "Is this what they give you here for penance, d'you reckon – three Hail Marys and show us a leg?"

Both men started laughing while Roseen very hurriedly finished rolling up her garters over her black lisle stockings.

"Had your eyeful, the pair of you?" she demanded angrily, her voice carrying in the empty stillness; and putting her skirts to rights, she snatched her hat and bag from the pew and went flouncing back along the aisle.

There was a rattle of scaffold pipes behind, and the noise of somebody jumping down and coming after her.

"Hang on a mo' – " A brawny, broad-shouldered shape appeared between her and the porch door. "You haven't took offence, have you?"

"Push off," Roseen said rudely, trying to side-step him. He side-stepped with her. "Don't be like that now, girl! We was only having a joke, Eddie and me. Here, tell you what – let's knock off for a bit and buy you a drink, eh? Just to show we didn't mean no harm."

About to tell him what he could do with his invitation, she looked the young chap straight in the eyes. They were the bluest she'd ever seen, and set in a face that wouldn't have shamed a picture-film actor.

"Well . . ." Despite herself, she hesitated.

"That's OK then. Eddie – ?" he called to his mate on the scaffold, miming his intention by raising an elbow. "The White Rose. You coming?"

His name was Billy Kelly. The youngest of a family of seven. Mother dead, father absconded, brought up by an elder sister. Ran away at twelve to see the world and spent a year in prison for petty theft – 'nicking from market stalls, mostly'. Somewhere along the way he'd acquired better sense and some gumption. Earned his living by hiring himself as a building labourer, navvy, stevedore, fairground fighter . . . jack of all trades. Eighteen years old, and as handsome a lad – as the song went – as ever came out of Erin's green isle.

His pride and joy was a six-horsepower 'Zenith' motor bicycle which he rode everywhere with swerving, skidding, noisy over-confidence to the danger of all else on the roads. He hadn't a nerve in his body, had Billy. He was a brash, cocky, devil-may-care young bruiser, always ready for a laugh, always ready for a fight, always ready for a drink; always ready for a woman.

In Roseen O'Connor, though, he'd met his match.

That first meeting of theirs had been two months ago, in June. Her affair (if affair it was) with Mr Bennet had been dragging on and on, and the attraction of the motor-car had long since palled as boredom and monotony set into their relationship. For months at a time she'd ignore him and go out and enjoy herself with young folk more her own age,

76

dancing, going to picture-houses or the Empire Palace. Then he'd buy her something expensive that she couldn't resist, and she'd relent and start seeing him again; always the same thing, going for drives in the 'Sunbeam', sitting in some back street and letting him maul her.

It wasn't what she understood as making love. Love was a word Mr Bennet never used, except when he spoke of his invalid wife, and then it became an apology, an explanation. No, it was . . . using her body to relieve himself, she supposed. He would kiss her, touch her breasts, stroke her legs, and then he'd start groaning and press himself against her while whatever it was happened, as it always did when he got over-excited.

Physically Roseen was still a virgin. It was innocence she'd lost; and that had been taken from her years ago in childhood, deflowered by her background and her upbringing. What she learned from Mr Bennet was that men were putty when it came down to the promises of sex. As long as a girl behaved as though she *might*, she'd have them eating out of her hand with eagerness – it was that tantalising *may be* that kept them coming panting back for more.

Ironically enough, their relationship hadn't attracted notice till it was over. He'd been very circumspect about their meetings; if he came into Dennison's never drawing attention to himself by being overly familiar with her, always picking her up in different side-streets and setting her down somewhere else. Not even the other shop-girls ever guessed for certain who it was she'd been seeing all this time. But then, after she met Billy Kelly and they'd started walking out together, Mr Bennet grew most upset that she was refusing to go with him any more, and he'd come barging into Dennison's one day the worse for drink and made a scene in front of all the customers. Mr Sims the manager had escorted him politely off the premises.

And that was how George Dennison came to hear of it.

"If he bothers you again, just you tell me, Roseen," Billy warned when she gave him a self-interested account of Mr Bennet's activities. "I'll soon sort the old bugger out for you. I'll knock his bloody block off, so I will."

She liked to hear this kind of violent strong-arm talk.

Billy's toughness made her feel protected; protected, and yet oddly vulnerable, as though the very presence of his strength left her weaker, softer, more helpless. It was an entirely new experience. She played upon his pride in his powerful muscular physique, saying there wasn't a man in all the Midlands could hold a candle to him for fitness and good looks; and Billy would flex his shoulders and square his jaw and wink at her.

On August Bank Holiday Monday – the day after George Dennison had called – they went together to the fair at the rear of the Wholesale Market. It was glorious summer weather and half the town had come out to enjoy itself, the younger women bare-armed under their Oriental paper parasols (all the go this year) and the men in shirt-sleeves and braces, collars left off, caps pushed to the back of their heads. The air was layered with an acrid, oily smell of hot machinery and baked potatoes and human bodies, and the volume of noise half-deafened the ears from carousel music, stall-holders' shouts, the staccato rattle of the rifle range, and the excited squealing of children on the Whirligig.

Billy had a go on the coconut shy and won a china dog which he gave to Roseen. He tried his hand at the hoop-la and claimed a bag of shelled nuts which both of them ate. After, there came the swing-boats, and the Big Wheel, and the merry-go-round, and then he had a couple of turns on the 'Try Your Own Strength' machine, hitting the peg so hard with the wooden hammer that the marker smacked into the bell on top with the force of a bullet. For that he was given the choice of a prize – either a vase or a picture.

Roseen chose the picture. It was in a nice gilt frame and had a drawing of exotic orange flowers with dark spots, identified below as tiger lilies. It would look lovely on her bedroom wall, she said.

The crowning triumph of this magic afternoon came towards its close, when the summer dusk had streaked the pale green sky with cloud-drifts of vermilion and gold, and the flare of naphtha torches licked the booths and alleyways with flickering light.

One of the fairground attractions was a boxing ring inside a canvas tent: sixpence to pay for a three-minute round with

'The Former County Champion Battling Joe Brennan' and five shillings to the man who could finish on his feet.

This was a challenge which many of the younger fellows couldn't resist, especially those who'd been drinking in the beer tent, and the ring was crowded round with others who'd paid to see the fun as a queue of Dutch-courageous hopefuls each clambered in turn through the ropes looking for an easy scrap, only to be casually despatched with a clip to the jaw or a bloodied nose or a drive to the stomach which left them breathless and retching. It was like watching flies being swatted.

Until it came to Billy Kelly's turn.

Billy knew a bit about boxing; enough to take care of himself in a proper fight. He'd weighed up 'Battling Joe Brennan' while observing the proceedings, and decided it was worth a go to win five bob. Roseen didn't try to hold him back. She watched him climb into the ring, pulling his braces down and stripping off his shirt to show the crowd his strong young body; and she'd felt so proud of him that it brought the tears to her eyes.

"Go on, Billy – " she shouted. "Hit him, Billy. You can do it!"

And hit him he did. Not with his first punch, nor even his second, but his third caught Joe Brennan smack beneath the ribs, winding him so badly that the 'Former County Champion' was doubled in half with pain and had to retire from the round to recover. The tent erupted into applause, the crowd's eager, laughing, sweat-streaked, drunken faces reflecting the naphtha light as they cheered their approval when Billy received his five shillings.

Roseen thought her heart would burst with happiness.

★

It was that same night, lying with Billy Kelly in the grass beneath the moon-silvered shadow of the Big Wheel, that she lost her virginity.

 8

"You know there's talk about you and Robert Wells, don't you?"

Sidney Hathaway had his hands clasped behind his head and was lounging back at his ease on the stone bench, cream flannel trouser-legs crossed, eyes half-closed against the smoke from his cigarette.

So casual was his statement that for a moment Flora failed to appreciate how sharp was the barb it contained.

"Perhaps you oughtn't to be seen about with him so often, old girl."

"*So often!*" Astonished, she shifted herself to regard the young man's profile. "But I'm not! And whose business is it, besides, how often I'm seen with him?"

"Nobody's. Everybody's." He removed the cigarette from his mouth. "In a place like this, things get noticed, you know. If two people are frequently in each other's company, the fact attracts comment."

Her astonishment was overtaken by a mixture of indignation and embarrassment. "But I'm seen equally as often with you – and Jessy – and Winifred. Does *that* attract comment?"

"Don't be a goose, Flora. You know what I mean." Sidney turned his head lazily to glance at her. "Mr Wells has a wife at home. And however much the pair of you love spouting poetry at one another, it simply doesn't do, my dear."

She bit her lip and looked away, towards the lily pond beneath the sunlit trees. Had her conscience been an easy one she'd have dismissed Sidney's criticism as niggling jealousy at her lukewarm reception of his own attentions; but the fact was that she so much preferred to be with Robert. In a way which she didn't understand, Robert appealed to everything romantic in her nature – but *nicely*, without being in the least bit forward or over-familiar. His behaviour was always impeccably that of a friend who was also a gentleman.

"I don't see that Robert's marriage has anything to do with . . . shared interests," she said defensively. "There's no impropriety can be attached to our association. It's perfectly blameless. We both happen to enjoy – "

"I know. You both happen to enjoy wallowing in the lush verbiage of A. C. Swinburne." Sidney drew on his cigarette and let the smoke trickle through his lips. "But when does a pleasure become a self-indulgence, I ask. Answer: when it's engaged in to an excessive degree."

Flora picked up the books from beside her and rose to her feet.

"I'm going back inside."

"Why – because of a friendly word of admonition? A fine teacher you'll make, dear thing, if you can't be done by as you'd do – if you won't receive what you're expected to dispense."

"Oh – " She looked down at him, quite tempted to stamp her foot. Sidney Hathaway could be the most exasperating person. Why she suffered his company, she couldn't think. He was cynical, he smoked too much, and he *never* cleaned his teeth!

"Don't let us quarrel." He sat up, flicking the spent cigarette into the grass. "I only came into college this afternoon to say cheerio before you go home for the Easter hols. Show a fellow a little kindness, won't you?"

Now that he'd finished the two-year course at Moseley and gained his Certificate, he was doing his probationary period in teaching at an elementary school in Edgbaston, and returned to see Flora frequently.

"I have sacrificed the delights of volunteering myself for country dancing practice in order to steal an hour of your company – and how am I rewarded? With cruelty and cold looks. Ah me."

"Stop being an ass, Sidney." In spite of herself she couldn't resist a smile. "But really, I *must* go now. I've a lecture on the theory of education at three o'clock."

"How infinitely dull. And an utter waste of time." The young man got up from the bench to accompany her back through the college grounds. "Believe me, old thing, no amount of theory can prepare one for the mortifying experience of facing a classful of noisy little wretches, and knowing that one's future livelihood depends upon controlling them sufficiently for the next three-quarters of an hour so as to impart some small amount of knowledge to their mutinous minds."

He offered his arm.

"Instead of theory, it would be of far greater use to us would-be teachers to cultivate a thick skin, a deaf ear, and a technique with the cane which would bring joy to the heart of the Marquis de Sade."

"I hope you're not trying to put the kibosh on my aspirations," rejoined Flora. Though she tended still to be shy, she'd managed to conquer much of her nervous reticence during this year and a half spent at Moseley, and now thought nothing of using the kind of modern idiom which her mother would tut-tut as 'sloppy speech'.

"But I do agree with you," she went on, matching her step to Sidney's as they went down on to the path, "that the application of proper discipline ought to be discussed more with the students. There should be other methods of corrective punishment than caning, for instance."

"Name me one."

"Well – withholding privileges – giving black marks. I don't think beating does any good at all. It's brutal and it's degrading."

"That's as may be. But it does the trick."

"Robert doesn't think so." As soon as she'd said his name, Flora knew she'd done the wrong thing to bring Robert Wells into the conversation again.

"I mean – " she corrected herself hastily as Sidney gave her a look, "I mean, quite a lot of schoolteachers would prefer to use the cane only as a last resort. I know that I would. The idea of thrashing some poor child who's probably just as ill-treated at home – well, it's really rather horrid."

"Thrashing is all most of 'em understand, old girl." He paused to light another cigarette from the yellow Turkish Abdullah packet produced from his blazer pocket.

"You can't *reason* with an eight-year-old whose only appreciation of right and wrong is whether it earns him a beating or not. He's been conditioned from birth, d'you see. Speaking kindly to a child when he expects corporal punishment will only confuse him. Which school is Robert Wells at, by the way?"

The question was lobbed so casually that Sidney made it sound an afterthought.

"Robert? Oh – oh, somewhere in the Lozells area, I believe." Flora glanced at him a little awkwardly. "Why do you ask?"

A shrug. "No reason. Curiosity. It seems a trifle odd, that's all, that his wife and family should be living away down south yet he chooses to do his probationary teaching here in Birmingham."

She made no response. She herself had thought it strange of Robert to elect to enter a school in Lozells – one of the poorest areas of the city – instead of returning to rural Hampshire. His reason, he'd told her, was that he relished the challenge. She'd been tempted to ask whether he wouldn't have found an equal challenge in Southampton, perhaps; but the question was never voiced. His decision to remain in Birmingham meant they could continue meeting socially, have tea together, enjoy the occasional theatre play and concert.

"Oh, before I forget – " Sidney went on, flicking ash from his blazer lapel, "there's a Tango tea-dance on next week in Tettenhall. That's close to your place, isn't it? If you're not doing anything much in particular during the hols, perhaps you'd let me take you."

★

Flora saw Sidney several times during that Easter of 1914. His family lived at Quinton, not too far a journey from Wolverhampton, and now that he'd learned to drive a motor-car he borrowed his father's. It vexed her that he should come to the house, because courtesy dictated that she introduce him to her parents, thus setting a kind of seal of official recognition upon their friendship.

Not that she actually *disliked* Sidney, she hastened to assure herself in the small hours of the night when thinking kept her awake. He was reasonably good-looking (apart from his awful teeth) and intelligent and interesting; but he wasn't *romantic*. He didn't gaze into her eyes and hold her hand, and say things like, 'Has anyone ever told you, my darling, how dashed beautiful you are in the moonlight,' as did the heroes of Elinor Glyn's novels. No, Sidney crashed her round the dance-floor, slapped her on the shoulder, told her appallingly unfunny stories, and referred to her constantly as 'old girl' and 'old thing'.

Compared with Robert Wells, he was just an overgrown boy playing at being a man.

In her not-quite-nineteen-year-old innocence, Flora was unaware that she was more than a little infatuated with Robert. All her life she had tended to fix her heart upon one special person – as in the case of Roseen O'Connor – and give them her undivided attention; and if, in those wakeful small hours of the night, she let her thoughts dwell upon Robert Wells it was only to reflect how much she admired him, how much she enjoyed his company, how much of a like mind they both were.

It never occurred to her to consider that her reason perhaps for failing to acknowledge Sidney's affection might owe a good deal to the fact that in her heart of hearts the suitor of her dreams was Robert.

Just occasionally, when the existence of his marriage intruded, she might remind herself that it was a mutual fondness for literature and nothing else which attracted them to each other; but to what extent this was self-excuse she never realised until one evening late in June that year. The two of them had been to a concert of Sir Edward Elgar's music, and with time to spare before the arrival of Flora's tram to take her back to college, they'd sat together in the terminus waiting-room.

For the rest of her life she would always remember that room. The green-painted walls decorated with peeling, dog-eared posters, the flickering gas-jets, the wooden slatted benches, the lugubrious whistling of someone outside; the empty, impermanent atmosphere. She was wearing a narrow hobble skirt with knife pleats around the ankle, and a hip-length belted jacket over a cream silk blouse. Her hair had been recently shortened into a fashionable 'bob' which suited her face, so everyone said.

For a while they'd sat discussing the concert – the breadth and sweep and dignity of Elgar's Second Symphony which so wonderfully fired one's patriotic fervour – and then Robert said suddenly, completely out of the blue, "You know that I'm falling in love with you, don't you."

A gentleman seated opposite looked up from his magazine and made a noisy clearing of the throat. Two young women next to him eyed Flora and Robert curiously, then glanced at one another and smirked behind their gloves.

He rested his arm along the back of the bench and leaned closer, lowering his voice.

"It's true. There's no other way to put it. I simply can't help myself."

The colour flamed in her cheeks. Overwhelmed by a rush of confused emotion, she couldn't think what to say, how to answer him.

"I'm sorry," he went on. "But I had to tell you. It will help you to understand why I've decided I must leave Birmingham and go away."

She turned her eyes to his, disbelieving. "*Go away?* But why? Why?"

"Why do you think? If I stayed I should want to see more and more of you. At least by removing myself back to Hampshire I'm putting myself beyond temptation's reach."

"But *why* must you go?" she repeated fearfully, not caring whether she was overheard or not, so great was her anguish at the thought of losing Robert's company. "Couldn't we – oh, couldn't we continue as we are? Still be friends?"

He shook his head.

"Please?" she pressed him, almost piteous in her appeal. "It doesn't matter that you love me. I don't mind, really I don't."

"It matters to me. Look – " He took her by the hand and

stood up to draw her to her feet. "We can't talk properly here. Let's go outside."

Half a dozen pairs of eyes followed their exit.

It was a beautiful evening. The weather had been wonderful so far this summer, the best anyone could remember, and the warmth of the day lingered still in the air, in the cobbles of the street, in the red-brick walls. Beyond a roofline of gables and chimneys, the grape-coloured dusk held a sliver of crescent moon.

Robert put his arms round Flora's shoulders and held her close. "It's my fault, I shouldn't have stayed here in Birmingham. Once I'd got my Certificate I should have done the decent thing and gone home to Helen."

"Why didn't you, then." Flora was close to tears. Had this been Sidney Hathaway, it wouldn't have mattered; but it was Robert . . . Robert who meant so much to her . . . Robert who was leaving her. Her heart felt as though it were breaking in two.

"Why didn't I? Because I was selfish. I didn't want to be apart from you, Flora. I realised I was growing much too fond – and thought I was strong enough to suppress my feelings, channel them into something else. But these past months – oh, I don't know, every time we've met has only made things worse. I'm a married man. I can't afford to be in love with you."

Miserably she hid her face against his jacket. It was the first time outside her dreams that a man had held her in his arms this way. The experience was far from being the blissful one she'd imagined. She didn't know which was worse – her confusion that he should care so, or her wretchedness that he was going.

"Can't you stop . . . I mean, stop *loving* me, Robert? Can't you simply *like* me instead?"

"No, that would be impossible. God – I feel so damn' guilty about all this. I wish it hadn't happened, believe me." He pressed her tighter, resting his cheek against her soft toque hat. "These last eighteen months of knowing you have been among the happiest of my life. I'll never forget them. But I have a duty to my wife – and to Meggie and little Jack – and for their sakes I've got to do what's right and sacrifice that

86

part of me which longs to stay here, with you. You do understand that, don't you."

Too choked by unshed tears, Flora could only nod. They had done nothing immoral, either of them. They had met openly as friends, as fellow-students, and their pleasure in each other's company had been entirely innocent. What had caused him to fall in love with her? She wasn't beautiful, or vivacious, or exciting. She was simply herself. She wished that she had the courage to ask him, but perhaps he wouldn't want to tell her; perhaps he didn't even know.

Almost as though reading her thoughts, Robert began quoting from Swinburne's *Erectheus*:

"Many loves of many a mood and many a kind
Fill the life of man, and mould the secret mind;
Many days bring many dooms, to loose and bind . . ."

She recognised the lines.

"It's best that we don't see one another again," he went on dully. "I shall be leaving Birmingham at the end of the summer term next month."

When she still remained silent, he put a finger beneath her rounded chin and raised her face to his.

"Oh, my darling, don't cry. Please don't. I can't bear to see you distressed. Blast it, I've made such a fearful mess of everything. I shouldn't have sprung this on you at the last minute. What you must think of me I don't know."

He looked into her brimming eyes, and there was an expression in his own of such bleakness that she was moved to whisper through her tears, "I think that . . . that you are the nicest man I've ever known . . . and I'm so terribly, terribly sorry . . . that our friendship has to end."

"I don't *want* it to end!" he answered, hugging her to him again. "There are some things in life too fine and too precious to be cast away. The links forged between us during this last year or so can't ever be broken. Whatever happens – remember this – I want you to know that I'll always be your friend, Flora, and I shall always think of you with deepest affection."

In silence they clung together, no more words left to say. The people in the waiting-room were starting to come out to queue for the tram which was due to arrive at any minute; and as they passed the young couple there outside the door, one or two of them must have wondered what unhappy story lay behind the tears.

In the distance the rattle and clank of the electric tram could be heard growing louder as it approached the terminus.

"Will you be all right now, dearest?" Robert asked her quietly.

She sniffed, and nodded. "Yes."

"I won't say goodbye – "

His lips brushed her cheek, and then, as she clung to him still, he gently took her hands and clasped them in his own to kiss them; and with something almost like his old smile for her, turned and moved away, walking quickly across the cobbles into the shadows beyond the lighted windows of the waiting-room.

Flora took out her handkerchief from her pocket and gave her nose a good blow. She blamed herself. She ought to have realised, when Robert chose to stay here in Birmingham. She should have seen the way things were developing. Even Sidney had said that people were starting to talk . . .

Oh, but how *could* she have known? He'd never given a sign of his true feelings, never. Not by so much as a word or a look or a gesture. But then, she told herself bitterly, she was so naïve, so stupid, that she wouldn't have noticed if he had.

And now it was too late. He was going away, leaving her life for ever, just at the very moment when her own feelings were beginning to crystallise into something deep and wonderful.

The tears welled again and she had to turn her face so that those waiting in the queue wouldn't see how upset she was. By the time the tram had arrived and they were starting to climb aboard, she'd managed to control herself sufficiently to follow, biting her lip to keep it from trembling, head bowed so that hopefully nobody would stare too much.

"Fares please!"

She found a seat at the back, opposite a woman reading the evening newspaper. Once they'd started away, the conductor began moving down the aisle; and reaching Flora, took her money, punching the ticket and looking at her with a kind of indifferent sympathy. Young females had wept on his tram before.

The woman opposite shook out her paper to turn to another page. Her thoughts all of Robert, Flora stared sightlessly at the banner headline splashed across the front. It was only after several minutes that she realised what it was she was looking at, the black letters clamouring meaninglessly for attention:

AUSTRIAN ARCHDUKE ASSASSINATED AT SARAJEVO.

9

If Archduke Franz Ferdinand of Austria had not been shot at Sarajevo on June 28th it is unlikely that Billy Kelly would have married Roseen O'Connor in Wolverhampton on September 5th.

Between these two incidents lay a chain of events which in the course of the next four years was to affect the lives of millions, reshape the map of Europe and sweep away for ever the pomp and panoply of the Victorian world.

Exactly a month after the assassination of the Archduke – heir to the Hapsburg Empire – by an idealistic young revolutionary, Austria declared war against Serbia; and such were the ramifications of national treaties that Austria's ally Germany in turn declared war on Serbia's ally, Russia.

Virtually overnight Great Britain found herself being sucked into the gathering maelstrom.

On August 4th the Prime Minister Mr Asquith announced to an anxious nation Britain's entry into the conflict. The following day eighty thousand German troops attacked the city of Liège in Belgium, and Europe was plunged into internecine slaughter on a scale which was to make an abattoir of an entire generation.

Everywhere young men were being mobilised for active service. Jingoistic fever was high. It was about time the Kaiser was given a bloody nose – he'd been asking for it long enough!

"It'll all be over by Christmas," said Billy Kelly together with thousands of others. "I'm going to enlist – I don't want to miss the fun."

"But you might get killed!" Roseen protested.

"Don't talk so daft. Who's going to kill me? Fritz? Not bloomin' likely."

"What about me then, Billy? What am *I* supposed to do while you're gone?"

"Wait for me, o' course."

"And if I don't – ?"

That made him stop and think a minute.

"Well, there's only one way o' settling that. How d'you fancy it if we was to get wed?"

"*Billy* – ! Oh, I thought you'd never ask me!"

There was a nuptial Mass at St Mary's and St John's, Roseen a picture in oyster satin brocade, Billy very handsome in his new Staffordshire Regiment uniform. George Dennison was among the congregation to see them married; and afterwards they held a reception in the back room of the White Rose, paid for out of the money he'd given them as a wedding present. The whole of Raby Street was there, and so were Billy's brothers and sisters and their families, spilling out into the public bar in one direction and into the garden in the other. The landlord swore later they'd drunk him clean down to his last barrel of beer.

Roseen was deliriously, ecstatically, head over heels in love. The only blot on this euphoric day was the fact that her Billy – her *husband*! – was going away to fight the Boche in France. But she wouldn't allow herself to think about that as she sat on his knee in the White Rose, alternately kissing him, laughing, and admiring the plain gold band on her finger.

Billy's mate Eddie, himself in private's uniform, made some sort of a speech as best man; but being almost too drunk to stand up, much of what he said was unintelligible and halted by a need to be helped outside to relieve himself. The children shrieked and fought and played and ran about; the old folk gossiped and cackled their toothless gums and supped their beer; and the bride's mother, having wept throughout the church marriage service, fuelled her emotional state with generous helpings of gin and required to be propped in a corner seat to keep her from falling over.

All in all, it was quite a celebration.

As the long, warm summer afternoon wore on, the sentimental nature of the exiled Irish soul crept into the songs being played on the back room piano, and the strains of 'Kathleen Mavourneen', 'Oh Erin, My Country' and 'The Hills of Connemara' rose in maudlin chorus from well-lubricated throats. There was a fight or two, but no heat in them to be serious, and nobody took much notice: after another pint it was arms back round each other's necks and sing along together, boys.

Billy had been granted a twenty-four-hour pass for his wedding day. That was all the Army would allow him. At six o'clock tomorrow morning he and Eddie Quinn must report back to their company officer at the Whittington Barracks in Lichfield to complete their basic training in preparation for active service in France. In the blazing heat of an August day just over a week ago, Allied troops had been thrown back by the Germans at Mons and forced to retreat to the Somme. This was no time to be thinking of a honeymoon.

Leaving the party on its final legs in the White Rose, Billy and Eddie between them got Billy's new mother-in-law down the road, home to Raby Street, with the bride bringing up an unsteady rear, her satin brocade hitched round her ankles to keep it from trailing in the dust and her wilting bouquet shedding petals on the cobbles. All four of them were rather the worse for drink, and the procession was anything but dignified, but since most of Raby Street was still carousing in the pub the only witnesses were a few incurious cats and dogs and the Bunns at number six, who were Temperance.

After a good deal of pushing and sweating, Connie was finally laid out upstairs on her bed, semi-conscious and still in her hat. Not trusting her own balance on the narrow staircase, Roseen had stayed below in the kitchen to put the kettle on for a pot of tea. Billy had recently bought her a gas stove – the first cooking stove she'd ever used – a black-lacquered 'Albionette', which did away with the need to keep a fire burning all day in the range. Now that she'd got the knack of it to make Billy his meals she was proving quite a good little cook.

"Well, I s'pose we better turn in," her husband said thickly once the pot was empty, " 's nine o'clock jus' gone. We got to be up again at four, you an' me, Eddie ol' mate."

Eddie was already dozing off, his head down on the

pegged-rag rug in front of the empty hearth where he was having to sleep the night. Had they thought about it sooner, he could have used Connie's bed. The state she was in, she wouldn't have noticed whether she was upstairs, down, or still at the White Rose.

Leaving him to make himself as comfortable as he could with a cushion and blanket, the bride and groom took themselves off to Roseen's small room overlooking the yard at the back. Although they'd now been lovers for several months and Billy came to the house every day, he'd never before set foot upstairs, and despite being half-fuddled with beer he managed to look round him with bleary curiosity once the bedroom door was shut.

There wasn't much to see in the dimness of the summer dusk. A chest of drawers, a chair and a brass bedstead; a piece of carpet on the floor, net at the window. On the wall above the chest was a mirror reflecting an oval of twilight sky; and next to it (which surprised him slightly) a battered wooden crucifix with a string of rosary beads looped from it. He knew Roseen went to Mass but she'd never struck him as being at all religious.

What pleased him, though, as he started taking off his khaki uniform, was the little fairground china dog on the fire-grate shelf, and the picture of tiger lilies hung above the bed.

★

"Billy – Billy, love, c'mon, wake up. I've brought you a bite to eat."

Roseen shook him gently by the shoulder.

There were a couple of protesting grunts, and then a groan; and then he half-propped himself on an elbow, rubbing his eyes with the back of his hand like a child, yawning in the pallid glow of the paraffin lamp.

"What's the time?"

"Just after three." Roseen sat on the side of the bed, a mug of steaming tea in one hand and a plate in the other.

"Here – " pushing the plate towards him. "I've done you and Eddie some fried black pudding on bread. You might not get any breakfast at the barracks."

Her husband hauled himself up against the pillows and

93

yawned again and stretched himself, his naked arms flexed behind his head. The Army barber had shorn his unruly, thick mop of hair to the regulation short back and sides, cropped close to the skin above his ears to leave a bristle-shadow of dark new growth. Roseen said it made him look like a convict.

"Ta, sweetheart." He took the mug from her, slaking his thirst with noisy gulps of the hot, sweet tea; then balanced the plate on his stomach and started eating.

"You manage to get some sleep?" he asked indistinctly through a mouthful of bread. "There's not much room for two in this bed o' yours."

"I had a couple of hours. Before you started snoring." She grinned at him. "No, I think I was too excited to sleep much. What with being married, and everything else . . . I hope I didn't keep you awake talking."

"Talking?" He shook his head. "I never heard you. What was it you was talking about?"

"Oh – nothing important. Silly things, really."

"Like what?"

Roseen looked down at her wedding ring and twisted it round her finger. "Well . . . you know, like how much I love you, and how much I'll miss you while you're gone . . . and how much I want you to look after yourself for me."

She glanced up at him again, her eyes shining suspiciously bright in the lamplight. "You *will* look after yourself, won't you, Billy. I couldn't bear it if anything was to happen to you."

Returning the look, he swilled down the last of the black pudding with his tea, then put plate and mug aside on the floor.

"Come here, and I'll show you what's going to happen to *you* – " Grabbing her round the waist, he tumbled her down beside him and started kissing her, playfully at first and then more ardently as healthy young desire began to arouse him. He'd been too drunk last night to enjoy his new wife as well as he'd have liked; but he was about to remedy that.

"What you doing?" Roseen giggled, the fears forgotten as he pulled undone the ribbons of her nightgown.

In reply he licked the lobe of her ear and ran his tongue

round the line of her jaw to her chin and down to the base of her throat.

"I'm going to finish what I started at half past nine, Mrs Kelly. I'm going to consummate this marriage well and bloomin' truly, that's what I'm going to do."

She felt his breath warm on her skin, her own desire quickening as his work-rough hands stroked the nakedness of her thighs and hips and buttocks. Throwing off the night-gown she climbed into bed and lay with her arms around him, mouth open to his kisses, moving her body slowly and sinuously against his and deliciously aware of his excitement growing in response. Billy was the first man she had loved or made love with, the first man to show her how much pleasure her own body could give her, and as she felt the sweet ache beginning, she thought she could never have enough of it; never, never.

Afterwards, when their passion was slaked, their need of one another sated, they lay together in the rumpled sheets, Roseen's head cradled in the hollow of her husband's shoulder and her legs entwined round his.

"How long d'you reckon you'll be away?" she whispered at last. The question had been asked before, but now it held an especial poignancy.

Billy pushed the tangled curls from her forehead and turned his head to kiss it. "Dunno. Depends. A month or two, I suppose."

"God . . . what'll I do without you."

"You'll be all right, don't worry. They'll give us plenty o' leave."

"I hope so." She stroked his shoulder, loving the touch of his skin like smooth white velvet beneath her palm, and supple with muscle. "I hope so."

"Tell you what, sweetheart – next time I'm home we'll go away together somewhere, eh? Would you like that?"

"A proper honeymoon, you mean? Oh, Billy – yes! That'd be lovely!"

"We'll take the motor bike. Go to the sea, p'raps. Anywhere you fancy."

Roseen smiled. She'd already given the thought her consideration and knew exactly where it was she wanted to go.

"Aberystwyth."

"Aberystwyth?"

"Mm. I went there once for a holiday when I was a kid. It's the only time I've ever been to the seaside."

He gave her a hug. "OK, well, we'll go to Aberystwyth the next leave I get. And I'll show you how to swim."

She smiled again, for a moment thinking of the Dennisons and Flora. A right little pernickety prude that one had been. But it was a good holiday; she'd never forgotten it.

"When this damn' war's over, d'you know what I'm going to do – " Billy went on quietly. "I'm going to get myself a decent reg'lar job as a garage mechanic. Earn enough money to put a bit by, like. I don't want us living from hand to mouth the rest of our lives."

He kissed his wife's forehead again. Never one to say much for himself, he was leaving her some dream for both to share while they were parted.

"I got it all worked out what we'll have. A nice little place to live, with a patch o' garden I can dig of a Sunday. Nice things to wear. I'll make a good husband, sweetheart, you just see if I won't – aye, and I mean to be a good dad, an' all. No kid of ours is ever going to know the kind o' poverty I was born to."

"Oh, Billy . . ." Roseen pressed her face into his neck. "Oh, Billy, I do love you . . . such a lot I do. Promise me you'll come back safe – *promise* me, please."

" 'Course I'll come back! I got a wife waiting for me, ain't I. D'you think I'd let some ruddy German bullet come between me and this – " He cupped her naked breast in his hand. And then, at the click of the staircase door opening below, "There, that's Eddie coming up to shift me."

Gently withdrawing his arm, he slid himself out of bed and reached for his clothes on the chair. There was a creak of mounting footsteps, and after a moment, a cautious tap-tapping.

"Billy – ?" Eddie kept his voice down to a hoarse whisper for fear of disturbing old Connie in the other room, still sleeping the sleep of the drunk.

The doorknob turned.

"It's gone four," he said, coming inside and careful not to

look too hard at Roseen. "I waited till I heard the bed stop creaking."

"You're a good mate, Eddie Quinn. I'll do the same for you, first chance I get." Billy gave his wife a wink and pulled his khaki shirt on over his head.

"Oh – there's some hot water left in the kettle," she told him, not caring whether Eddie had heard the bed springs creaking or not. "You can swill yourself in the scullery while I put some clothes on."

The two men went down, Billy with his boots in his hand, taking the paraffin lamp with them and leaving her alone in the ghostly grey darkness. She got up and went to the window, pushing aside the piece of net. Dawn wasn't far away. She could just make out the silhouettes of factory stacks against the night-pale sky.

Seized by a sudden need for comfort, she turned away and fastened her eyes on the wooden crucifix above the chest of drawers on the wall. It was the only thing she had which had ever belonged to her dead father, her only link with him apart from her name and her blood.

'Keep an eye on Billy for me, won't you,' she prayed silently. 'Don't let him get killed out there in France. I love him too much to lose him.'

By the time she'd dressed herself and gone downstairs, the pair of them had finished their ablutions in the scullery and were having another mug of tea before leaving to catch the early morning milk train to Lichfield.

"I'll write to you as often as I can," Billy promised, buckling the straps of his kit-bag. "The Army'll send you most of my pay, so you won't go short."

What else was there left to say. Nothing . . . except good-bye.

Keeping her trembling chin up and a smile fixed on her lips, Roseen stood in the front doorway to see both of them off down the street, her eyes so blurred with unwept tears that she could hardly see her husband when he paused a minute to wave back from the corner.

Then he was gone; just the echo of his hobnailed army boots ringing on the cobbles in the stillness of dawn, fading gradually away into the birdsong of a new day.

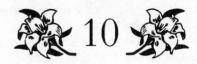

10

By Christmas that first year of the war, 1914, names which no one had even heard of six months ago were becoming daily more familiar in newspaper headlines. The sight of young men in uniform had ceased to draw attention now; indeed was commonplace about the streets as more and more volunteered for service. The Germans were on the run. Morale at home was high. There was every incentive to take the King's shilling and do one's bit for Blighty.

At sea, several fierce engagements were already being reported, with a heavy loss to life and shipping; but again it was the enemy who was faring worst, four of their warships being sunk on December 8th off the Falkland Islands (another place few people had heard of till now).

Imagining that Robert Wells must surely be among those enlisting for active service, Flora had read the news in the papers with more than usual concern. Since that evening together in June, the two of them had never met again, nor had any sort of contact. She had masked her grief, mourning in secret, hiding her feelings from family and friends and throwing herself into preparation for her Certificate exams at the end of her final term at college.

Whatever she might do to erase him from her mind Robert was always there, underneath her busyness, his image springing back into her thoughts the moment she relaxed, his memory filling her nights with restlessness. Only a few years ago she would have considered the whole episode of their parting as something wonderfully romantic – a married man – forbidden love – duty and sacrifice – the sad farewell; but she was older now, wiser and more sensible, and there was nothing romantic about heartache.

Over and over again Flora kept telling herself that Robert had had no choice, that he'd done the only thing a gentleman possibly *could* do in the circumstances. He had found himself in a most invidious position and withdrawn from it with conscience and honour intact. And he'd been completely, frankly, almost brutally honest about their situation: once the feelings of friendship had ceased to be platonic he must – as he said himself – put such emotions beyond temptation's reach.

What might have been the alternative? Flora did not know, and refused to allow herself the luxury of imagining. She hardly understood her own feelings; only that Robert's going had left a terrible emptiness, that there were nights when she wept for him into her pillow, and now that she suspected he was fighting for his country she carried the daily peril to his life like a weight within her breast.

★

Early in the new year of 1915 she had started as a probationary teacher at a small country school on the outskirts of Wolverhampton. Her pupils comprised an infant class of five-year-olds, the children of farmworkers mostly, whom it was her task to spend the next twelve months acquainting with the rudiments of reading, writing and arithmetic; and though the work would be at times difficult and demanding, from the very first week she knew she was going to love it.

There were three other teachers on the staff: the headmaster Mr Powell, a thin-faced man whose quiet authority inspired immediate respect; bespectacled, bookish Mr Holgate in charge of the first-year junior pupils; and Mr Gregory, keen on games and rather jolly, who taught the older infants. In the beginning, Flora had found it just a trifle disconcerting that she should be the only female, but she was treated in such an equable manner that the fact soon ceased to bother her.

The school itself was tucked away on the edge of a country village not many miles from her home at Stockwell End. Its four classrooms were heated by old-fashioned, pot-bellied stoves protected by fireguards which on cold, wet winter days would be hung with mittens, scarves, hats, socks and even gape-toed boots, all steaming gently in the warmth. Most of the children were up and about earlier than dawn, giving a hand in the byres and hen-runs before walking the several miles along rutted, muddied lanes in to school. They were poor, may be; but they had a wiry, robust health and hardiness which many a more pampered, privileged class of child might have envied.

Flora got along with them famously well. Once her infant pupils had overcome their first few days of tongue-tied wariness, they began to respond to her patient, smiling encouragement to learn; and well before that winter term had ended, Mr Powell's interim report to the education committee spoke of his probationer's natural aptitude for drawing the best from even the most backward pupil.

For the first time in many months Robert Wells was no longer Flora's foremost thought upon waking.

★

Being in Wolverhampton one Saturday afternoon to do some personal shopping, she'd reminded herself that the class would need sheets of coloured cartridge paper for a particular lesson she was planning. Rather than run the risk of finding there was not enough for her purpose in the school store-cupboard, she decided she'd buy some paper from the art and crafts shop in Victoria Street.

The February day was overcast with dull leaden clouds, and a thin, mean little wind seemed to spread itself in draughts round every corner and shop doorway. Having made her purchases with half an hour to spare before meeting her father to drive home together (since his heart attack he'd employed a chauffeur to run the motor-car), Flora thought she'd go into Beatties' store and wander round for a while. She'd always liked Beatties. The stock was invariably of the best quality, and one could browse there to one's heart's content in an atmosphere of unhurried comfort without being chivvied along by assistants.

She was looking at some rather smart frock material in the drapery department when she happened to notice a young woman a few yards away paying for an item at the counter.

Something about her struck Flora as familiar; and as the other turned towards her putting purse into bag, she realised at once who it must be.

In the same moment their eyes met. The recognition was mutual.

"Roseen – ?" Flora said, a little awkwardly, wondering whether or not she ought to speak. "It is Roseen, isn't it? Roseen O'Connor?"

She was given a quick up-and-down appraising glance. "Well, well, well. Fancy bumping into you." Roseen's expression of surprise was too artificial to be genuine. "I'd never have known you with your hair bobbed short."

She hadn't changed much, Flora remarked to herself. If anything, slimmer and prettier than she remembered, but still with that same slightly brazen touch of self-assurance.

Aloud she said, "You're looking very well," and then couldn't think what else to add.

Roseen tossed her head and smiled in a smug kind of way. "I'm married now, you know," she informed her.

"Oh – no, I didn't know." Flora's father had never mentioned it; why should he. "Congratulations!"

"Ta." (I don't suppose anyone's asked *you* yet, the tone implied.) "Yes, I got married in September. I'm Mrs Billy Kelly now."

"How nice. And – er – are your husband's family local people?"

"Sort of local, yes." A pause. "What about you, then? What you doing with yourself these days?"

"Me – ? Oh – " Flora indicated the roll of cartridge paper beneath her arm as though to explain its purchase. "I'm teaching at an elementary school – the infants' class – I gained my Certificate last summer."

"How nice." Was it imagination or was there just a hint of sarcasm in Roseen's echo of her own response. "Whereabouts is it you're teaching?"

"Out at Codsall. The village school. Perhaps you remember, we passed the place on one of our picnics – "

Why she said that, Flora didn't know. For some reason she felt stupidly nervous of this young, attractive married woman whom she'd loved once as a childhood friend and was meeting again today as a stranger.

" – one of our picnics," she continued gamely, "when you used to come to stay the weekend."

Roseen shrugged and examined her red-painted nails. "No, I don't remember." Then, inconsequentially, "My Billy's gone and enlisted as a soldier. He's serving with the Staffordshires."

"Oh, has he? I mean, is he?" Flora's nervousness made her tongue trip.

"Yes. He's somewhere out in France."

"Do you – hear from him at all?"

"Not very often."

The tone of voice altered, and all the confident chin-high swagger seemed just for an instant to drain from Roseen. She made a funny grimace, a tightening of the over-rouged mouth, and added quickly, almost aggressively, "But he's all right. I know he is. My Billy's all right."

"I'm sure he is." Flora looked at her, seeing the crumbling mask of self-conviction trying to re-establish itself. "I'm sure he is, Roseen."

Her own awkwardness left her all of a sudden and in its place there was a rush of sympathy. She thought of Robert Wells, possibly serving out there with the Navy in enemy waters; whether alive still, or maimed, or even dead, she had no way of finding out. In comparison with her own anxieties, what must Roseen be suffering, with a young husband on active service in France . . .

"He'll be home again, don't worry," she said, touching the other's arm in a little gesture of assurance.

"Yes. That's what I keep praying."

Roseen glanced away, towards a mannequin dummy positioned on a stand by the counter, displaying bolts of cheerfully-patterned cloth. "Well . . . I'd best be off now. I've got our Mam a bit poorly at home. The doctor's coming round to see her this evening."

Her eyes flickered back to Flora's face.

"It's been ever so nice talking. P'raps we'll bump into each other again one of these days."

"Yes. Yes, I do hope we will."

★

Whether or not it was because his roots were so firmly working-class, who could say, but George Dennison had always had an old-fashioned suspicion of what he called 'new-fangled lah-di-dah contraptions'. It was not an attitude which accorded well with business acumen in this dawning age of the petrol engine, and Mr Dennison was the first to acknowledge as much; in fact many of his horse-drawn delivery vans had already been replaced by motor vehicles. But when it came to *personal* use, he'd still preferred a pony and trap for his own transport, and it had taken his wife Maud many a weary hour of argument before finally, to shut her up, he'd agreed to the purchase of a private motor carriage.

(The telephone was a different matter. The telephone was *communication*. The telephone saved time; and time was money. Even so, he mistrusted using the thing.)

His present motor-car, the Wolseley 16/20, was the second one he'd owned. To be honest he'd never really enjoyed driving, viewing the whole performance as murderously dangerous, and had been quite happy to hand the job to a chauffeur. Young Craddock, now *he* was in his element behind a wheel. A smart lad too; knew his way round the innards of an engine like nobody's business. Saved Mr Dennison a small fortune in mechanic's bills, a fact reflected in his wages, which were generous enough to make sure he didn't get poached by any of the opposition in Stockwell End.

Craddock was parked now at the edge of Queen Square, sitting in the driver's seat with his employer behind him, keeping half an eye on the motor traffic and half an eye on the lookout for Miss Flora to appear.

At last – yes, there she was – just crossing over at the top of Victoria Street.

The young chauffeur got out of the Wolseley and stood ready by the rear door, immaculate in peaked cap and dark green uniform piped with gold.

"Thank you, Craddock." Flora smiled at him as he opened the door for her to get inside.

He touched his cap in salute, and once she was seated, secured the door firmly and went round to the front of the vehicle to begin cranking the starting-handle.

"I haven't kept you long, have I, Papa?" she asked, leaning

across to kiss her father's cheek. He'd not been looking himself for some months, and worry for him made her especially solicitous. "I thought I'd go into Beatties rather than wait about in the cold."

Her few bits of shopping were put on the leather seat beside her. Then, as the engine burst into juddering life and Craddock took his place again in front, she raised her voice slightly and went on, "You'll never guess who I met just now – "

George Dennison raised an eyebrow in enquiry. "Who?"

"Roseen O'Connor."

"Young Roseen, eh?" He didn't seem that surprised. "Really? And how's *she* keeping these days?"

Flora reached up a hand to grip the door strap, steadying herself as the car moved away from the kerb and turned into the flow of traffic.

"She was looking very well, I thought. You didn't tell me she'd got married."

"Didn't I? Must have slipped my mind. You and her have been out of touch for so long, perhaps I didn't think you'd be interested."

He looked through the window, trying to catch a glimpse as they drove past of the shopfront display of a rival grocery store. "What's her husband's name now, I've forgotten it."

"Kelly, I believe she said."

"That's it. Kelly. Hardly more than a couple of kids, the pair of them. Still, I don't know, with this damn' war – " He shook his head and left the sentence unfinished.

"She was telling me that he's serving out in France," said Flora. "Poor girl, I felt so sorry for her. She was trying to put on a brave face, but the strain of it was really rather obvious."

"Well, she's not the only one who's suffering. These days there must be thousands of women all over the place in the same boat. You just be thankful *you* haven't got a man out there, our Flora."

She thought of Robert Wells again; and bit her lip, shying away from the memory. Apart from mentioning his name once or twice in the early days of their friendship, she'd never spoken of Robert to her parents.

"Roseen's very pretty, don't you think," she observed, for want of something to change the subject.

"Pretty?" Her question seemed to bemuse Mr Dennison by its unexpectedness. He glanced towards young Craddock, then leaned forward and closed the glass partition separating the driving seat from the rear compartment.

"Yes, she's pretty all right. I remember even as a kiddie she could always turn heads in the street."

Perhaps it was Flora's heightened emotional state, but something about the way her father spoke those words, the tone of his voice, prompted her suddenly to say what she did next.

"Shall I tell you something, Papa? I've never mentioned this before, but when I was a child I used to envy Roseen O'Connor – yes, actually *envy* her."

"Good Lord, our Flora, that's a rum thing to admit to!" George Dennison was genuinely astonished. "What's made you tell me that?"

"I don't know. But it's the truth. I was such a dreadfully plain little thing – oh, I'm nothing much to look at now, I know, but then – well, compared with Roseen I always felt ugly and clumsy. She was the most fascinating individual I'd ever met, wayward and headstrong and yet so full of spirit. How I *wished* I could have been more like her. Perhaps then you would have loved me better."

Her father stared at her, the crease between his greying brows deepening to a frown. After all these years, to hear this . . .

"You did love her more than me, didn't you," Flora went on quietly, and he could hardly hear her for the noise of the engine. "I don't mind, really I don't, Papa. I can understand why, now."

He didn't answer at once; scarcely knew how to. It wasn't that he'd loved Roseen O'Connor more than this his own daughter, just that he'd loved her in a different way. And still did, if the truth were known, but with the harmless middle-aged affection of a fond relation. What shocked him a little, and hurt him, was that in all that time he'd never once given any thought to Flora's feelings – never imagined that as a child she could be so perceptive, so sensitive, of the fact that of the pair of them she hadn't been his favourite.

It made him feel uncomfortably guilty to realise that now.

He reached across the seat to take her hand, clasping it tightly. He couldn't look at her.

All he could say was, "You're my flesh and blood, our Flora. You've grown into a young woman I'm proud to have as daughter."

But it didn't make up for the past. They both knew that.

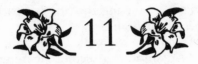

11

Sidney Hathaway was the first of the guests to arrive at the garden party the Dennisons were giving to celebrate their daughter's twenty-first birthday.

He'd motored over from Quinton, where he was living still; and, being Sidney, wasn't in the least put out that he was almost an hour too early and nobody else was there yet. Asked by the housemaid whether he would care to wait in the drawing-room until his hosts were ready to receive him, he decided he'd prefer to stretch his legs and take a stroll round the grounds for a while.

Mr Dennison had hired a marquee for the occasion. It had been erected on the lawns behind the house, its canvas dazzling white against the midsummer green of the trees and the paintbox blue of a cloudless sky. A scent predominantly of roses and philadelphus hung on the warm air. Everywhere the gardens were a blaze of floral colour – banks and beds and hanging baskets bursting with it, gravelled paths edged with it, stone urns spilling over with it. So much colour that the impression was almost unreal, like an artist's picture.

Sidney lit a cigarette and surveyed the scene. How extra-ordinary it was, he reflected, that just across the Channel young chaps were dying at this very moment in a screaming hell of noise and sweat and fear; yet only a few hundred miles away, here he was, in the peace and dreamlike stillness of a garden, looking forward to strawberries and champagne, his only cause for nerves being a mild anxiety about the state of his emotions.

He ran a hand down the thigh of his cream flannel trousers,

as though he could actually feel the blood beating through his veins; and it gave him a curious sense of elation that he should be alive and safe in this little English heaven while those poor devils were paying the price of patriotism in the stinking trenches of the Somme.

Thank God his old man had pulled some influential strings.

By the time he'd smoked a second cigarette people were just starting to arrive at the house, so he wandered back past the marquee to join them. Several he remembered from Moseley College – all female and all in Flora's year; the rest he didn't know. Of the male guests he seemed to be the only young man present apart from a fellow in spectacles with rounded shoulders and a peering, intellectual expression.

Flora introduced them.

"Sidney, this is Walter Holgate," she said, holding out her arms to bring the two of them together. She was looking utterly splendid, he thought, in a pale green, silky frock and a rather dear little hat. "Walter teaches with me at Codsall school."

The pair shook hands and eyed each other. Not much competition there, Sidney told himself. Any associate of Flora's was a potential rival; but Walter Holgate clearly was not of the stuff of which a maiden's dreams were made.

"Walter, this is Sidney Hathaway. You've heard me speak of him, I'm sure. We were students together at Moseley."

Walter blinked behind his pebble glasses and said, ah yes, of course, how very nice and how d'you do.

Sidney lit another cigarette; and when Flora had moved off to greet someone else, he started talking affably about his own teaching work in Edgbaston.

"I'm surprised a chap like you hasn't been conscripted yet," Walter remarked a while later in the conversation. "Practically everybody's getting called up since the Military Service Bill became law. Tom Gregory who was with us at Codsall, he's somewhere in the Dardanelles now. I'd be out there myself, except I failed the Army's medical exam."

"That must have been a relief!" Sidney's laugh underlined the smugness he felt. He'd managed to evade the obligatory examination himself: thanks to his father's string-pulling, some War Office clerk had put it on file somewhere that he suffered with a 'dicky' heart and so was exempt from active service.

"I don't know about it being a relief," answered Walter. "I'm almost as blind as a bat, so I guessed they wouldn't pass me. Tell you the truth, I was disappointed, though. I'd give anything for a chance to do my bit for the country."

Sidney looked at him as though wondering whether he wasn't half-mad as well as half-blind. "You've been listening to too much propaganda, old chap," he said lightly. "The Hun don't really eat Belgian babies for breakfast, you know."

"I never believed they did. But I hope you'll agree it's up to each one of us fellows to do what we can. There's no place for shirkers and cowards. They're calling this the war to end all wars – the only way to ensure we'll never have to fight another is by individual effort towards a complete victory."

Now he was starting to sound like Lloyd George, Sidney thought. Hey ho, how frightfully boring.

"Oh, I do agree, absolutely," he nodded, and looked around to see whether the champagne was being served yet.

Everyone said afterwards what a jolly good party the Dennisons had thrown. For a while one could almost forget that this was 1916 and that the whole of Europe lay under the shadow of wholesale bloody carnage. The sun shone; the girls smiled; the gramophone played ragtime music; even the food was pretty decent, considering the shortages.

Flora's birthday present was still in Sidney's blazer pocket. He was choosing the right time to give it her, not wanting it to be opened, looked at, admired, and then put aside with all the rest she'd received today. This present had cost him a good deal of money and he wished it to be properly appreciated; he was investing a lot, including his hopes, in how much Flora liked it.

His chance came towards the end of the afternoon when the other guests no longer claimed so much of her attention.

"You know, this won't do at all, old girl," he said, coming up behind her as she stood irresolutely on the lawn, making up her mind whether she should go into the marquee for something more to eat. "I'm about to make a complaint, so kindly give me your attention."

She glanced across her shoulder at him, the brim of her hat shading her face. "Very well. You have my attention. What's the complaint?"

"It's a most serious one. In fact, I'm not altogether sure it doesn't carry a hefty penalty. In a word, my dear, you've been causing unnecessary suffering to a fellow creature."

"Have I, indeed." Knowing Sidney as she did, Flora could guess where this was leading. "You mean, I've neglected to speak to you for the past twenty minutes."

"Precisely."

She turned fully towards him and smiled. "Well, here I am. I'm speaking to you now. What would you care to discuss? The weather, perhaps? So lovely for the time of year. Or how about the gardens – "

"Dash it, there's no call to be flippant. That demands a *double* penalty."

"It does?"

"Oh yes, and with immediate effect. You will take my arm, Miss Dennison – " he offered it – "and you will promise not to let go till I say that you may."

"I'm not sure that I wish to do any such thing!"

Still smiling, she belied her words by resting her soft small hand on the sleeve of his blazer jacket, permitting herself to be led across the lawn to the terrace steps. Sidney was such a clown; one could never take him at all seriously.

Reaching the far end of the terrace, they went down on to a path which led in the direction of the kitchen garden. The sound of laughter and chatter was muted here, and the background strains of ragtime drifted, faint and tinny, on the warm air.

Flora went to make some comment, but her companion hushed her with a finger laid to his lips, and it wasn't until they'd gone right along the path past a wall of espaliered pear trees that he stopped at last and turned to her.

For once his expression lacked its usual half-mocking humour, and in its place was a look she'd never seen before, an unsmiling earnestness which alarmed her just a little.

For several moments he gazed at her without speaking; and then the look altered, and his old expression was back again.

"Shut your eyes," he said.

"Why?"

"Do as you're told and don't ask questions."

She made a face, but none the less obeyed, her lids quivering slightly as she kept them closed.

"Now hold out your hand – the left one."

She did so, and after a second or two felt him take it, and something smooth being slipped on to her finger.

Her eyes flew open. The sunlight glinted like rainbow fire in the stones of a diamond ring.

"Sidney – !"

Flora's exclamation came out in a gasp, her breath quite taken away by astonishment.

"Do you like it?" he asked eagerly.

"Do I *like* it? Oh, it's – it's *beautiful!*" She looked up at him. "But I can't possibly accept it."

"Why not? You've accepted presents from everyone else today."

"But this is different."

"Because it's from me, d'you mean?"

"No, of course I don't mean that." She felt most embarrassed. He had put the ring on her third finger, her wedding finger; surely he must realise the significance of what he'd done. "I mean I can't accept it, Sidney, because – well, for a start it's far too expensive."

"That's my worry, old thing, not yours. I hope you're not suggesting perhaps I can't afford it?"

"Don't be silly. I'm not suggesting that at all. What I'm saying is, it's most awfully sweet of you to buy me such a lovely gift, but I'd really rather you hadn't."

She made to take the ring from her finger, but Sidney stopped her at once, closing his hand over hers and holding it tightly.

"I'm not much good at this sort of thing, am I," he said, and suddenly the earnestness was back again, in his face, in his tone, in the way he was regarding her. "The fact is, Flora old girl . . . the fact is, I'm terribly fond of you. Well – pretty smitten, actually. Have been for ages . . . ever since college, don't y'know. And the reason I bought you this ring – "

He came to an abrupt halt and swallowed awkwardly, his young face flooding with colour.

"Dash it, there's only one way to tell you. The reason for this ring, Flora, is that I love you and I want us to become engaged. There – !"

His relief at having got that off his chest was almost too painful to see. He continued to clutch her hand and gaze at her, but now with a silly lopsided smile which showed his unbrushed teeth.

Flora didn't know quite where to put herself. Sidney's sudden declaration had shaken her so much that she was completely at a loss how to answer. In the four years they'd known each other, he'd always treated her with a sort of pally affability, making a joke of everything, either being mockingly cynical or else teasing her unmercifully. There had never been anything romantic between them in the way of kisses or caresses; never anything tender like this.

"You don't have to say yes straight away," he said, beginning to recover his old self-assurance. "I wouldn't want us to be married, besides, until this beastly war is over."

And before she could catch her breath to speak, he was dashing on brightly, "I suppose the next thing is an interview with your Pater. He'll wish to know my prospects, how much I'm worth and all that. Whether I can keep you in the manner to which you're accustomed, eh."

He laughed loudly at the cliché.

"I'd rather you didn't see Papa," Flora heard herself saying, and she was surprised by the amount of firmness she managed to put into the words. "It wouldn't be at all a good idea."

"What – ?" Sidney gaped at her, all the amusement draining from his face. "I say, you're not turning me down, are you, old girl? You don't mean – you don't mean the answer's *no* to getting married?"

He looked suddenly so hurt, so crestfallen, that she felt quite sorry for him, and in an effort to make amends, replied, "I don't know. I shall have to think about it, Sidney. Please give me time."

"Yes . . . of course."

He was holding her hand still. Bending down, he pressed his mouth clumsily against it, his dark hair brushing the sleeve of her frock. Then, straightening himself, "But you won't take *too* long making up your mind, will you, dear?"

★

The war was changing Billy Kelly. Roseen had first noticed a difference that week they went away together to Aberystwyth in 1915 while he was on leave. It was meant to be their honeymoon, but instead of enjoying himself and having a good time, all he'd wanted to do was mope about by the sea, sitting for hours just staring at the waves. She couldn't understand it.

"What's the matter with you, our Billy?" she kept asking. "Why won't you talk to me? What's so blinkin' fascinating about seawater?"

He tried to explain to her; but he'd never been any use with words. How could you tell somebody about the scream that was filling you up inside, that never stopped, not even when you slept, but seemed to get louder and louder till you were frightened that one day soon your head would blow apart with it.

A doctor at the Front had told him it was nerves. *Nerves*. God, he'd seen enough sights to make him nervous, all right! But you got used to that, the blood, the stink of gangrene, the faceless corpses, the shell-spattered pieces of body. No, it wasn't the sights that had shocked his nerves, so much as the sounds. All the time, on and on and on, a never-ending bombardment of noise . . . the rat-tat-tat of machine-gun fire, the whistling scream of bombs, the *crump* of spewing earth, the shuddering roar of the batteries rolling across like thunder. And worse, because quieter, the cries of your mates out there in no man's land, left hanging on the barbed wire to die. In the stillness of the trenches at night you could hear them groaning, and there wasn't a bloody thing you could do to help.

But when Roseen asked him what was wrong, all Billy ever told her was, "I like it sitting here by the sea. It's nice and peaceful."

When he came home again in the summer of 1916 the change in him was more obvious. He'd suffered shrapnel wounds to his legs and after treatment in a field hospital had been recommended for 'Blighty' leave. Although the wounds were healing well, Billy seemed unnaturally depressed; somehow, all the stuffing had been knocked out of him and his face wore a look of weary defeat. Loving her husband the way she did, Roseen couldn't bear to sit and watch him of an evening slumped in his chair, apathetically trying to keep up some sort of conversation with her or Connie, his hands gripping the wooden arms till his knuckles showed bone-white, to stop himself from shaking.

She tended to throw the blame for his dispirited condition on poor Eddie Quinn, who'd been killed in the spring at Verdun. Billy had taken his best pal's death very badly. Perhaps that's why he wept at night, lying in her arms like some big frightened child; perhaps that's why he couldn't make love to her.

It was this impotence which worried her more than anything.

"What is it, Billy? What is it, love?" she'd whisper, as time after time he tried to take her, only to have his body fail him. "Is it me? Am I doing something wrong?"

He'd bury his face in the pillows, and wouldn't answer. He was too ashamed. It wasn't only his spirit this damned war was sapping, it was his manhood as well.

Roseen insisted they go to church while he was home, to see the parish priest and get a Mass said for Eddie. There'd been Zeppelin raids reported, and as they walked down to St Mary's and St John's that Thursday morning, she remembered Billy looking up at the sky in a nervous, almost cringing sort of way. Once outside the church, though, he squared his shoulders and lifted his chin and smiled at her, gave her a penny to buy some votive candles, and knelt beside her to pray before the statues of the Sacred Heart and Our Lady.

'Watch over our Billy for me, please,' she implored silently. 'He's had enough of it. Don't let him suffer any more.'

They had only those twelve days together before he went back again to Flanders. At the start of July heavy battles were being fought on the Thiepval Plateau and the second stage of the British advance on the Somme began, with German lines coming under steady attack.

Roseen's prayers were answered. Her Billy didn't suffer.

Had he been standing a few yards either side of his position, he could have been left a blind and mutilated cripple; instead he took the full brunt of the shell explosion and was blown apart into fragments.

 12

The letter from Billy's commanding officer was very nice, very thoughtful: 'Deeply regret to inform you . . . thoroughly decent chap . . . brave soldier . . . credit to his Company . . . every sympathy in your sad loss . . .' He probably wrote half a dozen such letters a week, the same formula of words each with a different name to bring heartbreak to mothers and wives and sisters; for every death, a whole family in mourning.

The letter had been waiting on the kitchen mantelpiece when Roseen got home from work that Friday night, worn out from standing on her feet all day and fed up with customers complaining about half-empty shelves and bad service. What did they expect, with a war on and most of the men gone away to fight in it.

"There's a letter come," Connie said, and something in the odd tone of her voice sent a sudden shiver of panic through Roseen as she followed the direction of her mother's eye to the mantelpiece.

She recognised the envelope. The Kavanaghs across the street had been sent one like it only this last week, telling them young Jack was dead. Her heart began to thump and she went cold, as though all the blood in her veins was turning to ice.

Please God, no . . .

She reached up to take the letter, hesitating a moment before snatching at it in a kind of fearful haste and thrusting it at Connie.

"You open it for us, our Mam. I don't think I can. You open it for us and read it."

Perhaps it wasn't what she thought; perhaps there'd been a mistake and the post office had got the wrong address.

Her mother's fingers fumbled at the sealed flap, seeming to take for ever while Roseen waited in an agony of impatience.

"What does it say – quick – tell me," she urged her.

There was a second envelope inside, thumbed-over and creased; and inside that, a single sheet of paper. Connie's lips silently shaped the words as she read. When she finished she looked at her daughter, and there was no need to say anything; the tears welling up in her eyes were enough.

"No – oh, God – *no!*" Roseen snatched the page from her hand and read it for herself, disbelieving. No, it couldn't be true – it *couldn't*. Hadn't she been praying night and day for Billy to come home safe?

'I deeply regret that I must write to inform you that Corporal William Joseph Kelly lost his life during an attack on enemy lines on July 15th . . .'

The words became jumbled together and blurred.

July 15th, that was almost three weeks ago. Three weeks, and all that time she'd been going around not knowing that her Billy was lying dead somewhere. They had even celebrated his birthday down at the White Rose.

She felt her mother's hand on her arm.

"Oh, Mam . . ." she whispered brokenly; and it was more than she could bear, remembering how they'd drunk his health that evening, toasted his promotion and wished him luck in his absence. If he'd lived, he would have been twenty-two.

"Oh, Mam . . ."

The tears scalded her throat. Turning to her mother she buried her face in the comforting shoulder and burst into a sudden uncontrollable frenzy of weeping, her small body shaking with the force of its grief.

Connie cradled her in her arms, adding her own noisy sobs, rocking backwards and forwards on her heels.

"Oh my poor child, my poor child, hush yourself now. Dear God, but 'tis a wicked world we live in. Such a fine young fellow he was – the Lord have mercy on his soul. Hush now, there, Roseen, hush now."

She continued this threnody for several minutes, and might

have gone on longer had not a better idea proposed itself.

"Come and sit you down," she said between her tears, "an' I'll pour us both a glass. Sure, but we're needing a drop o' something to console us after such black news."

Like a sleepwalker, her daughter released herself slowly from the enfolding arms and fumbled for the chair behind her; and when Connie brought a generous measure of gin, she put it to her lips and drank it down as though it were nothing stronger than water. Then she sat slumped with her head in her hands, shuddering with sobs, until gradually the alcohol started to dull the shock-sharpened edge of her grief and deaden its agony.

Between them both, they saw off the best part of a whole bottle that night. At least it helped Roseen to find some respite in the insensibility of stupor, sprawled fully-clothed across her bed after being violently sick; and when she didn't turn up for work the next morning – well, who could blame her. She was a widow. And this was the season of widowhood.

During the weeks that followed she continued drinking heavily in order to blot out the worst of her gnawing sorrow. What had affected her more than anything was the fact that she had no body to mourn over: her Billy lay in some temporary grave in northern France, along with many other young husbands and sons whose lives had been snatched from them to feed the rapacious appetite of war. The latest estimations reckoned the cost of hostilities to Britain at six million pounds *a day*; what it was costing in terms of human carnage was inestimable.

The only time she went near St Mary's and St John's was for the memorial Mass, and after that she vowed she'd never set foot inside the place again. So many hours she had spent there on her knees, so many novenas she'd recited, so many candles she'd lit – and all for what – to have her prayers thrown back into her teeth and her happiness destroyed. What was the point of believing in something that could play a trick like that on you? She'd never been greatly religious, but she'd always had a kind of superstitious trust in the help and intercession of the saints and the Blessed Virgin.

A fat lot of use it had done her.

"Why don't you go down to church and see the priest?"

Connie would urge when Roseen's misery drove her into bouts of dreadful depression. "He'll pray wi' you and help you mebbe find a bit o' comfort."

"I'm done with priests," she'd answer. "It's all a load of rubbish that they talk. Rubbish and lies."

Her only source of consolation, apart from the drink, had come from her Uncle George Dennison. He'd heard from Mr Sims his store manager that she was having days off work, and called round to see her. No one had thought to tell him that her husband was dead, or he'd have called a lot sooner.

The minute he saw Roseen he realised how badly she'd taken her bereavement. She was downstairs in the kitchen, wearing an old dressing-gown and reeking of gin; her hair hadn't been brushed and hung in a tangled mess over her shoulders, and her face was pale and sunken. She looked as though she'd aged ten years overnight.

Oddly enough, of the pair of them her mother seemed in much the better shape. Connie was still a blowsy, bloated alcoholic, but at least she appeared to be making an effort to keep the place – and herself – a bit tidier; and George Dennison wondered whether it wasn't because Roseen needed so much of her love and support that she'd managed to pull herself together.

"Don't worry about your job at the shop," he said. "It'll wait. I'll tell Sims to keep it for you till you're fit to start work again. Give yourself time to recover, Roseen. You can't just pick yourself up from a thing like this and expect to carry on with life as before, not when all the stuffing's been knocked out of you."

She started to weep, hiding her face in her hands, and he wished there was something more he could say to ease the burden of her wretchedness. He wanted to put his arms round her, hold her; and moved by this impulse even went so far as to get up from the chair where he'd been sitting. But Connie forestalled him, going across and pulling her daughter to her, patting her on the back as though she were a child to be pacified.

"See here, if there's anything you want or need," he offered, torn between pity and some stronger, indefinable emotion, "you'll let me know, won't you, Roseen. Don't run yourself short of money, like."

She looked at him over her mother's shoulder, her face a crumpled mask of misery; and then she said a curious thing – it stuck in his mind for ever after.

"I wish you'd been my dad, Uncle George. I really do. It's turned my life inside out, wishing that."

And he'd swear she wasn't so muddled with drink that she didn't know what she was saying.

★

By the winter of that year, the third of the war, Roseen had begun to pick up the threads of her life again. She was very young still – only just twenty-one – and her youth and natural resilience were working to heal the heart which Billy's death had shattered. She would always love him, always cherish the happiness they'd known; and because he'd died so soon, always look back on the days they'd shared together as a precious and golden memory.

But she wasn't the type to put on widow's weeds and mourn for ever. Roseen was one of life's corks, destined always to bob to the surface no matter how far down Fate pushed her. She started going out again, filling her evenings with the distraction of company to take her mind off Billy, frequenting the pubs and dance parlours and picture-houses; anything rather than sit at home, remembering.

Like everywhere else, because of the war Wolverhampton had become a town emptied of young men, and it was the rule now rather than the exception to see groups of women out together for a night's enjoyment. Through one of the girls at Dennison's Stores, Roseen had soon found herself drawn into a clique that met regularly at a pub called the Posada in Lichfield Street. It was here that she struck up acquaintance with another young widow, Annie Sutton, who'd lost her husband at Gallipoli and was working on the trams as a conductress.

Annie was a type after Roseen's own heart – bold as brass, fond of a drink and a joke, and always ready for a good time.

"Come on," she'd say, "I got a couple o' bob in my purse.

Let's go down the Empire Palace and have us a bit of a laugh, eh."

The fact that she was a widow was a matter of some relief to her rather than a tragedy. As she admitted, she'd only married Bertie Sutton because he'd got her 'up the stick' and when she miscarried three weeks after the wedding, "Well, that just about put the kibosh on the whole perishin' effort."

It was Annie who tempted Roseen to start smoking – a habit still regarded as socially improper for women – and showed her how to crayon her eyes in black to look like a 'vamp'. Vamps were all the rage just now. The two of them had been to the picture-house in Bilston Street several times to see Theda Bara or Vilma Banky in the role of alluring *femme fatale*, and with her lips painted scarlet and her hair tucked up inside a feather-trimmed turban, Roseen captured the image to a 't'.

She was still too raw from her grief over Billy to worry about taking up with any other fellow – not that there was a great deal of choice – but after months of mourning it was nice to be in the fashion and know from admiring glances that folk still found her rivetingly attractive. For somebody who had always thrived on attention, she *needed* the flattery of complimentary looks to put her on her feet again.

"You're wasted at Dennison's, you are, Roseen," Annie Sutton told her. "Stuck behind a flippin' counter all day. You ought to be doing some'at else, some'at more exciting."

Annie was right; perhaps it was time for a change. She'd been at Dennison's Stores ever since she left school, and seven years was a long time to be selling tea and bacon. What other kind of work could she do, though? It was all very well to hanker after 'some'at more exciting' but even with so many women employed because of the war, the openings were limited. She could go into one of the factories, except she didn't fancy the noise and grime; she could work on the trams, like Annie, or the railways, but that meant clocking-on at five of a morning. On the other hand, if she went along part-time to the Adult Institute and learnt to be a type-writer, there were plenty of clerical jobs to be had in offices – well-paid ones too, and clean.

"*Office*? You don't want to go in no office!" Annie protested. "Bostin' wench like you? It'd drive you barmy. What you need, Roseen, is some'at with a bit o' class, a bit o' glamour – "

She found it, one Saturday night at the Posada, while glancing through the personal column of the weekly *Wolverhampton Chronicle*: 'Young ladies required to act as hostesses at private *thé dansants*. Must be of nice smart appearance. Apply in first instance to Box no 219.'

The same edition of the newspaper had also carried a further item of interest. An announcement of the engagement between Miss Flora Dennison and Mr Sidney Reginald Hathaway.

★

It is one of those vagaries peculiar to the female sex that once aware that a man has fallen in love with her, no matter how lukewarm her own feelings may have been, a woman must begin to view him in a totally different light.

So it was with Flora.

Sidney Hathaway's proposal of marriage had come like a bolt out of the midsummer blue, but having recovered from the astonishment, her reaction was to treat the matter as an aberration and wait for him to recover his senses. Sooner or later he'd be bound to admit he was only indulging in one of his preposterous leg-pulling japes, and the episode could be – well, disregarded if not forgotten.

Sidney admitted no such thing, however. He had made his proposal in absolute sincerity. He loved Flora, and at some future date wished her to be his wife. She was not the first young woman for whom he'd felt an attraction – there'd been others, though not many, and none serious: minor flirtations along the primrose path of emotional experience. But compared with Flora they were merely a foretaste of the real thing.

He planned his courtship with a lover's single-minded dedication. He wrote her poetry – not bad poetry either; composed letters of a surprising maturity considering their flowery content; he bought her small, simple gifts so innocuous that she could scarcely refuse them without seeming ungracious; he took her on pleasant country drives to pleasant country places; told her frequently how much he cared, how happy he was when with her, how unhappy apart.

Flora could not fail but be impressed; even slightly flattered.

Gradually as the months of 1916 passed and the long, warm summer evenings gave way to the misty melancholia of autumn, and then to the first hoar-frosts of winter, her doubts about Sidney's earnestness began to waver; and a still small voice at the back of her mind started nudging her with a whisper of perhaps . . . perhaps . . .

She was a tender-hearted young woman and hated to think that she might be causing him hurt; indeed he often complained in his letters that her unresponsive attitude wounded him more than she realised. She was also romantic, and the notion of being loved in itself appealed to her greatly. What was more, it made her feel somehow very special to be told that she was beautiful (even if she disagreed), to be sent bouquets of flowers, and to receive on Christmas Day a telegram which stated quite simply, 'Darling Flora Dennison I love you'.

Flora knew from personal experience how distressingly painful the bonds of affection could be. In her heart of hearts she still yearned for Robert Wells; but sense and sensibility had taught her that such yearning was a foolishness and it was time she learned to put him from her thoughts. Robert was a married man. Their relationship had had to end before it truly started; so why continue to wound herself by hankering after its dream.

Once or twice Sidney had said to her, "There isn't somebody else, is there, old girl?" and she answered no, of course not; but it was a lie. Robert was lost to her, she must accept that, and in his place, life – or destiny, perhaps – had given her the consolation of another young man's love, someone of equal social status and shared interests, someone she genuinely liked, a schoolteacher as she was, and (if one must forget romance for a moment and be practical) a bachelor available for marriage at a time when available young bachelors were being slaughtered by their thousands in the fields of Flanders.

Flora *wanted* the security of a warm and tender relationship; she wanted children, the joy of motherhood; she wanted to

forget Robert Wells – no, not forget him, forget her attachment to his memory.

So when, in February 1917, Sidney had asked her yet again
to marry him, she had said yes; yes, very well, she would.

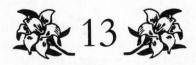

13

Horseley Fields was one of those town areas in whose name may be descried some faint echo of its origins.

Once upon a time, when Wolverhampton was younger and very much smaller, this had been a pleasantly rural open space abutting on to the countryside and used as common grazing land. But progress in the shape of commercial expansion and the requirements of a growing population had swallowed up the fields, burying them beneath a townscape of elegant Georgian squares and artisan terraces.

During the long years of the Victorian era this elegance had suffered a decline, little by little turning shabby and down at heel; manufactory yards were opened, and in place of the rural views of old there was now the iron works, the Union Mill, the canal wharf, the railway junction, each contributing its noise and smoke and industrial ugliness to the scene.

By the time of the Great War, Horseley Fields was the name of an area of narrow, gaslit alleys burrowing between tenements whose faded architectural gentility struggled to survive the dilapidations of poverty. One such building, a double-fronted house in Little Park Street, had been converted from domestic use into a private licensed premises known as the Shanghai; and it was here that Roseen and Annie Sutton were told to come after responding to the advertisement for *thé dansants* hostesses.

When she'd first seen the advertisement in the *Wolverhampton Chronicle*, Roseen hadn't a clue what *thé dansants* were supposed to be.

"It's French," said Annie, airing her knowledge. "Teatime

dances, that's what it means. Like a dance parlour, only you get served with cups o' tea and cake, and they have what they call hostesses to partner you round the floor. Ever so posh, some o' these places are."

The Shanghai wasn't 'ever so posh'. Its main room was on the first floor overlooking the street, and in the raw grey shadows of the February morning it had a seedy, drab appearance which Roseen found depressing. She was about to mutter to Annie that she didn't think much of the place, when the electric lighting came on suddenly; and the transformation was so magical she had to blink twice to believe it.

The lights were cleverly concealed behind a false cornice round the edges of the ceiling and gave off a diffused rose-pink illumination, something like the 'morality' lights in picture-houses. Bathed in this glow the entire room seemed to change and take on an atmosphere of warmth and intimacy, with a comfortable, cosy softness that made everything in it – the cane furniture, the bamboo lattice screens, the paper parasols and coloured Chinese lanterns – look romantically inviting.

Even the terms of employment sounded reasonable enough. Hostesses were expected to be smartly turned-out in afternoon dance frocks. They must be pleasant and courteous to the clientele. Any over-familiarity must be discouraged, and if persistent, reported to the management. No children allowed. Hours from two to seven, or by arrangement.

"What arrangement?" Roseen asked the proprietor, a dapper little man named Browne.

"We can discuss that once I'm satisfied you're both quite suitable," he said. He had a curiously affected way of speaking, strangling his vowels to make them sound 'refayned' and wore his hair parted in the middle and lacquered flat with brilliantine. Annie said it was dyed.

When Connie learned her daughter was giving in her notice at Dennison's to work as a dance hostess, she'd done her level best to dissuade her; but all to no avail. Since Billy's death Roseen had been growing more and more restless and unsettled. Not even George Dennison himself could change her mind. He came round to Raby Street for an earnest talk, and ended by suggesting that if she wasn't happy at the shop she could always move to one of the other branches.

Roseen said thank you, Uncle George, it was kind to be concerned, but no. She just wanted – well, to see more of life, was how she put it, but what she really meant was that she was after something offering her a bit in the way of excitement and adventure. Since meeting Annie Sutton all the dissatisfaction and discontent of the past months had gradually come to a head, and this, mixed with the emotional unrest of grief, made her feel she had to escape from her present existence if she wasn't to suffocate.

"Well, you know your own mind," he said. "I can't say I'm happy you've come to this decision, but I suppose I understand why. And the Shanghai's a respectable enough place by all accounts."

She and Annie started their new job together the second week in March. The daily papers were full of the outbreak of revolution in Russia and the overthrow of the Tsar's government: Roseen glanced at the headlines as she was getting herself ready that first day, then used the pages to wrap up her satin dance shoes. She had more pressing things on her mind than affairs in Russia.

The work at the Shanghai was hard; but it was interesting, and it was fun. There were two other girls, Myrtle and Nora, and the four of them were kept on their feet virtually all afternoon partnering gentlemen round the floor to music provided by three middle-aged ladies on piano, violin and cello. Roseen was surprised by the number of people attending these *thé dansants*, most of them men of a certain age who came in alone to pass away the time between shift-work or whatever. She soon got to know the regular faces, the ones who danced well, the ones who trod on her feet, the ones who held her too tightly.

After a while it was like living in another world. Out there beyond the window were the grey streets and the rationing, the never-ending news of death and disaster; but here inside the Shanghai the atmosphere always seemed nice and warm and cheerful, perhaps because people smiled and looked re-laxed – they'd come to enjoy themselves, after all, to forget for a while what was happening, to try and recapture a little of the gaiety of the days before the war.

And in the cosy, rose-pink glow of make-believe, dancing

to the music of a waltz or a tango, for an hour or so they could do that.

Roseen had been working as hostess for a couple of months when Mr Browne raised the subject of evening overtime. He'd been keeping his eye on her, he said, strangling his vowels as usual, and was very pleased with the way she'd fitted in so well. There'd been complimentary remarks; obviously she was a popular young lady. Would she consider doing an extra few hours if he offered another two shillings a week?

By this time she and Annie Sutton were aware that the Shanghai was being operated in the evenings as a club – rather exclusive by the sound of it, with its own private membership.

"What would you want me to do?" she asked.

"Oh, exactly what you're doing now," he told her.

It was an offer too good to refuse, especially since she needed the money. Dance frocks were expensive and Roseen never liked to look anything less than stunning.

For some reason Annie was put out about it when she heard, and the pair of them had their first exchange of words, with 'favouritism' and 'jealousy' bandied back and forth, leading to coolness on Annie's side for several weeks after.

So it was that she missed the beginning of a relationship which started almost at once between Roseen and someone else – a relationship that would in time have effects which none of them, least of all Roseen herself, could possibly have imagined.

*

She never knew what it was about Maurice Lines that attracted her so much the first time she saw him. He was neither tall nor particularly good-looking; just another man on the dance floor. Roseen was partnering someone else in a fast-paced Turkey Trot, and as she swung past him their shoulders brushed and for just that quick second he caught her eye; and that was the start of it.

There's something in the way a man looks at a woman that tells her whether he fancies her: if the chemistry between them is right, his glance will hold hers a moment longer than necessary, and in a way impossible to describe except to say that it carries a certain subtle recognition. Roseen had caught that look many times, and always got a *frisson* of satisfaction from its unspoken acknowledgement of her desirability. So when she went back to her seat at the end of the dance, she wasn't in the least surprised to find herself approached by this particular gentleman to ask if she would partner him in the next one.

He was a wonderful dancer. He took her through the tango as though he knew every line and curve of her body, flowing along in perfect time with the music and moulding her to his own movements with just the slightest pressure of the hand against her back. As partners they fitted together perfectly, and when he requested the following dance as well, she said yes, even though it was one of the rules that a hostess should make herself available for someone else.

The trio of middle-aged ladies who played during the daytime were replaced for these night-club dances at the Shanghai by a proper six-piece band, with a bar serving alcohol set up in one corner of the room. Half-way through the evening there was always an interval to give the band a break and the chance of a drink; and it was while Roseen was taking a rest herself that the same man came across to join her.

She was examining the damage of somebody's clumsy feet on her white satin shoes, and hadn't realised who it was standing there behind her till he spoke, asking if she'd care to join him in a glass of something.

"Thanks, but we're not allowed to," she said, turning to look at him over her shoulder.

Their eyes met again, and held.

"In that case, d'you mind if I sit here – ?" He indicated a chair next to hers at the small round table. "Or isn't that allowed either."

Roseen cast a quick glance towards the bar. Hostesses were supposed to keep themselves to themselves during the interval; but Mr Browne had his back to them both and was talking to the band leader.

"No, that's all right. I don't mind."

He took the chair and sat down facing her. "Cigarette?"

offering one from a silver case produced from his inside pocket.

She shook her head. That was another thing not allowed. The Shanghai was very particular about being run as a 'respectable' establishment.

"The name's Maurice," he volunteered, lighting the cigarette and turning his head to blow the smoke away from her. "What's yours?"

"Roseen."

He had dark straight hair slicked back from the forehead and a neatly-clipped moustache. "Roseen, eh? That's a pretty name. Goes with the rest of you. I haven't seen you here before. You must be new."

"I've been working afternoons, doing the *thés dansants* – " she knew how to pronounce that now and gave it emphasis, just to show off. "Mr Browne put me on this evening job at the start of the month."

"You dance very well."

"So do you."

He smiled. "Well, so I should. It's all part of my profession."

"Oh?"

"Yes, I'm in the entertainment business. Revues, musicals, exhibition dancing, that kind of thing." He inhaled another mouthful of smoke, and after a pause went on, "With a few lessons I reckon you could be really good yourself, Roseen. You know how to move. You've got what they call an instinct for rhythm."

"Have I? D'you think so?" His little compliment pleased her and she tilted her head flirtatiously to smile at him. "Honestly?"

"No kidding. You've got talent all right. Have you ever thought of using it to get work on the stage?"

"*Me – ?*"

"Yes, why not," he said, seeing the green eyes widen slightly at his suggestion. "Listen, all you need is the right connection, someone who'll put a word in for you."

He left the cigarette in his mouth and felt about in the pockets of his navy serge suit.

"Here – " finding what he wanted and holding it out across

130

the table. "Next time I'm in Wolverhampton I'll let you know if I've heard of anything. Hang on to this so's you won't forget me."

She looked at the card he'd given her. 'Maurice Lines Esq. Stage and Screen. Lower Essex Street, Birmingham.'

"Birmingham, is that where you live?" Opening her sequined evening purse, she slipped the card away inside, at the same time remembering to give Mr Browne another quick glance. He was still at the bar.

"I'm on the move so much I seem to live all over the place," Maurice Lines answered, and with a nod of the head towards her purse, "That's the address of my agent's office."

Roseen was impressed. Wait till she told her Mam she'd met somebody in the entertainment line at the Shanghai and he'd promised he might be able to help her. What a turn up for the books! This wasn't the sort of thing that would ever have happened at Dennison's.

"I'll have the next dance, if I may." He got to his feet, leaning over to stub out his cigarette, and she registered the fact that the well-manicured fingers were bare of any wedding ring.

Almost as though he'd read her thoughts he added casually, "Doesn't your husband mind you working as a hostess?"

"My husband's dead," Roseen said, and for a moment all the sparkling brightness went out of her expression. She looked down at her own ring. "He was killed ten months ago in France."

"I'm sorry I asked."

"That's all right, you weren't to know."

She raised her face; and once more there was that too-lingering glance between them both.

★

She didn't see Maurice Lines again for almost three weeks. It was the middle of June; national morale had been boosted with news of a British victory in the Ypres salient with Messines Ridge taken; and the first American troops had just arrived to add extra fighting weight to the Allies' thrust against the Boche.

It seemed to be the turning of the tide at last.

The summer weather was sticky and humid, and despite a light breeze at evening, the narrow streets around Horseley Fields retained the heat, their stagnant air soured by the smell of factory effluence. Roseen had treated herself to another frock, a cool one just right for this time of year, in a greeny-blue georgette with bugle beads sewn on to the bodice and the hem raised a stylish couple of inches above the ankle. It had belonged to Myrtle, who had had to give up her job when Mr Browne found out she was pregnant, and Roseen had bought the frock from her when she left. In her condition she wouldn't be doing much dancing for the next six months: the tragedy of it was that Myrtle needed the work – her husband hadn't long come back from the Dardanelles with an arm and half a leg blown off.

(That still hadn't stopped him enjoying his oats though, had it, remarked Annie Sutton, now back again on friendly terms.)

She was wearing this particular frock the night she encountered Maurice Lines for the second time. He came into the Shanghai late, about half past nine, just after the interval was over, and Roseen didn't notice he was there till he got in ahead of someone else to claim her for a hesitation waltz.

"You'll have me in trouble doing that," she said, feigning a petulant tone as he took her in his arms. "Jumping the queue – "

"Jumping the queue's not allowed. Don't tell me." He laughed, showing his white teeth. "Be honest, though, I bet you'd rather dance with me than that old buffer."

Despite herself she couldn't help but smile at such a nerve; and then he was holding her close and guiding her with his wonderfully smooth, professional touch between the other couples on the floor. Just before the waltz ended he put his mouth against her ear and said, "By the way, you're looking really beautiful tonight, Roseen."

After that there were other men to be partnered; most of them reasonable dancers, but nowhere near being a patch on Maurice Lines. Every time the two of them passed each other they'd exchange little glances, and something inside Roseen seemed to give a jumping tingle of excitement at the look in those dark eyes of his. It had been ages since she felt so exhilarated by a man's response to her attractiveness.

He claimed the last dance (she was hoping he would); and as they moved together to the rhythm of the band music, he said, "If I waited for you downstairs, would you come and have a drink with me?"

The question startled her. Flattered her as well. "I don't know . . . Mr Browne doesn't like us keeping company out of hours."

"Oh, come on. There's that business I want to talk about, remember?" He swung her round in a giddy triple turn, holding her tightly to balance them both; and then he went on, "I'll be at the end of the street. No one's going to see us meeting there."

Their cheeks brushed, and she smelled the cologne he used, felt that little tingle of excitement again; and heard herself saying coolly, "Well – yes, OK, I suppose it'll be all right. Only for half an hour, though."

14

George Dennison would never have admitted it, not even to himself, but his feelings for young Roseen were decidedly ambivalent. That day a couple of years ago, coming back from town in the Wolseley, his daughter Flora had just about hit the nail on the head when she made the comment that he'd always favoured Roseen more than her. And then that comment of Roseen's herself, about always wishing he could have been her father; somehow the two things added up to one and finally brought the truth home to him.

Throughout his life he'd been a man who lived by his own rules. He'd come up the hard way from poor beginnings and put his sweat into building a prosperous business – and by God it *was* prosperous – yet for all his success he wasn't too proud to remember the days when he'd walked to school with no shoes on his feet. He was that sort of man.

It wasn't his wife Maud's fault that she was barren after Flora, and it wasn't Flora's fault that she hadn't been born a boy. George Dennison would dearly have wished for more children, but then wishing and getting were different things entirely in his book and he wasn't of the nature to pine for the impossible.

There was a time when he'd seriously thought of adopting young Roseen O'Connor – in fact, if Maud had been a woman of less pride, he might well have gone ahead and done so; but that would have meant dragging out his relationship with Connie, so things were probably best left as they were. Whatever her faults Maud had always been a good wife and he wasn't going to belittle her by making her rear some other woman's child against her will.

Right up to the time of Roseen's marriage his feelings had been – well, how could you say, paternally benevolent. He'd kept a close eye on her, fostered her development, seen to it she had a fair start in life; a roof over her head, a steady job. He'd stinted her nothing, not even though his affaire with Connie had been over and done with for years.

And then suddenly she wasn't a child any more. Mr Dennison could remember looking at her one day and thinking, good Lord, you're grown up, Roseen, and it was like seeing her for the first time as other men saw her, as a woman. All that early promise of heartbreaking loveliness had been fulfilled and she knew it herself, knew how to make the most of it. She'd had the sense to leave her hair alone: while everyone else was following the fashion and having theirs bobbed, Roseen wore it in its natural curly state caught back from her face in a ribbon, either that or left loose so that with every movement of her shoulders its smouldering copper tones seemed almost to catch fire. It was the sort of hair you longed to reach out and touch.

She'd developed into a charmer, all right. Delicate features with something almost feline about them – the slant of the eyes, perhaps – and a slender, well-proportioned figure. But more than this, what made her so altogether *different* was the look she had about her, of provocative invitation, of promise; the look that said, 'You want a good time? Then try and catch me first.'

George Dennison recognised all this; and in the same moment felt ashamed of himself that his sexuality should have responded to the recognition, however natural it was for a man to have such feelings.

After she'd gone to work at the Shanghai he saw nothing of her for six months; and then they happened to meet one lunch-time in what was known locally as 'Boney Park', St George's churchyard in Wolverhampton. He had spent the morning discussing business with a wholesaler along Bilston Road, and, after the stuffy office full of pipe-tobacco smoke, thought a walk would clear his head as well as please his doctor: walking was an exercise he'd been prescribed for his heart trouble.

Roseen was seated by herself on a bench at the side of the path. People were glancing at her as they passed, but she didn't pay them any notice, being more occupied with a book propped on her knee.

"Well – and how are you, young lady?" he said, coming up beside her and sitting down. She was dressed in a thin summer frock of some gauzy print material, and had a little straw hat with flowers round the brim. Very pretty.

"Uncle George!" She gave him a quick, surprised smile. "Hello, what brings *you* into Boney Park?"

"I'm just on my way back from a meeting. Thought I'd stretch my legs a bit. You're keeping all right, are you?"

"Yes, thanks. Mam's not been too grand, though. She says it's this heat that makes her swell up, so she's taken to stopping in bed."

"It'd do her more good to cut down on the drinking she does."

"I know, but you try telling *her* that." Roseen closed her book, marking the page with a square of white card.

"How's your Flora?" she went on brightly. "I saw it in the *Chronicle* about her engagement. Have they named the day yet, her and her young man?"

He shook his head. "They've said they want to wait for the war to finish first. Wisest thing, as I told them. There's no knowing what could happen yet."

"That's true. Is she still working at the same school?"

"Codsall. Yes, she's still there."

"I suppose her young man's serving as a soldier some-where."

"Sidney? No, he's kept well out of it." A faintly grudging note sounded in the answer. "He does the same job as Flora – schoolteaching. Well, somebody's got to stay behind and keep the education system going, that's what he says." Then, changing the subject, "And how about you, Roseen? Still at the Shanghai?"

She sketched a shrug. "For the moment, I am."

"Oh – you're thinking of leaving?"

136

"I don't know yet. It all depends. There's this chap." She bent forward to pick a thread from the hem of her frock. "He's promised to get me work on the stage."

"The *stage* – ?"

"Oh, he's quite genuine," she said, looking at him quickly. "He's in the entertainment business."

The expression slid too easily off her tongue.

"I see. And what kind of work is it he's offering?" George Dennison didn't much care for the sound of this. It was one thing for her to quit his own employment to become a dance hostess (and if truth be told, he'd never been altogether happy about Roseen doing what she did), but quite another to swallow the bait of a promise made by some fellow 'in the entertainment business'. Entertainment was a word which encompassed a multitude of categories. It could mean anything from theatre or music hall to sleazy backstreet studios and worse.

"He says he might be able to find me something as a dancer. They're always looking for girls to join the chorus line, he says."

"Is that so? Where does he come from, this – what's his name?"

"Maurice Lines. He's from Birmingham." Roseen dipped into the book on her lap and produced the card she'd been using as a marker. "There you are – 'Stage and Screen, Lower Essex Street' – that's the address of his agency."

"Can I have a look?" Mr Dennison held out a hand to examine the card for himself. He knew Birmingham. If his memory served him right, Lower Essex Street was somewhere near Holloway Circus. He made a mental note of both name and address before giving the card back.

"And where did you meet this Mr Lines? At the Shanghai?"

"Yes. He comes in about once a week of an evening."

The more he heard, the more he was inclined to feel suspicious. "You want to be careful, Roseen. Some of these characters, they can lead you up the garden path – "

"Oh, not Maurice! He's ever so charming and sincere."

"I'm sure he is. That's part and parcel of the way they operate." He paused, leaning over to place his hand on hers. "You won't do anything silly, will you. I mean, you won't go agreeing to whatever this man offers without talking to me about it first. Will you promise me that?"

"Well . . ." She looked away with a little pout and he knew what she was thinking, that it was really none of his business. "Well, all right, if I'm offered something for definite, I'll let you know."

He gave the hand a squeeze of thanks and released it.

"It's just that – well, I've got nobody to look after me now, Uncle George," she went on after a moment. "Not since Billy died. And what with Mam so poorly all the while . . . I'm on my own, like. Maurice says I could earn a lot of money dancing."

"What d'you need money for? *I'll* always help you out, you know that."

"But I don't want you to. It'd make me feel I was sponging off you. All these years you've been taking care of Mam and me – " she stopped and made a gesture of helplessness. "I can't expect it for ever. You're not some bloomin' charity."

He pressed her hand again in reassurance. It felt small and soft and feminine; and made him think of the young woman he'd been visiting lately out at Albrighton, whenever the strain of his enforced married celibacy needed some relieving. She was hardly older than Roseen nor – God help him – than his daughter Flora.

He pushed the thought away from him.

"As long as I'm alive," he said, "you've always got me to depend on. Just you remember that, Roseen."

★

There *was* an agency calling itself 'Stage and Screen' in Birmingham – George Dennison checked – but further than that there wasn't a lot he could do. He didn't want to start drawing attention to Roseen's connection with this Maurice Lines by asking questions at the Shanghai. The management was known to be very particular about that sort of thing, and she wouldn't thank him for getting her dismissed for flouting regulations.

It looked as though he'd have to leave things as they were and hope she had the commonsense to watch what she was getting up to.

Mr Dennison might have had rather more to think about had he happened to catch the title of the book she'd been reading that day. It was *The Rainbow* by an up and coming young author, D. H. Lawrence, and had been suppressed as obscene not long after its publication two years ago. Enough copies had been sold, however, for the literate public to be aware of its modern treatment of sexual love. Maurice Lines asked Roseen if she'd come across it, and when she said no, he had given her his own well-thumbed copy to borrow, telling her it wouldn't hurt to have her mind broadened a bit.

She was no reader, and never had been; and she'd never heard of D. H. Lawrence; so it smacked of naïvety that she should have been in possession of such a work in a public place like Boney Park, unaware that she ran the risk of getting herself arrested. She was only reading *The Rainbow* because it was Maurice's and Maurice was clever, and she wanted to impress him when he asked her questions about whether she'd enjoyed it. As a matter of fact she wasn't enjoying it at all. The parts she could understand of the story were 'mucky', and the rest was too boring to hold her attention.

But she persevered.

For the past few weeks, since the start of August, she and Maurice Lines had been meeting every Sunday night (her one night off) in the Station Hotel, where he stayed whenever he was in Wolverhampton.

"You want to be careful," Annie Sutton warned her, echoing George Dennison. "Hotel rooms have beds. And beds as a rule get laid on, specially when you've had a drop too much."

So far, though, the two of them had kept to the lounge bar, and it wasn't until the third weekend that Maurice wondered if she'd like to go upstairs and have a drink with him in private. He'd come by a few bottles of French champagne, he said, bought off an officer home on leave; it'd be a crying shame to let it go to waste with no one to share it.

Roseen had never tasted champagne in her life.

"But are you allowed to entertain upstairs?" she queried.

He tapped the side of his nose, and winked. "Only if it's business."

Much of the space in the small top-floor room was taken

up by a big old-fashioned bed which she had to skirt past to reach the only chair, near the open window. The sky outside was still filled with an afterglow of sunset, its dark violet distances banded with vermilion swathes of cloud, and the dying ember rays of daylight were reflected in the mirror of the wardrobe door.

Maurice lit the gas bracket, adjusting its flame to give a shadowy warmth to the room.

"Cigarette?" Sitting down at the foot of the bed he leaned over to pass her one from his case, then struck a match to light it, his hand on the arm of the chair.

"Isn't it draughty for you by that window? Wouldn't you rather sit here next to me?"

"No, I'm all right, thanks."

"Suit yourself." He inhaled deeply, keeping his eyes fixed on hers. "I might have some good news for you next week, by the way."

"Oh – ? What – about a job?"

"Mm. I'm meeting a chap on Thursday who does all the hiring for touring revues. I mentioned you to him on the telephone and he said he might just be interested."

A quick flush of pleasure showed in Roseen's face. "D'you think he will? Take me on, I mean?"

"He'd be a damn' fool not to. You can dance, you've got the figure, and the looks and the style. Believe me, sweetheart, there's not many girls around like you."

She leaned her head against the chair and smiled, letting the cigarette smoke trickle out between her half-closed lips. Talk of this kind was like music to her ears.

"How about that champagne!" Maurice jumped up again suddenly and went round the bed to the wardrobe, and as he opened it she caught a glimpse of the navy serge suit he usually wore at the Shanghai. Tonight he was in grey flannel trousers, and a tweed jacket which he'd taken off to hang on the door hook as he came into the room.

"I've had this standing in a bucket of cold water from the kitchen," he said, holding up a dripping bottle to show her. "The chambermaid must have wondered what the heck I was playing at, keeping a bucket in the wardrobe. Perhaps she thought I preferred it to one of these – "

His shoe kicked against something on the floor which gave off a dull china *ping*.

Roseen started to laugh. She liked Maurice's sense of humour – it was down to earth and funny without being crude.

"Now then," finding two glasses from an inside shelf and bringing them round for her to hold, "let's try and ease this cork out nice and quiet so we don't give the show away – "

Cigarette in the corner of his mouth, he stripped off the foil and undid the wire cradle, using his handkerchief to wrap round the neck. Then, "Here we are – quick, where's your glass!" as the cork popped and the wine came bubbling up from the bottle.

"What shall we drink to?" Roseen asked excitedly.

"To Lady Luck," he said.

"Yes – to Lady Luck!"

The champagne had a sharp-sweet taste that made her pull a face at the first mouthful, and then it caught the back of her throat and went into her nose, starting her laughing again.

Maurice sipped his like a connoisseur.

"Not bad . . . mmm, not bad at all."

When the fizz of bubbles had subsided he topped the two glasses up and leaned back on the bed, cradling the bottle between his knees.

"Well, what d'you think – do you like it?"

She rubbed her nose with the front of her hand, like a child, and took another drink. "It's sort of . . . different."

"I'll say it is!" He grinned at her, showing his teeth beneath the dark moustache. "Only the best for the best, eh, darling?"

They smoked another cigarette each; and when the first bottle of champagne was empty, he opened another.

Roseen was starting to feel wonderfully light-headed and happy. Suddenly it was as though she hadn't a care in the world and the more she drank, the lovelier everything seemed. She hadn't felt as elated as this since – well, not for a long, long time. All the dreariness and weariness and misery of the war receded into the background, and the only thing that mattered was the deliciously dizzy present, the here and now of euphoria with its promise of a glamorous and golden tomorrow.

She lolled back in her chair, and kicked off her shoes, already imagining herself up there on the stage of the Empire Palace, dozens of men falling madly in love with her – her face in the newspapers – everyone admiring her. The dream was so rosily vivid that she didn't mind at all when Maurice put his glass aside and pulled her into his arms and fell over backwards with her on to the bed.

It only made her laugh even more.

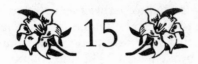

15

I don't know whether you'll ever read this. Perhaps it doesn't matter. The simple fact that I'm writing to you, my dearest, is enough to bring you closer, just as it's enough for me to speak your name and find a little comfort.

When I look back on those days at Moseley and remember the time we shared in one another's company – those moments of which memories are made – it seems it happened to someone else in another world entirely. All that's left now is a ghost that haunts me – no, not a ghost, it's more tantalising than that – some story I read in a book, perhaps, so well-written and evocative that I can't get its scenes out of my mind.

I have been through hell, Flora, like so many of the fellows in this dreadful war; and not just us, but *Them* as well. We're all in it together, whatever our uniform or language or allegiance. Nothing will ever be the same again – whatever we had before, it's gone for good. This damn' business has altered each and every one of us; and since it's us – the little cogs in the machinery of war – who are the shapers of history, then by our change the pattern of the future is changed likewise. One thing I know for certain, that there's not a man of us would go through this again, so perhaps the world will be a safer and a better place once the madness is finally over. It's the politicians and the generals – 'old men, grey borderers on the march of death' – who make war, not the chap who has to do the killing and the dying.

I've been laid up over here for the past fortnight nursing a broken shoulder and fractured ribs and wishing to God I was dead. Does that sound ungrateful? I've seen death so often that it's ceased to bother me, so many fine lads alive one minute and blasted to kingdom come the next. If one's going to go, that's the way to do it, not skulk about with a couple of broken bones like me, of no damn' use to anyone including myself.

Do you know what I wish? That I could be home again, with you, my darling, held safely in your arms in the peace and quiet of the English countryside and no sound but birdsong and the strong deep beat of your heart against mine. I cling to that image for the sake of my sanity while I'm lying here malingering among the maimed and the dying.

I've misplaced my book of Swinburne, but somewhere (was it in *Erectheus*?) I seem to recall how:

> . . . the light that gleams
> On the faces of men falls faint as the dawn of
> dreams,
> The dayspring of death as a star in an under sky
> Where night is the dead men's day.

That's how it feels, as though all the light has gone out of the world; not the sun, the moon and the stars, but the shining brightness of hope and innocence.

Do you still spare me any thought at all, I wonder? Perhaps you don't. I gave you so little to remember; only a love which wasn't mine to give, and yet you had it all and always will, Flora, my darling. I've longed for you so often.

One day we might meet again, do you think? When all this is over and the world's got its senses back. God, how I wish things could have been different for us.

It was almost two months before Flora received Robert Wells's letter, written from a field hospital in Palestine. By the time she read it he'd been patched up and sent back into naval service, patrolling the dangerous waters off the Dardanelles Straits aboard HMS *Raglan*.

His letter moved her profoundly. Its tone of despair contained a cry for help which she was powerless to answer; and the tenderness expressed between that despair drew to the surface all her own buried yearnings. That he should write after all this long time with such pleading affection wrenched at her heart, causing her a grief and bewilderment which she could not, dared not, reveal for fear of betraying herself.

Many a night she lay in the darkness of her bedroom weeping silent, hopeless tears of longing, torn between surrender to the past and duty to the future. Her over-vivid imagination painted a picture of Robert wounded and weak in some hospital ward in the alien surroundings of a foreign land, dreaming of the long-ago days at Moseley and reliving through his mind's eye the scenes of their friendship. She thought of him whispering her name, needing her in his loneliness; and it was like probing into a wound which had never healed.

From her grieving and heartache there rose the spectre of guilt to add to her torment: guilt that Robert should mean more to her than Sidney her fiancé ever could; guilt that she might have stolen from Robert's wife and children the love which rightly belonged to them alone; guilt because she hadn't the strength of will to shut him out of her life and forget him.

His letter, read and re-read until she knew every word and nuance of it, was hidden away within the pages of her own copy of Swinburne's poetry, marking a passage from *Tristram of Lyonesse* which in her present mood of melancholia seemed especially evocative:

> Hath he not plucked from death of lovers dead
> Their musical soft memories, and kept red
> The rose of their remembrance in men's eyes,
> The sunsets of their stories in his skies . . .

Hardly the sort of thing to 'jolly her out' of herself, as Sidney would say. He'd noticed how withdrawn and pensive she appeared, and a number of times had enquired if anything was wrong; but what could she answer? The truth would have hurt him terribly – maybe enough to put a question mark over their engagement. So she fobbed him off with some excuse or other and made an effort to seem happier, throwing herself into her school work and the preparations for Christmas.

Heaven knew, there was enough to keep her occupied – the children were performing a little nativity play for their families, and costumes had to be found, scenery painted, parts rehearsed and carols learnt, not to mention seeing to the planning and provisions for the party afterwards. With only three teachers now (jolly Mr Gregory, so keen on games, had died at Gallipoli in the autumn), much of the arranging was thrown on to Flora's shoulders.

At home too there was a lot to think about. This year Sidney's parents and elder sister had been invited to spend Christmas with the Dennisons at Stockwell End, arriving on Christmas Eve and staying till Boxing Day. The Hathaways were crashing snobs in George Dennison's opinion, but since they would soon be related by marriage he felt obliged, as he put it, to 'shell out a bit' and put on a decent show.

Despite the ache concealed within her heart, Flora did her best to join in the festive spirit and be attentive to Sidney's parents, sympathetic towards his sister (her husband was serving in France) and affectionate with Sidney himself.

On Christmas Day the whole party went to morning service at St Michael and All Angels on the Lower Green at Tettenhall. There'd been a light dusting of snow during the night, just enough for the wintry sun to give a sparkle to the naked trees in the churchyard, turning the scene into a tinselled cameo. Moved as she always was by the beauty of the service, Flora prayed for Robert, and for herself; and then hurriedly, in case God should notice her order of priorities, for Sidney and their future life together.

Afterwards they all walked home, up the hill again, to open the presents and warm themselves with glasses of spiced rum punch before sitting down to what Mr Hathaway, in his hearty, patronising manner, called 'the groaning festal board'.

Flora could tell that her father didn't care overmuch for Sidney's people. Their middle-class affectations irritated him, as did their unconscious ability to remind him that he was a social inferior, even though the word Trade was never mentioned. He thought Mrs Hathaway, especially, too stuck-up for her own good, and because he was annoyed at having to be pleasant to those he despised, each time the lady referred to her late father, a Member of Parliament and junior minister at the Foreign Office, Mr Dennison countered with some comment about his own family which emphasised their plain ordinariness.

His wife Maud, on the other hand, cared very much for the Hathaways' good opinion, and couldn't do enough to make them feel she was honoured to have them as guests. Flora noted how she seemed to ape Mrs Hathaway's fluted inflections of speech and her over-exaggerated gestures (was not mimicry the sincerest form of flattery?) and, for the first time in her life, realised how much it mattered to her mother to be accepted as a social equal by those of innately superior class.

She realised something else too – that because she loved her mother she could never do anything discreditable or improper which, if it came to public ears, might be likely to cause talk. Since receiving Robert Wells's letter she had sometimes in moments of wishful yearning imagined him coming back again to the Midlands to find her and asking her to break off her engagement and go away with him. It had been a deliciously lovely daydream; and of course hopelessly impossible. More than any pain she would cause Sidney, the shaming effect upon her mother's social standing would be unforgivable.

Yes, but what if Robert *did* return? He'd hoped in his letter that one day they might meet once more. If that happened and the dream came true, could she trust herself to deny him? She greatly doubted it. Oh, why did she have to *care* so much for people, she asked herself despairingly. Why couldn't she be the sort of person who didn't give two hoots – like Roseen O'Connor – someone whose only concern in life was to please herself, and none of this nonsense about suffering pangs of guilt and remorse. How easy to say yes to Robert then!

These preoccupations with her inmost thoughts finally started to show through the façade which Flora had been at such pains to wear over Christmas.

"Dash it all, I do wish you'd say what it is that's worrying you," Sidney reproached her on Boxing Day. His parents and sister had departed from Stockwell End immediately after luncheon, leaving him to follow later. "Whatever's on your mind, old thing, you may as well come out with it and tell me."

"But there's nothing – !" she started to protest.

"Yes there is, I can see there is," he insisted obstinately. "You've been down in the dumps for a couple of weeks now. It's not *us*, is it? I mean, you're not having second thoughts about the engagement?"

"Oh, Sidney, don't be such an ass." She pushed her arm through his and gave it a reassuring hug. "I've told you, there's really nothing wrong. I'm probably a little tired, that's all."

"Now you can't fob me off again with that excuse," he said, kissing the tip of her nose. "I can read you like a book. It's all this hanging about, that's what it is. All this shilly-shallying. You'd rather us be married, wouldn't you."

And without waiting for an answer, "Well, to speak the honest truth, Flora, so would I. Perhaps it wasn't such a good idea, putting off our wedding indefinitely. Tell you what, let's get married in the New Year, shall we? What d'you say, old girl – would that make you happier?"

She didn't know whether it would make her happier or not, but marriage would certainly put her beyond temptation's reach; and maybe Sidney's ring on her finger would exorcise the ghost of Robert Wells from her heart.

She looked up at him, and managed her brightest smile.

"Yes, let's do that, darling," she agreed. "We'll set a date for the New Year. There seems such little point in waiting."

★

On Easter Saturday 1918 she walked down the aisle of St Michael and All Angels on her father's arm to become Mrs Sidney Hathaway. It was a quiet wedding followed by a private family reception at Stockwell End – not what George Dennison had envisaged for his only child, but the effects of the war were being felt everywhere these days. At least the local press turned out in force to report the event in their newspapers.

Flora had not realised quite what an upheaval marriage

would be. When she and Sidney had started making plans in January, it had all seemed so simple and straightforward: because she very much wanted to remain near her parents rather than move to Birmingham, he'd decided to give up his teaching post at Edgbaston and apply for Mr Gregory's vacant position at Codsall school. But that would take time, and in the meanwhile where were they to live? The choice was either renting furnished accommodation until Sidney's transfer was settled, or staying at Stockwell End – and the latter appeared the most sensible arrangement. Its only drawback was the distance Sidney would have to travel each day; but he'd manage, he said optimistically; with his qualifications he was bound to get the post at Codsall, and if not – well, if not, they'd just have to think again.

The first night of their marriage was spent at the Kensington Court Hotel in London. Paris would have been far more romantic for a honeymoon (when she was younger and in love with love's ideal, Flora had always dreamed of going to Paris as a bride), but of course the war made that impossible. The late March weather was cold and unsettled, and they arrived off the train in an absolute downpour which veiled the city streets in a curtain of rain and rather dampened their plans to see a show.

Though neither was hungry, they each pretended they were, and to please each other stayed in for dinner at the hotel. Conversation between them was nervously trite. They were man and wife in name now, but the physical unity of their marriage was yet to be achieved, and it was as if this evening were the minute hand of their lives' clock pausing just a fraction before the midnight of their separate past before it moved on to start a new hour in a new day of all their shared tomorrows.

Flora kept meeting Sidney's eyes, and smiling, and glancing hastily away with some silly comment about the weather, or the journey, or the meal; anything rather than suffer the awkwardness of silence. She'd never felt so timorously shy, nor yet so filled with excited apprehension. The whole day had seemed unreal, as though she'd been a spectator watching it happen to somebody else; and now here she was, Mrs Sidney Hathaway, sitting opposite the stranger whom that somebody else had married at St Michael's church this morning.

For a moment her mind flitted to Robert, and she found herself wondering whether she'd have felt the same had it been *him* she had vowed to love, honour and cherish until death. Then, instantly angered by her own weak disloyalty, she reached across the table and pressed Sidney's hand.

"I hope I've made you happy," she said.

"Happier than I've ever been in my life."

He grinned at her like a small boy and emptied back his glass of wine. He'd been drinking steadily throughout the meal and was feeling a good deal less nervous than earlier, when they'd first arrived and been shown to their hotel room. The sight of the double bed had made him break out in a sweat of anticipation.

"I'll love you to the last breath in my body, dearest little wifey darling."

He was trying to remember all the things he'd heard from other chaps about taking a girl to bed and – well, doing IT. The nearest he'd ever come to sexual intimacy was putting his hand up a few skirts and fumbling about with stocking garters. His barber kept some books which were pretty graphic in their diagrams and drawings, but all he'd learned from them were the clinical details of the female body and nothing about actual performance.

He was terrified of hurting Flora in case it put her off the whole business. Women could be like that, apparently.

"I say, darling, did your mother have a little talk with you before the wedding?" he enquired casually when at last they were upstairs, and the bedroom door with its 'do not disturb' notice firmly locked behind them.

She was seated at the dressing-table unclasping the string of pearls he'd given her as a gift.

"A talk about what?" she asked, glancing at him from the mirror.

"Well . . . you know, about babies and all that."

Her face flooded with embarrassment. She shook her head.

"What – nothing? Not a word?" This was a bit of a blow; he'd been counting on Mrs Dennison. "You mean you've absolutely no idea what happens once people are married?"

"I know a few things. Jessy Craig told me at college."

"Oh, well, that's all right then!" He started taking out his collar studs. "Only I didn't want you to be alarmed. It's all perfectly natural and everybody does it. Even the King and Queen."

The effort at a joke fell flat. Flora took up her brush and began using it on her hair with quick, nervous little strokes, avoiding meeting his eye.

"And you don't need to worry about getting pregnant, old girl," he rushed on. "Not for a while, anyway. I've brought some of these." Digging into his trouser pocket he produced an unidentifiable packet. "They're French – best quality."

She didn't ask what they were; from Jessy's intimations she could guess. It all seemed so terribly unromantic, somehow, and not at all how she'd dreamed her first experience of making love would be. In the imagination of innocence she'd so often conjured up in her mind an idyllically rapturous moment of bliss when the man she adored would take her into his arms and kiss her; the air would be full of the scent of roses swooning in the summer evening's warmth; and after a while he would draw her down beside him with tender whispered words of endearment, and enfold her within the strong and safe protection of his embrace. What followed afterwards would be the most beautifully, wonderfully thrilling sensation . . . the fulfilment of every dream of womanhood.

She put her brush aside and stood up. Sidney had lit a cigarette and still had it stuck in his mouth while he undressed himself, eyes screwed up from the smoke, face glistening with nervous perspiration. To make things worse, he'd tangled his trousers round one leg and was hopping about in an effort to keep his balance, not helped by all the wine he'd drunk at dinner.

Later, with the lights off, when he took her too quickly in a clumsy, fumbling, over-eager fashion, she only cried out once; and that was with the pain of disillusionment

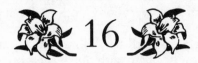 16

Connie had spent the evening enjoying herself at the White Rose; one of those evenings just like she'd always enjoyed in the good old times, with a sing-song at the piano and free drinks all round to celebrate somebody's birthday. *Her* birthday. Twenty-one again, that's what she told them. Anything for a laugh.

A pity Roseen couldn't have been there as well; but she'd got herself this new job last year and she had to be working till late of a night. Dancing, it was, like at the Shanghai, only different. Connie couldn't properly understand. Something about being on the stage, kicking her legs up for a lot of fellows to watch and hardly a stitch upon her. It paid well, though – there was always a bottle of gin in the cupboard for her old Mam.

Old.

She was that, all right, and feeling it. Forty-eight. Mother o' God, what wouldn't she give to be thirty years younger again, the handsome red-haired colleen who'd first stepped ashore off the boat from Dublin. She could have shown Roseen a thing or two at dancing! Sure, nobody ever did the Irish Jig with such high-stepping boldness as Connie, raising her skirts for the men to admire her ankles.

One of the Kavanagh boys saw her home from the White Rose, singing 'Goodbye Dolly Gray' all along Raby Street and the tears running down her face for the old days. She gave him a kiss by the backyard gate for his trouble; then fell over herself drunk into the kitchen, and had to gather her wits together to turn on the gas under the kettle for a pot of tea. They still had the black-lacquered 'Albionette' their Billy (God rest him) had bought for Roseen. Connie had never got used to the thing; and the state she was in tonight, she had a job even remembering whereabouts she'd put the Vesta matches.

By the time she found them thrown at the back of the shelf she was starting to feel a bit wobbly in the legs, so she sat herself down to shut her eyes for five minutes.

She must have dropped off a while, because she was roused again by the noise of her own snoring; and thirsty for that pot of tea, hauled herself with some effort out of the chair to put a match to the kettle. Sure, but there was an awful smell of gas about the place, she thought vaguely . . . didn't turn off the tap while she was searching about for the Vestas . . .

Even as the thought occurred, it was already too late. The flare of the match ignited the pocket of gas which had formed, and though the explosion wasn't enough to cause much damage, it blew Connie backwards across the floor.

Her heart, weakened by years of drink and self-neglect, was unable to cope with the shock. Hearing the bang a neighbour came round to investigate and found her lying there; but there was nothing to be done. She'd never take another drink again.

★

The loss of her mother had the effect of driving Roseen further into the relationship she'd formed with Maurice Lines. Up until the midsummer of 1918 they'd been lovers, but now that she was left entirely alone, orphaned as well as a widow, she began looking to Maurice for something more than the superficial gratification of their affaire. What she needed was the permanency of marriage to a stable partner who could give her the security of an emotional anchor, just as Billy had done. She wanted to feel that she and Maurice were two halves of the same whole, not only in bed, where they had sex together with almost insatiable abandon, but in their everyday separate lives as man and woman.

He told her often that he loved her, in that semi-serious manner which means nothing; and true to his promise he'd found her work on the stage. Not exactly what she had

153

dreamed of, but as he pointed out, all professionals had to start somewhere, and while the Colosseum on the Dudley Road wasn't the Folies-Bergères, it was a step at least in the right direction.

"Have you ever thought about getting married, Maurice?" she would ask him sometimes, deliberately offhand as though it didn't matter; and he'd laugh and look at her with those dark eyes of his and say he wasn't rich enough, or hadn't the time, or something like that, just in fun. Her friend Annie Sutton, who didn't care a great deal for him, reckoned he wasn't the marrying sort.

"Them kind never are, so long as they can get it for nothing and there's wenches daft enough to gi' it them," was her tart response to Roseen's grumbling at the situation. "If you wanted his ring on your finger, you'd ha' done better keeping your legs together."

"But then I wouldn't have got the job at the Colosseum."

"Well, make your mind up! You can't have it both ways."

After her mother's death the tenancy of the house had passed to Roseen, and George Dennison obligingly paid to have the place redecorated and repaired for her. He also gave her the money to choose some new curtains, but that got spent instead on clothes and cheap paste jewellery. Maurice forsook his room at the Station Hotel in favour of spending weekends enjoying free bed and board at Raby Street; and gradually as the months of 1918 wore on into autumn and a settled domestic routine developed between them, Roseen became increasingly determined that he was going to marry her.

Getting pregnant, however, was more difficult than she'd imagined. Maurice was always particularly careful about taking the right precautions and kept note of the date of her monthlies, so she couldn't too easily lie about being 'safe'. In the end she resorted to pricking holes with a hat-pin through the packet of protectives he kept conveniently to hand under the pillow.

That did the trick. And he never even noticed.

*

Suddenly – unbelievably – there was talk of victory. At the start of November Austria surrendered; a week later the

154

Kaiser's abdication followed; and on Monday, November 11th, an armistice was signed and the guns of the Great War fell silent. After four long years, the brutal and bloody conflict which had cost the lives of millions and swallowed up the accumulated capital of generations, was finally over. In its death throes it took with it not only kingdoms and empires and dynasties, but a tradition of nobility, graciousness and social order; an entire phase of history.

It was the closing of an epoch. The war to end all wars. Never again, were the words on everyone's lips as the grief and tears of a widowed land turned into joy and thanksgiving. Never again.

Roseen learned the news at the Colosseum while getting changed into costume for the evening performance. There were six of them in the chorus line, and it was always a bit of a crush in the fly-blown, dirty backstage dressing-room. One of the musicians in the pit orchestra stuck his head round the door and with hardly a bat of the eye at so much unclad flesh, sang out excitedly, "Oi, you lot – have you heard? The war's over. The Boche have signed the armistice!"

There was a moment's disbelieving silence; and then somebody said, "Thank Gawd for that – about blinkin' time," followed by, "Nip an' fetch a couple o' bottles o' beer, Fred, an' we'll have a quick 'un to celebrate!"

Half the world was celebrating. People were running out into the streets hatless, embracing strangers as well as neighbours, singing and dancing in a mass delirium of relief that the shadow was lifted at last. It was like Mafeking Night all over again, on a vaster scale. The spectre of death which had been stalking Europe shrank to a row of signatures on a piece of paper. The Germans had signed the armistice!

The Colosseum's audience that evening was smaller than usual, but, fuelled by celebratory alcohol, what it lacked in numbers it more than compensated for in rowdiness; and once the curtain went up there was a job even to hear the orchestra.

Arms linked round each other's waists to form a line, the dancers pranced out on to the stage amid a chorus of whistles and shouts to start their opening routine.

One – two – three – kick *– one – two – three –* kick *– one – two – and back –* kick.

Their costumes, skin-tight and flesh-coloured, had tassels sewn to each breast, and every bounce sent the whole lot jiggling up and down to the noisy appreciation of the audience. It wasn't the most glamorous way for a girl to earn her money, but Roseen didn't care: her dancing days at the Colosseum were numbered. When she saw Maurice Lines at the end of the week she was going to let him know she was pregnant, and once they were married she could stop at home and put her feet up. Permanently.

One – two – three – kick.

She froze a happy smile on her face for the benefit of the sweaty ovals gawping up at the other side of the limelight. It would be just her luck if all this jouncing around brought on a miscarriage. She'd never been one for babies and had a job imagining herself with some squalling little kid tied to her apron-strings; but what she carried inside her was her certain guarantee of getting Maurice to the altar.

And back – and kick.

Should she wait till she was fully three months gone, to be on the safe side, she wondered? She'd look a bit stupid if she told him she was pregnant and then found out it was only a false alarm – knowing Maurice, he wouldn't be very pleased. Still, she had to face it, he wasn't going to be all that pleased in any case. No, best stick to what she'd already decided, and tell him this weekend. Give the junket chance to set, as old Connie used to say.

With a final saucy twirl of the tassels, the line finished their number and pranced off again into the wings, pursued by applause and good-natured obscenities.

The days till Friday seemed to pass in a haze of merry-making and drinks parties, and Roseen hardly had time to worry about what she'd say to Maurice: never in bed before three of a morning and up again at eleven to meet Annie Sutton at the Posada. In spite of the dripping, dank November fogs which hung about the streets, there was a euphoric feeling of happiness in the air that the war was over, and an almost desperate need to let off steam and have a cracking good time.

By Friday evening, when she left the Colosseum after the performance, all the jubilation was beginning to catch up with her and she felt tired and a bit out of sorts as she made her way home to Raby Street. Sometimes Maurice would turn up at the theatre to walk back with her; but not tonight. Instead she found him sitting in the gas-lit kitchen with his feet up on the fender, picking his teeth, and a dirty dinner plate shoved aside on the table.

"Hello, Maurice," she greeted him, trying to sound a lot better pleased than she felt. "What time did you get here, then?"

"Around nine." He jerked his head in the direction of the plate. "That all you've got in for me to eat? Cold ham and pickle?"

The hint of criticism stung her. "If you'd been at the Colosseum to meet me, we could've popped in to the pie shop on the way home."

"I didn't fancy mutton pie again. I had one of theirs the other week and it tasted rancid, more like horse meat."

"Well, there's a heel of bread and some cheese if you're still hungry." Roseen unbuttoned her coat and went to hang it behind the door at the foot of the stairs. She wasn't in much of a mood for his complaints tonight, but she needed to humour him. "I'll go out in the morning and get us a nice piece of something from the market."

There was a grunt in reply.

"Anyway, how are you?" she went on, shutting the door and coming round behind his chair, leaning over with her arms round his neck to kiss him. "Been busy this week, have you?"

"About the same. We made a night of it on Monday when we heard the news of the armistice."

"You and who?"

"Oh, just me and a few of the chaps. While you're on your feet, put some more coal on the fire, will you. It's blasted chilly in here."

She bit her tongue on a sharp response and releasing him, went across the hearth to the scuttle. "D'you want a drink?" she asked over her shoulder, bending down.

"I'll have another whisky." He didn't offer to get up and

fetch one. He was like that just lately. Idle. Expecting to be waited on. She'd soon alter that once they were married.

While she was pouring his drink, and a gin for herself, she said as casually as she could, "Maurice, how long are we going to go on like this?"

He'd taken out his cigarettes and was lighting one. "Like what?" he asked, blowing out the match and tossing it into the grate.

"Well – you coming here of a weekend and treating the place like your own."

He shot her a look, and after a moment said, "It was *you* invited me, sweetheart. If you hadn't wanted me here, why the hell ask me?"

"But I *do* want you here! All I'm saying is, how long are we going to carry on seeing each other casual-like just a couple of days at a time. Why don't we make it more permanent?"

"How d'you mean?" He was being so deliberately obtuse she felt like swearing. She handed him the whisky and took the cigarette he offered.

"I mean why don't we get married, Maurice. We've been together over a year now. Don't you think it's time we talked about settling down?"

He drew heavily on his own cigarette and gave her a long, weighing-up kind of examination. "I'm not the settling sort, Roseen. I told you that right at the start. No ties, no promises, no demands, I said, and we'd get along like a house on fire."

"Yes, I know. I remember. But I thought p'raps . . . well, you're knocking on a bit, Maurice. You're thirty-two. You want to get married some time or other, don't you?"

He gave a shrug for answer.

Seeing she wasn't going to get far on that particular tack, Roseen decided she might as well save herself bother and give him the truth. She swallowed her gin off straight and went to pour herself another to drum up a little Dutch courage. For all her cocky self-assurance, Maurice had a way at times of making her feel insecure and nervous, and tonight's combination of tiredness and alcohol wasn't helping much, either.

"I think I might have to go round and see the doctor in a

week or so," she said, watching his face over the top of her glass. "I suppose you can guess why."

The dark eyes narrowed a fraction. He returned her look carefully, but made no answer.

She waited a moment; and then, almost angrily, "Well, don't you want to know? Aren't you interested?"

"You can't be pregnant. That's impossible," Maurice said, and there was something in the tone of his voice that she didn't like. "You can't pull an old trick like that on me."

"We'll soon find out – I've missed two months already."

"I don't believe you."

"But I have! You never asked me when my monthly was due – '

"You told me you were regular."

"I was, until September. If I don't show next week it means I'm three months gone. So what you going to do about it?"

He ran a finger over the neatly-clipped moustache. "Find you a bloody abortionist, what d'you think. You're not catching me out that way."

Roseen couldn't believe she'd heard him aright. In all the times she'd rehearsed this scene to herself, she had imagined Maurice accepting the situation if not with good grace at least with nothing worse than a bit of a grumble. He'd soon come round to the idea, and then everything would be all right between them again.

She felt suddenly sick.

"Is that all you can say?" she asked aggressively. "Have an abortion and get rid of it? Your own child?"

He drew hard on his cigarette before flicking the stub into the fire. "That's all. As far as I'm concerned, if you're pregnant it's not mine."

"But I haven't been with anybody else except you!"

"Then the only way you can be up the stick is by immaculate bloody conception."

Her temper started to rise, fanned by the gin. "If you want to know how it happened," she said a little wildly, "I did it on purpose. I had a go at those preventives you're always leaving around. I'm fed up waiting, Maurice. I want to get *married*, d'you hear?"

He took his feet from the fender and sat up. In contrast with her noise, his own voice was cold and level, and thin with contempt.

"You silly cow. Doing a thing like that. I told you I'd never marry you. Why couldn't you leave well alone and be satisfied with what you'd got."

"Because I'm sick of being your weekend bit on the side!" she flung back. "If you're going to use me to serve your bed and belly, I don't see why you shouldn't give me your name and make it legal."

"Silly cow," he said again, almost matter-of-fact. "Didn't it ever occur to you I might have a wife already."

It was like running full tilt into a brick wall. Roseen opened her mouth to shout something back at him – and then realised in the next split-second exactly what he'd said. Her mouth stayed open.

Maurice casually drank off the rest of his whisky and stood up.

"You disappoint me, Roseen, you really do. I thought you had some gumption behind that pretty face of yours."

That was as far as he got. With a scream that could be heard half-way down Raby Street, she flew at him round the kitchen table and caught him by the shoulder; and before he could manage to push her off, she'd raked his cheek with her crimson-painted nails.

"You bastard, Maurice Lines – !"

He caught her by the wrist and slapped her so hard round the side of the head that she saw stars for a minute as she staggered back. Then she came at him with her fists and feet in the grip of such wild rage that she would have killed him if she could.

"You *bastard* – "

He hit her again with calculated brutality, splitting her lip wide open. This time she fell over backwards, hitting her head on the chair seat as she went down.

"That's enough," he said tonelessly.

Stunned by the blow, she lay there on the hearth trying to wipe the blood from her mouth with the back of her hand. Maurice went upstairs. When he came back down he had some clothes and belongings bundled under his arm.

He looked at her indifferently, the reddened scratches pin-pricked with beads of drying blood on his cheek.

"We're finished, you and me, Roseen. Understand? I never want to see you again."

She managed to give him a reply which had all the feeling of the gutter packed behind it.

 17

"What did I say? What did I tell you? Just you be careful, I said. He's up to no good is that 'un, I said. And did you listen?" Annie Sutton threw up her eyes. "Did you heck!"

It was Sunday, midday, and she and Roseen were sitting in their usual place in the public bar of the Posada. Roseen's mouth was still swollen and bruised from the punch she'd been given two days ago, and she looked pale from lack of sleep, and undernourished.

"All right, don't keep rubbing it in," she said irritably. "I went and made a mistake. And now I know better. It's my funeral not yours, Annie, so shut up saying I told you so."

"I could see what he was after, that Maurice Lines, first time I met him," Annie went on, ignoring her to glance towards the street door at a stoutish middle-aged man just coming in. "They're all alike, them sort. Think they're doing a girl a blinkin' favour swanning around her wi' their smarmy antics." She gave Roseen a quick nudge in the ribs. "We're in luck. Mr Podmore wants to buy us a drink – what you having?"

"I don't want anything. He'll only come over and start being a nuisance." Roseen shot the middle-aged man a sullen look. He was the proprietor of a photographic studio in Berry Street, and a regular at the Posada. "Pretend you haven't seen him, Annie. You know what he's like once he gets talking."

"He's lonely, that's all. You got to feel sorry for the poor old codger." The other raised her voice. "Yes, thanks ever so, Mr Podmore. We'll have the same again – port and lemon."

She touched her brassy-blonde hair and straightened the fox fur round her neck. "His old woman died last year. He probably misses the company. Anyway, we don't have to stop, we can always go round the Wheatsheaf after he's treated us."

Roseen said nothing. Ever since Maurice Lines walked out on her last Friday night she'd been in a really angry mood, mainly with herself for believing all his lies. She'd run them over and over again through her mind; and each time she thought of the way he'd managed to gull her with his sweet-talk and his flannel she could have screamed aloud at her own stupidity. To think he'd deceived her so easily – taken advantage of her – *used* her. And she'd been daft enough to imagine *she* was the one who was being so almighty clever!

If ever their paths crossed again, so help her, she'd kill him. No wonder he hadn't wanted to talk about settling down – he must have been laughing fit to choke at the way she'd run around after him, cooking his food, buying him presents, washing his shirts, giving him a good time in bed. Well, nobody was ever going to pull a trick like that on her again; *nobody*. He'd made a right damn' fool of her.

And to crown it all, she'd gone and got herself deliberately pregnant by the so-and-so. It was that which just about vexed her more than anything. Instead of making her life, she'd managed to ruin it completely.

God alive!

"Roseen, are you listening to me?" Annie complained, giving another nudge to get her attention. "I said d'you want some pork scratchings to eat. Mr Podmore's asking."

"What – ? Oh . . . no. I'll throw up if I eat anything."

"You'll make yourself ill, you will, the way you're carrying on. Starving yourself's not going to help, the condition you're in." (She'd told Annie, of course; no point keeping it a secret.) "And I bet you had no breakfast this morning neither – "

"Stop your nagging, I'm all right." Roseen turned her face away petulantly. Annie had been in her element since Maurice Lines cleared off: there'd been a bit of jealousy there, with him being such an obvious good catch.

What a joke. That bird was dead, sell the cage, as Connie would say.

She moved her feet to let Mr Podmore get past to the table.

"Here we are then, ladies," he said, setting down their glasses of port and lemon and planting himself next to Roseen. "Your very good health!"

He took the head of froth off his own pint of ale and sucked his lips in noisy appreciation.

"How are we keeping, then? All tickety-boo, eh?" His suit was of brown and mustard checked cloth and he was wearing his usual coloured-silk bow-tie with a winged collar. There was a large solitaire diamond on the little finger of his right hand.

"*Me*, I'm doing very nicely thank you, Mr Podmore," Annie told him archly. "And yourself?"

"All the better for seeing you, m'dear."

He put his glass down and bent his head forward to look at Roseen. She didn't respond. She was thinking what she'd say to Maurice Lines if he walked into the Posada at this moment.

"Dear me, Mrs Kelly, that's a nasty cut lip you've got there," he observed. "Been in the wars, have you?"

"Her fancy man did that," Annie informed him, getting in first. "She's been having a terrible time wi' him, I tell you, Mr Podmore. Haven't you, Roseen. You just tell Mr Podmore what that blighter's been and done across you."

Roseen treated them both to one of her dark looks.

"There, she don't really want to talk about it," said Annie, taking a sip of her port. "A whole year she was knockin' about wi' him and what d'you think he told her, Mr Podmore, when she raised the subject o' marriage. He only went and told her he'd got a wife already, didn't he. I ask you! Whole bloomin' year he's been leading her up the garden path, and now – well – !"

She rolled her eyes expressively, and took another sip.

"And he marked your face like that, did he?" Mr Podmore asked Roseen in a concerned manner.

She glanced at him, and shrugged.

"Then you're well rid of him, m'dear. Any man that can lift his hand against a woman isn't worth a brass farthing. Best you forget him."

"Oh, but she can't, Mr Podmore," Annie got in again.

"He's left her wi' a sight more than a split lip to remember him by, if you take my meaning. And now what's the poor wench to do, I ask you. Another month and her job's gone along wi' her reputation – "

"Mind your tongue, Annie, it's running away with you," Roseen told her sharply. "Mr Podmore's not interested."

"Well, pardon *me*, I'm sure!"

There was a moment's awkwardness. The public bar of the Posada was beginning to fill now, and Annie covered herself by waving to a couple of regular customers at the bar. "Hello, Gert! Sid! No, we're all right for the minute, thanks – " raising her half-full glass in response to their mimed invitation.

Mr Podmore gave his attention to Roseen. His round, moon face with its bushy eyebrows and drooping moustache conveyed an expression of speculative interest that was not without sympathy.

"That's – er, that's a ticklish predicament you're in, Mrs Kelly," he said, leaning towards her and sinking his voice. "What are you going to do, have you thought?"

She made a grimace, the bruised and swollen mouth pulled down at the corners. "There in't much I can do, is there."

"You'll be leaving your job at the Colosseum, I suppose." A nod.

"Will he support you, this fellow you've been – " Mr Podmore sought about for a tactful way to phrase it, "this fellow you've been friendly with?"

"*Support* me? Don't make me laugh!"

"If he won't, you could always take him to court, you know."

"That's just what I told her," Annie chimed in again. "Make the perisher cough up, that's what I said. It's him as put you in the family way, Roseen, I said, and it's him as should bloomin' well pay for the inconvenience."

Roseen looked at the untouched port and lemon in front of her, then after a moment picked it up and drank it straight off.

"I'd sooner beg in the street than take a penny-piece off *him*," she said savagely, wiping the back of her hand across her mouth. She hadn't told Annie she'd deliberately contrived to put herself 'in the family way'. No court on earth would hold Maurice Lines to blame for that. "I've got my pride. I'll manage."

"And her only just lost her mother, an' all," Annie said, examining her own now-empty glass. "It's a hard life for some, Mr Podmore, especially for us young widows."

A shake of Mr Podmore's balding head expressed agreement. Since Mrs Podmore died last year, he'd learned the cost of loneliness, and that in itself was hardship enough.

"Can I put you another one in there, Mrs Sutton?" he enquired, indicating her glass. "Mrs Kelly – ?"

Their *yes* and their *no* were simultaneous. Roseen stood up as though it was time to think about leaving; but whether the amount of drink she'd already had this morning went to her head, or whether the fact that she'd hardly eaten since Friday made her weak, whichever it was, she came over suddenly dizzy and half-sat, half-fell down again in an untidy sprawl across Mr Podmore's lap.

"Goodness me, Mrs Kelly – are you all right?" he exclaimed, propping her up with an arm about her waist. "Here, let's get you a brandy!"

He fumbled in his waistcoat pocket for a half-crown piece and thrust it at Annie, who was hunting for her handkerchief to flap in Roseen's face.

"Best *you* go and fetch it, I think, Mrs Sutton."

Annie required no second bidding. By the time she returned with two double brandies (her own nerves needed some calming with all the excitement) Roseen was sitting up very pale in the face and trembling like a leaf.

"Here y'are, my wench, get this down you," she said solicitously, handing a glass across the table.

It was Mr Podmore who took it from her. His arm still supporting Roseen by the waist, he put the brandy to her lips as though she were some infant invalid; and when she tried to hold it for herself he said, "No, no, just you let me, m'dear," in a way that made Annie raise her eyebrows.

"And when you feel a bit better recovered," he went on after she'd taken a few sips, "you, me and Mrs Sutton here are all going round to the Molineux for a slap-up luncheon. No expense spared, mind, the treat's on me. You order what you like, m'dear – beef, boiled mutton, or how about a nice piece of dressed tripe? You look as though a square meal wouldn't come amiss – "

He managed to move his legs out of the way only just in time before Roseen was violently sick on the floor.

★

The Great War had not been such an ill wind for everybody: it had blown a little good into the life of Aubrey Podmore, for one. His photographic studio behind the Grand Theatre in Berry Street had done brisk business in portraits of young men in uniform for their families to have as mementoes while they were gone (many of them, alas, for ever) and as long as the war went on he could expect to turn out a dozen or more of these studio portraits a week.

With the return of peacetime, however, he was back again to a staple commercial diet of weddings and babies, and his own particular speciality – postcard photography of the 'what the butler saw' variety.

He had had some success in this field before the war with his *Bathing Belles* and *Mam'selle Mimi* series; but the young woman he'd been employing as a model ran away with a comedian from the theatre, and Mr Podmore had found some difficulty replacing her. Not every female was willing to take off her clothes for the camera; and of those who would, very few had figures to justify the exposure, let alone the knowingly naughty expression required for this kind of work.

He had a connoisseur's eye for faces and figures, had Aubrey Podmore, and that eye had been admiring young Roseen Kelly for a good twelve months or more, ever since she started frequenting the Posada. She was of exactly the image he had in mind for a new series, to be called *Boudoir Beauties*. With her wonderful hair rippling loose down her back, and her shapely, voluptuous body and sensual features, she could make him a fortune in *risqué* postcards if only he could persuade her to pose for him.

He'd been following her career at a distance, first at the Shanghai and latterly at the Colosseum; and it seemed a fortuitous coincidence bordering almost on Fate that at the very time military portraits were petering out and he was

167

thinking of launching the *Boudoir* series, Roseen should be in need of someone dependable to turn to in her troubles.

Accordingly Mr Podmore had invited her a few days after the incident in the Posada to call upon him at Berry Street to discuss a matter which might possibly be to their mutual advantage.

Curious to find out what was in it for herself, she'd decided to accept. The studio was on the first floor, over a tobacconist's shop, and reached by a stairway door off the street. On the attic floor above it was the somewhat poky living accommodation formerly shared by the proprietor and his late wife, and displaying that lady's florid taste in wallpaper and furnishings.

"Here we are, Mrs Kelly," announced Aubrey Podmore in his most avuncular manner, settling Roseen with a cup of tea among the busy chintz of the sofa, "let's make ourselves nice and comfortable, now."

The sunset light of the November afternoon caught the glint of his gold Albert watch-chain as he bent to seat himself opposite.

"I've a proposition to put to you, m'dear. And when you've heard me out, you can say yes or no whichever you wish. The decision's yours entirely."

There was a pause. The same light threw shadows across the chimney breast in sullen competition with the flames of a small fire burning in the grate below.

"As you're aware, Mrs Kelly," he began again importantly, "I'm a photographer by profession. And while most folk think there's nothing more to the job than pointing a camera and pressing the bulb, I can assure you they're in error. My work is an art. An *art*, Mrs Kelly. I emphasise that. What I do in my studio is to take a set of ordinary facial features attached to an average body, and using my creative expertise, turn them into something *extra*-ordinary, something unique and individual. Do you follow?"

Roseen gave a half-shrug and nodded, wishing he'd hurry up and come to the point.

"There is a particular form of artistic photography in which I happen to specialise," he continued. "Indeed, Mrs Kelly, I don't think I'm boasting too much to say that my work in this line is very highly thought of – sufficient to sell by the thousand all over the country and earn me a tidy little income."

"Very nice, I'm sure," she said, without much interest.

"Well now, m'dear, what I'm proposing – " hands on knees, Mr Podmore leaned towards her from his chair, "is this. I'm looking for a young lady to use as a model for my photographic work. Not just any young lady, you understand, Mrs Kelly. This one must be beautiful – no, more than beautiful – *striking* is the word. Striking. And with that special quality you don't find in many, the ability to *present* herself. She's got to be the sort of female to turn men's heads to stare at. In short, Mrs Kelly, I'm looking for a young lady I can create into a living masterpiece – a sublime work of the photographer's art."

There was a second pause, longer this time. Roseen finished drinking her tea, her shrewd little mind beginning to busy itself as illumination dawned.

Putting cup and saucer aside, she glanced at Mr Podmore. His eyes beneath the bushy brows were fixed upon her with a waiting, hopeful, somehow greedy expression.

"So what's your proposition?" she asked casually.

"In a nutshell, m'dear – in a nutshell, I believe *you* are the lady to fit the bill."

"*Me* – ?" She managed to feign a look of astonishment.

"No doubt of it. I knew it the moment I made your acquaintance. You've all the attributes rolled into one, m'dear. Appearance – presentation – confidence. What do you say, now? I can promise, with you at the other side of my camera I'd be inspired to produce photographs that would make you into one of the leading lovelies of the decade."

Roseen pursed her lips, pretending not to be greatly impressed, while her brain worked furiously. *A leading lovely of the decade.* She liked the sound of that. Yes, she liked the sound of that very much.

"Before you give me an answer," said Mr Podmore, rising cumbrously to his feet, "I'll show you an example of the specialised work I've been talking about."

He went across to a dark oak dresser against one wall and opened a drawer to take something out. During Mrs

Podmore's lifetime he'd had to keep this kind of thing locked away downstairs in the studio.

"Here you are, m'dear, have a look through," handing her the leather-bound album, "see what you think."

She rested the album on her knee. *Bathing Belles Series 1* was embossed in silver lettering on its cover. Inside she found what she'd half-expected, postcard pictures of a pertly vicacious young woman wearing a happy smile and very little else, disporting herself in a variety of inviting poses. Eddie Quinn, Billy's mate, had had a collection something similar: she could remember him showing it round at the White Rose. These pictures of Mr Podmore's were obviously in better taste and more imaginatively photographed; and though sexually provocative, she didn't find them all that offensive (unlike Eddie's, which had been downright crude).

"Well – ?" asked Mr Podmore cautiously once she'd reached the end of the album.

"Well – " The thought of having *him* look at her with not a stitch to cover her body made her skin creep. Still, it couldn't be worse than dancing half-naked for a lot of gawping men at the Colosseum . . . She looked at him and smiled. "Well, Mr Podmore, how much had you thought of paying me?"

"Five pounds a week," he said, straight off.

Five pounds? *Five pounds* – ? Blimey, that was a flippin' fortune! She'd be mad to turn down an offer as good as that, Roseen told herself.

There was just one thing . . .

"What about me being pregnant, though?" she asked him bluntly.

Mr Podmore took the album from her and went back to the dresser.

"It's up to you what you do about that, m'dear."

"How d'you mean?"

"If you want the work I'm offering, you'll have to get rid of it."

"I wish I ruddy could! Annie Sutton got me some pills off a friend of hers, cost me twelve-and-six they did, and a fat lot of use it was taking them."

"Pills are no good, Mrs Kelly. You want to do the thing properly. I'll give you the address of a woman to go to, m'dear. She's very discreet about this sort of business."

Mr Podmore re-seated himself on the sofa next to Roseen, and patted her hand.

"Just you trot along and see her tomorrow. And don't worry about the payment. I'll settle that for you."

His plump hand closed over hers again; and this time didn't release it in a hurry.

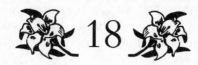 18

In the spring of 1919, shortly after their first wedding anniversary, Sidney and Flora Hathaway had moved from Stockwell End to their own home in Albrighton, a small country village some eight miles or so outside Wolverhampton. Sidney was now teaching with his wife at Codsall school, and patting himself on the back for applying for his transfer with such opportune timing: the cessation of hostilities had released thousands of men from military service to seek re-employment in civilian jobs, and had he delayed his application he might well have found himself pipped to the post by some better qualified teacher.

It was George Dennison who'd bought the house for them, a neat little whitewashed Victorian villa along the lane to the station and overlooking water meadows towards a distant skyline view of the Wrekin.

There would be no awkwardness caused by his daughter and son-in-law coming to live in Albrighton: the young woman Mr Dennison used on occasion to visit here had since left the village, and with her departure he'd decided to call it a day, so to speak, and hang up his hat. He was now in his fifties, with a worsening heart condition. No point in inviting an early demise. Better to forfeit a little pleasure and gain a few extra years, was his doctor's advice.

It wasn't the only pleasure he was being required to forfeit. In fact his life was undergoing a general change all round.

The deterioration in health, accelerated by a further heart attack just before last Christmas, had persuaded George Dennison that the time had come to unburden himself of the responsibility of his grocery stores. Had he had a son to inherit the business, he would have handed over the day-to-day running and remained at the helm in some minor advisory capacity; but as it was, he preferred to 'get shot of the whole kit-boodle' as he put it, and early in the year had started negotiating the sale of Dennison's Stores to the national Home & Colonial Company.

'What do you intend doing in your retirement?' was a constant irritating enquiry, producing the terse reply, "Bury myself in the greenhouse, I suppose. It's about all I'm good for."

Maud Dennison was of a different opinion. Throughout their married life she and George had gone invariably to Aberystwyth for their annual holiday, and whilst she enjoyed Aberystwyth very much, she had longed occasionally for something different, a change of scenery abroad, perhaps.

She began reminiscing about her cousins Phyllis and Hilda who had emigrated to Canada and were now married and settled with families of their own: how nice it would be to see them again after all this length of time, and what a pleasant part of the country to live in, so close to the Great Lakes. She even went so far as to borrow a selection of books on the subject from the public lending library and leave them beside her husband's armchair to be glanced through; and she started writing more frequently and rather more affectionately to Phyllis and Hilda in the hope of eliciting an invitation to visit.

"A long sea voyage would do us both the world of good, George," she said several times a week. "Once you've retired from the business we really ought to think about taking one together."

It wasn't only George Dennison whose health was causing concern just now. Sidney too had problems. Since their marriage Flora had insisted that he take better care of his teeth; but the years of neglect were starting to take their toll, causing painful inflammation of the gums which made him all the more reluctant to use a brush. To make matters worse, he had a morbid fear of dentists and refused to seek treatment, preferring to dose himself with commercial prophylactics and mouth-washes, despite anything Flora could say to change his mind.

"Oh, do stop nagging on about it, old girl!" he'd protest.
"If I go to a dentist he'll only pull all my teeth and leave me
looking like the village idiot."

There was another thing too. Flora had hoped to be able
to continue teaching for at least a couple of years before
starting a family, but shortly after she and Sidney moved to
live in Albrighton she had 'missed' for the second month in
succession, and suspected that she might already be pregnant.
The discovery both vexed and excited her. She loved her
school work too much to want to give it up; and yet at the
same time the notion of having a child of her own to care
for, and rear, and instruct, filled her with feelings of pleasure.

At the end of May her pregnancy was confirmed, and
Codsall school would need to look for a replacement after the
summer holidays.

Sidney was like a dog with two tails when he learned the
news; and he insisted on celebrating his impending fatherhood
in grand style, announcing it in a self-congratulatory speech
at a dinner party they happened to be giving at the house that
same weekend. Flora had hardly known where to hide her
face. She would have much preferred to tell close friends first,
quietly, rather than suffer the embarrassment of having her
husband trumpet his achievement quite so volubly to all and
sundry.

However, she accepted the congratulations – with a murmured aside to her friend Jessy Craig, staying as guest, that
Sidney might have thought to give *her* just a little credit for
the conception while he was at it.

The next day being a Sunday, she and Jessy and Philip
Venables, Jessy's fiancé, went to St Mary Magdalene's church
in the village for morning service; and after luncheon it
was left to Sidney to decide what they should do with the
afternoon. Since the weather was so perfect for walking, he
proposed that they visit Boscobel House a few miles away.
Philip was history master at a preparatory school, and would
no doubt appreciate seeing the site of one of the past's more
colourful incidents, where King Charles II had hidden in
an oak tree from pursuing Roundheads after the Battle of
Worcester.

They made the country walk leisurely, enjoying the peace

of the lanes and the soft green vista of barley fields bending to the breeze in wave-rippled patterns of shadow.

The two men walked along ahead in the glittering sunlight, leaving the young women following arm-in-arm some yards behind. There was such a lot to talk about. Jessy and Flora had not seen one another for some time, and wanted to catch up on news of old friends from Moseley College – all the little bits and pieces of female gossip which there hadn't been an opportunity to exchange at dinner the previous evening.

Winifred Unsworth was now at a missionary college, of all places, and hoping to go out to Africa with an evangelical organisation, "The Society for the Propagation of the Gospel, or something," said Jessy. "Can you imagine! She's proposing to live in a straw hut amongst a lot of savages and convert them single-handed, to hear her talk. Watch out for the crocodiles, I told her. If the cooking-pots don't get you, more than likely *they* will."

"Which must have encouraged her enormously," laughed Flora.

"No, she merely agreed she'd heard their bite was worse than their bark. She always did have a dry sense of humour, did Winifred."

Conversation then turned to May Prothero, who had done very well for herself by marrying into an aristocratic family.

"Only the younger son, of course," said Jessy, "but a title's a title for all that, and you know what a frightful snob May liked to be. *And* what do you think, but she's jumped aboard the suffragist band-wagon and is campaigning like billy-o for equal rights to the vote."

"But I thought we had equal rights now?"

"Yes, women over *thirty*. May declares that's blatantly unfair – oh, you should hear her! – and she says we should be allowed the same privileges as men, and not be treated like inferior chattels. We women worked to help win the war, that's her argument, not just those over thirty but *all* of us, so we should jolly well enjoy equal status."

"I wonder whether her father-in-law agrees," was Flora's comment.

"Apparently he does! A good thing too, or there'd be

ructions in the stately residence. He's a very liberal Liberal, says May."

Jessy was interrupted at this point by Philip Venables, calling back to draw her attention to the house whose farm buildings they were just passing – a particularly handsome example of Tudor half-timbering with mullioned windows and herring-bone brickwork on the chimneys.

"That's Humphreston Hall," Flora told her. "Sidney and I walked across the fields at the back not long ago and noticed what looks like the remains of a moat. I'd love to know the history of the place. Once I've time to spare I'll try and find out whether anyone's written a paper on it – the local historical society, perhaps."

"Yes, I suppose when you've stopped teaching there'll be a chance for things like that," said Jessy a little abstractedly, more interested to see what Philip was now pointing out beyond the Hall.

"By the by," she went on, having admired the silhouetted view of the Wrekin in the sun-hazed distance, "did I tell you I'd heard from Reggie Bellamy? You remember him – he was in the year before ours at Moseley. Played tennis a lot – partnered Muriel Rowley."

Flora frowned, trying to recall.

"Yes, you *do* remember him," persisted Jessy. "Our Winifred was frightfully keen on him at one time."

"Oh, yes – of course. I know who you mean. He grew a moustache that made him look exactly like Lloyd George."

"That's the one. Well, I had a letter from him about a month ago wondering if I'd like to meet again – I suppose he hadn't heard I was engaged – and passing on his news. You know poor Frank Dawes was killed, don't you? And Vivyan Edwards?"

Flora nodded. "Passchendaele. Sidney told me."

"And someone else Reggie mentioned was that chap *you* used to like – you know, the one who was married. What was his name. Robert – " Jessy paused a moment to think, "Robert Wells, that was it. Now, you remember *him*."

"Yes . . . I remember him."

There was nothing in Flora's voice to betray the sudden heart-jerking snatch of hurt at hearing Robert's name so unexpectedly. She'd last heard from him – that letter written at the field hospital – almost two years ago. Since then there'd been only silence. After the tenderness and longing he'd expressed, she couldn't believe he would have neglected to write again for so long unless the worst, the unthinkable, had happened; and for the last twelve months she had forced herself to face the bitter, terrible fact that Robert was probably dead.

It had not been easy to accept. He lived in her heart and in her memories as the one true romantic love she had known, and even if neither of them had ever met again, it was consolation of a sort to feel assured that somewhere, wherever he was, he still thought of her, as she of him, both treasuring the same shared feelings.

But death – death was final; such a total separation. There were no memories, no hopes, no dreams, in the cold, eternal darkness of the grave.

"He had a jolly close shave, Reggie says," Jessy was chattering on blithely. "His ship was torpedoed – only a handful survived. Your Robert was lucky to escape with his life, apparently – "

She stopped. Flora had seemed to sway and lose her balance at that moment, and if their arms hadn't been linked she could have fallen.

"Flora – ? Dear, are you all right?"

"I – I . . . oh, can we just stop a second, Jessy? I feel suddenly faint. How stupid."

Putting an arm around her to support her, the other called to the two men ahead, then looked again at her friend. Beneath its glossed-chestnut fringe of hair, Flora's face was ashy white.

"You don't look too chipper, old thing. I hope you haven't gone and overdone it, walking all this way in your condition," Sidney said on turning back, and equally concerned by her paleness.

She managed a brave smile. "No, of course not, darling. Walking's good for me. I shall be perfectly recovered in a minute or two."

Robert was alive. He'd been spared. Oh, thank God! When she'd believed him to be dead, for a while it felt almost as though something within her had died too; and now – now her dreams had been given back to her. He was *alive!*

★

The place looked just as untidy, but at least it had been kept clean since Connie went, he thought to himself. The window-net had been washed; the brick floor swept. On the mantelpiece above the fire was propped a picture of some exotic kind of flowers – tiger lilies, could be – with a cheap little china dog to one side, and a framed sepia photograph of Billy Kelly on the other, staring out at the world in the frozen pose of a soldier. A table against the opposite wall carried a 'Zonophone' horn gramophone with a wind-up handle.

"Sorry about that – " Roseen said, coming back into the kitchen from the scullery, where she'd gone to answer somebody's knock at the yard door. "It was her from across the alley wanting to cadge half a loaf. She's round every other day scrounging food for those kids of hers."

She looked at herself in the mirror above the gramophone, and touched a finger to her crayoned eyebrows. "Did you say you'd like a cup of tea?"

"No, I won't bother, thanks," George Dennison responded. "I haven't long had my dinner." He never referred to it as luncheon unless he was at home. "I was in the neighbourhood, so I just thought I'd call on the off-chance to see how you were."

Roseen smiled at herself in the mirror, and keeping her eyes fixed on her reflection half-turned towards him. "I'm glad you've come. I was going to write to you, anyway. About the house."

"What – this house?"

"Yes. I probably won't be living here much longer, you see." She seemed fascinated by herself, arching her neck, touching her hair, moistening her full red lips. "I'm thinking of moving."

"Moving from here? From Raby Street?" She hadn't invited him to sit down, but Mr Dennison did so now, taking the Windsor armchair that used to be Connie's. "Why? You're not getting married again, are you?"

178

Roseen shrugged, then moved away from the mirror, smoothing her hands over the hips of the expensive-looking winter frock she was wearing. She'd lost weight, he remarked to himself. She seemed older too, and her face had lost its last lingering traces of roundness, so that the fine bones were more pronounced, the greenish eyes more catlike – beautiful, but there was something just a little hard about their expression.

"I don't know about marriage," she said. "But if he asks me – *when* he does – I suppose I might consider it."

"Who's this we're talking about – somebody at the Colosseum?"

"Blimey, no, I left that place the end of November! I'm with Mr Podmore now – you know him, he's got the photographic studio in Berry Street. I've been working there as his assistant the last couple of months."

George Dennison digested this information. "I see. So who's the fellow you might be marrying?"

She examined her crimson-varnished nails. There was a gold ring set with a large square garnet on the right hand.

"Aubrey Podmore."

There was another pause while he took in what she'd said. He must have met this Mr Podmore a number of times at Council of Trade meetings, but only recalled him vaguely – a thickset, middle-aged chap who never had much to say for himself.

"*Podmore* – ? But he's old enough to be your father, Roseen!" As soon as the thought struck, it was out of his mouth in a burst of almost accusatory disbelief. "You can't go tying yourself to somebody that age. It wouldn't be right, not for you!"

"Why not. What's age got to do with it." She gave him an odd, sidelong look. "He knows how to spend his money, that's the main thing. He pays me five pounds a week for sitting around doing san fairy ann except smile."

"Five pounds a week – good God!" A leaden knife of pain curled under George Dennison's heart, warning him against excitement, but in his concern for Roseen he ignored it. "If he's paying all that amount, he's *buying* you."

She shrugged again, pulling her face into a so-what ex-

179

pression. "He fancies me. And you know what they say –
better to be an old man's darling than a young man's slave."

Something had happened to her. This wasn't the Roseen
he'd known all these years since childhood. A tough, independent, assertive little madam, yes, but never the sort to throw
herself after money. She'd always had too much pride.

The pain beneath his heart dug deeper.

"And what's this Podmore getting in return?" he asked,
hearing the harshness and something else – could it be jealousy
– in his own voice. "You're going to live with him, I suppose,
is that it? Is that why you're leaving this place?"

She didn't answer directly, but gave herself another glance
across the shoulder towards the mirror, and said, "There's
nothing for me here. Not now Mam's gone. I'll be better off
with somebody who'll look after me and spoil me."

"But I've always promised you *I'd* be the one to look after
you!"

"It in't the same thing, though, is it, Uncle George."

The way she said that held a profundity of meaning. Slowly
she turned her head again to look at him.

"It in't the same thing at all. You more than anybody ought
to know that."

19

The snow had been falling all night. With morning it had started to thin to large, solitary flakes drifting softly against the bedroom windows and shedding a still, white light upon the room's interior.

Seated at the side of her father's bed, Flora turned for a moment to listen. From somewhere along the landing corridor beyond the closed door came, faintly but persistently, a baby's protesting wail as little Imogen was settled down for her mid-morning rest. Born in November 1919, Flora's daughter was now fourteen months old, a happy and tractable infant, but the routine of her nursery world had been disrupted by all the recent to-ing and fro-ing between Stockwell End and Albrighton, making her fractious. She was teething again as well, which didn't help.

Flora's attention returned to her father. The gentle, pure light from the windows rimmed the sunken contours of his face and lent the skin a waxen pallor. He was very seriously ill, drifting in and out of consciousness. There was nothing anyone could do now but hope for the best, and be prepared for the worst.

As she watched, the eyelids fluttered and half-opened and he moved his head a little on the pillow, saying indistinctly, "Maud – ?"

"No, it's me, Father. Flora." She leaned forward and took his hand. Despite the warmth of the fire burning cheerfully in the cast-iron grate, he felt cold to her touch. "Mother's downstairs. Shall I call her?"

"No . . ."

He was silent again for a while; and then, "What time is it?"

She glanced at the clock on the chest of drawers opposite. "Twenty to eleven. You've had a good long sleep. Is there anything you'd like? Can I fetch you a drink?"

He made a slight sound like a sigh, turning his eyes towards the windows. Even in his helpless, weakened state he hated to feel a burden to those who were nursing him. "Just a drop of water . . ."

"Nothing more? Some warm milk, perhaps?"

"No . . . just water."

Releasing his hand, Flora got up from the bedside to reach across for the carafe, and half-filled its companion glass. Then easing her arm gently behind her father's head, she raised him enough to hold it to his mouth for him to take a few small sips. "There now, is that better?"

When he'd had all he wanted, she rested him carefully back against the mound of pillows and wiped the corners of the mauve-blue lips with her handkerchief. Even that slight exertion had seemed to drain him. He lay with his eyes closed for a while, and just as she thought he was drifting off to sleep again, he said suddenly, "There's something I want to tell you. Is the door shut?"

"Yes, Father. It's shut." She looked at him, wondering.

"Good . . ." He moved his head, seeking the pale blurred oval of her face there beside him. "Now, listen. This is secret between you and me, Flora. Your mother mustn't know."

"I understand."

Slowly, and with long laborious pauses, a man making his final confession, George Dennison began to speak of his twenty-year association with Connie O'Connor and her daughter. There was no time now for niceties. His strength was running out, together with his life, and each sentence told the plain unvarnished facts. Connie had been his mistress. And he'd loved the child Roseen as if she'd been his own flesh and blood. For that reason he'd clung on to his relationship with her mother long after it was finished, refusing to give Connie up entirely, for fear she should marry another man and thereby rob him of Roseen.

That was wrong. Very wrong. She'd needed a proper

father, a kiddie like her, not somebody playing at part-time parent. He knew that now, and felt a terrible guilt about it. Contrary to what he'd intended, he had cheated Roseen of the love and security she might have received from a settled family upbringing. Instead, she'd had no direction in life, no guidance . . . she was getting herself into the wrong sort of company, through his fault, his selfishness . . .

Flora heard him out in stunned silence. She had always loved her father very much, and respected him, and it hurt her beyond words that with his dying breath almost he should expose himself as a man who had led a life of such deceit, an adulterer, unfaithful to her mother and practising the kind of hypocritical double standards which he'd so often spoken out against in others.

At the same time, however, she could begin to understand at last why Roseen O'Connor had always seemed the more favoured of the two of them. It didn't lessen her pain; merely placed it in a better perspective. And it explained, too, all those puzzling little incidents from her childhood, right back to the still-remembered visit to Raby Street at the age of ten when she'd first set eyes on Roseen, leaning from the upper window and laughing as she waved goodbye to her father leaving the house.

"Why did you want me to know this?" she asked briefly when at length George Dennison fell silent. "Was it to clear your conscience?"

It had taken perhaps fifteen minutes, no more, for the entire story to be told, and now he lay back against his pillows, drained to the point of exhaustion by the effort of such a catharsis.

He didn't respond to her question; not immediately. The fire was starting to burn low, and Flora got up automatically to attend to it, adding more coal from the scuttle, glad of the diversion. Then, instead of going back to the bedside she went over to stand at one of the windows, looking down into the silent snow-shrouded garden, faint powdery-blue in the morning shadows.

"Why, Father – why?" she asked him again without turning, striving to control her voice through a little knot of tears. "Do you want my forgiveness, is that it?"

"Yes . . ." he said after a moment, so quietly that the word was no more than a breath.

A flock of sparrows wheeled across the lawn in a sudden burst of flight, scattering snow from the bushes.

"Well – you have it. I can't speak for Mother, of course, but – if it's any use, *I* forgive you." In the circumstances what more could she say.

"And Roseen . . ."

For a second she thought he meant forgive Roseen, too, and wondered why. None of this was *her* fault, after all. The girl was more to be pitied than blamed, coming from such a background.

"Help Roseen," he said. "If she's ever in trouble, try and help her, our Flora."

Help her? Why should I, she thought bitterly. She's nothing to do with me any more. Why should I be expected to feel responsible.

"Promise me you'll help her . . . promise me that."

Flora turned from the window, ready to say no, she couldn't, it was impossible; but the look on her father's face stilled the protest. No matter how he'd behaved, he'd always been the best of parents, the kindest and most loving of men; her friend as much as her father. He had denied her nothing. How in heaven's name could *she* deny *him*, and at such a time.

"All right, Father. I promise. If ever I'm in a position to help Roseen, I will do."

George Dennison smiled.

"That's my girl."

And as she went towards the door, "Give the baby a kiss from me," he said.

Those were the last words she ever heard him speak.

★

Despite the sadness of the occasion, it was a beautiful day for a funeral. The February skies lost their grey web of cloud and a milky-pale sun did its best to brighten the afternoon and lend colour to the mass of floral wreaths decorating the chancel steps of St Michael and All Angels.

Its light spilled through the stained-glass windows in a prism of soft, warm tones like watered jewels, edging the

184

sombre-cloth shoulders of the mourners, falling across the polished oak coffin almost like a benediction to echo the theme of the vicar's eulogy, that life was but changed, not ended, by the body's death.

The church was packed with people. Being early closing day in the area, many employees of the old Dennison's Stores (now the Home & Colonial) had come to take their last farewell of a Guv'nor who had been not only a noted citizen of the town but held in respect as a fair-dealing and benevolent employer, a self-made man who had reaped the profit of his own hard work without ever once forgetting his lowly origins.

Flora lost count of the number of messages of condolence received at the house since her father's death a week ago. They had come by every post following the obituary announcement in the *Express and Star* and the subsequent newspaper articles. 'God bless him, he was a real gentleman, one of the best' seemed to be the general verdict. Nothing about his private life, of course; no one knew the full truth of that except herself – and Roseen.

She sat at the front of the church, black-veiled, between Sidney and her mother, staring numbly at her gloved hands and trying to push from her mind the memory of her father's self-confessed misconduct; willing herself to remember only that even in his failings he had always tried to do his best for everyone. He had been a man like any other. No one was perfect. Far be it from her to apportion blame or condemnation when she herself was guilty of unfaithfulness, even if it was only the infidelity of imagination.

Afterwards in the churchyard, when the final prayers had been said and the coffin lowered, she wept a little as she helped her mother to cast a handful of earth into the open grave. Then, making an effort to regain her composure, she glanced around the crowd of faces standing in respectful silence a short distance off, waiting for the family's last rites to be completed before they drew near. The undertakers' men were bringing out the wreaths from the church, and as she looked distractedly across in their direction Flora found her gaze arrested by someone she vaguely recognised.

At that moment Sidney touched her arm. People were just

beginning to approach now for a word or two of murmured sympathy, and she had to give them her attention, thank them for attending the funeral, shake hands, accept their commiserations. It was some time before she recalled to mind the figure near the porch, and looked about her for another glimpse.

Yes, there – hanging back on the path as though waiting for the numbers to disperse – a young woman with pretty auburn hair and a fox fur thrown around the shoulders of her fashionable calf-length coat.

Flora recognised her now.

It was Roseen.

Giving her mother into the care of Sidney, she left the graveside to go down on to the path, excusing herself to those nearby; then stood there uncertain, wondering whether Roseen would approach her or not. The other had obviously seen her, because after a slight hesitation she began walking slowly along, adjusting the veil on her small, close-fitting hat and not looking towards Flora but sideways, as if not particularly interested in a meeting.

The distance between them narrowed.

"Hello." Flora couldn't think what else to say. "Hello, Roseen."

There was a little nod of acknowledgement. Behind the veil the other's eyes were expressionless, failing to reflect the tight smile which was offered in response.

"How are you?" said Flora awkwardly.

"I'm keeping well. Sorry about your Dad. I hope you didn't mind me turning up here."

"Of course not. It was nice of you to come."

In fact, in view of the closeness between her father and Roseen, Flora had wondered whether she oughtn't to try and get in touch personally with news of his death; but there'd been so much to do, with the funeral and everything, and somehow the opportunity had never presented itself.

Roseen glanced past her. "Is that your husband?" with a nod in the direction of Sidney, standing with Mrs Dennison supported on his arm, in quiet conversation with the vicar.

Flora turned.

"Yes. Yes, that's my husband."

Roseen treated Sidney Hathaway to an indifferent appraisal. "My Billy died, you know," she said, as though discussing the weather. "He got killed in the war."

"Father told me. I was sorry to hear about it. You weren't married very long, were you."

"Two years."

There was a pause.

"And – and what are you doing with yourself now?" Flora enquired for the sake of something to break the silence.

"Oh . . . this and that. I'm a lady of leisure, as you might say. My fiancé doesn't really like me working."

"You're getting married again – ?"

She wondered whether she ought to add her congratulations, but Roseen forestalled her, responding at once, rather shortly, "I don't know about getting married. He keeps asking me, of course. But he's a good bit older than me."

There seemed something vaguely illogical about such a statement, and while Flora was turning it over, the other went on, "You got any children yet?"

"Yes, we have a little girl. Imogen."

Roseen's lips shaped the name as though savouring it to see whether she liked it or not. Sidney had wanted to christen the baby plain ordinary Jane after his mother; but Flora had put her foot down and chosen something altogether more romantic and original, something out of the fairy tales of her childhood.

"A bit fancy for me," Roseen remarked off-handedly; and then, "Well, I'd better be saying cheerio now. Aubrey'll be waiting with the car."

Again there was that tight little smile.

Flora watched her walk away along the path towards the lychgate, a focus of attraction for the eyes of those men still in the churchyard. She knew it, too. Her head was up and she looked neither to left nor right as she tossed the tail-end of her fox fur across her shoulder, moving with a particularly fluid grace which emphasised her shapely femininity.

For a moment or two before she rejoined Sidney and her mother, Flora experienced a little pang of envy. Since Imogen's birth she had put on extra plumpness, and examining her appearance in the mirror only this morning while dressing for the funeral, she'd told herself she was getting to look downright dowdy. She was twenty-five, the same age as Roseen, and in comparison felt suddenly ten years older. Her life had settled into a comfortable routine of husband and baby and home, a routine which must shortly deepen by daily repetition into a groove to carry her through the rest of her days.

It was all very warm and safe and cosy. And very dull.

What must it be like to be Roseen, she wondered. To be slim and beautiful and have the daring to paint her face and show her legs beneath fashion's rising hemlines; to accept the admiration of the other sex with such a wonderful disdain, refusing to follow social convention and give up her independence to marry merely for the sake of marrying.

Oh, what must it be like to be Roseen!

With such thoughts as these running through her mind, Flora would have been astounded to know that, in turn, Roseen Kelly was envying *her* as she'd walked away just now along the path.

Her relationship with Aubrey Podmore wasn't a happy one. When she'd first gone to work as model in his studio, he was the employer, the boss, calling the tune, so to speak; but gradually over the months, as he'd fallen under the spell of her sexual attraction, their roles had been dramatically reversed, and now it was Roseen who held the upper hand. Mr Podmore was that rather sad spectacle, a lonely middle-aged man whose love for a much younger woman had turned him into a doting fool grateful for the smallest crumb of kindness.

Roseen had become his mistress in the summer of last year, not because she loved him but because the arrangement suited her. After Maurice Lines, and the awful harrowing experience of her abortion, she harboured a contempt for men which she made no pains to conceal. She shared her lover's bed, but refused to let him touch her unless he'd been extra generous with his money; or unless she was too drunk to care.

It was a vicious circle. The more she despised Aubrey Podmore, the more he pleaded for affection and showered her with gifts; and then she would feel a momentary prick of conscience and be nice to him for a day or so, until his pathetic show of gratitude began to irritate. It was in one of these ephemeral moods of conciliation that she'd agreed to their engagement. The ring he'd bought – emeralds and diamonds – had set him back a tidy sum of money, and she wasn't about to forfeit it by changing her mind.

The latest thing was a car. She wanted one of her own now that she'd mastered the mechanics of driving, and Mr Podmore had promised he would buy her one as a wedding present. Just as soon as she named the day. Well, Roseen had no intention of being waltzed up any church aisle for the sake of a motor-car, and there'd been several heated scenes in recent weeks, with accusations thrown around on both sides.

In the end it had come down to this: no marriage, no car; and for once Aubrey Podmore meant it.

She had come to George Dennison's funeral today in a peevish frame of mind, having spent the previous evening trying to wheedle her lover out of his stubborn resistance. She needn't have bothered. Even after he'd enjoyed her in his greedy, fumbling way, he'd refused to alter his ultimatum, and she'd ended up sleeping on the sofa, hating herself as much as him for mis-using her body in such cheap pretence.

Added to this, George Dennison's death had depressed her deeply. Uncle George was the nearest thing Roseen had ever known to a father, and when she'd read in the papers about him dying, she had felt the same cold thrill of shock as when she lost her husband Billy. For as long as she could remember, he'd always been there in the background of her life, ready with advice and help and generosity; and now he was gone. Her Uncle George. There was nobody, *nobody* to replace him.

She had found his funeral service harder to bear than she'd thought, and afterwards had had to stay behind in the church for a bit, alone with her memories, sniffing back the tears and wishing she still had the faith to pray for his soul.

The trouble was, she had no one to turn to now. With Uncle George Dennison dead, it was as though some door had been closed for ever on her past, and all she was left with to see her through the future was a shoddy relationship with some ageing man she didn't love. No home of her own, no family; no security.

Driving back to Berry Street with Mr Podmore, she had

189

experienced a feeling of sudden and total devastation. All her life she had envied Flora Dennison, and now she found herself longing with all her heart to change places and actually be her, with a nice young husband to console her, and a baby in her arms to love, and a cosy little house to live in.

Somewhere to *belong*.

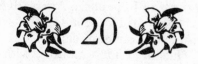

20

On August 31st, 1921, almost three years after the armistice brought about a cessation of actual hostilities, the final signatures were appended to the final documents ending the Great War.

The reason for this lengthy delay lay in German reluctance to comply with the terms of the agreement resulting from the Paris Peace Treaty, ratified the previous year. It was only after the Allies delivered their ultimatum, to occupy the industrial heartland of the Ruhr unless Germany undertook to act in accordance with the agreement, that she was finally forced to capitulate.

All this, though, was comparatively stale beer to what was happening at home, where, like a thorn embedded deep in Britain's side, the festering problem of Ireland was an ever-present source of political inflammation.

'Home Rule' had been a vexed question ever since the 1850s, with bills repeatedly debated in both Houses of Parliament; and but for the outbreak of war in 1914, the Irish dream of self-government might in fact have been realised. The six counties of Ulster, however, predominantly Protestant and loyal to the monarchy, had no wish to be separated into an independent Irish state, and this proved a major sticking point to final settlement.

The result was predictable – more violence, more insurrection, more bloodshed, as republican fought against loyalist. Attacks on police barracks grew increasingly frequent, and in June 1920 the 'Black and Tans' – armed recruits so-called for their uniforms – were sent across to Ireland to reinforce law and order. Their presence served only to exacerbate the situation. The outrages went on, and the death toll continued to mount.

In May 1921 the Irish Republican Army (IRA) burnt down the beautiful old Customs House in Dublin, centre of British administration; and, an even more sinister development, there were Sinn Fein raids in London suburbs, with the cutting of telegraph wires, which caused considerable alarm to those who thought the 'Irish problem' belonged exclusively across the Irish Sea.

As if the Lloyd George government hadn't already enough on its plate, the coal miners had gone on strike in March, supported by the railwaymen and transport workers. This had the effect of crippling the country's power supplies, and a state of national emergency was declared. In June the northern cotton mills were closed because of a disagreement over wage reductions; and the worsening unemployment situation brought mass demonstrations of protest on to the streets of the capital.

The Great War might indeed be officially over; but its economic legacy was only just now starting to be felt.

There was another legacy too, and one even more costly in terms of human suffering: almost ninety-four thousand officers and men were still missing and unaccounted for from the war, and for each of that grim number there was a family in a limbo of uncertainty about their possible fate. For those who survived as cripples the situation was hardly better; and it was becoming commonplace to see blinded or limbless men begging at street corners for money to support their wives and little ones.

Robert Wells could count himself luckier than many. He had been one of the few to escape the sinking of his ship HMS *Raglan* at Imbros in January 1918, and saw out the remainder of the war learning to walk again on a leg shattered by torpedo shrapnel. Once released from the Navy, he'd returned to Helen and the children at Freshwater on the Isle of Wight, and to his old teaching career; but picking up the threads of a life disrupted by four such terrible and punishing years of service proved more difficult than he had supposed.

He was thirty-five now, seasoned by experience into a quieter, more introspective, yet stronger personality than hitherto; he had gone away to war a dreamer, full of the self-heroics of idealism, and came back a realist with no illusions left to rose-tint the future.

Once he'd had time to readjust himself to domesticity, the first painful fact he felt he must face concerned his marriage. There was no point in running from the truth: he loved his wife Helen, but as a brother rather than a husband. What slight passion had originally fuelled their relationship had burnt itself out within the first six months, and physical affection had grown to be a habit rather than an expression or a need.

She was a good housewife and a good mother; a good woman. She had kept hearth and home together during the time he'd been away, never complaining at the hardship, never reproachful, accepting whatever must be endured in that patient, placid, unemotional manner which was the chief hallmark of her character.

Her children Margaret (called Meg) and young Jack had grown up while Robert was gone, and now seemed almost like strangers to him. Meg would soon be leaving school to go to Southampton to start her nurse's training. Suddenly she appeared a young woman, not the jolly little girl he'd left behind four years ago. And Jack – well, Jack had turned surly and resentful after being the only male about the house for so long, and Robert was finding it hard work to get along with him.

The only thing left in his life of any constancy was his deep and unalterable love for Flora Dennison; and even that must now belong to the past. He had learnt after writing to her that once that she was now a married woman. The news had not especially surprised him, but for several weeks he'd suffered the most desolate sense of loss. But then, what had he expected, after all – that she would wait for him, not knowing when, or even whether, he might ever be free?

The rationalist in him could accept that they were unlikely to meet again; but the memories of love were not so easily disposed of, and Robert Wells knew in his heart of hearts that as long as he had life and breath within him he would think of Flora with the utmost longing and regret.

★

Tiger lily.

It was a funny name to call a flower. Tiger and lily were such dissimilar things; like fire and moonlight, or passion and tranquillity.

Or Roseen and Flora.

A combination of opposites, linked together by the very nature of their contrast.

George Dennison had said something much the same, that day last year when he called to see Roseen at Raby Street; the last time she ever saw him. He'd picked up his hat from the table, ready to leave, and then paused a minute, taking a closer look at the picture on the mantelpiece.

"That's nice," he'd said. "Tiger lilies, is it?"

"Yes. Our Billy won it for me at the fair one year."

"Tiger lilies." He'd repeated himself with an odd little laugh. "Reminds me of you and Flora, that does."

She hadn't understood then what he meant; but she did now.

She'd been drinking most of this afternoon, ever since leaving Annie Sutton at the Posada and coming back to Berry Street, to another row with Mr Podmore. He didn't like her going into public bars without him. He was jealous she might meet somebody younger and better-looking.

Well, she'd had some news this morning that was well worth the celebrating; and if it wasn't that pubs had to close after lunch under the new licensing laws brought in during the war, she would have stayed put at the Posada till last orders – and Aubrey Podmore could have gone to hell.

By five o'clock the bottle of gin on the sideboard was considerably emptier than it had been, and Roseen had reached that state of drunken stupor when obscure and half-formed thoughts suddenly acquire a most profound significance.

Lying sprawled on the sofa, her Chinese red-silk wrapper hanging off one bare shoulder to reveal a swell of breast, she had her eyes fixed in glazed concentration on Billy's picture, now adorning Mr Podmore's wall.

Tiger lilies . . .

She breathed the words to herself, her mind flickering round them in connection with the news she'd had today.

Tiger lilies . . .

She repeated them aloud, ending on a noisy hiccup that made her giggle.

Yes, *now* she knew what Uncle George had meant, about her and that Flora. A tiger was graceful – and untamed – and had sharp claws. And a lily – a lily was just a silly lily.

This set her giggling again.

"What are you finding so funny all of a sudden," Aubrey Podmore said sullenly. He'd been matching Roseen almost glass for glass – whisky, not gin – and was still nursing the wounds and slights of their argument with peevish, self-pitying resentment.

She cast him an unfocused glance across her shoulder.

" 'S private. You wouldn't un'stand. Here – gi' us 'nother drink – " draping her arm over the back of the sofa and waving her empty glass.

"You've had enough to drink. You're not getting any more."

"Ah, shurrup, you miserable ol' coot, an' gi' us 'nother one." The diamond and emerald ring on her hand caught the sunlight in scintillations of fire as she brandished the glass at him. "Jus' one more, eh."

"No."

Half-drunk as he was himself, Mr Podmore hated to see her like this, blowsy and dishevelled, cigarette ash spilt everywhere, slack-lipped from too much booze. She drank because she despised him, because she was unhappy, because she couldn't bear him touching her; her drunkenness was the testament of his own failure as a man.

"No, come on, Rosie – " he always called her that, "show a bit of sense, for God's sake. Go and lie down till you've slept it off."

"Don't wan' lie down. Wan' another drink." She dragged herself upright on the sofa, not caring whether the silk wrap covered her or not, her peachy-copper hair spilling in a tangled mess of waves over her face. "Wan' another drink – d'you hear!"

She was having some difficulty now in seeing straight, and the room kept sliding sideways up towards the ceiling. Her head felt odd too, as though it was only loosely connected to her neck and might fall off if she moved it in a hurry. She let the glass drop from her hand and rested her cheek on the back of the sofa, gazing dizzily towards the window, eyelids twitching against the glare of the afternoon sun. The window frame swung away to the left, leaving a ghostly double on the wall; and the light seemed to burst into splinters of kaleidoscope-colour inside her head.

After that she must have passed out.

When she opened her eyes again she was lying in the bedroom, with the curtains half-drawn, and everything so still and quiet that she could hear the clank of the trams in Prince's Square and the tinkling strains of a barrel-organ playing 'Nelly Dean' somewhere near. That would be the blind lad down at the corner. A wife and three small kids, and his war medal pinned to his coat. Roseen gave him sixpence sometimes.

She licked her tongue round her parched lips. Her brain felt like a piece of hot jelly rolled in grit, and it was almost too much effort even to move. Stupid blinkin' idiot, she was . . .

Then she remembered the reason for this morning's beano at the Posada, and immediately regained a little more interest in life. There'd been a letter for her in the post from a firm of solicitors, executors or whatever of Mr Dennison's. If she would care to call upon them at their chambers in Lichfield Street, she would 'learn something to her advantage'.

Which could only mean, surely, that Uncle George had left her some of his money in his will.

The bedroom door opened.

"Oh, you're back in the land of the living at last," Aubrey Podmore said, looking in. His own sour mood had evaporated along with the effects of the whisky, and his concern was now all for Roseen. "Could you drink a cup of tea if I made one?"

She shifted her head on the pillow, and winced. "Mm. Ta."

She heard him go down the passage to the kitchen, floorboards complaining at his bulky weight. He had put her to bed naked as well as unconscious, and for a moment she wondered whether he'd touched her at all; or just sat and looked at her. He liked looking at her. He was a bit of a *voyeur* was Mr Podmore. It was part of the pleasure he got from his work.

While he was busy boiling the kettle she managed to struggle up and reach for her wrapper, left draped over the brass rail at the foot of the bed. Judging by the amount of light outside it must be almost dusk and the room was turning chilly now that the sun had gone.

"Here we are, m'love." He came back after a while with a tray, which he put on the table beside her, seating himself on the bed to pour them both a cup.

"I suppose you had your eyeful while I was flat out, did you?" Roseen remarked, not really caring.

"I cleaned you up, that's all. I don't like you looking a slattern, no more than I like you behaving like one."

"And what's that supposed to mean." She curled her fingers round the cup he passed her and raised it to her lips, at the moment only interested in slaking her awful thirst.

"I mean going into public houses by yourself. It's only tarts that do that."

"Oh, for crying out loud – " She seemed to remember it was this which had started the argument between them earlier. "You're not carping on about that again, are you."

He caught the irritation in her voice and his big fleshy face took on a hangdog expression. "I'm only telling you for your own good, Rosie."

"Well, let me tell *you* something. If it wasn't for me going into pubs, how the hell d'you think you'd ever have met me – eh? I don't recall you being so bloomin' finickety that first time you picked me and Annie Sutton up at the Posada."

"I didn't pick you up. I bought you both a drink, that's all."

"And there's a difference, is there?"

She shot him a look of contempt and held out her cup to be refilled. The barrel-organ at the corner had stopped its melancholy tinkling now, and in its place was the sound of the paper-seller raucously bawling the evening headlines from his pitch at the end of Berry Street.

Mr Podmore leaned against the bedhead rail, his shoulder just brushing Roseen's, watching her gulp down the tea.

"Don't let's have another argy-bargy, sweetheart," he said pleadingly. "I've stuck about enough of it for one day. I wouldn't be so concerned for you if I didn't think the world of you, you know that."

She ignored him, not even bothering to shift away from his body's contact.

"You're such a lovely, sweet creature, Rosie," he went on again after a moment. "It always worries me that something might happen to you. I mean, look at the dreadful things you read about just lately – women shanghai'd off the streets for this white-slave racket – "

Despite the thumping pain in her head, Roseen started to laugh, not because he'd said something funny, but because the idea of Aubrey Podmore, of all people, worrying about women being snatched away to a life of debauchery was so risibly far-fetched. The white-slave trade had been much in the news recently, supposedly procuring concubines for the harems of Arabian sheikhs.

"You're a fine one to talk, Podmore! What about those postcards of yours? I'd hardly call *that* a respectable way to carry on, neither, getting young females to stand about in their drawers for you to photograph."

"That's different. It's art."

"My eye and Betty Martin it is. I know which I'd prefer, given the choice between you and Rudolph Valentino in a desert tent."

Her sarcasm stung him on the raw. "Oh, you can laugh, m'girl, but I mean what I say. These are dangerous times we live in. Once you're my legal wedded wife there'll be no more gadding off to public houses by yourself. You'll stop at home where I can keep a watch on you and know you're safe."

God, what a prospect, she thought!

"Well, thanks for warning me, Podmore. At least I know now, I'm doing the right thing."

Because he wanted so much to believe she loved him, he

misunderstood her, thinking she meant she would welcome the security of a proper married relationship. He twisted himself awkwardly on the bed to put his arms round her.

"You won't regret it, Rosie sweetheart. I'll make you a good husband, I swear I will. I'll look after you, and spoil you, and pet you – " In his sudden happiness, Mr Podmore began kissing her face, his loose wet mouth sucking at her cheek and his hand reaching for the warm nakedness of her breasts inside the wrapper.

"Oh, my darling . . . my little angel . . . I love you . . . be kind to me, please be kind – "

Roseen shoved him off irritably. "For God's sake stop mauling me, will you. You make me sick, the way you carry on."

"But I need you – "

"Too ruddy bad. You make my flesh creep, you do. I don't want to be prodded and poked and gawped at all the while. I hate it, d'you hear. *Hate* it."

She gave him another shove for good measure, and rolled over to the further side of the bed to get up, hanging on to the brass rail for support. The gaslamp had been lit outside in the street by this time, its light shining between the half-drawn curtains and spilling a dingy yellow wedge across the room.

It touched the side of her face as she turned away. "You're nothing but an old bore, and if you want the truth, I'm fed up to the back teeth with you."

"You don't mean that." Mr Podmore's expression was abject with hurt. "Rosie – tell me you don't mean that. Look how good I've been to you."

There was no answer. She tugged the red-silk wrapper round her body and tied the belt, not even listening to him.

"Sweetheart – " He tried coaxing. "Haven't I always been good to you? I've given you a nice home here with me, I've pampered you, bought you whatever you fancied – "

"You can't buy affection," she interrupted shortly. "You can't buy respect. I've stuck with you only because it suited me to."

His hurt quickened, lashing his pride into anger. "You can be a cruel bitch!"

She ignored that. "I'm going to have a cigarette," she said,

199

starting to walk somewhat unsteadily round the bed to the door. "And then I'm getting myself dressed and I'm going out."

"You're not going anywhere – " Mr Podmore moved to intercept her, catching her by the arm. "You've been playing games with me quite long enough. I want an answer from you, m'girl, and I want it now. Do you intend to marry me – yes or no."

She pushed the hair back from her face and looked at him; and then very deliberately, as though picking off an insect, removed his hand from her arm.

"Podmore," she said, "let me tell you something. I wouldn't marry you if you was the last man left on earth. I've got plans for my life. And you're not included. You see, the fact is, I don't need you any more."

★

Roseen kept her appointment with George Dennison's solicitors. She was right in her expectation: her Uncle George had indeed left her money in his will. One thousand pounds, to be exact; together with an outright gift of the property in Raby Street, 'so that she will always have a secure roof over her head'.

That same afternoon she packed her bags and left Aubrey Podmore and Berry Street for good. She was a woman of independent means at last – and by heaven, she meant to make the most of it.

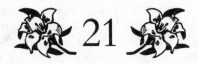

21

Maud Dennison had always been a strong-willed woman, but her husband had tempered that will to a great extent by the force of his own personality. Now that he was gone there was nothing to act as a check; and what had initially been tolerated, excused and explained as behaviour due to bereavement was in fact Maud Dennison's natural character finally at liberty to manifest itself.

She missed her husband George; of course she did. They had been married for almost thirty years. Despite the difference in social background they'd enjoyed a partnership based upon respect, consideration and fondness – qualities which had stood the test of time. It was true that after Flora's birth and Maud's failure to bear more children, physical intimacy had ceased; but it was a vastly overrated thing in Maud's opinion and (again in her opinion) they were probably more content having an only child than suffering the inconvenience of raising four or five.

In any case these days it was only the labouring class who had large families.

Mrs Dennison was of that type of woman to whom appearances meant everything. To be of good standing in society was a paramount objective, and one she had worked hard to achieve and maintain. Because her husband was in Trade, throughout her married life she had had to fight the stigma of snobbery among her more upper-crust neighbours, and to give her her due she had fought it with their own weapons of tone and taste and traditional values.

Now, at last, she had succeeded. Once her husband was

dead and decently buried she was no longer 'the Grocer's Wife'. She was Mrs Maud Dennison, wealthy widow. The difference was a subtle one, but none the less important – a social distinction between actually *making* money and *inheriting* it – and having finally attained full entrée into the jealously-guarded coterie of Stockwell End, Mrs Dennison was not about to surrender it at her daughter Flora's prompting by removing herself from her prestigious address to some dowager's cottage in rural Albrighton.

In this she had the support of her son-in-law.

Sidney agreed entirely with Maud that she should remain at Stockwell End if such was her wish; and as for the domestic staff, why, of course she should keep them on – it wasn't as though she couldn't afford their wages. In fact it was Sidney who planted the notion in Mrs Dennison's head that he and Flora and little Imogen might instead be the ones to move. A shame to let so large a house go wasted, after all, when the place would make an ideal family home for all four of them.

Flora herself was inclined to resist this proposal. It would mean in effect two mistresses under one roof, and her mother would never tolerate that, no more than Flora could tolerate being treated as the daughter of the house again. Besides, she actually liked her own little whitewashed villa in Albrighton, and she liked the circle of friends she'd made there – other young mothers who understood and shared the joys and worries and stepping-stones of babyhood. She even liked the girl they employed as housemaid, and the woman who came to do the heavy laundering.

But then, late in the autumn of 1921, two things occurred to force a change of mind.

The first the discovery that she was pregnant again. As with Imogen, the conception was an accident, and as it was going to mean having two very young children about the house, the necessity therefore arose of finding somewhere larger to accommodate a proper nursery.

The second thing was Sidney's deteriorating health. For the past year he'd been complaining on and off about feeling run down and tired, and had started taking days from school to stay in bed with 'a bit of a temperature'. Their doctor had prescribed a holiday at the seaside, and they'd duly gone away to Aberystwyth; but hardly were they home again than Sidney had succumbed to a very unpleasant attack of swollen glands.

What with the nausea of early pregnancy, an ailing husband and a small child to care for, Flora was beginning to feel increasingly run down herself, and wondered whether indeed they might not be wiser going home to Stockwell End – for the time being, at least. So it was that they found a tenant for the villa in Albrighton, and moved back to live with Mrs Dennison just before the close of the year.

Sidney managed to struggle along with his work at Codsall school during the following term, but by Easter it was obvious that his illness was worsening. He began to lose weight and appetite, complained of lethargy, and had feverish headaches which developed gradually during the day and were severe by evening. On top of this he continued to be troubled by swollen glands, and his breath often had the most offensive odour, as though he'd eaten something rotten.

Concerned, and not a little irritated by her husband's apathetic attitude, Flora sought the opinion of another doctor. This time the diagnosis was septicaemia – blood poisoning – caused by chronic dental neglect.

"Your mouth is in a most deplorable state, Mr Hathaway," he was told none too kindly. "In fact, I've seldom seen worse. I don't need to tell you that the gums are badly ulcerated, and there's a lot of associated tenderness and bleeding. It's the discharge from the ulcers that's causing the problem by producing the sepsis which is attacking your system. My advice to you, Mr Hathaway, is to seek proper dental attention as soon as possible. And I must emphasise that. *As soon as possible.*"

It was advice which Sidney was loath to act upon; but the choice was either to continue suffering the unpleasant effects of his body's own self-damage, or to take his faint courage in both hands and go to a dental surgeon.

In the end he was forced to yield to common sense and Flora's insistent badgering, and went along to a place at Tettenhall, where on May 18th he was given nitrous oxide anaesthetic for the removal of his teeth.

The operation was unfortunately not straightforward.

Some of the larger roots, weakened by decay, broke off within the jaw, and post-operative bleeding was heavier than expected. Arrangements were made for Sidney to go to the Royal Hospital in Wolverhampton for further treatment; but this he refused, and even though groggy and in considerable pain, insisted on discharging himself and returning home to Stockwell End, where he took to his bed.

By May 20th, a Saturday, he was obviously very ill. The haemorrhaging had slowed, but not stopped, and Flora still needed to keep changing the towels which covered his pillow.

"Sidney, you *must* let me call the doctor," she told him repeatedly, vexed by his stubborn refusal to admit to anything seriously wrong. "Or at least let me tell your parents how sick you are."

The answer was no. He didn't want any fuss, he insisted fretfully; once his mouth healed up he'd be as right as rain. It was difficult to hear clearly what he was saying, and Flora was scarcely in any mood to be patient: she was seven months pregnant, and what with the worry and the lack of sleep, she felt tired and on edge. It would have helped had her mother not been abroad at this time, but Maud Dennison was on a three-month visit to the Canadian cousins, and in her absence the responsibility of nursing, cleaning and spoon-feeding Sidney fell entirely upon his young wife's shoulders.

In the end she could stand it no longer.

"Don't you realise how selfishly you're behaving?" she said, turning on him suddenly one morning. He had asked her to rub his feet, something which seemed to give him comfort; and it was while she was sitting there at the end of the bed that she realised she'd had quite enough of this exhausting situation.

"You lie here day after day," she expostulated, "watching me run off my legs with fetching and carrying – you refuse to let anyone else do a thing to help – you won't even have the doctor in to see you – "

The force of her anger astonished her, the way it exploded.

"You're worse than a child, Sidney. You've made yourself ill entirely through your own stupid fault, and it's *me* you seem to expect to make you well again!"

She thrust his feet out of her lap and stood up, hands

pressed against the small of her back to relieve the ache of pregnancy.

"If only you'd listened in the first place and looked after your teeth, as I kept telling you. Don't you see how unfair it is? I'm bone weary. In my condition I should be spared all this. But no – it's *you* that's more important – *you're* the one demanding the attention – *you're* the one that needs the rest and sleep!"

Sidney's dull, sunken eyes returned her a martyred look. In his present helpless suffering he'd been under the impression that Flora enjoyed fussing round seeing to his comfort and helping along his recovery. She was his wife, after all said and done. What else was a wife for, if not to minister to her husband's needs. In sickness *and* in health – that was what the institution of marriage was about.

He tried to say as much, but his mouth and throat were so swollen and excruciatingly painful that all he could manage was a disjointed gargle.

"I don't care whether you'll see him or not, I'm going to telephone Dr Perry," Flora said, ignoring his efforts. "And I'll tell him how insufferably stubborn you're being – oh, yes I will!" as Sidney tried to lever himself up in weak protest. "You're sick. You need proper care. You'll *never* get better the way you're going on."

With that she turned away and went across the room to the door, refusing to take notice of the feeble cries of appeal coming from the bed. Going downstairs to the telephone in the study, she asked the exchange operator to connect her to Dr Perry's surgery.

It was several hours before the doctor arrived, and his initial concern upon entering the house was for Flora herself. The strains and stresses of the past days had bruised her eyes with dark circles, and her features were pale and drawn, obvious signs that she'd been overdoing things.

"Bed and a good rest for you, young lady," he ordered, following her up the stairs. "You should know better at the moment than tire yourself out playing nursemaid. I'm surprised at you."

Stung by the rebuke, Flora reminded him a little sharply that it was her husband's silly obstinacy more than her own lack of sense which was to blame; and showing him into the bedroom added, "See for yourself what he's like. I'm afraid I've completely lost patience. He really is becoming quite impossible."

Sidney himself proved that. Having been roused from sleep by the sound of the doctor's voice, he first insisted on struggling up in bed, weak though he was, and would have tried to get out if he could, except that the effort brought on a paroxysm of retching coughs. Flora had to fetch a cloth to wipe the blood from his chin. Then, when Dr Perry asked to examine his mouth, he stubbornly turned his head aside and started to cry, mumbling something about being all right if he could just have some medicine to clear things up.

It took a good deal of coaxing and firm insistence before he could be persuaded to do as requested.

"When actually were the teeth extracted?" the doctor enquired of Flora.

"Last Thursday."

"I see. Hmm. Well, let's take a look there, Mr Hathaway. If you could just turn your head to the light, please – "

For the next few minutes, apart from the ragged gasp of Sidney's breathing there was silence while Dr Perry conducted a careful examination. When he had finished he got up from the bed to soap his hands at the washstand in the corner.

"I'm going to have to refer you straight to hospital," he said over his shoulder. "I'm afraid the condition you're in is potentially very serious. In fact, without the proper medical attention – "

He left the sentence unfinished. The gravity of his tone was sufficient to convey the rest.

★

The irony was that, believing himself to be in perfect health, Sidney Hathaway had contrived to avoid military service in 1915 by a fraudulent claim to have a 'dicky' heart.

Had he been less of a coward, less anxious to stay safely out of uniform and leave the fighting to the other poor devils, a thorough physical check-up would have revealed the truth of his condition early enough for him to seek treatment, and that might perhaps have extended his life by many more years.

As it was, no one had reason to suspect that Sidney's health had been on a tightrope for some time past, and that it was only his young man's strength which had kept him apparently fit. Once that strength began to fail, eaten away by the corrosive effects of blood poisoning, his fitness likewise deteriorated, and the more it worsened, the faster his constitution weakened.

Not even the doctors could say for certain whether at the end it was heart failure that killed him or pneumonia. It was left to the post-mortem to decide.

★

To lose a father was devastating enough; but to lose a husband too, and within so short a time, was almost more than Flora's emotional state could cope with.

The unexpectedness of Sidney's death came as such a dreadful jolt that she couldn't – wouldn't – believe it at first, not even at the funeral. She kept thinking it was her father they were burying all over again, and that Sidney was still in hospital. And then she would remember that last visit, and Sidney's parents and sister looking accusingly at her, saying, "Why couldn't you have told us in time?" and she in turn crying out to the doctor, "Why didn't I have any warning?"

That was the way with heart disease, though. Unless one knew the little signs to watch for, life pursued its course in ignorance of the fact that at any random moment it might suddenly gutter and go out like a candle. Sidney's uncle had died at the age of forty-three; just dropped dead one day playing cricket. It didn't seem fair that a man in his prime could be snatched away like that, but then he too, apparently, had had a 'dicky ticker', so perhaps it ran in the family.

Once Sidney's death was learned, the immediate concern was for Flora's unborn child and whether the shock mightn't bring on premature labour. Jessy Craig (now Mrs Philip Venables) came to stay at Stockwell End with her own new baby, to be with Flora until her mother's arrival from Canada – Mrs Dennison had been informed of the sad event by telegram and was on her way back on board the White Star liner SS *Berengaria*.

"If only I'd known he was so ill!" Flora kept saying over and over again. "If only I'd cared for him better!"

"You did all you could, dear," Jessy soothed her. "You mustn't blame yourself, now. No one could have done more. Not even the hospital had any idea he might go the way he did."

"I know – but oh, Jessy, I *do* blame myself. I resented poor Sidney being sick. I showed him no patience or sympathy. I even told him it was his own fault entirely – in fact I was *beastly*."

"And now I suppose you're feeling guilty," came the practical comment.

Yes. Yes, she did feel guilty; horribly guilty. The memory of that final week of her husband's life would haunt her for ever, she was sure. But then in the midst of her widow's breast-beating, Flora would occasionally recall things about Sidney which she'd never liked – his constant cigarette-smoking, his childish sulks, his selfish too-quick love-making – and her guilt would evaporate for an hour or so to be replaced by a rebellious sense of relief.

She *had* loved him; she had, she had. But when her son was born, healthy and full-term in the second week of July, she didn't name him Sidney in remembrance.

Instead she called him Robert.

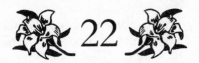# 22

"Flora, dear, this is Gerard Lansby."

Jessy Venables had come over from the other side of the room arm in arm with a tallish, well-built young man whose fair hair framed pleasantly engaging features.

"He's been pestering me for an introduction on the pretext that the pair of you have met before."

"Oh, have we?" Flora returned an uncertain smile to the one Gerard Lansby gave as he offered his hand. "I'm sorry . . . I'm not altogether sure I remember the occasion."

"Christmas 1908," he said promptly. "One of the children's parties Dennison's Stores gave. You pinned a number on my jersey."

"Goodness – did I?" Despite herself she started to laugh. This evening's dinner invitation was the first proper social event she'd attended since her husband's death four months ago, and oh, the relief to escape from the dreariness of widowhood for a while and be with people who were enjoying themselves. "What an extraordinary memory you must have to recall a thing like that!"

"Well, you see, I fell in love with you for the entire afternoon." The blue eyes held hers and the smile deepened. "And I've had a predilection for soft, shy little creatures ever since."

"Don't believe *anything* he tells you," Jessy came in, catching his final words just as she was turning to speak to someone else. "He has the most dreadful reputation with women – haven't you, Gerard?"

"If you say so, my dear. I never argue with a lady."

Flora felt her cheeks beginning to warm a little, as much in slight embarrassment that he should continue looking at her so attentively, as for that reference to 'falling in love' and 'soft, shy creature'.

"And how did you happen to be at a Dennison's Christmas party?" she enquired politely, her tone putting just a touch of distance between them. "Did you have any connection with my father's stores, Mr Lansby?"

"Mm. A relative was manager of the Bilston shop. And my name's Gerard."

By this time Jessy Venables had moved away to attend to other guests, leaving them standing alone together, otherwise Flora might have chosen to ignore the reminder in that last remark. As it was, she heard herself answering a shade astringently, "Yes, I did catch the introduction."

Her coolness brought a rueful lift to the corner of his mouth. "Oh dear. I see the shy little girl I met that Christmas has learnt to be wary. How sad. I rather preferred her the way she was."

He turned aside a moment to take two glasses from the sherry tray the Venables' maid was passing round; and handing one to Flora, went on, "My reputation isn't as bad as Jessy made it sound, you know. Actually I'm quite a decent sort of chap, but I suppose the fact that I'm not yet married makes me a prime target for the ladies. After all, there are not many of us eligible bachelors left to grace the social scene."

It was difficult to judge at five minutes' acquaintance, and Flora couldn't decide whether Gerard Lansby entertained an extraordinarily high regard for himself, or whether his self-confident approach was a natural part of his character.

Thinking to put him in his place, she replied, "Then I suppose you must be rather grateful that so few young men returned from the Front to provide you with competition," and took a sip from her glass.

"Yes. I count myself one of the lucky ones. All *I* came home with from Ypres was a scratch or two and chilblains."

He stepped back to let a couple of people pass, responding to their apologies with a friendly word of banter; then turning again to Flora, "By the way, I was sorry to learn about your husband. Jessy told me. Jolly bad luck, that . . . what with a new baby and everything."

Now it was her turn to feel put in place. In the most effortless manner Gerard had succeeded in making her feel at once ashamed of her snide aspersion on his courage, and guilty of forming instant adverse judgement. He had shrugged off his experience of Ypres lightly, as though it were nothing, instead of the living hell few men had survived; and his tone when he spoke of her bereavement had held the genuine warmth of sympathy.

Not knowing quite how to respond, she looked past him towards the drawing-room windows, open wide to let in the soft evening air; and misinterpreting her silence, he went on quickly, "It isn't easy for a chap like me, without family, to appreciate the devastation of losing someone very close. I think you're wonderfully brave to pick up the pieces and soldier on."

"What other choice do I have? I can't sit at home and weep for ever."

How disgustingly noble that made her sound, Flora told herself. The truth was, she'd wept hardly at all for Sidney; indeed she had felt very little beyond the first shock of her loss and the sense of guilt that she'd never cared quite enough.

"Life must continue, as they say," she added, looking back at him and taking another sip from her glass; and then, changing the subject abruptly, "Are you a friend of Philip Venables? Where do you live? What do you do?"

"Is the answer to the first question dependent upon the other two?" Gerard asked, amused by this sudden rush of interrogation. "As a matter of fact, I've known Philip for years – we were at school together in Stafford – so yes, you might say we're friends. As to where I live and what I do, well, I'm a farmer and I've a house and a few hundred acres not far from here at Brewood. I should be glad to show you round the place, if you like."

He would have gone on to say something more, but just at that moment general conversation was interrupted by the deep reverberation of the dinner-gong from beyond the room, and Philip called cheerfully to everyone to go through and sit down if they would; and so it wasn't until much later in the evening, when they'd all eaten, that Flora and Gerard found themselves once more in one another's company.

This time they sat together in a small group at one end of the drawing-room, digesting an excellent meal over coffee while one of their fellow-guests entertained them quietly at the piano. Talk at first was of generalities – the weather, the garden, this year's holiday in Deauville – and then moved on via the expulsion of Mr Horatio Bottomley from his seat as a Member of Parliament, to the confused situation in the Irish Republic, and thence to the recently-opened assembly of the League of Nations in Geneva.

It was the opinion of one of the gentlemen present, raising his voice somewhat to air his views above the background strains of Liszt, that the members of the League were living in cloud-cuckoo-land if they thought they could eradicate warfare in the world – one had only to look at the situation in Asia Minor at this very moment, with Turkey fighting Greece over its territories. Depend upon it, they'd be expecting our young chaps to go over there to sort the trouble out and clear up their mess for them, just as they always did, damn' impudent foreign beggars.

His hectoring volubility, fuelled by cognac, brought a little yawn of boredom to Flora's lips.

Seeing her fingers politely try to conceal it, Gerard leaned sideways from his chair and said in an undertone, "He's probably never been closer to a real fight than a clerk's desk. I'm going out on to the terrace to smoke a cigar. Would you care to keep me company?"

"Don't you think that would be a trifle rash?" she whispered back, emboldened by the several glasses of wine she'd drunk at dinner. "I have my reputation to consider, Mr Lansby."

"So have I, Mrs Hathaway. And I can imagine no better way of enhancing it than by being seen à deux with you."

The teasing manner in which he said this brought colour again to her face. She was tempted to refuse him, but the flattery of his invitation was somehow too appealing to resist, and, besides, the voluble gentleman opposite was warming ominously to the sound of his own opinions. Before she had time to reconsider she found herself rising to her feet with a murmured, "If you would excuse me, please," to those seated nearest.

Every eye in the room seemed fixed upon her as she moved away towards the terrace doors, Gerard just a few close steps behind; and it crossed Flora's mind to wonder what on earth they must be thinking, all of them, what conjectures and conclusions were being drawn.

Then – suddenly – she discovered that she didn't really care. Let them look, she thought defiantly! What does it matter. I'm giving no cause for offence. I'm breaking no social taboos.

It was a moment of startling self-revelation.

For the first time since Sidney's death she realised that her only responsibility now was to her darling children, and that in every other way she was free to be her own person, to do precisely what she wished: no longer the daughter subservient to her parents, no longer the wife in submission to her husband, but a woman whose pattern of life was from henceforth entirely her own to control.

★

The following weekend there was quite an argument between Flora and her mother over Gerard Lansby. He had telephoned to invite her out for a spin in his motor-car that Sunday afternoon, and perhaps to have tea at the farmhouse afterwards if she wished.

She had accepted.

Maud Dennison was shocked: it had been bad enough that her daughter refused to wear black after the first month and was seen to be cultivating social engagements when she should still be in mourning, but to start encouraging the attentions of another man only four months into her widowhood and with an eight-week baby barely weaned from the breast was so scandalously in breach of moral propriety as to be almost unheard of; and what would the neighbours think.

Flora said she didn't give a fig for moral propriety, and the neighbours could mind their own business. Little Robert had a perfectly reliable, well-trained nurse to see to his feeding and care, and as for her 'encouraging the attentions' of Gerard Lansby, that was absolute nonsense, and in any case it wasn't

213

going to bring Sidney back to life whether she stayed in mourning one year or ten.

Her mother countered by complaining that she really couldn't understand what had come over Flora lately to make her behave in such an inconsiderate, headstrong manner; the effects of Sidney's sudden tragic death and the baby's birth must have turned her wits – to which Flora responded tartly that she'd no intention of taking notice of anything her mother said; she was accepting Gerard Lansby's invitation, and that was that.

All in all, it was quite a heated exchange. Mother and daughter had always been far more alike than either was aware of, and it had taken the close proximity of living as two widowed women beneath one roof to make them begin to realise that fact.

As a conciliatory gesture, which was not quite an apology, Flora wore black silk for the outing with Gerard, its sobriety enlivened by a deep, white lace collar. Hemlines this year had crept up to mid-calf, and with the female leg so much on show there was a vogue now for artificial silk stockings in the newly-fashionable beige and flesh tones. She had acquired her first pair only recently, and was feeling really awfully daring to be wearing them today.

Gerard thought she looked "very sweet, like a convent schoolgirl" when he came to pick her up from the house. He was driving a smart little Arrol-Johnston tourer which he used "just for knocking about", he said, and in his leather motoring cap and goggles looked more like a dashing young airman than a farmer, Flora decided, as he handed her into the car.

He really was rather handsome. Several times she found she was sneaking little sidelong glances at his profile, and had to tell herself that she'd better take care or she'd find her head being turned.

It was a beautiful afternoon, with Nature conspiring in their favour to produce one of those glorious early autumn days when the air holds the sparkling clarity of wine and the golden sunlight spills across the fields from a cloudless sky. They drove westwards from Stockwell End into the country-side, taking quiet little back lanes which meandered round ancient parish boundaries and dipped through shallow water-splashes, signposting them towards rural hamlets as yet untouched by the modern red-brick ugliness of progress.

By the time Gerard turned his motor-car towards Brewood and home, the mellow September light was already beginning to thicken into shadows beneath the trees, and a honey-coloured sun was rimming the tops of the far away Clee Hills.

It was in this late afternoon loveliness that Flora first saw Cowpers, standing on the edge of the beechwood at the end of a long grassy drive, its windows reflecting the dying warmth of the day. At one side was an old walled garden, full of seasonal colour from beds of chrysanthemums and dahlias; at the other, a paddock where a few yearling lambs were grazing in company with Gerard's hunters.

"I'm keeping an eye on them for the shepherd," he said with a jerk of the head towards the lambs as he opened the car door for Flora. "They're not doing as well as they should – better they're here than out in the fields."

She was prepared to be impressed; and found the house itself enchanting.

"Good. I'm glad you like it," he replied, ushering her through the entrance hall, walls hung with sporting prints, to a snug parlour overlooking the garden. "Myself, I'm biased, of course, having lived in the place all my life – but no doubt about it, I'd rather be here at Cowpers than anywhere else on earth. It's *home*."

There was an unconscious emphasis of affection on that final word which did not escape Flora.

"You must have missed it awfully while you were away at the Front," she said, taking the brocade-covered wing-chair he indicated for her.

"Miss it – ? I'll say I did. You've no idea." He gave her a look over his shoulder as he bent to put a light to the logs laid ready in the grate. "It was the only thing that kept me sane half the time, thinking about these four walls . . . and the farm, and the land, and the woods. Thank God I was spared to come back. Now then – "

He straightened himself to his full height and smiled down at her. "A pot of best India tea, I think. And some of Mrs

Barry's seed cake. She's the cowman's wife – does all my cooking and cleaning. Wouldn't be without her."

He excused himself and went off somewhere towards the back of the house; and while he was away Flora looked round the room in curiosity. It was very masculine, that was her instant impression. More sporting prints on the walls, foxed a little with damp and old age; a stuffed badger in a glass case on the sideboard; copies of field sports and farming magazines strewn untidily across the window-seat; a pair of well-worn slippers beside the log basket; and overall, permeating the air, a faint scent of apples, leather and woodsmoke.

In fact it was a room which showed no influence whatever of a woman's touch, and Flora found this somehow reassuring. She was prepared to like Gerard Lansby, and like him very much; but the idea that he might be a social gadabout had acted as a curb upon the attraction he held for her.

This house, however, was his home, the place where he belonged. Its atmosphere held nothing of a predatory character: rather that of stability and comfort, and strength. And just as all homes bear the individual stamp of their occupant, so Cowpers seemed to reflect most faithfully the type of man Gerard was behind his public façade.

Not a philanderer at all, Flora told herself, with a little catch of pleasure at the realisation; but someone entirely different.

★

News of Sidney Hathaway's sudden and unexpected death reached Robert Wells some months overdue in a letter from his old college friend, Reggie Bellamy.

"What do you think," Reggie had written, "he never was much of a go, was Sidney; and now he's left the delectable little Flora all on her ownsome and a real catch for somebody quick enough to give solace in her widowhood. They say she's worth a mint of money – wouldn't mind taking a gamble on her myself!"

The flippant tone of the letter annoyed Robert considerably; but overriding his annoyance far more was a desperate longing frustration that Flora should again be free, while he himself remained fettered by the obligations of marriage. The thought

216

of her alone in life, and with two little fatherless children to raise, brought out the protective side of his deep and abiding love for her; and for a week or more after hearing from Reggie he wrestled with the urge to go and see her, make physical contact once more, an urge so strong that several times on his way to school of a morning he deliberately bicycled instead towards the railway station with the intention of catching a train up to the Midlands.

It was only his sense of duty – to his pupils as much as to his wife – which restrained him from actually giving way to his compulsion.

In the end he took the less drastic decision to get in touch with Flora by letter, and during the final week of October wrote to her as follows:

My dear Flora

Forgive my silence. There seemed so little point in continuing to assure you of my love; but now, having learnt recently of your husband's death, I feel I must write to you again. Please accept my deepest condolences, and believe me, you are constantly in my thoughts and prayers – never more so than at this time.

I have reflected a great deal upon the influence of Fate in our lives, and have come to the conclusion that its purpose is a mystery. Of one thing I am sure, however: that God doesn't create us to be clockwork toys which He can wind up to go round and round in our own little particular space of time until the mechanism runs down. He made us out of love, not out of amusement; and therefore I can't believe that He places us in certain situations only to sit back and say, 'now get out of that if you can'. There *is* a pattern and plan to life, otherwise the whole thing degenerates into a meaningless jumble, with neither rhyme nor reason to it.

The problem is, Flora, that we allow ourselves to become so blinkered by convention, by strictures, by self-imposed guilt, by fear, that we waste the opportunities which that individual life-plan, if you like, presents to us. We saddle ourselves unnecessarily with a burden of unhappiness because we think in our own arrogance that we have an obligation and duty to continue along one particular course, from which there is no deviation; and very often we so mismanage events that we only realise our mistakes when it's too late to repair them.

When you married Sidney, I thought you were lost to me for ever, Flora, my darling, and I blamed myself bitterly. These past few years I've been living in a strait-jacket of frustration and misery. You can't believe how I've suffered. The heart-wound of my love for you never healed, and I couldn't grow used enough to its pain to be able to ignore it. I still miss you – love you – need you so very much.

It's said that those who do not change the pattern of their lives are condemned to repeat it for ever. I want my life to be with you, Flora, and yours with me. Not yet, perhaps, but one day. Will you give me that assurance?

Please reply to me. You can send a letter care of the post office in Freshwater.

Yours, always and for ever

Robert.

Flora wept when she received the letter. To hear from Robert again after all this long time re-awakened the poignancy of old memories – memories which, to be truthful, marriage and the fulfilment of motherhood had tended to blur perhaps a little. *Could* she give him the assurance he asked for, her promise that one day she would share her life with him? Surely she'd been sharing it already, all these years she had kept his remembrance alive, wrapped round with love and held warm and safe against her heart.

But things weren't the same any more. Suddenly the future was beginning to take on added dimension, new interest. Her burgeoning friendship with Gerard Lansby was at an early stage still, but she enjoyed his company immensely and had been very flattered when he telephoned a few days after the visit to Cowpers, asking if he could see her again.

There was a time when she had believed that nothing could ever change the constancy of her love for Robert. He would be with her for ever, imprisoned in the amber of her past. Perhaps that was the trouble, though, that he *was* in her past;

218

and it irked her to feel that by saying yes to Gerard she might be betraying something precious and beautiful – not only the love but the memory.

She could live the rest of her life looking back over her shoulder, but was that what she really wanted? Wouldn't it be true to say, if she were being really honest with herself, that Gerard Lansby was beginning to edge Robert just a little out of her thoughts?

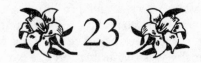

Roseen Kelly ran her fingers over the naked shoulders of the young Frenchman making love to her. After Aubrey Podmore and the flabby grossness of an ageing body, it was ecstasy to feel the sensuous strength of hard, smooth muscle giving her pleasure again.

His skin had the pungent smell of masculine excitement; not the rancid odour of an old man's perspiration, but sharp and clean and fresh; and the thick black hair falling over his forehead was still glossy with moisture from the swim he'd taken in the sea a short while before.

Roseen hadn't the slightest idea who he was. Nor did she care. Until half an hour ago she'd never even met him. She had been leaning on the rail of her first-floor balcony, looking at the moon reflected on the silver waters of the Channel and wondering whether it was worth her while getting dressed again to go down to the hotel lounge for a drink and a bit of company; and just as she made to move away, she'd noticed someone coming out of the sea, a pale shape naked in the moonlight.

The beach at this point ran almost from under her balcony. There was only the road and a low wall, and then the shelving sand to the waves' edge. As the shape resolved itself into the slim figure of a young man, Roseen could see him quite clearly and leaned her elbows forward on the rail to watch. Presumably he'd left his clothes by the wall, because he stopped there and bent down; and when he straightened again, in the act of pulling on his trousers, she couldn't resist giving a cheeky whistle of admiration.

This was France, after all, so who cared.

The whistle attracted him. He looked about quickly, turning his head to find where it had come from, and Roseen laughed aloud in sheer devilment.

"Mind you don't catch cold, you, doing that," she'd called out.

Her voice drew his attention to the balcony. He could see her now, outlined against the glow of the bedroom light, and there was the sudden gleam of teeth as he smiled.

"*Holà* – you warm me, yes? Then I no be cold."

She laughed again. "Saucy blighter, aren't you."

But she didn't say no; and something in her tone, and the way she touched the loose waves of her hair, must have given him encouragement, because he did a one-handed spring over the wall, still holding up his trousers, and crossed the road to stand under her balcony.

"You – me – *y mettons le jus* – yes?"

"You me *what?*"

Roseen leaned further over to look at him. The moonlight shone on the wetness of his face and hair, and she liked what she saw; just for an instant he reminded her somehow of Billy, the same cocky, carefree arrogance.

"I show you!" Before she could open her mouth again, the young man had made a grab at the thick, ropey stem of an old vine growing against the hotel wall and began hauling himself with considerable agility hand-over-hand till he reached the balcony rail. The next minute he'd pulled himself up to get a foothold, and was standing precariously facing her, his trousers fallen back around his ankles, and not a stitch to cover his nakedness.

Roseen tried to keep a straight expression. This was just the sort of escapade that appealed to her, with the spice of danger adding to its excitement; more than that, there was something deliciously attractive about the whole situation – being in a foreign place where home rules didn't apply, and on the verge of a sexual adventure with a good-looking Frenchman whose interest in her was becoming unashamedly evident.

"Haven't you got any buttons on those trousers?" she said, looking him directly in the eye.

He glanced down, at the trousers, at himself; then stepped out of them and threw them across the rail before vaulting over in a single easy movement.

"Buttons – *pop!*" he answered with a snap of the fingers, laughing.

Roseen laughed with him; she couldn't help herself.

"Saucy blighter," she said again. "You don't waste time, do you."

He shrugged. He was younger than she was, about eighteen, and his moustache was hardly more than a dark fuzz of hair on his upper lip.

"You ought to get dried off. You're dripping all over the floor."

He gave her a look that managed to combine impudence with erotic invitation, and reaching forward, pushed her feather-trimmed wrap from one shoulder and began stroking the soft warm skin beneath.

"You like dry me, *ma cocotte chérie?*" His eyes slipped past her to the bed in the room behind. "You like make me warm?"

"You get much warmer and you'll burst into ruddy flame," Roseen told him archly, taking a step backwards. It was quite obvious what was going to happen between the two of them, and she wanted to enjoy it, not have it over and done with all inside five minutes and him gone again. Apart from Aubrey Podmore, who couldn't knock the skin off a blancmange as a lover, the last man to have sex with her was Maurice Lines, and that was too long ago.

The young Frenchman cupped his hand round the nape of her neck and pulled her gently towards him. When he kissed her, his lips were cool and salty. It was only the lightest little kiss and then he drew back again and looked into her eyes, and smiled; and Roseen could feel her legs begin to tremble.

"*Si tu ne m'avais pas aguiché je t'aurai laissée tranquille,*" he murmured.

She didn't know what it meant, and she didn't care as he kissed her again, his arms tightening and his mouth this time hungry and hard on her own.

★

222

Roseen had been determined to enjoy herself with the money George Dennison left her in his will – and enjoyment in her book meant doing things in the biggest and most expensive style. There'd been a certain amount of delay, of course, while the estate was administered, but she had enough put by from Aubrey Podmore's besotted generosity to keep her afloat financially until the legacy came through; and with the house in Raby Street now her own property she was more soundly secure than she'd ever been in her life.

It was an indescribably *satisfying* feeling.

The first thing she'd done was to go out and buy herself a little motor-car – a Star touring model with 'perambulator' hood which folded down, and a brass radiator grille, and smart black wheel-guards; and she would stand for hours looking at it parked in the street outside her door, thinking to herself, 'that's mine, that is – all mine', while the neighbours twitched their parlour net-curtains in nosiness and envy.

For the satisfaction of giving them something else to talk about, and because she'd never been anywhere more exotic than Wales, Roseen next took it into her head to treat herself to a holiday in France; and because she'd read in some magazine or other that Deauville was *the* place to be seen this year, she made up her mind that that was where she'd go. Only the best for her, that's what she told them all.

In her naïve ignorance, she had imagined Deauville as Aberystwyth with a French accent and palm trees. What she hadn't been prepared for as she disembarked off the Southampton ferry at Le Havre was the utterly alien sense of *foreignness* which had overwhelmed her. Everything looked so different from what she'd expected – sounded different, even smelt different. It was just like being removed to another world.

Her sexual escapade with the young Frenchman had been all of a piece with this strangeness, this difference. It could never have happened back home; or at least, not in the same romantically exciting way. Anyone hauling himself dripping wet and naked into somebody's bedroom in Raby Street would either need to be drunk, or else barmy.

She never did find out his name. He had disappeared at dawn over the balcony of the hotel room, and that was the last she saw of him. For the next two evenings she'd waited, hoping; but on the third, when he still hadn't reappeared and the sight of the empty sea was starting to bore her, she consigned their passionate night of love to the back-drawer of memory and took herself downstairs to the lounge bar in search of more sociable entertainment.

The Hotel Océanique in Deauville had recently been refurbished throughout in the new angular, colourful style known as *art décoratif*, and attracted a lot of the younger and livelier sort through its doors. Roseen had been staying a week now, and was on smiling terms with the other guests; but the people who came in just for a social drink tended to be different faces every evening.

Tonight the lounge bar was crowded: it was somebody's birthday, the barman explained in his careful English when Roseen went to order herself a gin sling. Sipping her drink, she rested one elbow behind her on the magenta-topped counter and surveyed the noisy scene. There was one particular group at a corner table, three young men and four girls toasting each other in champagne, and for a moment she felt almost envious of their gaiety and the fact that they had friends to share their laughter; and then the barman touched her arm lightly, distracting her.

"*Pardon, m'mselle*, there is a gentleman who wishes to ask if you would permit him to buy for you a drink."

Roseen turned to glance along the bar counter. There were quite a few people standing around, and the low lighting and blue wreaths of cigarette smoke made it difficult to see faces clearly; but at the far end was a man by himself leaning casually against the bar and looking in her direction.

She hesitated a second. Then, with a quick bright smile, "OK. Tell him thanks, I'll have another gin sling," and raised her empty glass in acknowledgement to the stranger.

He raised his own. Suddenly she didn't feel quite so much a wall-flower as she had a minute ago. When her drink came she looked towards him again, and saw that he'd moved from the bar and was edging his way through the crush to join her. Well, why not, she thought with a mental shrug; two people alone in a crowd. Why not.

He was well-dressed, that was the first thing Roseen noticed about him as he approached. He was wearing a very smart double-breasted charcoal-grey suit, which made a change from all the blazers and flannels, and his silk tie had the discreet stripe of regimental or old school colours.

"Hello," he said, holding out a hand. "I hope you don't mind the informal introduction. The barman told me you were English." There was a disarming grin, and as they both shook hands, he added, "My name's Johnnie. Johnnie Driscoll."

"Pleased to meet you." Roseen treated him to one of her glances from under her eyelashes, thinking to herself, God alive, where have *you* been all my life! He was certainly handsome, all right. She'd always had a weakness for dark wavy hair, and the pencil-thin moustache set off his debonair good looks to perfection. "You're English as well, then, are you?"

It was a stupid question, but she couldn't think for a minute what else to say.

"Yes. I'm staying down the road at the Royale, but it's pretty dull compared to this place. You're on holiday, too, I take it, Miss – er – ?"

One eyebrow was raised in query.

She was about to correct herself to 'Mrs', but changed her mind. "Roseen," she informed him. "Roseen Kelly."

"Roseen? I say, what an awfully nice name. And you're here in Deauville by yourself, are you?"

A nod.

He took a flat gold case from his pocket and opened it to offer a cigarette. "That makes two of us. I've been travelling round France on business and thought I'd allow myself a couple of days to relax before going back to London."

The gold case was matched by an identical gold lighter. The cigarettes were Turkish Abdullah. Roseen, who never missed a trick, noted all this; and was glad she'd taken the bother to put on her most expensive frock, a hip-line-waisted affair in emerald crêpe de Chine with swirls of sequins sewn on to the bodice.

She waited until he'd lit his own cigarette, then asked casually, "Is that where you live – London?"

"Northolt, actually. Just beyond Ealing. And you? You

225

have the most intriguing hint of accent, but I'm not sure I can place it."

That made her smile. She turned her head to blow away her smoke, then looked back at him and said, "I'm Wolverhampton, out of Dublin." And when he frowned, not taking her meaning, "My mother was Irish."

"Ah. That would explain it. The red hair, I mean. And the green eyes. They *are* green, aren't they?"

He leaned towards her as though for closer examination, and Roseen could smell the clean, fresh scent of shaving soap. She gazed up disarmingly into his face. His own eyes were brown, fringed by dark lashes, and as their gazes met she felt a little shiver of pleasure run through her. He's probably got a wife and kid waiting for him in Northolt, she told herself; but I don't care. What was it Annie Sutton always used to say – there's no such thing as a married man a hundred miles from home.

She smiled again, feigning a touch of coyness, and looked down.

"So tell me, Roseen, what's a girl as enchanting as you doing alone in Deauville?" Johnnie asked her, leaning back on the bar and drawing on his cigarette; then quickly, apologetically, through the smoke, "Oh, I may call you Roseen, mayn't I? You don't mind?"

"No, course I don't." Their gazes brushed and held once more. She decided a little self-advertisement wouldn't hurt. "Somebody I knew left me a lot of money in his will when he died – and I mean a *lot* of money. I've got my own house, I've got a car, clothes, jewellery . . . no husband nor kiddies . . . I thought, well, Deauville's supposed to be a posh place for a holiday, why don't I treat myself – "

She made a shrugging gesture.

"So here you are," he finished for her.

"Yes. Here I am."

"No boyfriend, though, to enjoy it with?"

"How d'you mean?"

"I mean a pleasure shared is twice as much fun. Why come by yourself?"

"You ask a lot of questions, you do." She put her glass to her lips to drink off the rest of the gin, eyeing him sideways

226

as she did so. The truth was, she'd *wanted* to come by herself, but now that she was here, she was finding herself growing hungry for company. There was only so much sea you could look at alone, only so many shops you could walk around, only so many pavement cafés where you could sit drinking coffee before the on-your-ownness began to get in the way of the enjoyment. That was why the young Frenchman the other night had been such a welcome distraction.

"Anyway, I've met you now, so I'm not by myself, am I?" she added glibly, putting down the empty glass and glancing away across the bar.

No sooner were the words out of her mouth than Roseen wished she hadn't said them. That sort of remark made her sound a bit cheap, a bit too easy, which wasn't the impression she'd intended or wanted to give. She tried to cover up her slip with a show of indifference, pretending it didn't really matter whether the two of them shared this evening together or not, saying carelessly, "Come on, drink up. I'll buy you one in return before I go."

An expression of instant disappointment registered itself on Johnnie Driscoll's face. "What, you're not depriving me of your company already? Oh, surely not – we've hardly got to know one another! You don't *honestly* have to dash away so soon, do you?"

"Well . . ."

Her false play of hesitation brought out his smile again. "No, of course you don't. And in any case, I wouldn't dream of allowing you to buy me a drink. Here – " he drained his own glass and placed it on the counter next to hers. "Have the same again?"

She went through the motions of giving this her consideration, even to glancing at the marcasite watch on her wrist.

"Well . . ." she repeated mock-reluctantly.

"Another gin sling on its way. And then I'll tell you what, Roseen. I've just had the most marvellous idea. I haven't eaten yet this evening – I was thinking of trying that little place opposite the Casino. Would you care to join me in dinner there? Please – ?"

Blimey, you don't hang about much, do you, Roseen

observed to herself. First it's a drink, and then a meal. I wonder what you do for encores?

"Thanks for asking, but actually I'm not all that hungry," she told him, stealing another sidelong look as he signalled to the barman for attention. "I had something earlier on."

He gave his order for their drinks, then turned his head to regard her.

"Don't you like me very much? Is that what you're trying to say?"

The blunt manner in which he put the question caught her off-guard, and she heard herself answering quickly, "'Course I like you! It's just that – "

"It's just that nothing. We're two people – two *English* people – alone in a strange place. Why on earth shouldn't we share one another's company for a few hours? Where's the harm?"

Suddenly he sounded almost angry; and in an attempt at appeasement she said jokingly, "Your wife might not like it if she ever found out."

"I don't have a wife. I'm not married." He continued to look at her. "Are you? You said just now there was no husband, but I notice you're wearing a wedding ring."

"I'm a widow, that's why."

"Ah."

He turned away again for a moment to pay for the drinks; and then as he handed hers to her, he gave a little rueful smile and said apologetically, "Look . . . I'm sorry. I oughtn't to have made that comment. It really was the most frightful bad manners."

"That's all right." Roseen wondered what else he might have observed about her. She raised her glass with a little flourish of bravado. "Chin-chin!"

"Yes. Chin-chin." Their eyes met once more. "Now you really *will* have to have dinner with me. Just to show I'm forgiven."

She thought of her young Frenchman; then shrugged off the memory. Once bitten was never twice shy with Roseen. Suddenly the holiday in Deauville was starting to live up to her expectations.

24

Deauville had never been as popular with the English as Nice or Monte Carlo or Biarritz, but the French adored it. With its Casino, its Hippodrome, its elegant villas and luxurious hotels, it was one of their most fashionable watering-places and a favoured northern resort of Parisian society. The height of the season was August, when Deauville's horse-races attracted the cream of both aristocracy and racing fraternity to spend lavish sums of money at the tracks, the restaurants, the discreet *maisons closes*, and the gambling-tables.

Roseen Kelly had arrived on holiday just as this year's annual season was nearing its end. The September weather was still pleasant enough to bring visitors to enjoy the beaches and beautiful Calvados countryside, but with the departure of the *haut monde* much of the sparkle had gone, and the town was wearing a slightly weary, end-of-party atmosphere.

It was far from dead, however. There was still fun and glamour and gaiety to be found in the night-clubs which had been springing up since the war as places of late-hour entertainment, catering mainly for the young and rich, a favourite haunt especially of the 'flapper' – those defiantly emancipated socialites whose flighty style of life kicked over the traces of convention. Roseen's only experience of this sort of venue had been the Shanghai in Horseley Fields, but the Shanghai was hardly to be compared with the night-clubs of Deauville into which Johnnie Driscoll now started taking her.

That first evening together, after a very expensive

champagne dinner, he had suggested going on to a place called the Janzy d'Or. It never occurred to Roseen to wonder how he'd managed to discover so much of the town's night life after only a couple of days: she was enjoying his company far too much to bother about things like that.

The Janzy d'Or had turned out to be a single large, low room in the basement of a cobbled back street *estaminet*. It was hot, it was noisy, it was crowded; its smoke-filled air throbbed to the music of a Negro band playing Dixieland jazz; and she had loved it.

They came again the following night, staying till three in the morning; and the night after that Johnnie took her to another club, the Coquelicot, where he taught her a sensational new dance called the Fox Trot and held her so close in his arms on the dimly-lit floor that Roseen's head had spun with an exhilaration which left her breathless. The more she was with Johnnie, the more she liked him; and the more she liked him, the more she wanted to be with him. It was as simple as that.

They never met during the day. Going to bed so late now, Roseen was seldom awake before noon, and Johnnie's business affairs appeared to keep him fully occupied. What it was exactly that he did he never explained, beyond the occasional passing reference to deals and profits: Roseen gained the impression that he worked for himself, since his hours and activities were apparently of his own choosing, and because instead of returning to London as he'd originally intended, he was now proposing to stay in Deauville for a further few weeks 'to consolidate new contacts'.

Unusually for Roseen, she didn't ask questions; she was happy to accept whatever she was told, and added two and two together by way of her own conclusions. When Johnnie suggested that she might like to extend her own fortnight's holiday to keep him company, she'd accepted at once. No point in going back to Raby Street when she could be having the time of her life dancing away the night in the arms of a man as irresistibly attractive as this one.

Besides, he hadn't yet attempted to make love to her – hadn't even *kissed* her – and Roseen's pride in her own feminine sexual allure refused to let her leave until at least she'd proved to herself that Johnnie Driscoll was no different from any of the rest.

★

"Put your jewels and your glad rags on tomorrow," he'd said. "I'm taking you somewhere special – a best-bib-and-tucker affair. It's time you were introduced to something a little more sophisticated than night-clubs."

The 'somewhere special' had proved to be the Casino, and Johnnie was right about it being sophisticated: the glitter of its crystal chandeliers vied with the sparkle and wink of diamonds, and its *fin de siècle* décor of royal blue and gold reflected the opulence of Russian sable evening capes, satin-faced dinner jackets and Paris-designed gowns. In Deauville money was never out of fashion, nor ever out of season.

Roseen had taken her companion at his word and spent the afternoon choosing herself a new outfit at one of the larger costumiers. The money she'd brought with her from England was now virtually exhausted, but Johnnie had arranged for her to sign a draft for fifty pounds made out to his own credit, exchanging the money for her into francs. She had no idea what the price of the frock was that she eventually bought. French currency meant nothing to Roseen. All that mattered was that she wanted to look her most desirable, wanted Johnnie to feel proud of being seen with her; and the frock she'd chosen certainly did that. It was in mauve, with a low V-cut neckline in the style known as a 'glad neck' and it fitted like a glove to her hips, then fell in a series of knife pleats to just below her knees.

To finish it off, at the assistant's recommendation she'd treated herself to a pair of strap-front shoes with Louis heels and pointed toes, and a long necklace of purple glass beads; and with her hair tucked up inside a fashionable evening turban, she looked, as the assistant said, *très chic, très ravissante.*

Johnnie thought so, too. Roseen had never knowingly blushed in her life, but the admiring way in which his eyes lit up as he watched her descend the hotel staircase to meet him in the foyer that night made her go hot with pleasure.

231

"I say, Roseen, you're looking an absolute bobby-dazzler!" he exclaimed, coming forward to meet her at the bottom step. "I can see I'm going to have my work cut out this evening fending off admirers."

He gave her one of his disarming smiles as he took the coat from her arm and draped it round her shoulders before conducting her across the foyer to the revolving entrance doors. He himself was quite dashingly turned out in black evening suit, starched dicky and white bow-tie, and Roseen's small chin went up a fraction with pride as she pictured what a striking couple they must make.

Arriving at the Casino by taxi-cab, they had dinner together before going through to the gambling rooms. The air here held a warm, expensive drift of perfume and cigar-smoke, and the noise of conversation was subdued, all attention being on the green-cloth roulette tables and the serious business of winning. There was an undercurrent of nervous tension, expectancy, excitement, almost tangible in the atmosphere of the place.

It was all entirely new and unfamiliar to Roseen, a world away from the kind of social scene she was used to in Wolver-hampton; and for a while at first she felt slightly out of her depth as her normally assertive self-assurance deserted her. Fortunately Johnnie seemed not to notice; in fact for the first half-hour he was far too busy enthusiastically explaining to her the rules of roulette, its methods of play and various systems, and the meanings of *pair, impair, manque* and *passe*, and the black and red diamonds.

"It's purely a game of chance, you see, Roseen. Once you've put your stake on whichever of those thirty-seven numbers, and the croupier's spun the wheel, whether you win or lose depends entirely on the whim of Lady Luck."

For a moment he'd put his hand on her arm to indicate one of the tables closest to where a new game was about to start, and Roseen felt a *frisson* of desire for him, not only because he was so handsome, but because he was so completely at ease in this glittering, affluent, upper-class setting. She pretended to be absorbed in proceedings, but at the back of her mind she could hear a small voice very like Annie Sutton's telling her to be careful, because if she didn't watch out, before she knew where she was she'd be falling in love with Johnnie Driscoll.

Since he obviously knew so much about roulette, she was about to ask if he'd ever won a lot of money at the game – in fact she'd even got so far as to utter the first two words of her question – when her eye just then happened to fall on the young croupier bending forward at the table to start the wheel.

Her mouth stayed open.

"You were saying – ?" Johnnie prompted.

She looked at him. Then, hurriedly, "Oh – er, nothing. Nothing. It doesn't matter. Shall we – go and have another drink or something?"

She turned her back on the table. What rotten blinkin' luck, here of all places, to run into that young Frenchman she'd had in her room last week! It *was* him; she was certain.

She risked another quick glance over her shoulder.

"*Messieurs, faites vos jeux.*" He had spun the wheel into motion now and sent the ball bouncing and rattling against the black and red segments; and straightening from the table, looked directly across at her, as though he'd known all along that she was there.

Yes, it was him all right. And what's more, he'd recognised her too.

"Well, have another drink if you really must," Johnnie was saying. "But I thought you said you'd fancy a little flutter at the tables?"

"I might . . . in a bit."

The young croupier raised one eyebrow in silent, intimate greeting. Roseen pretended not to see.

"Come on, take me out, it's getting close in here. It's starting to give me one of my headaches," she said fretfully, putting a hand to her forehead.

"Damn' it, Roseen, you *are* a bore." Now it was Johnnie's turn to sound fractious. "I brought you here to enjoy yourself and have some fun. I might just as well have saved myself the trouble. If you want a drink, there's the bar out there – but you'll excuse me if I don't join you. I need to keep a clear head for playing."

Had she been with any other man, in any other place,

233

Roseen would have been tempted to let fly with the sort of response that didn't mince words. As it was, she walked off a few steps, limiting herself to an exaggerated sigh and a shrug.

"Look – " immediately recovering from his spate of annoyance, he tried to make amends. "Why don't I order you a gin sling to be brought over while you watch me play. Will that do? We'll go across to the side table near the window. It ought to be somewhat cooler for you there."

It would also be well away from any embarrassing, tell-tale eye-play from the French boy. Johnnie might not notice, but Roseen didn't want the awkwardness of being anywhere too close to someone she was trying to pretend she didn't know from Adam.

"OK, thanks," she said, switching off the headache for one of her sudden bright smiles; and in a gesture meant naïvely to impress, "Tell you what, Johnnie, if I give you the money, will you bet it for me, eh? And if you win we'll split the difference."

"I never play with other people's money."

"Oh – go on! It won't matter if you lose." Her smile turned to one of teasing. "I shan't hold it against you."

For a moment it looked as though he would still refuse; then, reluctantly, "Well . . . just this once, perhaps. How much do you want to stake? The minimum is ten francs."

Roseen dipped a hand into her bead-embroidered evening purse and produced two French bank notes, all she had with her.

"Is this enough?"

He took them from her with a cursory glance at their value. "It'll do. But I hope you'll remember what you promised."

"What was that?"

"That you won't hold it against me if I lose."

As it happened, though, he didn't lose. He played steadily and with concentration, placing his stakes decisively, his entire attention given to the game; and Roseen sat near him nursing her glass of gin, her eyes hardly leaving his face as she absorbed every little change of expression, every tightening of the lips as the wheel spun, every half-smile as the croupier announced a winning number.

Anyone watching her in turn would have discerned in her yearning gaze the look of a woman poised on the brink of that melting self-abandonment called love.

When finally he'd finished playing, Johnnie carried his winnings clutched in both hands like a jubilant small boy and emptied them into her lap.

"You've brought me luck, Roseen," he told her excitedly. "Now put that lot away in your purse, my girl, and come on – we're going to celebrate with a bottle of champagne at the Coquelicot!"

When she'd done as he bade her, he caught at her and pulled her to her feet, hugging her to him; and as they went out through the doors of the gambling room, arm in arm and laughing, Roseen saw they were being watched by her young French croupier.

Catching her eye, he smiled at her, and spread out his hands in a loser's gesture.

★

"I wish I could be there with you, wherever it is," said Gerard Lansby quietly, not looking at Flora but out across the lake. The two of them were standing together on the arched stone bridge which spanned an inlet of the rush-fringed waters, and the silence between them had been lengthening into minutes before Gerard finally broke it with his remark.

"You wish you could be where with me?" Flora glanced at him from beneath the rim of her felt cloche hat.

"Oh, I don't know . . . that private place you go to in your thoughts." He returned her glance with a smile, then leaned forward to rest his elbows on the parapet. "That place that's such a long long way from here . . . and from me."

He fell again to contemplating the view, his fair hair ruffled slightly by the breeze soughing across the water. The misty autumn sun was just sinking behind the trees on the further shore and its light shed a glow upon the scene, dyeing the surface of the lake a steely red and silhouetting in black the little bobbing shapes of moorhen and wild duck. Where the woodland crept down to encroach upon the water's edge, the pale trunks of silver birch were flushed a delicate rose by the sunset's fading warmth.

Flora waited some moments before responding to her companion's comment. It had seemed to hold a hint of criticism, of resentment. They had spent a lovely afternoon together walking in the woods around his farm at Brewood, and she didn't want the memory of this day to be spoilt at parting.

"We all have our little dream-worlds," she said at last, gently. "Perhaps we need them as an escape from reality."

"*This* is reality, Flora." Gerard nodded his head towards the scene about them. "So why not share it with me? Why leave me with the feeling that I may as well be alone here, that the person I'm with is absent somewhere else, probably preoccupied with other thoughts."

"I'm sorry if I gave you that impression." She tried not to sound too guilty, but it was perceptive of him to read so much of the truth into her silence. She *had* been preoccupied. The stillness of the woods, broken only by the patter of falling leaves and the sudden wing-clap of pigeons taking flight, had served to evoke a mood of nostalgia. Much as she enjoyed being with Gerard, it was no use her trying to make chatty, cheerful conversation about trivialities when her thoughts were turned inward upon themselves, remembering.

She had responded to Robert Wells's letter, the one written after Sidney's death – nothing too personal, simply an acknowledgement of his kindness in writing, and hoping that he and his family were well; that sort of thing. He had written again almost at once, lines so tender and beautiful that all the old poignant feelings of love for him had come rushing back into her heart, overwhelming her to such an extent that she'd been moved to act upon the impulse of its emotion and in turn send him a confession of all that he'd meant to her over the years.

Now, however, she was rather beginning to regret having written quite so intimately . . . wishing she'd been more prudent, allowed herself more time to consider the implication of her words. What was her affection for Robert, after all? Wasn't it simply an echo of something, a shadow-love, a memory of a stranger? His voice still spoke to her through the lines he wrote, but when she tried to recall his face it was like peering into a misted mirror and seeing only a blur.

She turned away from the lake-reflected sunset, fading now

to coral wisps against the ivory evening sky, and for a moment or two her eyes wandered over Gerard's profile. More and more frequently of late she'd caught herself looking at him like this and thinking how attractive he was.

"Please don't suppose I'm not appreciative of the time you've given up to spend with me this afternoon," she said; and she wanted suddenly to touch his arm, to hold him, feel the warmth of physical contact between them both. "If I haven't been very good company, forgive me. I'll try to be jollier next time."

"So long as there *is* a next time, Flora." He straightened up from the parapet and gave his attention to replacing his cap which he'd earlier removed. "Be careful you don't go away so far inside yourself that you forget to come back."

The lightness of his words belied his expression as he glanced at her.

"There are people who rather care for you, you know. Perhaps more than you realise. Try and remember that, won't you."

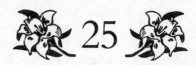

25

The Lansbys had farmed over at Brewood since the time of the Civil War, when Gerard's ancestor, being one of the Midlands county gentry who had sided with Cromwell, acquired the estate known as Cowpers – a former Royalist property – as reward for his support. Upon the Restoration of Charles II it seemed that he would be forced to relinquish all title to the land; but the bankrupt Crown was sorely in need of money, and a little opportune palm-greasing had resolved the matter expediently, if not entirely honourably. Cowpers had remained in Lansby ownership ever since.

Over the intervening years the estate had dwindled somewhat in size, but by the time Gerard inherited it there still remained several thousand acres, of which he farmed a few hundred, the rest being rented to tenant farmers.

But for the grace of God and the bad aim of a German sniper, the Lansby line might have ended at Ypres. Gerard was the last in direct descent, and until he took a wife the land had no heir. He was the only child of his parents' marriage, his father having broken his back in a hunting fall which rendered him incapable of further exercising his duties as husband: for the next twenty years until his death the elder Lansby had been confined to a wheelchair, paralysed, a man with all the endowments of intellect, class and wealth, dragging out his days with a cynical, bitter contempt for his useless body.

It was incumbent upon Gerard to marry: that was his duty, to ensure that the line continued, not only the Lansby blood but ownership of Cowpers. His father had drummed into him from adolescence this responsibility; and Gerard had accordingly obliged at twenty-one by getting engaged to the daughter of a neighbouring landowner. It was a match more of convenience than affection; and only his pride, not his heart, had been hurt when the young lady broke off their engagement some time later and scandalised the district by eloping with her father's under-gardener, an unprepossessing brute of a fellow with the muscles of an ox.

Gerard had solaced himself with a few fleeting affairs, and then, with the outbreak of the Great War, had followed his conscience and taken a commission in the Army. People said afterwards that he'd been blessed with a charmed life. Gerard himself always claimed, albeit facetiously, that heaven wasn't ready for him yet. He tended to be philosophical about his chances of survival, especially at Ypres, and that sniper's bullet which, luckily, had gone wide, was not the nearest he'd come to death; but perhaps it was some measure of the young man's character that it was the only time he'd been fully conscious of his escape.

He returned home to Brewood, to Cowpers; and to an altered world. His mother had died during the terrible flu epidemic which had ravaged the country hard on the heels of the war. Some of the farmworkers had gone away to fight and not come back – it was the same story everywhere – the land had been neglected, the estate run down, the flocks depleted. For the next couple of years Gerard had had his work cut out restoring his inheritance to something like a profitable concern. It was no time to look for a wife, even had he felt inclined.

That same luck, though, which had brought him safely through the war seemed to stick to him still and reward his efforts. By 1922 Cowpers had managed to get its head above financial waters, and Gerard was able to turn his mind a little more to friends and social life. Within a surprisingly short period he had acquired the reputation of a ladies' man – unfairly, perhaps, but the choice of female company was disproportionately large with so few eligible fellows in competition, and it was his joke that gallantry required him to pay equal attention to all so that none should feel neglected. The truth was that most of the ladies he met by introduction virtually fell over themselves in their eagerness to become Mrs Gerard Lansby and mistress of Cowpers; and nothing put a man off so much as being the pursued rather than pursuer in the game of romance. There was no sport in courting some young woman who made her ambitions instantly clear by cooing at him about marriage and babies and such. To whet his appetite what he had to have was the thrill of the chase, the gradual wearing down by tally-ho of something soft and sweetly pretty who would allow herself to be captured only after she'd given every indication of escape.

It was precisely this aspect which so attracted Gerard to Flora Hathaway.

If he were forced to put hand upon heart and be honest, he'd have to admit that she wasn't *quite* his sort, not physically. Usually what most appealed to him was a combination of fair hair and blue eyes and long slim legs, whereas Flora was dark and small and plumply comfortable. She had a sense of fun, however, which he liked, and a gentle femininity which made him protective towards her; and he respected her dignity too, as well as her intelligence. It was refreshing to be in the company of a young woman who was able to stimulate him intellectually while arousing in him feelings of tenderness for her vulnerability.

Added to this, Flora was wealthy enough in her own right not to chase after him for what he had; and too recently a widow yet to consider remarriage.

The strongest lure of all, though, was her detachment from their friendship – a detachment which wasn't aloofness or indifference, but as near as he could explain it to himself, an air of elusive preoccupation elsewhere. Sometimes, for example, when he was with her a look would come over her face as though she longed to hear some other voice than his, and at other times she would smile at him then at once glance away with an unconscious little sigh. The curious thing was, it had nothing to do with her late husband, Gerard was sure of that. Whenever she spoke of the departed Mr Hathaway her manner was entirely matter-of-fact.

In the beginning these occasional fits of abstraction had annoyed him enough to bruise his pride, and he'd caustically apologised for being too much of a bore; but now Flora's behaviour was starting to intrigue him, keep him guessing, make him wonder about her. And by allowing her thus to engage his thoughts Gerard broke one of his own cardinal rules: never to let a woman gain the advantage by occupying his attention in her absence.

For a man who had hitherto liked to keep his fancy free, it was proving a most unusual experience.

★

"If only Winifred could have come this evening," Jessy Venables said, and not for the first time, "it would've been absolutely topping – all of us here together again, exactly like the old days."

She tucked her hand more firmly into the crook of Flora's elbow and paused outside the double doors which led into the main assembly hall, raising herself on tiptoe to peer in through one of the porthole windows. Moseley College was giving a formal reception to mark the retirement of its principal, Dr John Rankin, and those former students who were members of the college's Alumni Society had been invited to attend. Already there was quite a jam in the corridors from arrivals queuing to discard fur evening stoles and capes and overcoats, and blocking the way with groups of noisy reunions as they recognised old faces from the past.

"Good Lord!" exclaimed Jessy, her nose still pressed to the window, "there's May Prothero! I never expected *her* to come, not all the way from Sussex. And see who it is she's with!"

Still keeping hold of Flora's arm, she pushed open the door and made her way into the hall in the direction of the elegant figure of the Honourable Mrs Courtenay Fytche, standing in conversation with a portly, red-faced young man. To judge by the slight yawn hovering about her lips, May was finding his company less than absorbing; and indeed the moment she espied Jessy and Flora she broke away towards them, her hands held out in greeting.

"*Darlings* – !"

Her voice had the slightly theatrical emphasis which Flora remembered.

"Darlings, how perfectly heavenly."

Marriage to Lord Buckland's younger son had polished her sophisticated manners to a hard gloss and there was exactly the right amount of condescension as she leaned a little forward and permitted them each in turn to kiss the air on either side of her cheek.

How too divine, thought Flora waspishly, trying not to meet Jessy's eye in case she gave herself away. When they were students together she'd always found the former May Prothero unbearably intimidating; but not now. Now she merely admired her for her style.

While Jessy monopolised the conversation, rushing in at once with a dozen questions, Flora found herself with the red-faced man May had just discarded. She'd recognised him instantly, even without his Lloyd George moustache, as Reggie Bellamy, a college friend of Sidney's; the same Reggie who had once broken Winifred Unsworth's heart by partnering Muriel Rowley at tennis.

"I say – by Jove!" he declared, seizing her hand and conveying it to his wet lips in a clumsy gesture of gallantry. "If it isn't the adorable little Flora, and grown lovelier than memory e'er served me. My word, but you're a vision worth beholding, m'dear!" There was the slight smell of alcohol on his breath as he bent his head towards her and in a hoarse whisper added, "Sorrow, if I may say, has lent you a luminous dignity."

She released herself with a smile. "How very kind of you, Reggie." At close quarters she could see the unnatural flush of his cheeks which gave him such a florid appearance. He had always drunk more than was good for him, and now the indulgence was beginning to show.

"You're looking remarkably well yourself," she added in turn, lying tactfully. Then, "There's quite a crush here this evening, isn't there. Have you seen many we know?"

Before he could answer, Jessy interrupted to speak to him and ask how he was, leaving Flora to an exchange of conversation with May; and by the time they'd each listened politely to the other's small talk Reggie had spotted someone else among the crowd and temporarily deserted them.

"Winifred should thank the Lord for Muriel Rowley," Jessy said, watching him go. "D'you realise, if it hadn't been for a game of tennis, she might have found herself married to that crashingly awful bore."

"Hardly a fate worse than what she's doing now," May remarked, fitting a cigarette into a long, carved-ivory holder. "Living in a snake-infested hut in the African jungle. Teaching Scripture to a lot of barbarous natives. Not *my* idea of bliss, darlings."

She glanced about her indifferently, as though waiting for someone to attend on her with a light.

Jessy started to say something in defence of Winifred. Whatever it was, Flora herself didn't hear. At that very second a small gap had opened near the hall doors. She looked across between the shifting heads – and the next moment her heart had been sent leaping wildly into her throat.

The suddenness of it shocked her into rigidity. It was quite the most extraordinary sensation. The noise around her seemed to be receding to a great distance, and she felt faint yet at the same time intensely alive, as though each nerve were keyed to a vibrant trembling pitch.

The whole thing lasted only a few seconds. It was a dream; but it was real. And then her heart began to beat again in hard quick thuds, and the sounds returned, rushing back upon her in a tide of laughter and voices.

It was him.

It was Robert Wells.

He was here.

Here!

Flora couldn't believe it. He wasn't a member of the Alumni Society. Why hadn't he written to tell her he'd be coming? What was he doing? Why hadn't he given her any warning? A kind of panic seized upon her, and she wanted to turn and run, get away before he saw her there. It wasn't fair; she wasn't ready, wasn't prepared to meet him again.

Oh God!

Then Jessy had her by the elbow and was saying, "Flora, just look who Reggie's bringing over to join us!"

★

It was like seeing again a face only half-remembered from a faded photograph. A stranger's face, almost. Robert had

243

changed, grown older, and the man who had lived in Flora's heart and mind all these years only vaguely resembled him. She had forgotten so much, the way his thick, dark wavy hair fell forward over his forehead, the exact shade of brown of his eyes, the shape of his mouth . . . to look at him now was a rediscovery.

The passage of time had left its mark on him, and so had the war. He walked with a slight limp, a legacy of Imbros, and there was the thin white line of a scar from cheek to temple. Flora ached to reach out and touch it, stroke away the hurt; but for ten minutes now all she'd been able to do was stand apart in a silent daze and listen while the others made inane conversation, chit-chatting on about themselves as though that were the most absorbing topic in the world.

Every so often Robert would glance at her, and she could feel her heart turn over again, the colour warm her cheek, and a shiver, half-fear half-happiness, curl down her spine.

At last he managed to edge her away. People were starting to drift in the direction of the dining hall where a cold buffet was being served, and no one appeared to notice that they'd lingered behind.

"Eight years and four months," he said quietly under his breath. "It's been a long time, my darling."

"Yes . . . a long time. So much has changed."

"But not our affection. You told me that in your wonderful letter."

"Oh, the letter –" Flora had to look away from the intensity of his gaze. That spur-of-the-moment letter she had sent, pouring out her loneliness of feeling, all the pent up memories of her love.

"I shouldn't have sent it." She forced herself to say the words. Now that they were alone together she was over-whelmed by a sense of unrealness, as though this whole encounter were a dream, a delusion. "I should never have written it."

Pain showed for a moment in his face, then was gone again. He seemed unnaturally calm. "All the same, I'm glad you did. For both our sakes. You *needed* to write it."

"Did I – oh, did I, Robert? Wouldn't it have been fairer had I left well alone?"

"Fairer to whom?"

"To your wife and family, I suppose." She was demanding the impossible of herself, trying so hard to be sensible and self-controlled when inside something was crying out to be released, all the emotion she'd harboured, all the longing she'd suppressed. "Did you – did you come here this evening because of what I said?"

"Of course. I had to. What did you expect, my sweet? Wasn't this what you wanted? I managed to wangle an invitation from the college – it seemed the perfect opportunity. I knew you'd be present tonight."

"How?"

"Reggie Bellamy."

"He told you?"

"He let it slip. I suspect he's rather got his eye on you. Never mind that, though – I'd already planned to visit the Midlands and try to see you. I couldn't keep away any longer, not once I knew how much you cared."

"Robert – "

"No, listen." His voice took on a sudden urgency. "We love one another, *love* one another, Flora. We share something extraordinarily beautiful that can't be denied, however much distance we've tried to keep between us all these years. Neither distance nor time can ever alter our feelings – you know that as well as I do."

The same tired old argument sprang to answer for her. "Yes, but we must accept that there's nothing we can do about it. Nothing! You have Helen and the children – "

"That's one of the things we have to talk about. That's why I'm here."

"To discuss Helen?"

"To discuss *us*, my darling. I'm not prepared any longer to go on letting things drift and wasting both our lives."

Flora looked about her helplessly. Her feelings were in such confusion, so many conflicting emotions buffeting her – happiness, wonderment, guilt, nervousness, bewilderment, tangled up inside; and what made it ten times worse, everyone around was cheerful and relaxed, making normal friendly conversation with each other, and she must try to control

245

herself sufficiently to put on this facade so that none of them should guess . . .

Oh, what if she hadn't allowed the impulses of her heart to overrule her head and spur her into writing that letter of confession! Robert would never have been tempted to see her – he'd have stayed far away with his family in Freshwater, and their love remained for ever undisturbed, woven into the background pattern of their lives, an integral part but not the most important.

And yet – and yet she was glad he was here. Yes, *glad*. After so long, actually to be with him again, and know that he was alive and real, not a figment of her imagination – it seemed almost unbelievable.

He was watching her closely, his eyes never leaving her face, looking at her as though he could never have enough of the sight, as though he needed to imprint upon his mind every detail of her features.

She made an effort to compose herself.

"I suppose . . . we really ought to go and join the others," she said breathlessly, and that little tremor of the voice betrayed her.

"They can wait another minute. Listen," he touched her arm, and she was intensely aware of the warmth of his fingers through the thin silk of her sleeve. "I'm staying at a hotel on the Edgbaston Road. Will you have dinner with me there? There's so much needs saying that can only be said in private. I'll speak to you on the telephone tomorrow and we'll arrange an evening."

He smiled at her in just the way he used to in the days of their first acquaintance, the days of their innocence; and Flora knew then why it was that she had loved him for so long. Why she hadn't the strength nor the will to refuse his invitation.

He offered her no choice.

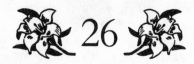 26

Johnnie Driscoll wasn't his real name. That was as phoney as his accent and the old school tie he wore. The police in London knew him as Charles Fereday; but the name under which he'd actually been born hadn't been used for over a dozen years and belonged now to the detritus of his past. No one would have recognised in the suavely sophisticated Mr Driscoll the runny-nosed little boy from Bermondsey whose father was an out-of-work drunkard and whose mother sold cockles from a pail in the street.

That little boy had finally passed out of Johnnie's life just before the Great War. In his stead appeared Charles Fereday, product of hard schooling as gigolo to a succession of wealthy middle-aged matrons who had rounded the rough edges of his manners and his speech and taught him to ape the gentleman in exchange for his handsome young body in their beds.

It wasn't long before the gigolo had turned confidence-trickster, gambler and petty thief; and in 1920 had narrowly evaded arrest by decamping to the Continent, living on his wits and his winnings among the affluent British champagne set of Biarritz. Within a year, implicated in a rather unpleasant suicide, Charles Fereday vanished in turn, to suffer a change of identity and to resurface some while later in Monte Carlo as Johnnie Driscoll, professional roulette player.

Women adored him, especially the bored and the lonely who could afford to solace themselves for the theft of their youth and their husbands' attention by buying the flattery of his company. Johnnie gave them value for money: he had the golden tongue of a good liar, and that rare ability to make each female he was with feel not only beautiful but the most desirable creature in the world; and as long as the bedroom lights were off, he could make love so well to order that he grew almost bored hearing women tell him he was the best, the most fantastic, they'd ever been with.

The odd thing about Johnnie was that he liked gambling far better than making love. It satisfied him more in every way. Winning money was doing something entirely for oneself, pitting expertise and wits against the system; whereas sex was a thing any brainless fool could enjoy. It wasn't that he disliked women in any way. He'd made a livelihood out of providing them with a service, after all. No, it was just that he had no respect for them, especially the over-painted ones who flaunted themselves with their money and their jewels and their swank, expecting him to be their performing poodle.

He had learnt the trick of dissembling, however. If a woman could afford to finance his gambling habits and keep him in Savile Row suits, crocodile-leather shoes and gold cigarette cases, who was he to cavil at her fading, ageing charms. And if she started complaining about his expenses, well, there were plenty of other rich old trout in the sea; and some not so old, either.

The night he came across Roseen Kelly in the bar of the Hotel Océanique, Johnnie had just extricated himself profitably from a short-lived affair in Paris, and had come to Deauville to enjoy the fruits of his labour at the Casino. He wasn't bothered about female company. The gambling was more important. Something about Roseen, though, had taken his attention sufficiently to prompt his approaching her.

A few minutes' conversation told him all he needed to know: she was unattached, she had money, and though she wasn't stupid, she was vain. She was also dirt common, liked her drink, and had an eye for the men.

Johnnie had decided to amuse himself.

For a girl who'd acquired her sense of survival in the back streets of the Midlands, it was extraordinary how easily she'd played into his hands. He was disappointed, in fact, to find her so gullible. She gave him cash for gambling – as much as he needed – and bought him tasteless presents; and when he'd suggested they travel to Monte Carlo for a week at the tables there, it had taken only a kiss and a squeeze to make her say yes.

She was hot for him, all right. He could feel the desire coming off her in waves when they danced together, see it in her eyes when she looked at him. Not that he wouldn't have minded taking her to bed – lamb would make a palatable change after so much mutton – but sex was his trump card, to be played only in the last resort should her generosity require some encouragement. After all, every well had its bottom, as his father used to say, and she'd already given him a nice little contribution.

Unfortunately the run of luck which had smiled upon Johnnie in Deauville seemed to evaporate into the blue in Monte Carlo and he started losing heavily, a thing he hated because it dented his self-esteem as well as his wallet. To recoup his losses he borrowed again from Roseen, and even won back fifty pounds; but the dice stayed obstinately against him, and every further loss saw him gambling rashly and ever more recklessly to try and regain his winning form. On the final evening he staked every last franc he could raise.

If he'd won, he would have broken the bank.

As it was, he took Roseen back to their hotel and made love to her.

★

"What d'you mean, they won't let you have any more?" He stared at her face reflected behind him in the dressing-table mirror. "Did you see the bank manager? Did *he* tell you that?"

Roseen lit a cigarette from the case on the bedside table. "He said he had no authorisation, or something. Don't ask me what he was on about. I explained just how you told me, about the arrangement with the bank in Deauville. Tight-fisted old bugger said it didn't make a ha'p'orth of difference."

Johnnie finished grooming his hair and threw the brushes aside as he turned from the mirror.

"You *have* got the funds in your account to meet that cheque, I suppose?"

"I don't know. I think so."

"You *think* so! Can't you remember? You're very careless with your money, Roseen."

The remark was cruel as well as unfair, and it stung her.

"Hark who's calling the kettle black! For a blinkin' ruddy genius at winning, you made a fair old job of kissing goodbye to that fifty quid I lent you last week – *and* the two hundred you had off me in Deauville. If that's not carelessness I don't know what is."

"You'll get it all back, I told you. Damn' it, my luck's bound to change. All I need is the stake for a few more games."

"And in the meantime we've got to pay for this hotel room," Roseen reminded him through a mouthful of cigarette smoke.

When Johnnie first revealed that he was a professional gambler, it had seemed such a glamorous and exciting thing to be – like an actor in a motion-picture story. She felt as though she were being caught up in some wonderfully crazy adventure – the night-clubs, the champagne, the expensive lifestyle, the Casino; together with falling in love, it had all gone whirling to her head to divorce her from reality.

She would have given Johnnie Driscoll anything he asked for, even the moon itself if she could; so what was a few hundred pounds . . .

Even now, the fact that he'd managed to lose everything didn't really bother her that much; not until this morning, when she'd gone down to the Monte Carlo branch of Lloyds Bank to arrange another withdrawal, only to be informed after being kept half an hour that a stop had been put on her account. Roseen hadn't the faintest idea what a 'stop' was, but it sounded pretty sinister. She couldn't have gone through Uncle George Dennison's thousand pounds that fast, could she?

Maybe she could, though. She'd been spending her money like water. Thinking about it on the way back to the hotel, she tried totting up in her head how much she'd splashed out these last months, and on what – her car, of course; things for the house, clothes, jewellery, the cost of her holiday, presents for Johnnie; and on top of all that the loans she'd been making him.

It came to quite a lot.

"The bank manager said I ought to go and see the council, whatever that is," she said, watching her lover's face as he lit a match to his own cigarette. "He said they might let me have some money for the fare back to England."

"It's the Consul," he told her shortly. "Not the council. The British Consul. And I'd stay the hell away from there if I were you."

"Why?"

Because I don't want the name of Johnnie Driscoll being brought to their attention, he told himself.

"Because they're more than likely to detain you and ask a lot of awkward questions. Look, if you're so worried about things – well, go and pawn some of your jewellery, why don't you. That ought to make enough to see us clear."

"Pawn my jewellery – ?" Roseen's voice went up on a disbelieving note. "Why the flippin' heck should I? What's wrong with taking something of your flippin' own down the pop shop? It was *you* got us into this mess, Johnnie. Blowed if it's up to me to bail you out!"

"Oh, for God's sake – " He glared at her as though he were about to lose his temper. What a damn' stupid thing to do, saddle himself with some common little tart without first making watertight sure she could afford to up the ante as required.

He controlled himself with an effort, drawing hard on his cigarette. Argument and accusation would get neither of them anywhere.

After a second he went on in a more conciliatory tone, "Darling, I know I'm responsible for this temporary little embarrassment. If I'm angry, it's with myself, not you. I simply can't fathom out what's gone wrong with my method of play – it's *never* failed before, never. So . . . won't you be a sweet pet and do as suggested? Please?"

Roseen was too much in love, otherwise she might have told him to go and take a running jump out of the window. If she counted the price of her folly, Johnnie had cost her something like three hundred pounds – which was a very expensive love affair.

She wanted him so badly, that was the trouble; wanted his

hands, his lips, his body, his handsome face above her in the dawnlight as he roused her to greater heights of ecstasy than she'd ever known. She had guessed they'd be good together – he'd kept her waiting for it till the frustration was driving her mad – but not until the first night they'd made love did she realise she'd met her sexual match at last.

Johnnie Driscoll was simply the best man a woman could ever want in bed; and Roseen had a very healthy, very demanding appetite.

He must have read these thoughts, because a smile appeared, and pitching his half-smoked cigarette casually into the wash-basin, he came over to her. He hadn't long been out of bed – Roseen had left him sleeping while she went out to the bank – and was wearing only a pair of cream flannel trousers.

"Be a good girl for Johnnie – mm?" Running his hand over his muscular chest he looked at her in a way that enkindled the sudden quick spark of desire. "All I want is enough for a decent stake, and we're home and dry. That ring of yours is all you'd need to pawn."

She knew which one he meant. The emerald and diamond ring Aubrey Podmore had given her.

Roseen's sexual hunger fought with the more practical considerations of common sense. If she pawned that ring and gave Johnny the money, what guarantee did she have of ever seeing it again? He was on a losing streak at the moment: he could go on losing for another week, another month, and keep coming back to her holding out his hand for more every time.

Oh, but she *wanted* him! She could feel the throbbing warmth of arousal starting up inside as she stared at his mouth and imagined it moistly, gently, caressing her body's most sensitive places.

"No, not that ring – " she said, a little breathlessly, backing away from temptation. "What about your cigarette case and lighter? They're solid gold, they'd fetch more."

Johnnie's eyes went cold.

"I thought you loved me, Roseen."

"I do love you!"

"You have an odd way of showing it."

"No more than you. Haven't I given you enough already?"

"And haven't I given *you* enough in return?"

He made his innuendo clear by reaching for her suddenly and pulling her into his arms, one hand going round to snatch her head back sharply by the hair so that her face was tilted only an inch from his own.

When he kissed her there was no tenderness or affection, only the desire to bruise and hurt.

Roseen struggled violently to free herself. Despite the pain, there was a pleasure in his cruelty which she'd never felt before with any man, and it shocked as well as startled her.

She jerked her head away.

"You bastard, Johnnie," she said, and the smile she gave him bared her teeth. "You'll say sorry for that."

He didn't answer, but his face wore the same smile.

Releasing her hair, he caught at her by the collar of her blouse and deliberately ripped it open down the front, tearing the buttons from the material. Then, thrusting his hand inside, he began squeezing her breast, fingers kneading hard into the soft flesh.

This was developing into a dangerous game, a sexual foreplay that took its enjoyment from aggression and the urge to inflict pain.

In retaliation she made to claw at Johnnie's cheeks with her nails, catching him slightly – not enough to draw blood, but enough to score the skin and make him loose her.

"Bitch," he grinned.

Dodging under his arm, she ran round the bed and seized up one of his discarded hairbrushes, hurling it at him; and followed this with whatever came within reach – scent bottles, ornaments, shoes, coat hangers, cushions.

He fended them off, ducking from side to side and laughing in malicious glee at the damage she was causing, taunting her to aim better.

"I'll show you – " Roseen panted.

The dressing-table stool was just behind her. She grabbed it up, holding it over her head; and then deliberately threw it with all her strength. Johnnie raised an arm as it came sailing straight towards him, and gave a shout of pain when it caught him full on the elbow.

"Right – you're going to pay for that, my lady!"

He flung himself full-length across the bed and clutched her by the torn edge of her blouse, roughly pulling her over struggling, kicking and thrashing about in an effort to beat him off. Roseen was a strong young woman, and this aided her resistance; but Johnnie had her down on her back on the bed without much trouble, holding her there with bruising force while he knelt on top of her, thighs straddling her heaving body.

Before she could grab at his hands to defend herself, he had her by the hair again and gave her several quite vicious slaps across the face, hard enough to stun her for a second.

"Bitch," he repeated, almost pleasantly, still smiling. "Now we'll see how much you really love me."

What happened next was the closest experience Roseen had ever had of rape. Johnnie was brutal, callously brutal, turning what should have been the most intimate expression of pleasure into a prolonged endurance of assault, plunging himself into her with such aggressive ferocity that she swore every obscenity she could think of to make him stop. When that failed to work, she gritted her teeth and fought him hurt for hurt, raking his back and shoulders with her nails until the blood ran.

It only served to excite him the more. Sweat dripped from him on to her face, into her eyes; and gradually, in spite of his savagery, Roseen felt her body starting to respond in an equally brutal, animal kind of fashion – not with the slow, sweet ecstasy of love-making, but with a pain that seemed sexual satisfaction in itself.

Wrestling, punching, scratching, biting, they fought one another to exhaustion; and when finally they'd expended themselves in the satiation of their violence, they fell apart on the bed like two drunkards, heads lolling, mouths panting open, hardly able to move.

Long minutes went by. Monte Carlo's lunchtime noises drifted up from the streets below in a background of muted sound.

After what seemed an eternity, Roseen groaned and stirred, trying to lever herself up on her elbows. The room looked as though a bomb had hit it . . . precisely how she was starting to feel herself.

She glanced at Johnnie. There was blood all over the sheets and over his body.

She licked a split lip. "What the blinkin' hell was all that about," she said sullenly.

He groaned in turn and rolled over. "A lesson. Teach you not to say no."

"I'm still not pawning my emerald ring."

There was silence for a few moments before he began to laugh, a cynical sound which held no trace of humour. He squinted up at her and shook his head as though in admiration; then, reaching out an arm to the bedside table for his gold case, took two cigarettes, lighting them together, and gave one to Roseen, saying, "All right. You win. We'll forget about the pawnbroker. We'll try something else instead."

"What sort of something else?"

"You'll see, my pet. I'll show you. And who knows, with your appetite you might even enjoy it."

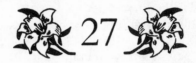

27

Mussolini.

The newspapers wouldn't let you get away from the name. Every time you looked at one, there it was, in bold black letters all over the front page. Benito Mussolini. *Il Duce.*

Roseen had nothing else to do with herself at the moment but glance through newspapers; and though she was far more interested in the fashion pictures and cinema celebrities, this Signor Mussolini was too much the centre of attention to be ignored, even by her.

Apparently there had been some big political gathering in Naples a week ago, on October 24th, 1922, of Mussolini's strong-arm supporters. *Squadre d'Azione*, they were called. Action squads. From Naples they'd marched all the way to Rome to take over the government, and the upshot was that the Italian king had been forced to make Mussolini his Prime Minister.

Roseen didn't understand, and couldn't care less, what it was all about. Politics bored her. The only thing which really took her attention were the photographs showing a lot of handsome Italians in black shirts waving their fists in the air. She had all the time in the world to pore over them: there was little else to do while sitting around in the foyer of the Hotel Georgic waiting for what Johnnie called 'a nibble'.

He had chosen the Georgic because it was one of Monte Carlo's busier, more popular hotels and had a quick exchange of guests, a mixture of visitors and commercial travellers. The ruse he proposed was simple. Using Roseen as a decoy, he would wait until she had lured one of the unattached gentlemen guests into the lounge bar, and having ascertained their room number, would then calmly go upstairs and pick the door lock . . .

He had played this game before, in London. He knew the risks. He enjoyed the challenge, the tension, the steel-cold nerve. It was like gambling; it made him feel *alive*.

"But it's criminal, that is!" Roseen had protested when he'd first outlined his plan. "It's thieving. What if we get ourselves caught?"

"We won't get caught, not if we're careful. Listen, the whole thing's so fantastically easy – "

All she had to do was dress herself up in her best and most expensive, and sit with a newspaper in the hotel foyer. If approached by any of the staff, she should say she was waiting for someone. Sooner or later along would come a chap on his own and give her the eye; and if he looked as though he were worth a bob or two, she should show herself interested. Over a drink together in the bar she'd make a point of letting him learn she was staying there by herself at the hotel.

"But how will that help?" Roseen had wanted to know.

"Use your head, my darling. Nine times out of ten he'll ask you for your room number. You won't tell him, of course. Why should you? So he'll tell you his."

"How do you know he will?"

"Because they nearly always do. Why do you think he's bothered to pick you up in the first place. He's looking for female company, isn't he."

"You mean he'll think I'm on the game, a tart or something?"

"Oh, come on, Roseen – where's your imagination. A well-dressed young lady in a reputable hotel?"

"But I don't speak any French. I'll stick out like some ruddy sore thumb."

"No you won't, not in Monte Carlo."

She had swallowed Johnnie's bait, hook and line down to the sinker, allowing herself to be blinded to the fact that he was using her in the most unscrupulous manner. Had she been less sexually infatuated, less in love, she might have asked many more questions before agreeing to become an accessory to theft. She had done enough pilfering as a child

257

– it wasn't that which worried her; her concern was all for avoiding detection, and how on earth she was going to extricate herself from trouble should the gentleman insist on more than just a drink.

Johnnie reassured her that it would be all right as long as she kept her head, and patiently rehearsed her in her role. Having obtained the room number, what she had to do next was excuse herself for a moment to go and powder her nose. By this time, he himself would be waiting outside in the foyer but on no account must she betray the fact that they knew one another. The entire success of the operation hinged upon that. As she passed she must drop a handkerchief or glove, he would courteously retrieve it – and in thanking him she'd pass on the information.

That was all.

Johnnie would do the rest.

"How long d'you think you'll need?" Roseen asked anxiously.

"Give me fifteen minutes. Just time enough for you and your friend to enjoy another little chin-wag in the bar."

"And then what do I do?"

He grinned. "You'll think of something."

"But supposing I can't –?"

"Oh, don't be a toot, Roseen. You were meant to be waiting for friends, remember? Well, lo and behold, suddenly there they are out in the foyer, and really, so sorry and all that, but you have to dash away now," he mimed exaggerated apology, "so thanks awfully for the drink, another time, perhaps – "

It sounded simple, the way Johnnie enacted it; but the real thing hadn't proved quite as straightforward. For a start, Roseen's first 'encounter' spoke such appallingly bad English that she couldn't understand him, and the second – who claimed to be a millionaire – had had nothing in his room worth stealing.

To avoid any suspicion they moved their operations to another hotel, La Barcarole near the Lido, and it was back to looking at Signor Mussolini. Here they had better luck, though; or perhaps Roseen was gaining confidence with practice, because the gentleman she found for Johnnie this time provided such rich pickings that it seemed the wisest course of action to decamp from Monte Carlo ahead of the hue and cry, and return once more to Deauville.

Once back, they took rooms in separate hotels – best to play safe by not being seen together, said Johnnie. Anyway, it would only be for a little while (when Roseen protested) – as soon as he'd won enough to pay what he owed they'd leave France together, the two of them, and go home to England. And then – and then, well, maybe he'd think about settling down and finding himself some proper, regular employment. In the motor-car trade, perhaps. A job with a bit of class.

Roseen's hopes had taken off on wings of fancy upon hearing this, and she started indulging herself in day dreams, imagining it wouldn't be long now before Johnnie did the decent and showed his gratitude by putting an engagement ring on her finger. It seemed the likeliest outcome – didn't it? – to their relationship. Oh, he could be cold and even cruel at times; but when he was loving it was *wonderful*, and because she wanted so much to convince herself, she clutched at straws and closed her mind to the little voice of doubt which whispered that he might be using her.

Once they were home, they could set up together in Raby Street . . . she'd be Mrs Johnnie Driscoll . . . he needed her, he did, to share his life and help him make a go of things . . .

That dream had lasted just forty-eight hours; the time it took Johnnie to double his winnings at the Deauville Casino, and then because he was feeling so lucky, push that luck too far and lose everything again on a single throw of the dice.

He didn't even have the grace to apologise when they met much later that evening at Le Coquelicot night-club. Fuelled by the amount of gin she'd had to drink while waiting there, Roseen showed her disbelief with the sharp edge of her tongue, letting temper take the place of love as the freshly-painted vision of her future evaporated into disillusionment. To add insult to the injury to her pride, when she asked what bright idea he proposed coming up with this time, he had the gall to suggest they could always 'pull the same trick' used in Monte Carlo.

Her response was to round on him furiously, accusing him

of being a cheat, a spendthrift, a liar, and whatever other unflattering epithet anger could throw at him. What followed was an argument so acrimoniously violent that people at nearby tables halted their own conversation to enjoy the rumpus.

"You can go to blazes!" Johnnie had shouted finally, slamming back his chair to get from the table. "I'm sick of you. I'll be a damn' sight better off without you!"

Roseen didn't attempt to follow him when he left. She sat in Le Coquelicot crying inconsolably into her gin until the night-club closed, and then, maudlin drunk, wandered the darkened streets of Deauville shouting up at the shuttered windows what she thought of men and the whole bloody world in general. Finally she'd collapsed in the doorway of a church; and the priest, coming to open for early morning Mass, found her there, a piece of human flotsam cast up by the breaking dawn upon his step.

He had offered her coffee and the spartan comfort of his presbytery before finding someone to see her back to her hotel; and in the cold, pitiless light of a new day Roseen had looked at herself in the mirror of her room and for a moment seen reflected there the blowsy, drink-ruined features of her mother.

The sight was enough to sober her.

Nor was that all. Johnnie Driscoll had left a note at the reception desk. No thank you; no goodbye. Just an IOU for three hundred pounds.

It was the last she was ever to hear from him.

★

"Well, well, well," said Annie Sutton, standing there outside on the wet pavement, dressed to the nines in a very expensive fur coat. "So it's true what I heard. You're back from your travels at last."

Not waiting for Roseen to invite her in, she pushed past through the door on a cloud of gardenia scent, and giving the coat sleeves a brush to get rid of the raindrops, went on, "They told me at the Posada you'd been seen around. I thought I'd come and pay you a call, ask how you was, like."

"For old times sake?" Roseen responded hostilely. She and

Annie hadn't set eyes on one another for over a year – the last time they'd met, Annie had made some poisonous remark about her morals – and she wasn't particularly pleased to see her now, not in the mood she was feeling. "Or have you just come for a good nose round, is that it."

Annie didn't appear to take any offence.

"Haven't you got a fire going? It's perishin' cold in here," she observed, looking about the room in a patronising manner, and letting her eye dwell on the bits and pieces of ornaments Roseen had bought.

"There's one in the kitchen – I suppose I better ask you through now you're here."

"I suppose you had."

"And I suppose you want a cup of tea," Roseen went on after they'd gone into the back room and she'd pulled the curtain across the door to stop the draught.

"That'd be nice, ta."

She didn't offer to take Annie's coat, and Annie didn't offer to remove it. Instead her visitor went and sat herself by the glowing range in the high-backed Windsor chair old Connie had always used, and glancing at Roseen, commented mildly, "That gadding about in France ain't done you much good, by the look on you. Didn't you get much sun?"

"They don't have sun this time of year."

"What you want to go for, then? You could've saved yourself the money and gone off to Blackpool instead."

Roseen didn't choose to answer.

" 'Course," the other went on, watching her light the gas for a kettle of water, "I didn't expect no letter nor nothing like that, but as I said to Aubrey, well, you'd ha' thought she'd remember to send us a post-card at least."

"Aubrey – ?" Roseen stopped in the act of reaching for the tea caddy, and looked round. "Aubrey Podmore?"

Annie smirked, patting a hand to her brassy blonde hair. "Oh, I forgot. You ain't heard, have you – about me and him, I mean."

"Heard what?"

"He's asked me to marry him, has Mr Podmore. We got our engagement notice put in the *Express and Star* while you was away."

The news took Roseen completely by surprise. Annie had called round to Aubrey Podmore's studio in Berry Street a few times while she'd been living there as his mistress, but the two had never seemed especially friendly with one another. In fact from what she could recall, Annie had been unpleasantly catty about her taking up with him in the first place.

"How long's this been going on, then?" she enquired, trying to put the right amount of indifference into her voice as she reached to open the cupboard for cups and saucers.

"Oh . . . since you walked out on him. He took it ever so bad in the beginning, he did. I had a job cheering him up, I can tell you. But after a bit – well, we started getting fond o' one another and it seemed daft, me living in lodgings, when he needed somebody there wi' him to see to his meals and the like – you know, somebody to do his bits o' shopping and his washing and keep the poor lonely old soul company of an evening."

Annie made herself sound like a charitable institution, a cross between Florence Nightingale and Snow White. No wonder she could afford to come here throwing her airs about: with an eye to the main chance, she'd wormed her way into Aubrey Podmore's affections by playing upon his loneliness and hurt, representing herself as a tender-hearted, understanding female who wanted nothing more from life than to share it with a gentleman who'd love and cherish her.

Roseen could see it all.

"Well," she said sarcastically, "I suppose I ought to congratulate you, Annie Sutton. You was never the one to miss a trick, I'll say that."

"I know which side my bread's buttered. And what's more – " the other went through the motions of drawing off her gloves, "you don't get this sort o' thing scrimping and scratting around after ha'pennies."

She held up a hand for Roseen to look at. The firelight caught the stone of a ring on her left finger, making it wink.

"Sapphire, that is. Sapphire and diamonds. He bought it me for our engagement, said it matched the colour o' my eyes. He's ever so kind that way, is Aubrey, ever so generous."

Roseen's mouth turned down at the corners. He'd said

exactly the same words to her when he'd given her the emerald. She could remember the moment as clearly as anything; remember the thrill of wearing something so beautiful. She had loved that ring. It had broken her heart to have to sell it, but she needed the money to pay her hotel bill in Deauville and to buy herself a ticket back to England . . .

"He bought you the coat as well, did he?" She couldn't resist the question even though she knew the answer. It was like turning the screw of her own irritation.

Annie stroked the soft fur and snuggled herself inside it. "What d'you think? He saw it in the window o' that place in Lichfield Street and he said I could have it for my birthday if I wanted."

"I didn't think your birthday was till April."

"It ain't."

There was another smirk, so self-satisfied that Roseen felt like throwing the kettle of boiling water all over the smug expression. *She* could have had a fur coat if she'd wanted – Aubrey Podmore had been so besotted with love for her he was like putty in her hands, he'd have given her anything. But she'd never asked him for a flippin' fur coat, had she . . .

For a moment there was a sharp prickle of jealousy.

She poured the water into the teapot and said in a couldn't-care-less tone of voice, "When you getting married, then, you and him?"

"Oh, some time in the spring. We ain't quite decided on the day, but it'll have to be at St George's o' course – Aubrey wants it done proper. Only the best for us, our Annie, he says. And then we're going to have a week away somewhere nice. Bournemouth, p'raps. I've always fancied Bourne-mouth, haven't you?"

Roseen said nothing. In her mind she was asking herself the 'what if' question: what if it was *her* getting married . . . what if she hadn't walked out on old Podmore when she had . . . what if she'd decided to stop with him instead. She wouldn't have gone traipsing off by herself to France . . . she wouldn't have met Johnnie Driscoll . . . wouldn't have lost all her money . . . wouldn't have got in the mess she was now.

And *what* a mess!

Mechanically she started stirring the tea in the pot, hardly listening to what Annie was saying next. She could have made a complaint to the police, of course, about Johnnie going off and leaving her stuck in the lurch; but she was too scared they'd find out about him, about what they'd been up to together in Monte Carlo. So she'd come back home to Raby Street, putting a brave face on things for the neighbours' sake and pretending she'd had a lovely, wonderful time.

Thank God, at least she'd still got a roof above her head, and a door she could shut on the world.

Suddenly she stopped stirring. The spoon fell with a little clatter from her fingers.

"Roseen – ?"

Halted in mid-flow by the sound, Annie interrupted herself to twist in the chair to look at her.

"Roseen, you feeling all right? Here – you've gone ever so pale, you have."

"I'm . . . I'm OK."

"You sure? I don't like the look on you at all. You ain't sickening for some'at, are you? You ain't gone and picked up some'at in France and brought it back wi' you?"

If she hadn't been feeling so unexpectedly ill all of a sudden, Roseen might have found this remark bitterly funny. As it was, she made an effort to fight down the attack of nausea, and fixing a frozen smile on her face for Annie's benefit, got on with pouring her a cup of tea.

"No, I told you, I'm OK. Really, I am."

Not for the world would she give Annie Sutton the satisfaction of knowing how near the truth she'd come. She *had* picked up something in France. Something serious.

She was three weeks late with her period. And now she'd started being sick.

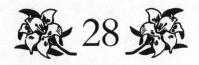# 28

The night after her meeting with Robert Wells at Moseley College Flora had the most extraordinarily vivid dream. Like most dreams it was nonsensical; and yet the images were powerful enough to evoke real emotion and remained fixed in her mind long after waking.

She was in a motor-car with Gerard Lansby. They were somewhere in the countryside, driving very slowly along a lane which seemed to be getting narrower and narrower. We'll have to turn back, she kept saying; but Gerard took no notice, and suddenly they were going down the drive to Cowpers and she realised she had on nothing more than her underclothes.

There was a figure waiting by the gate. It was Robert. You can't go any further, he said; and in her dream Flora felt acute embarrassment that he should find her there, like that.

Then she was inside the house looking through the window on to the paddock. Robert was there again, and this time he had someone with him – a woman with long, loose hair holding his arm and wearing Flora's clothes. They're trespassing, said Gerard, they want the omnibus to Brewood, you'd better go and tell them.

The next thing, she was running back along the drive; but the faster she tried to go, the slower her legs were moving, and though she called out to him to wait, Robert was drawing further and further away. Then suddenly they were in the omnibus together, and the woman with Robert had turned into Roseen O'Connor. She was seated on his knee, stroking his hair and kissing him; and looking over his shoulder she said to Flora, if you want to change places you'll have to ask the conductor at the next stop.

It was at this point that the dream ended. One of the housemaids, knocking on the bedroom door to come in and draw back the curtains, had roused Flora from sleep.

For several minutes afterwards she lay drifting, half-way between waking and dozing, the image of Robert still vividly imprinted upon her mind; and in this vulnerable, unguarded state of semi-sleep she was possessed by the most astonishing jealousy and insecurity that he should betray their love in the arms of another woman – someone not even his wife (which would have made sense, perhaps) but *Roseen*, of all people.

Then the maid returned, this time to light the fire, and Flora was wakened completely.

Throughout that day, though, she couldn't shake off the after-effects of her dream. It was almost as if subconsciously she were reminding herself of those times past when she'd actually wished she could change places with Roseen, or at least adopt something of the same 'me first' self-assertive attitude.

Placed in Flora's position, would Roseen have thought twice about accepting Robert's invitation to meet at his hotel? Of course not!

She was being neurotically over-sensitive, she chided herself. She *wanted* to see Robert; *wanted* to be with him; *wanted* to discuss the things they should have talked about together at the very beginning. So what was holding her back? Prudence? Timidity? Doubt? Or the fear of being placed in an ambivalent position?

What would Roseen have done?

Ah, ask rather, what would Roseen *not* have done . . .

It was really quite eerie how a young woman she hadn't seen – hadn't thought about – in months could none the less sway Flora's judgement. Like living with a ghost upon her shoulder. The last thing she had heard of Roseen O'Connor – or Kelly, she now was – was through her father's solicitors, conveying the terms of his will regarding the property in Raby Street. It hadn't surprised Flora that he should be so generous to his mistress's daughter; nor had she forgotten her own promise, extracted by her father on his deathbed, to do all she could to assist Roseen if she were ever in need.

It was a relief to think that she would not be required to keep that promise now. With a house of her own and money enough to live comfortably for a while, Roseen's future had been secured, and her association with the Dennison family ended.

Well . . . not entirely, perhaps.

When Flora lifted the telephone receiver to speak to Robert Wells at his hotel and accept his invitation, whether she knew it or not there was something of Roseen's example and influence which had coloured that decision.

★

It would be a much better idea to meet for luncheon, they agreed. That would give them the entire afternoon, not just a few hours together over dinner.

"I suppose, really, I ought to have travelled to Wolverhampton and met you there," Robert said, taking her into the residents' lounge of the Calthorpe Hotel, "instead of putting you to all this inconvenience."

"It's no inconvenience. Craddock brought me over in the Wolseley."

She wondered whether it was necessary to say that Craddock was the chauffeur; then remembered Robert already knew this from yesterday's 'phone conversation, and rushed on awkwardly, "He'll be calling back for me at six o'clock . . . he has to go to a garage somewhere this afternoon . . ."

"Well, at least that eases my conscience a little." Robert smiled at her. He looked tired, Flora thought; tired and strained, as though he hadn't been sleeping properly. "I wish you could stay longer, though, my darling. We might have had the evening together, perhaps."

"No – I must be home for the children." She said that a fraction too quickly, making it sound an excuse.

"Of course. I'd forgotten. They'll be needing you." He showed her to a chair in the window looking out on to the hotel garden. The soft, pale light of the autumn morning seemed to glow in the russets and reds of beech leaves scattered in thick drifts across the lawns.

"You never told me, by the way, what you'd called your little boy."

Flora sat down and took off her gloves. "I called him Robert," she said. "I named him after you."

There was a moment's silence. Another couple came in and settled themselves in armchairs to peruse the luncheon menu. "It was something to remember you by."

Robert kept his eyes fixed on the garden, as though he couldn't bear her to see his expression.

"Thank you," he said quietly. "What a generous, beautiful thought, and how like you, my darling." And then, looking at her again, "I wish to God I could have been his father."

"Yes. I wish that, too . . . but I'm afraid he resembles Sidney to a complete T."

She said this in such a rueful way that despite the circumstances she couldn't help but laugh at herself. "It's true, though. I absolutely adore my little boy, but I can't look at him without being reminded whose son he is. Poor Sidney. He would have been so proud."

Robert seated himself beside her. "Do you miss him – Sidney, I mean?"

She gave a small shrug. "In some ways I do. He was my husband for four years, after all. I grew . . . used to being married, I suppose, used to his company. Isn't that really what marriage is? Growing used to someone?"

"Yes. That's about the gist of it." He reached across and took her hand, holding it between his own. "The problem is, though, unless you're in love with that someone to start with, there's no foundation to build upon, and in a few years the getting used to becomes – well, just another description for boredom and complacency. That's what happened to me and Helen. We were never in love. Never."

"Then why did you marry?"

"Duty. Expediency. Who can say. Why did you marry Sidney?"

"Because . . . it seemed the right thing to do at the time. And because I needed to forget about you, I suppose, if you want the truth. It was pointless hanging on to something I knew I could never have."

Robert's fingers tightened. "If only I'd been less of a fool

– less full of pious principles and ridiculous juvenile notions about moral obligation – I would have cut myself adrift eight years ago and stayed with you. Why didn't I, for heaven's sake? I've asked myself that so often."

"Because you *do* have principles, you *do* have moral obligations," Flora came in quickly. "Why do you think I've loved you, Robert, if not for those very values? I couldn't have spent all this time caring for a person I didn't respect, someone who could throw aside his marriage – " She glanced at the couple across the room. They were still discussing the menu. "Someone who could throw aside his marriage," she went on in a lower voice, "and abandon an innocent wife and children. I loved you precisely because you were selfless enough to sacrifice your own happiness in order to secure theirs."

"But at what cost? I've lived like a man half-dead these past years."

"I can't believe that!"

"You must. Otherwise you're condemning me to a future that's hardly worth staying alive for. I *need* you, Flora. I can't go on without you . . . not any more."

He looked at her, and there was so much sadness, so much longing in that tired face that it was as much as she could do not to draw him into her arms and rock him like a child.

"Would you like to see the luncheon menu, madam? Sir?"

Perhaps it was just as well that the dining-room maid interrupted at that moment, smiling politely as she offered the handwritten bill of fare.

"Oh – er, yes, thank you – thank you." Robert took it from her; and when she had gone, "We'll talk about things later, my darling. This isn't really the place. Let's decide what we'll have to eat, and then perhaps we might go for a walk or something, if you'd like."

"Whatever. I don't mind."

Flora leaned towards him to study the menu, and misinterpreting her movement he bent his head and kissed her very gently on the cheek.

"I love you so much," he whispered. "Never doubt me."

Luncheon was a sedately civilised affair, with both of them making the effort to appear relaxed and normal, occasionally catching each other's eye in the middle of small talk and for a second losing the thread of their conversation. Robert chatted about his school work – he was deputy headmaster now – and about his return as part-time amanuensis to the poet Charles Anthony la Motte, for whom he'd worked as secretary before the war.

"Oh yes, I remember that," said Flora. "You gave me a copy of his book, *The Flowerless Fields of Heaven.* I've always treasured it . . ."

In return she spoke to him of her children, and of the voluntary work she'd lately undertaken as a hospital visitor.

"It gives me something to do with myself – gets me out of the house a couple of times a week. Now that I'm no longer teaching I need the distraction. And it's interesting, as well as being rewarding and truly worthwhile. There are so many patients who never see a visitor from one day to the next, you'd be surprised."

It was almost two o'clock by the time they'd finished their meal. The October day had brightened, and the sunshine tempted them out for a stroll around Cannon Hill Park just a short distance from the hotel. They had come here occasionally together in the old days, and for both of them it was like stepping out of the frame of the present into the past again.

Flora held Robert's arm. She had been anticipating today with mixed feelings of nervousness and euphoric excitement, knowing that after this meeting their relationship would be altered; whether for good or otherwise was impossible to foretell. They had a choice to make, a decision to reach, perhaps the most important of their lives since the outcome would affect their future – and not theirs alone, but the future of others too, those innocent pawns in this complicated game of emotional options.

"Do you remember – ?"

They must have said that to each other a score of times as they wandered round the park by the lake, sharing their memories.

"Do you remember," said Robert finally, "the last evening we spent together, my darling? I took you to hear Elgar's Second Symphony – "

"Yes, and then you walked with me back to the tram terminus – "

"And as we sat in the waiting room I told you I'd fallen in love with you."

Flora bent her head and a little smile of nostalgia touched her lips. "How I remember that. Could I ever forget."

They had reached the bandstand now, and in the shelter of its shuttered wooden sides, were out of the breeze which ruffled the surface of the lake and sent fallen leaves whispering along the empty paths. Robert led her to a wrought-iron bench. The sun was warm here, and it was peaceful to sit with the touch of its autumn rays upon their faces, listening to the companionable calls of ducks and waterfowl vying with birdsong above the distant noise of city traffic.

With Robert's arms around her and her head against his shoulder, Flora told herself that this was the happiest moment she had ever known. Nothing else mattered, nothing at all. For as long as she lived, she would always remember these few precious, perfect minutes and cherish them as the most beautiful experience of her life.

It was a time outside time, outside reality; a time of dreams come true.

How long they remained like that, held wordless in one another's embrace, neither could tell. After the first kiss it was so natural, so easy to be secure and safe and let go of the fears for their future, the pain of their past. The whole world seemed to shrink to this little space of park bench in the sun as though nothing existed beyond it, no separate lives, no families, no obligations; just the two of them together wrapped around in the strength of their own love, their own need, their own wanting.

It was Flora who was first to break the stillness at last.

"I wish time could end for us here, now, at this moment," she breathed softly, her mouth against Robert's cheek. "I wish we could stay just as we are for ever, don't you . . ."

"Mm."

He moved his head to kiss her again. His lips were warm and strong, and yet tender, and their caress sent a renewed shock of excitement pulsing through her body, making her tremble. She had never known anything like this with Sidney,

271

never felt the sweetness of sexual arousal and the longing to offer herself completely to the ardour of a man's love-making. With Robert it was all so wonderfully new, so wonderfully natural.

She returned his kiss, cupping his face in her hand.

"Oh, my dearest one," she murmured, "my dearest, sweetest, love . . ." They were words spoken in her dreams in the lonely darkness of the night, words whispered to his memory. "How I wish we never had to part again."

He released her with sudden abruptness and sat forward, shoulders hunched, hands thrusting into the pockets of his overcoat.

"What is it? What have I said?" She stared at him, dismayed. "Robert – "

He shook his head.

"What *is* it?" she asked again, more urgently, not understanding.

"It's me . . . us . . . It's, oh God, it's everything," he said at last, not looking at her. "Sometimes I think it might have been better if I'd never come back from the war – at least that would have been an honourable way to end it all."

He sounded so despondent, so flat, that in an instant the bubble of Flora's happiness burst and she was back in the world of reality, jolted out of her dream by Robert's total change of mood.

"What are you talking about?"

She took his arm and gave it a little shake.

"Tell me what's the matter," she begged. "Don't let today be spoilt for us. Tell me what's wrong, darling, and I'll try and understand, really I will."

He reached across for his trilby hat on the bench beside him; then, elbows resting on knees, began turning the brim round and round between his hands in an agitated way as though he needed something to occupy him while he spoke.

"Sometimes I feel so guilty . . . so guilty I can't live with my own conscience when I think of how I've conducted my life. I never wanted to be the cause of hurt or offence to anyone, and yet everything I've done seems wrong – wrong for the wrong reason, the wrong motive. I shouldn't have married Helen. I didn't love her. I only did it because I was full of some noble idea of duty, and noble ideas don't put happiness into a marriage, not without love to make it work."

"But you've always been a good husband," Flora interrupted loyally in defence.

"No, I haven't. I provided Helen and her children with a home and saw that they never went without. That's as far as my role as husband stretched. But I've been unfaithful to her every day, every hour, every waking moment since I fell in love with you – and that's what I have to carry on my conscience. I have *not* been a good husband, my darling. Helen has never been anything other than your substitute in my life."

The confession touched Flora more keenly than she realised, bringing a sudden knot of tears to her throat.

"Then I'm as guilty as you, Robert," she whispered, burying her face against his shoulder. "Don't blame yourself entirely – you mustn't. It's just as much my fault as yours."

"I won't accept that."

"It's true, though. If I hadn't encouraged your friendship in the beginning – "

She stopped, unable to go on for a second; and then, swallowing hard and drawing a quivering breath, "Does she know? About me, I mean?"

"She's never said. But yes, I think so – hope so, anyway. It will make things . . . perhaps not easier, but less unpleasant to accept. You see, I know what I must do now – "

He turned to Flora as he said that. The suspicious brightness of her unshed tears betrayed her; and seeing them, Robert uttered a little groan of hurt.

"Oh, my darling," he murmured with quiet intensity, drawing her back into his arms and kissing the tears away, "I love you . . . I love you more than you can possibly believe. Whatever the cost, I'll pay it willingly. When I go back, I'm going to ask Helen if she'll divorce me . . . if she'll free me from our marriage so that I can spend the rest of my life with you."

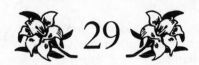 29

A few days after his return to the Isle of Wight, there was a
letter from Robert waiting for Flora on the hall table as she
came down to breakfast. He had told her he would write
rather than telephone his news, and she'd been watching each
post with mounting apprehension, so great was her anxiety
to know the outcome of his talk with Helen.

The instant she saw the expected envelope there on the
table, her heart took a leap into her throat, and for a silly
moment she felt almost too scared to go and pick it up. The
whole question of their future lay contained within its pages.
What did Robert have to say? Was the news hopeful? Had
Helen agreed to their divorce – oh, had she? Would he
otherwise have written quite so soon?

It was a rule in the Dennison household that mail was never
read until breakfast was finished; and for the next half-hour
Flora had to sit in nerve-racked suspense making polite
noises to her mother's conversation, the letter burning a
hole through her pocket.

As soon as she could she excused herself and fled upstairs
to her room. By now she was reduced to such a state that the
racing thump of her heart set her hands shaking as she fumbled
with a paper-knife to open the envelope.

Feverishly she glanced through the closely-written pages,
looking for a sentence to end her agony. Then she read them
again, more carefully, more coherently.

And again . . . only this time with growing disbelief.

The most terrible, leadweight feeling seemed to sweep over
her. Robert's letter was loving and warm, but its contents

were an utter anticlimax. He had arrived back in Freshwater to find Helen very ill and running a high temperature, he wrote; obviously in the circumstances he couldn't raise the question of divorce immediately, but would have to bide his time till she recovered. He was sure Flora would understand, and be patient for a while.

All the keyed-up tension of waiting shrivelled slowly away, leaving an after-taste of bitter despondency. She laid the letter aside and sank on to the bed.

How often had she hoped it might all be resolved by now, all the unpleasantness. How often these last days had she visualised the scene between Robert and his wife, heard them in her mind rationally and calmly discussing their relationship and agreeing it was better to part now as friends than let things continue to the point of future enmity.

Yet nothing of the kind had happened; nothing been resolved. Instead, all this time, Helen had been lying on her sickbed, with Robert at her side solicitous as ever and, as he put in his letter, making sure she ate properly and had everything she required.

"*Bother* it!"

Flora's exclamation was involuntary. She *hated* all this uncertainty. It seemed almost as though Fate were toying with them, her and Robert, leading them on so far and then suddenly, unpredictably, pulling the rug of their hopes from under their feet. If only she didn't have such a tender conscience; if only she didn't feel so guilty, wanting him as she did; if only she didn't feel that her existence in his life amounted to an act of theft, since she was stealing something which belonged to someone else – the loyalty and love of another woman's husband.

Oh, if only – !

Already the magic of their day together in Birmingham was beginning to lose a little of its golden glow as the reality of their situation dawned on her. She had wanted the whole thing over quickly – cleanly – fairly – like a surgeon's knife; the divorce heard and granted, everyone happy and satisfied.

Life wasn't like that, though. Nothing was quick or clean or fair, when it involved the breaking up of the family home, the separation of man and wife, the bewilderment suffered by children, the legal arguments . . . the whole distressing, tawdry, nasty business.

Besides, on what possible grounds could Robert obtain his divorce? Flora had wondered about this only last night, and it had exercised her imagination to the detriment of several hours' sleep. All she knew about the dissolution of marriage was what she read in the occasional newspaper report of cases involving desertion, adultery or cruelty. Since he was innocent of all such offence, how on earth was he legally to free himself?

The following afternoon she raised this subject in a casually roundabout fashion when her friend Jessy Venables came over to Stockwell End for tea. Jessy's own little girl Poppy had been taken upstairs to the nursery wing to join Imogen and baby Robert, and the two young women had the drawing-room to themselves in Mrs Dennison's absence at some committee meeting.

"I was reading the other day," Flora began carelessly, pouring tea for them both, "in one of the daily papers, I think it was, about a couple who wanted to separate because they'd fallen out of love with each other. And it set me wondering – you know – if one of them wished to marry someone else, how would they go about it?"

"The usual way . . . by getting a divorce," Jessy answered abstractedly, more interested in a plate of iced sponge cakes.

"Ah, but they couldn't, apparently. There were no grounds."

"Marriage itself is ground enough for divorce after a few years, that's what Philip's always saying." Fingers hovered a moment over one cake, then rejected it in favour of another. "Anyway, if one of them wanted to marry someone else that badly – well, a weekend in Brighton would always do the trick."

"A weekend in Brighton?" Flora pricked her ears. "Together, you mean?"

"No, you ninny. Don't you know what happens in Brighton? Or Blackpool, or anywhere, come to that." Jessy spoke through a mouthful of sponge.

"Well – people go there for holidays, don't they."

"They go for *liaisons*. And not with their spouses. Look,"

she went on patiently, finishing the cake and casting her eye at the plate again as she took up cup and saucer, "if people want to divorce and they haven't got sufficient grounds, what often happens – so I've heard – is that the chap goes off by himself to some cheap hotel, books a double room as Mr and Mrs, and engages the services of a lady of easy virtue. If you follow."

"You mean – ?"

For one horrified moment Flora had the image of Robert in some squalid, seedy bedroom making love in the arms of a stranger.

"You mean he goes to bed with a *prostitute?*"

"Mm. Of course, he doesn't have to *do* anything. The whole point of the performance is that the chambermaid finds them together next morning in – what's it called – you know – compromising circumstances."

Jessy was treating the conversation as though they might be discussing the weather.

"But how do *you* know so much about it?" Flora asked, careful not to let herself sound too appalled by the sordid picture this procedure raised.

"Oh, it happened to someone Philip knew – a friend in Stafford. His wife had hired a private detective to watch him, so he obliged her by going through with this rigmarole. Anything for a quiet life . . . I say, these cakes are jolly good! Don't mind if I help myself to another, do you?"

Flora passed the plate again. The idea of Robert possibly having to commit himself to the same course of action to get his divorce was so awful, it was quite unthinkable. She wouldn't let him do it – no, never – not for anything in the world!

There *had* to be some more civilised and honourable way . . .

★

November that year 1922 was an eventful month both at home and elsewhere. There was an exciting General Election with the Conservatives winning a large majority. In Dublin the Irish politician Erskine Childers – whom many of his countrymen regarded as a hero – was tried by court martial on the technical charge of possessing an automatic pistol without proper authority. He was found guilty of treason and executed, a sentence which aroused enormous controversy. Five days later the world's attention was switched to Egypt, with news of the discovery at Luxor of the fabulous tomb treasures of a young pharaoh.

No one had heard the name Tutankhamen – indeed no one knew how to pronounce it – but suddenly it seemed to be everywhere at once. The mysterious pyramids had always excited public imagination, and never more so than at this moment, fuelled by daily news articles about Lord Carnarvon's Egyptian expedition and his extraordinary feat in finding the tomb. A buried hoard of treasure hidden away for centuries beneath the desert sands – it was all wonderful *Boys' Own* stuff, especially the account of Lord Carnarvon thrusting a lighted candle into the blackness of the burial chamber and seeing its feeble flame illuminate the glorious golden riches of the Ancient World.

Such was the avid interest in Tutankhamen that by the end of the month catch-phrases had started to circulate (always a sign of popularity) including the rather awful 'toot and come in' which society's new darlings, the Bright Young Things, adopted as their own.

Even Robert Wells referred to the subject in one of the long letters he'd begun writing weekly to Flora. 'The pupils at school are so fired by the famous discovery that our history lessons are now devoted exclusively to pyramids, pharaohs, sphinxes and what-not, and at least three of the boys have confided to me their ambition to become famous Egyptologists!'

He wrote that Helen was still poorly and needing medical treatment for what had been diagnosed as a disorder of the blood:

I've been warned that she mustn't be excited, or upset at all, as this might retard her recovery. I feel so sorry for her – she's so pathetically grateful for the little use I am around the place, and is always apologising for making herself a nuisance. Sometimes I can't bear to be in the same room – it seems so horribly cruel that once she's well again, I'm going to tell her that I want to live with someone else. It makes me feel a thorough Judas. To be honest, but for the thought of you, my darling, waiting there so patiently for me, I doubt I'd have the strength or courage to do what I must. But chin up, eh. In a few more weeks this will all be behind us, and we can start making wonderful *wonderful* plans for our future together.

Flora wished she could share his optimism. The thought of someone sick being attentively nursed back to health so that her husband might tell her he was leaving her for another woman: somehow it seemed all wrong, callously contradictory, like getting the condemned man well enough for execution.

Besides, Christmas was approaching and Robert surely wouldn't want to spoil the family celebrations with talk about divorce; which meant that even though Helen might be recovered by then he would have to continue the charade and make things even worse – a mockery of what the season was meant to be.

These thoughts piled one upon another in Flora's mind and were reflected in the letters she wrote in return: tender and affectionate, yet betraying somewhere between the lines a plea for reassurance. Indeed this was a highly fraught period for her, made more difficult by the fact that she had no one to confide in, no one to whom she could turn except Robert himself. She had thought frequently of unburdening herself to Jessy Venables; but something – not embarrassment, certainly; shame perhaps – kept her from doing so.

If Robert was worth her love, then he was worth waiting for, she told herself. She would just have to cling on to patience and hope it would all turn out for the best.

She would have been deeply troubled to know exactly how difficult Robert was finding it to make the initial approach to his wife: his letters only hinted at the fact. After that beautiful afternoon the two of them had spent in Birmingham, he had been so fired by his love for Flora that he would have taken on the whole world and defied every single convention in order to make his future with her. Once home again, however, the down-to-earth practicalities of the situation had tended to rub something of the gloss from his eagerness and temper his resolve to act immediately. It was one thing to say 'I love Flora; I want to marry her' but quite another to tell his wife, and the children he cared so much for, 'I am leaving you for someone else; you are no longer part of my life'.

To do that would require all the courage he had, and all the conviction.

★

"You know, your attitude is enough to freeze a fellow off completely," Gerard Lansby told her, taking the corner of Histons Hill with a noisy clashing of gears. "Good job I'm not the type who takes no for an answer."

He and Flora had not seen one another for over a month, and, growing a little annoyed with her offhand manner to him on the telephone, he'd decided to confront her with a *fait accompli* and had reserved luncheon for the two of them at the Admiral Rodney Inn at Brewood.

"But I can't possibly come out with you today!" Flora had protested when he'd appeared without a word of warning upon the doorstep to collect her.

"Why not? Do you already have a lunch engagement?"

"No, but even if I did – "

"Right, that's settled then. I'll give you five minutes to go and fluff your hair – and no argument!"

She could have refused; but Gerard was a friend and she liked his company; and besides, she needed cheering up. After a moment's deliberation she'd said yes . . . as long as he returned her home for teatime. This evening was one of her duty-turns for hospital visiting.

"In any case," he continued now, swinging the Arrol-Johnston out to overtake a plodding farm-cart, "when a woman says no, she generally means perhaps. It's when she says yes that a fellow starts to worry."

"You're a dreadful cynic, Mr Lansby," Flora told him lightly.

"Not at all. I'm simply a realist. I don't believe in painting the lily."

"Gilding it, surely?" she corrected.

"Not according to Byron and Shakespeare, both of whom

knew a great deal about the fairer sex. 'To gild refinèd gold, to paint the lily, to throw a perfume on the violet' – obviously you don't know your quotations, and you a schoolma'am too. Shame on you, Mrs Hathaway!"

"I'm not a schoolma'am now, and I can't be expected to remember *every* quotation," she defended herself, trying to sound annoyed but not quite succeeding. Gerard had a way of making her laugh at herself, which was what made him such a marvellous companion. Darling Robert, for all that she loved him so, was always a little too serious and intense . . .

She pushed that disloyal thought firmly to the back of her mind and went on, changing the subject, "By the way, why are we going to Brewood for luncheon? Any particular reason?"

"Only that the Rodney is my local port of call." Gerard slowed the car and glanced to left and right, waiting for another vehicle to turn before continuing over the crossroads. "I thought it time that you were introduced there."

"Why?"

"Why? My word, what a lot of questions you do ask! Because I'd like to show you off to a few of my friends."

The compliment hidden behind that remark didn't escape Flora. She pretended to make light of it, however. "As the latest decoration to hang upon your arm, you mean?"

He returned her a look from behind his driving-goggles and said in a bantering manner, "On the contrary, my dear, you are its sole adornment," but there was something in his expression at odds with his tone.

Within another ten minutes they had reached Brewood and were turning off one of the village's steep, narrow streets into the courtyard of the Admiral Rodney. This was a mellow-bricked coaching hostelry of some considerable antiquity if one looked behind its Georgian façade, and a signboard hanging over the street still boasted 'Stabling for Fifty Horses' as well as 'Accommodation for Cycles' below its advertisement for J. & J. Yardley's Celebrated Ales.

Having parked his motor-car well clear of the courtyard entrance to allow for the passage of other vehicles, Gerard took Flora into a low-ceilinged room cosily lit by a log fire, and found them a table to themselves near the inglenook.

"It's game pie today," he said, reading the slate nailed up beside the counter. "Mrs Seal does all the cooking herself." He indicated the proprietor's wife, a buxom young woman crossing the room with tankards of ale. "She's an absolute wizard with pastry – her pies are famed for miles around."

Ensuring that Flora was comfortably settled he excused himself for a moment to go and speak to several acquaintances, young fellow-farmers by the look of them; and then returned with a pint of ale for himself and a glass of pale amber-coloured parsnip wine for his companion.

"Another of Mrs Seal's accomplishments?" she asked, sipping it a little warily and deciding that she liked it.

"Mm." Gerard took the head off his pint with a long appreciative gulp. "Parsnip, elderberry, dandelion and burdock . . . good old English country wines. You won't find a bottle of anything French at the Rodney."

Flora looked about her, beginning to appreciate why he'd brought her here. The place had a solid, settled atmosphere, a feeling of timelessness and unchange, as though Waterloo and Sevastopol and Mafeking were only yesterday away. Nothing had altered much in a hundred years. The talk was still of fatstock shows and corn prices, the perfidy of Parliament and the problems of tenant workers . . . there was a sense of continuity about it all, somehow.

"I'm glad you decided to come today," Gerard said, watching her face. "I knew you'd like it here."

Even he was of a piece with the place, she thought. Perhaps it was because he worked with the land that he had those enduring qualities for which she liked him. Not the flippancy – that was just top show – but the strength of character beneath it, the confidence and stability which she had sensed on her first visit to Cowpers.

It may have been the parsnip wine, but suddenly she felt a great affection for him; not the kind of affection she had for Robert, but something comfortable and safe and warm.

After the second glass, drunk with an excellent meal, this feeling seemed to spread to everything around, even to the smiling moon-face of the clock beside the door, and Landseer's 'Monarch of the Glen', mottled at the edges, on the wall opposite.

Then Gerard said, "Oh, I almost forgot, I've got tickets for us both for the Grand Theatre next week," and she was brought down to earth with a jolt.

"Sorry – ? What did you say?"

"The Grand. They're doing *Iolanthe*. I'd like to take you."

Flora felt her ears redden. Hastily she sought about for some excuse or other.

"I . . . I'm not sure. I can't recall which are my nights for hospital visiting."

How could she possibly go to the theatre with Gerard when she'd now promised herself to Robert? It wouldn't be fair to give him that encouragement; wouldn't be fair to any of them. Even being here today was breaking trust.

"Well, you can always change your evenings, can't you? It's only voluntary work." He sounded a little put out. "I've gone and bought the tickets now."

"You ought to have asked me first, really you should. It's very awkward . . . Can't you take someone else instead?"

"Now that's a fine way to treat a fellow, I must say! If I'd wanted to take anyone else, I wouldn't be asking you."

She had never seen him angry before. All the good humour had vanished from his face and his voice took on a sudden edge.

"Dash it, Flora, I haven't got the plague or anything, have I?"

"Of course not – "

"Then why give me the cold shoulder? Every time we've spoken on the telephone you've been fobbing me off with some excuse – admit it – you were in half a mind not to drive out today, and now you're saying you don't want to come to the theatre with me! Why not be honest and tell me the truth?"

Oh, if only she could! But that would sever their cherished friendship for good, and she couldn't bear that, to part under such a cloud. How was she ever to confess to him that she was involved with a married man who was prepared to abandon his wife and family for the sake of a love which had now lasted eight years?

She bent her head, pretending to fold her napkin, unable to meet his eyes.

"If there were some other fellow on the scene, I could understand it," Gerard went on, more calmly. "But I asked Jessy Venables, and she said no, there's no one else. So what is it about *me*, Flora, that you don't particularly like?"

"But I *do* like you!" She glanced up quickly. "Believe me, Gerard, I like you very, very much."

The sincerity in her voice showed how much she meant that.

"Then prove it. Come to the theatre with me." He took her small chin in his hand, forcing her not to drop her head again, and gave it a firm little shake. "Otherwise I shall be scrutinising myself in the mirror with the worried eyes of a man who fears his Douglas Fairbanks charm is deserting him."

The tension between them melted.

"The trouble with you," she answered, unable to resist a smile, "is that you're very vain."

The riposte came quickly. "And the trouble with *you*, my dear little Flora, is you're utterly adorable."

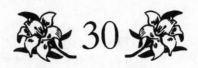 30

It wasn't a very happy Christmas for Roseen.

She was two and a half months pregnant now, and starting to get desperate.

Ever since realising her condition she'd been doing what she could to be rid of the thing. She'd swallowed castor oil by the cupful; taken a box of pennyroyal pills; sat sweating in tubs of scalding water drinking gin till she was sick; she'd even had a go jumping from top to bottom of the stairs. She'd tried everything.

Nothing had worked.

Except the castor oil.

Christmas Eve was spent alone by herself at Raby Street, getting very drunk and debating which was the simplest way out of her predicament – putting her head in the gas oven or having another abortion. Remembering the nightmare horror of the last time, the gas oven was probably a lot quicker and a lot less painful.

Who would care, after all, if she was dead? Not a soul. The only ones who'd ever really loved her were dead and gone themselves . . . her Mam, Billy, Uncle George.

She aimed an unfocused glance at the kitchen mantelpiece. Three Christmas cards, that's all she'd had. Three miserable flippin' cards. One from Annie Sutton 'with best wishes for the New Year from Aubrey and me'; one from that Flora Dennison 'hoping you are well'; and one from the chap who managed the off-licence on the corner 'in appreciation of your regular custom'.

Roseen put her head in her hands and had a good hard cry.

Even the neighbours didn't want to know her these days, not since she'd come into her money. They called her 'Lady Muck' behind her back and encouraged their kids to throw stones at her motor-car.

God, what a way to spend Christmas Eve!

It was all that Johnnie Driscoll's fault, leading her up the garden path with a load of lies and then robbing her blind of everything she'd got. Men – they all needed putting on a ruddy great bonfire and burning, they did. She'd known nothing but trouble from them ever since she could remember, smarming around with their fancy talk and their big ideas trying to impress her, just itching to get their fingers up her skirt.

And her daft enough to let them . . .

Well, serve herself right for the mess she'd gone and landed in. If she behaved like a whore, why be so surprised if she got treated like one – ended up like one, and all, the way she was going.

She'd poured herself another gin for consolation, and sat on the hearth by the fire smoking her last cigarette, tears reduced to half-hearted sobs, listening to the raucous shouts of Christmas revellers out in the street and the scratching of mice on the cellar steps. Then the bells of St Mary's and St John's began to ring for Midnight Mass, and Roseen decided. To hell with gassing herself, she'd go to church instead and say a prayer for her poor old Mam and Billy.

Staggering off along Raby Street in her best chinchilla-trimmed coat and hat, the crisp, cold air had soon sobered her up. It wasn't far, St Mary's and St John's; and by the time she arrived she was in no worse a state of alcoholic stupor than half the rest of the congregation. Connie had always brought her here for Midnight Mass: it was one of the memories of her childhood, standing under the gas lamp outside the White Rose pub, waiting for her mother to have a last drink before taking her to church.

She hadn't been for years now. Not since Billy died.

Funny how much better all of a sudden she felt, though, kneeling among the crush of steaming bodies and looking up at the candles shimmering there on the altar. It was like . . . like being with family again. Nothing had changed.

Even the Christmas Crib was the same as she remembered, with the ox and ass and shepherds gathered round the Holy Family.

When she was little Connie used to take her after Mass to say a prayer to the Baby and put a farthing in the collecting box for orphans of the parish. Perhaps it was because she was feeling so emotional tonight that Roseen had been prompted to copy that childhood memory, and after the service was finished push her way across into the side aisle to visit the Crib.

What was the prayer she used to say? Something about 'infant Jesus meek and mild, look on me a little child' and a Hail Mary to follow.

She stared at the faces of the carved figures with their stiff, painted smiles and their sightless gaze. Tears suddenly filled her eyes. What was the use of believing in anything any more when all the faith and trust had been knocked out of her by life's unfairness. She'd come here for a bit of comfort, a bit of company; not for religion. In any case how could she pray to a wooden baby in a manger about how to get rid of the baby she had in her womb . . . it didn't make sense.

The candle flames blurred into haloes of light as the tears spilled over and ran down her cheeks. She got to her feet, fumbling in her purse for something to put in the box beside the Crib.

"God bless our Mam and our Billy," she whispered. "God bless Uncle George." And then she'd turned and run blindly from the church, out into the darkness and the cold of Christmas Eve.

★

"Am you wanting Mrs Smith?" asked a woman, sticking her head from an upstairs window to address Roseen on the pavement below. " 'Cause if you am, her ain't here. Her's gone to stay wi' her daughter in Gornal what's had a new babby."

Roseen's heart sank. Wasn't that just her bloomin' luck . . .

"D'you know when she'll be back?" she called up.

"Not for another few weeks, cock." The woman began shutting the window again; and then, on an afterthought, added not unkindly, "If you'm in trouble, try Mrs Bailey in Pipers Row. Her can prob'ly help you."

"Ta."

The last time she'd been here to this house, pregnant with Maurice Lines's child, it was Aubrey Podmore who'd sent her. Back-street abortionists didn't advertise themselves: they and their clients knew they ran a risk of prosecution for what they were doing. But pregnant again, alone and at the end of her tether, Roseen hadn't known where else to go for assistance.

Wearily she retraced her steps into town, and by asking at a shop in Pipers Row found out the address where this Mrs Bailey lived. It was a filthy-looking place. The windows were grey with dirt and paint was flaking off the front door. Roseen had to screw up all her courage before she could raise her hand to the knocker.

The middle-aged female answering wore her hair done up in paper curlers under a scarf and was attired in a coat over a pinafore, and a pair of down-at-heel slippers.

"I've been sent from Mrs Smith's in Fallings Park," Roseen told her in response to the question. "Somebody said you might be able to help me."

"You'd best come in, then." The woman jerked her head.

Inside the place was even worse than it looked from the street. There was a piece of old curtain draped from ceiling hooks, half-hiding a bed in one corner of the room, and overall was the lingering smell of tom-cats and boiled cabbage.

"How far are you gone?"

"Nearly three months."

"Left things a bit late, haven't you?"

"I've been trying to get rid of it myself, but nothing's worked." Roseen looked around at the mess and the dirt, and felt her flesh crawl. Still, it had got to be done so she might as well get on with it. "D'you think you can do anything for me?"

"I can try. This your first time, or what?"

"It's my second."

"Then you'll know what to expect. Only I don't like a lot o' noise, see, or the neighbours start complaining." Mrs

Bailey took off her coat and hung it behind the door. "I can do you now if you like. D'you live very far?"

Roseen shook her head.

"That's as well. You'll start coming on in about an hour, so get yourself in bed as soon as you're home." It was all extremely matter of fact, like arranging to have a tooth out. "I charge ten quid – and you never heard my name, all right?"

She'd expected it to be expensive; lucky she was prepared. The sale of her little motor-car just after the New Year had brought in a useful bit of money.

"All right," she said. Her legs were starting to shake with nerves. God Almighty, let it be over and done with as quick as possible so she could get out of here . . .

The woman ferreted about, then hitched aside the curtain and spread half a dozen sheets of newspaper over the bare mattress.

"Take your drawers off and lie yourself down here. I won't be half a mo'."

Numbly Roseen did as she was told. The vile smell about the place as much as the fear of what she was going to suffer was starting to make her feel physically sick. She lay on the bed and stared up at the brown rings of damp mottling the ceiling. Outside in Pipers Row the world went about its Wednesday lunch-time business. She tried to concentrate on the sounds, to give her mind something else to think about; but the cold sweat of apprehension that kept breaking out from every pore made that impossible, and all she could hear was Mrs Bailey somewhere along the passage singing to herself as she ran a bowlful of water.

The twenty minutes that followed were the worst Roseen had ever endured in her life. The agony was so great that she had to stuff her mouth with her skirt to stop herself from screaming as the abortionist's instruments penetrated into her body. When it was all over, she lay trembling from head to foot like a spent animal, the blood from her bitten lips mingled with saliva and sweat.

"You'll do, my wench."

Mrs Bailey gave her a perfunctory wipe with a cloth, then bundled up the stained newspaper and shoved it under the bed.

"Let's have you on your feet now. You can't stop here. My old man'll be in for his bite o' dinner at one o'clock."

Leaving Roseen to tidy herself as best she could, she carried the bowl and its dreadful contents out of the room and cleared away the evidence before coming back to let the young woman out through the door.

"You hop off home and get yourself straight to bed," was her parting shot as the front door closed again.

How she ever managed to get back to Raby Street that day, Roseen never knew. The pain was a white-hot poker burning its way through her belly, and every step a conscious, terrible effort. People were looking at her as though they thought her drunk, the way she was forced to haul herself along by clinging on to the railings to keep upright.

She'd just got to the top of the street when she started to haemorrhage, the blood pouring out of her in a flood and running down her legs.

"Here, you all right – ?" she heard somebody call; and that was the last thing she remembered before the world turned black before her eyes and she fainted dead away.

★

It was like being drowned. Sometimes she could feel herself rising slowly towards the surface, towards light and echoing sound; and then she'd sink again, back into the suffocating darkness that contained her. She preferred it down there. It didn't hurt so much. The light brought pain, and the brighter it grew the more she suffered and tried to fight, though whether she was struggling to save her life or to save herself from further pain, she didn't know.

Every now and then her head was filled with swelling noise, like the sea on the shingle at Aberystwyth, fading away to a drawn-out sigh, then building again in waves of sound that crashed about her and sucked her back into itself.

She thought she could hear Billy calling, and Connie, their voices filled with water.

"Where are you?" she'd cry. "Mam – ? Billy – ?" but they were always too far off to hear her.

How long she lay wrapped in the drowning darkness Roseen couldn't tell. It was timeless here. Then gradually . . .

very gradually . . . she started to sense that it was changing, shrinking away, leaving her floating in a web of greyness which held her suspended just below the light. The pain had gone at last; and all she felt now was the drowsy lethargy of being almost asleep.

Sleep . . .

Was she dreaming? She must be. Billy was dead; and yet here he was, as large as life, sitting beside her and smiling, dressed all in white like an angel.

"Well, Mrs Kelly," she could hear him say, "who's been a silly girl, then? You've given us quite a scare."

What was he talking about? She screwed up her eyes. Why was everything so bright? Was she in heaven – blimey, what a thought!

She tried to lift a hand to reach him.

"No, you just lie still now."

Why? He was her Billy, her love . . .

"I'm going to take a quick look at you, see how you're getting on."

She felt movement somewhere, hands touching her softly and gently.

"You've had a bad time of it, Mrs Kelly. You've been very ill, you know. Still – I think we can safely say you've turned the corner at last."

Roseen was beginning to sort things out inside her head now. She wasn't in heaven at all – how could she be when she was still alive. And it wasn't Billy talking to her, it was some young chap in a white coat who looked a bit like him.

She heard a peculiar sound, a little croaking whisper, and realised it was herself trying to speak.

"Where . . . am . . . I?"

"You're in the women's ward at the Royal Hospital, my dear."

This was like doing a jigsaw puzzle. Each new piece that was fitted into it made the picture easier to see. She was in hospital because – because – yes, it was all coming back to her – because she'd had that abortion. That was it. She'd had the abortion and something had gone wrong.

"Excuse me a second, Doctor."

291

A nurse came up to speak to the young man in white, and after a quiet word or two went briskly on her way again.

He got to his feet. "Well, Mrs Kelly," he said, tucking his stethoscope into a pocket, "I'll come by and see how you are tomorrow. In the meanwhile I want you to try and drink as much fluid as you can. Will you do that for me?"

She croaked at him again, trying to focus her eyes on his face. The light still hurt, but she was getting slowly used to it now; and when he'd gone she even managed to turn her head and look towards the source of the brightness. It was a window, filled with January sunshine.

She drifted back to sleep.

★

When she woke next time, she thought for a minute she was having another dream. A plumpish young woman, smartly dressed with a fox fur round her neck and a felt cloche hat, was sitting next to the bed with her nose in a magazine. Roseen recognised her almost at once. What made the whole thing unreal was the fact that she should be here in the first place – *her*, of all people.

There was the rustle of paper as the young woman turned a page; and as she did so her glance fell on the patient. Immediately the same irritating sweet smile which Roseen remembered from childhood softened her features and she leaned forward a little, saying in a gentle, nervous manner, "Oh, hello, Roseen. How are you?"

Roseen didn't answer, except to pull a face.

"They told me you were feeling slightly better. You *look* better, I must say." Flora Hathaway closed her magazine and put it aside. "When I first saw you last weekend, well . . . you really were quite poorly."

She smiled again, genuinely sympathetic; and Roseen wanted to know what the heck it had to do with her, how ill she'd been. What was she doing here anyway?

"It was lucky you were admitted straight into hospital. That's why they've been treating you with all these drugs – blood poisoning can be very serious."

Blood poisoning . . .

Roseen recalled the awful room in Pipers Row, the filth and

dirt everywhere, the abortionist's tools, the whole disgusting paraphernalia. Her skin crawled at the memory.

She moistened her bruised lips with the tip of her tongue. At least she wasn't pregnant any more – thank God for small mercies – but that Mrs Bailey had blinkin' near half-killed her in the process.

"My husband Sidney had blood poisoning," Flora was saying. "That's how I know how bad it is. He got his because he neglected his teeth, though."

She went on talking in a friendly sort of fashion, but Roseen wasn't paying much attention. By the sound of it no one had mentioned the word abortion, or miscarriage, though it must surely have been as plain as a pikestaff to the doctors that she'd had something illegal done to her. Would they report her to the police, was what worried her most; she'd heard of the same thing happening to a barmaid at the Posada.

"I suppose you must be rather surprised to see me here," Flora was telling her now. She could say that again! "I've started doing hospital visiting – you know, a sort of voluntary thing to help patients. I thought . . . well, I mean, when I saw your name on the list I couldn't simply *ignore* you, could I, Roseen. We've known each other too long. So here I am – "

She spread out her hands and smiled that sweet little smile again, as though she meant it. "Anything you want, anything you need – "

Roseen looked at her out of the corner of her eye.

Anything?

That sounded like an offer that might be very useful. What was the old adage about every cloud having a silver lining . . .?

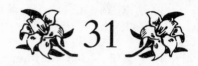# 31

"It was something I promised Father when he was dying," Flora repeated, facing her mother across the dining-room table. "He insisted I gave him my word – what else could I do?"

"You could try acting with a little more sense for a start." Maud Dennison's expression was a picture of irritation. "Any obligation your father may have placed you under was cancelled out by the provisions of his will. That young woman has received quite enough from our family over the years, and as far as I'm concerned she'd not getting a penny piece more."

"It's not the money Roseen needs," Flora protested, "but our help. She's all alone in the world – where else can she turn? Yes, I know Father was generous, but even so, a promise is still a promise."

"Oh, you're *exactly* like him! You'll believe any lame dog story – "

"This isn't a story, Mother, it's fact. Roseen is in the Royal Hospital recovering from a serious bout of septicaemia, and Dr Marshall told me himself she'll need a few weeks' care and attention while she recuperates. He can't just pack her off to Raby Street to a cold and empty house."

"So you propose she comes here, and enjoys free bed and board at our expense."

Flora threw out her arms in exasperation. "But we can afford it. We've got the room."

"She would *not* be welcome."

"That's a very petty attitude to take, I must say."

Maud Dennison rose imperiously to her feet. "I refuse to be spoken to in such a fashion. Remember I am still your mother, Flora, and that this is my house. *I* shall decide the type of person I consider suitable to be invited here."

"I see."

Flora stood up in turn, pushing back her chair. Suddenly there was something rather more at stake than the simple matter of Roseen's recuperation: ever since she'd returned to live at Stockwell End two years ago there'd been this silly jockeying between her and her mother over who should have the last word on a subject. Whether it be the domestic staff or the upbringing of Robert and Imogen or her style of clothes, or even her friendship with Gerard Lansby, her mother always had to be the one to make the final comment, the final point.

Generally Flora took not a scrap of notice and went her own sweet way, allowing Maud just enough margin to keep the peace between them. Even so, remarks like 'this is my house, *I* shall decide' rankled considerably because it served to remind her who was real mistress here.

Why she had suggested in the first place that Roseen should come to Stockwell End, she couldn't imagine. It was one of those spur of the moment impulses, prompted as much by pity as by that promise made to her father. For years now, she and Roseen had been brushing along on the fringes of one another's lives, and though they might not share much liking for each other, neither could ignore the fact that there existed a sort of illegitimate bond between them, forged by George Dennison's relationship with Roseen's mother.

So there it was.

"Come and stay with us for a couple of weeks," she'd offered in hospital, "at least until you're able to look after yourself."

What had surprised her was that Roseen should have accepted with quite so much alacrity.

"And there's another thing to be considered too," Maud Dennison was saying now, pretending to give her attention to the gardener digging a bed outside the window. "From what I recall of her, this person – this Mrs Kelly – comes from a very poor, ill-educated background, and I would certainly not wish it to be known that such was the class of woman I encouraged into my house."

"But who is going to know?" Flora responded on a note of some impatience.

"The staff will know, my dear. It only requires a remark here and a comment there for all of Stockwell End to hear of it. I guard my reputation very jealously in this neighbourhood. Just imagine the talk there would be."

Conscious of the store which her mother set on keeping up social appearances, Flora appreciated the point; but it still didn't deter her from pursuing her own argument.

"People around here are already aware of the voluntary work I do. Surely it wouldn't be stretching their tolerance too far if I were seen to be offering help where genuinely needed. Isn't that what charity is all about?"

"Charity doesn't come into it. Common sense should be the only practical consideration in a case like this. Open the door to one and you'd be expected to do it for every other Tom, Dick and Harry you felt sorry for. Before we knew where we were we'd find ourselves turned into a common lodging-house."

"Oh, don't exaggerate, Mother! All I've proposed is inviting someone I've known since childhood to stay here while she recovers. We're not talking about strangers – we're not talking about someone we've never met – we're talking about Roseen Kelly who used to come to this house as our guest, take holidays with us – "

"Yes, at your father's insistence, and *very* much against my own wishes," interjected Mrs Dennison, turning from the window. "As far as I was concerned she had no business being here, no more than she has any business now. She was a most unsuitable companion for you."

"Be that as it may, the fact remains," Flora went on doggedly, "that Roseen *has* been here, and often, and I can't for the life of me see that her coming again should arouse so much hysteria. Father always thought very well of her" (of her mother Connie too, she was tempted to add) "and if Stockwell End chooses to lift its snooty nose because she's working-class, then all I can say is, well – san fairy ann."

"*Flora!*" Maud Dennison was appalled to hear such a common expression used in her own dining-room. It was the sort of thing the gardener said. Really, what on earth was the world coming to when well-bred young women dared to address their parents in such a way.

She gave her daughter a withering look. Bobbed hair, lipstick, skirt-hem to her knees . . . fashionable Flora might be, but her appearance could scarcely be described as lady-like, no more than her behaviour, gadding out and about with some young farmer and not even widowed a year, and now this extraordinary business with Roseen Kelly. It could only end badly, of that Mrs Dennison was quite certain.

She drew herself up in her most dignified manner and moved towards the door, saying as she went, "I don't wish to hear anything further on the subject of this morning's conversation. I have said all I intend saying, and I trust that I have made my objections clear."

"Perfectly clear. But don't worry, Mother, I'll take full responsibility for what I've done. You see, what I haven't told you is that everything's already been arranged. Roseen has accepted my invitation to stay, and Dr Marshall is discharging her from hospital on Monday morning. I'm sure you'd agree it would be the most frightful bad manners to cancel the whole thing now."

★

The disagreement between mother and daughter continued; but in the end Mrs Dennison had been forced to concede defeat, albeit with a very poor grace. Flora might do as she wished, she said; she herself washed her hands of the matter entirely. It was a fine thing, though, when someone of her own high social standing was forced to receive so undesirable a type of person as guest beneath her roof.

Flora felt just a little guilty about her mother's protests. In a few more weeks – a few more months at the most – Maud would have far more to fret over once she learned that her daughter was planning to marry a man awaiting divorce. So far Flora had not said a word about Robert Wells; but her silence couldn't continue indefinitely. Once Robert and Helen had agreed to end their marriage, events would start to move and it would be most unfair if she didn't forewarn her mother of the outcome. That wasn't a thing which Flora looked forward to with any degree of pleasure. She could well imagine the disbelief, the indignation, the outcry of 'what will the neighbours think' – and worse, the shame she'd be bringing upon the Dennison name by going to live with a man who'd left his wife for her.

Her mother would never forgive her. Never. But that was the price she would have to pay and learn to come to terms with, if she wanted to be with Robert. Nothing was ever free, least of all a love demanding so much sacrifice.

*

Roseen gazed around her, and the smirk on her pale, hollowed face dissolved into a look of self-indulgent pleasure. Talk about living the life of Reilly – this was Buckingham bloomin' Palace compared to Raby Street! They'd given her a room all to herself, with a view between the trees to Tettenhall Rock and furnished very swankily in nice, soft, peachy colours that made it warm and cosy, somehow. The curtain material matched the cushions and bed-cover, and the carpet wasn't an ordinary piece of square, but completely covered the floor and felt like velvet moss to walk on.

Somebody had put a bowl of hyacinths in the window. They were white ones, her favourites, and the scent of them filled the room.

She snuggled further down between the sheets into the almost sensuous comfort of the goose-feather bed, and sighed with contentment. If only Annie Sutton could see her now, she wouldn't half be eating her heart out. It was worth it being so ruddy ill, to land up in clover like this. All she'd got to do for a bit was put on the agony act and roll her eyes like a dying duck in a thunderstorm, and she could stop here as long as she liked. They wouldn't be turfing her out in any hurry, to send her home to Raby Street, not yet at least: there was no food in the pantry, no heating in the place, and a pipe had burst and flooded the scullery. It would be like sending her to her death, it would – Dr Marshall had said that himself. Like sending her back to her death.

Roseen half-closed her eyes. A fire had been lit for her and it was lovely just lying there in the soft light of a winter's afternoon, watching the shadows of the flames flicker across the ceiling. When they were both kids sharing a room together, she and Flora Dennison had made up stories from the pictures they could see in the firelight's reflection; that was one of the things she remembered best about staying here in the old days, that and the way they used to sneak off to the attic, the pair of them, and dress up in Mrs Dennison's party frocks and things.

She'd been jealous of Flora then; jealous because she envied her – hated her almost, for having so much. Funny how their lives kept bumping into one another's. She didn't hate her now . . . didn't like her much either . . . felt nothing at all about her, really . . .

Roseen must have dropped off to sleep at that point. She was still ill and very weak, and the morning's journey from the Royal Hospital had sapped what little energy was left. It was Flora who had arranged the bedroom and prepared everything. She'd even had a special word with the cook and two housemaids, explaining the circumstances of their guest's temporary residence in case they should wonder, for Mrs Dennison herself had said nothing at all to the staff: still highly annoyed with her daughter, she'd taken herself off on a fortnight's visit to a relative over at Worcester.

The sound of the door being quietly opened disturbed Roseen from her nap. She opened her eyes again.

"Sorry if I've roused you," Flora said, as she shifted to turn over. "I've only come in to draw the curtains and see if you'd like anything to eat."

She wasn't hungry. Dr Marshall had told her to have as much as she could to build up her strength, but she'd lost all interest in food; it was like chewing cardboard. The only reason she forced herself to eat was because she looked such a scrawny, half-starved scarecrow with her sunken eyes and her thin white face and her bust as flat as a flippin' pancake.

She gave a wide yawn and pulled herself up on the pillows, resting her head against one arm.

"Would you care for an egg – or a piece of poached fish, perhaps?" Flora went on, pausing by the grate to give the fire a stir as she crossed to the window.

Roseen responded with a noncommittal sound. Having just

woken, what she wanted right at this moment was a visit to the loo and a cigarette.

"Or there's some hot beef tea, if you'd prefer."

"I think I could fancy a boiled egg, ta." She scratched her head and yawned again; then after a brief hesitation, "The lavatory's down at the end of the passage, is it?"

"Oh – yes. Sorry, I should have asked. Can you manage by yourself?"

" 'Course I can." She pushed aside the covers and swung herself awkwardly out of bed, trying to keep her legs covered with her nightgown. Had it been a man in the room she wouldn't have cared two hoots how much of herself was revealed, but she'd always had a curious reserve about that kind of thing in front of other women.

While she was gone Flora rang for one of the maids to fetch up another scuttle of coal and tell Cook to soft-boil an egg for their guest. Now that Roseen was actually installed she intended fulfilling her promise to her father as efficiently as she could, and to see that everything was carried out to the letter, as he would have wished it.

There was just one minor point, though.

"Do you think smoking is all that healthy for you?" she observed pleasantly when Roseen returned eventually, the stub end of a cigarette hanging from her mouth. "My late husband used to smoke a lot, but I could never see the benefit of it myself."

There was a shrug. Removing the offending stub, the other went over and threw it into the fire before getting back into bed with the laconic remark, "I've always smoked cigarettes, so I can't say. Our old Mam used to reckon it killed the germs and stopped you catching coughs and that."

Delving into the pocket of her nightgown, she produced a paper packet of Weights and offered it across.

"Here, want one – ?"

"No thank you," Flora said hastily. "And I'd really rather *you* didn't have any more, either."

"Why not? Where's the flippin' harm?"

"There's no harm, Roseen. It's just that – well, to be frank, I can't bear the smell. I used to hate it when my husband smoked."

There was a knock at the door and the maid came in to replenish the fire. Flora waited until she'd gone again, then went on in a conversational manner, "The very first thing Sidney always did on waking was light a cigarette. I can't tell you how that used to annoy me! When I was pregnant it made me feel really horribly sick."

"Did it? I wouldn't know, myself, o' course."

"Sorry. I'd forgotten. You've never been pregnant, have you."

No answer.

Yesterday afternoon, when Dr Marshall made his final examination, he'd had a quiet word with Roseen about the abortion. She'd suffered for what she'd done, he said, and that was punishment enough, whatever his private views upon the matter. The tragedy of it was that the infection she'd picked up might possibly have left her unable to conceive again. In other words, the likelihood was that she'd never have a baby. She was sterile.

The news had come as a relief, more than anything. With her sort of life pregnancy was an inconvenience she could gladly do without, thank you. She liked going with men, she liked having sex; what she didn't like was all the pain and the mess of paying for her pleasure later on.

Roseen had been reared against a background of working-class poverty where every new pregnancy meant a bit less money to go round, and a bit more scrimping and scraping, and a black eye from your old man for getting yourself in the club again. Given such an attitude, it wasn't surprising that she regarded babies as a nuisance and a burden.

Even so, mulling over Dr Marshall's words last night in the semi-darkness of the hospital ward, she had been overwhelmed by a sudden feeling of sadness. Yes, that was the only way she could describe it. *Sadness*. Just as though she'd lost some part of herself. At the back of her mind she'd always had this dream that one day she'd meet the right man and get married, and have the security of a happy family life – and being told she might well be sterile put the kibosh on it somehow, souring the dream. A woman who couldn't conceive her husband's child was cheating herself as well as him of the biggest proof of their love.

"If you like, I'll bring Imogen and Robert to see you tomorrow."

Flora had been carrying on talking, but wrapped up in her own thoughts Roseen only caught the final sentence.

"What – ? Sorry, what d'you say?"

"Imogen and Robert. My children. Imogen's two and a half now. She's dying to meet you – she adores having visitors to stay with us. If you like – I mean, if you don't mind – I'll bring them both for you to see tomorrow."

Her face held a look of love and pride in the little smile it wore; and Roseen had to turn away for a second to hide the pang of envy.

"No, I don't mind," she said, carefully casual. And then, in a rush of words which took her by surprise, "You don't have to put yourself out too much, you know. I'm obliged to you for having me here, really I am – I can't think why you're doing it, to be honest – but you don't need to be *nice* to me. It in't as if we're friends or anything."

"I'm not being *nice* to you, for heaven's sake." Flora's expression changed. "You're a guest here in our house – how else should I behave?"

They looked at one another; and in that moment something between them seemed to ease and soften, like the loosening of a knot.

"As for being friends – well, our acquaintance goes back a long time, Roseen. And that counts for something, doesn't it."

*

It did.

In the days which were to follow, both would find that it counted for a very great deal.

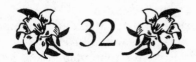

32

For two young women who had little in common beyond a few shared memories of childhood, Flora and Roseen seemed to get along together surprisingly well once the ice had been broken. Knowing what a good thing she was on to here at Stockwell End, Roseen put herself out to appear friendly and agreeable; and was astonished after a few days to discover that her play-acting wasn't all pretence. Far from being the stuck-up, silly so-and-so she'd always taken her for, Flora Hathaway was actually a very likeable person.

For her own part Flora found herself for the first time in her life able to see beneath the surface of Roseen's confident and self-assertive character and catch the odd glimpse of vulnerability, of uncertainty – weaknesses she could understand and pity, because they were part of her own nature too.

During the first week of Roseen's residence the two of them had gradually progressed through the various stages of familiarity, little by little relaxing their guard with one another; and by the second week they were sufficiently at ease to talk about things of a more personal and private aspect.

It was Jessy Venables who was the instigator of one particular confidence: she had come over to tea to meet Flora's 'patient' and had happened to remark during the course of conversation that Roseen ought to consider hiring a private nurse once she'd returned home to Raby Street.

"You know, that was a good idea of Jessy's," Flora commented later after her friend had left. "It wouldn't hurt to have someone coming in to keep an eye on you for another week or so."

"It wouldn't hurt if I had the money to cough up," was the somewhat cryptic response.

"Private nursing agencies aren't all that expensive."

"They are when you can't afford them."

Something in Roseen's tone made Flora look at her more carefully.

"But surely it isn't a question of *affording*. Father left you quite generously off in his will, I believe." Thinking that sounded a little too patronising, she added quickly, "I was pleased he did."

Roseen gave a shrug; then changed the subject slightly with the comment, "He was a good old stick, your Dad. Him and me hit it off like a house on fire, right from the start. He never saw me go short of nothing, nor our Mam neither."

"Yes, he thought a lot of you, I know. He told me. We didn't talk about you much, of course . . . well, I mean, there wasn't much to say, was there . . . but just occasionally your name would crop up in conversation."

Flora wondered whether it would be indelicate to mention Connie O'Connor's relationship with her father. After all, she had been his kept mistress throughout Roseen's childhood, a fact which all of Raby Street knew even if Stockwell End didn't.

She was on the point of making some tactful allusion when – almost as though reading her mind – Roseen saved her the trouble.

"You know there was something going on between them, don't you – our Mam and him?" she said abruptly, examining her fingernails in a way that suggested a certain awkwardness.

Flora took a deep breath. "He . . . told me that, too."

They glanced at one another quickly, like conspirators.

"*Everything?*"

"Everything. It was when he was dying. He wanted to make a clean breast of things, I suppose. He couldn't tell my mother – "

"What, you mean she never found out?"

"I don't think she ever even suspected. She wouldn't have let Father bring you into the house otherwise. That really would have set the cat among the pigeons!"

"She was always against me, though," Roseen said reflectively. "I could tell from the way she used to look at me she thought I was common. She was right, an' all. Compared with you I *was* common." She went back to examining her fingernails once more; and then added, "I was always jealous to death of you, you know, Flora."

It wasn't so much the candour of the admission as the way it suddenly came out which startled Flora – that, and the unexpectedly familiar use of her name. Not since they were children together had Roseen done that.

For a moment she couldn't think what to say.

"It's a fact. I hated you half the time, I was so jealous," the other went on, seeming not to notice her hesitation. "You had everything I'd always wanted. I'd got nothing. You had a nice posh house with servants to look after you. You had new clothes, not somebody else's hand-me-downs. You drove around in a motor-car, and went away on holidays to the seaside. Worse of all, you'd got a Dad – Uncle George – and I wanted him for *my* Dad, not just to pretend for a couple-odd hours a week, but all the time."

She glanced at Flora out of the corner of her eye.

"I hated it, sharing him with you. I used to wish you was dead, so's he'd adopt me."

"Well – that's honest, at least!" The reaction was immediate. This was a moment for frankness. "Would it surprise you, Roseen, if I said that I was always jealous of *you* – because my father loved you so much? Because he actually preferred you to me?"

"Go on – I don't believe that."

"It's the truth. You were a far prettier child than I ever was, far more lively and demanding. He liked that. I was a plump, plain, quiet little thing who wouldn't say boo to a goose. I lived in your shadow for years, wishing I could be the sort of girl that you were so that my father could love me just a little bit better."

Again, they looked at one another; only this time it was as though each was suddenly seeing the other through different eyes, not as enemies but as allies. Two young women thrown together by the circumstances of their lives.

"Is that why you've taken me in?" Roseen asked quietly. "On account of your Dad?"

"Yes. He asked me to promise I'd help you if you were ever in any trouble."

"And that's why your Mam's gone away, is it, me being here?"

A nod.

"You've put yourself out quite a bit, then, haven't you."

"It's been worth it."

Suddenly they were exchanging smiles.

"You're a chip off the old block, you are, Flora. You're just like Uncle George."

Coming from Roseen, it was one of the nicest compliments she could ever remember being paid.

★

The next day, while she rested in bed after luncheon, Roseen told Flora the story of her life. Some things she didn't mention at all, like the two abortions; or preferred not to dwell on, like her husband Billy's death; but in everything else she was candidly honest, even to the exact nature of her relationships with Maurice Lines and Aubrey Podmore.

"Given my time again, I don't suppose I'd want to change much," she admitted. "It's been a lot of fun mostly, in between the bad bits – and it's the fun you tend to remember, looking back. There's only one thing I've done I've ever *really* regretted."

"What was that?" Flora was sitting by the window in the pale afternoon light, doing some embroidery while she listened. Roseen's story had fascinated her; repelled her too, in parts. For all her confidence and vivacity – even, maybe, because of it – events had a habit of sucking Roseen to the bottom of the pile, she thought.

"There was this bloke. Johnnie Driscoll." Roseen linked her hands behind her head to rest against the pillows and stared reflectively towards the fire. "I bumped into him on holiday last year in Deauville. He bought me a drink – the usual tale – told me he was in business and the rest of it.

306

'Course, I believed everything he said, didn't I. My trouble is, I've always been a sucker for a handsome face, and Johnnie *was* handsome, blimey he was. Minded his manners, spoke nice, treated me to champagne suppers and nights at the Casino . . . before I knew where I was, he'd got me eating out of his hand, he had."

There was a pause.

"He sounds almost too good to be true," remarked Flora, selecting a different coloured silk from her box.

"Almost too *bad*, you mean! He proved himself a right proper charmer, did our Johnnie. Must've spotted me coming a mile off. D'you know what he was? I'll tell you. He was a gambler – a *professional* gambler. He'd beg, borrow and steal so he'd have enough for the roulette tables – it was like a disease with him – and so long as it was *my* money he was gambling, he didn't much care how often he lost, neither. Only trouble was, I was daft enough to believe he could win it all back again . . . that's why I kept lending him more and more."

Another pause. When she spoke again, Roseen's voice held a sudden bitterness.

"Everything I'd got he took off me. Skinned me to the bone, he did. And when there was nothing left, d'you know what he went and done across me, the stinker – ? He skedaddled, didn't he. Hopped it and left me there in Deauville all alone to face the music."

"What – without any money?" Flora looked up.

"Not so much as a ruddy brass farthing."

"But didn't you go to the police?"

"What could the police do, I ask you." Roseen drew a veil of discretion over her reasons for not wanting the French authorities involved. "He'd gone – done a bunk. They'd never've found him. He was too flippin' clever by half, was Johnnie."

By this time her story had captured Flora's entire attention. She put her embroidery aside.

"So what did you do?"

"Had to sell my best bit of jewellery to pay the hotel off and find the fare home. Ever since then – well, I've been scrimping along as best I can just to make ends meet."

"But why on earth do that? Withdraw some money from the bank, why don't you – that's what it's there for."

"No, you don't understand. I've got nothing left. It's all gone."

"Gone? What – *all* of it?"

Roseen nodded.

"But Father left you a thousand pounds." Flora stared at her, trying to make some sense of what she was saying. "You can't have spent that much already, not in six months. I mean – a thousand pounds is a lot of money."

"Don't I know it, an' all!" The other appeared not to resent the implied criticism. "I bought a car, and tranklements for the house an' that, but I'd still have had a good few hundred quid left to keep me going if that blasted twister hadn't nicked it."

"But how much *did* he have from you altogether?"

"Well . . . I didn't see much change out o' the three hundred I went and lent him."

"Good God –" Flora was so taken aback she couldn't think what else to say for a second. She'd imagined that the sum they'd been talking about was in the region of fifty pounds or so – but *three hundred*! It was a ridiculous amount of money to entrust in the hands of some complete stranger. Poor, misguided Roseen . . .

"No wonder you can't afford private nursing," she said at last in a worried voice. "What are you going to do – how will you manage for the future?"

There was a shrug and a pulled face. "I'll have to look for work, I suppose, once I'm on my feet again."

"You might find that difficult. There's hardly any work around at the moment, the state the country's in."

"Oh, I'll cope somehow. There's always public houses wanting barmaids. Folk don't stop drinking just because they're having to live off the dole."

"But you're not very strong, Roseen. That kind of employment calls for long hours, I imagine. Look, I tell you what – " Flora's generous nature rose impulsively to the occasion. "If Father were still here, I know what he'd do. He'd ensure you had whatever help you needed, at least to tide you over for a bit. Well, I'll do the same. I'll see that

308

another hundred pounds from the estate goes into your account. That should give you more than enough to manage on till you're able to find a decent job."

Roseen's eyes widened. Blimey, she thought, talk about the fairy with the magic wand – !

"You mean you'd *lend* me a hundred quid, just like that?"

"No, it wouldn't be a loan. It would be an outright gift."

Blimey again . . .

★

A few days later Roseen was pronounced well enough to go out for a short stroll in the fresh air. Flora wrapped her up against the wind in one of her own fur coats and made her hold her arm while they walked through the garden as far as the ornamental summerhouse. The weather had been quite mild this month, and thick clumps of snowdrops were already dotting the lawns, with here and there the first green thrusting spears of daffodil and crocus showing beneath the naked trees.

They sat inside the summerhouse for a while enjoying the sun's pleasant warmth through the closed glass. Somehow their conversation steered round to Flora's marriage and what a disappointment she felt it had been; and then Roseen said, "But you'll get married again, won't you? There must be dozens of chaps falling over theirselves to ask you."

"I don't know about dozens! There's one I see occasionally, a local man, just a friend. *He's* very fond of me."

"And d'you show him much encouragement?"

"No, not really . . . though I'd like to."

"Why don't you, then?"

"Because there's someone else. Someone I'm in love with." The words just seemed to slip from Flora's mouth. It was the first time she'd ever admitted her love to a soul except Robert himself.

"Go on! Who is he?" Roseen was agog to hear more. "What's he look like?"

"Oh, you know, brown eyes, dark hair. Quite tall." She tried to be offhand.

"How long ago was it you met him?"

"Ten – no, eleven years ago now. 1912. We were students together at college in Birmingham."

"Crikey. And you've been in love with him all that time, have you?"

"I suppose I have, *nearly* all that time, yes."

"So why didn't you get married to him? Instead of Mr Hathaway?"

Flora looked at the pool of January sunlight reflected through the glass door.

"If I tell you, Roseen," she said after a moment, "will you swear you'll never breathe a word of it to anyone else? It's a secret, you see. No one else knows."

"*I* won't say anything – promise I won't." Roseen crossed her hands on her breast in the old childish gesture of oath-taking which they used to use together. She never took her eyes off Flora's face. "Fair's fair. You've heard all *my* secrets, haven't you."

There was another pause. It would be such a relief to confide in someone after keeping her feelings for Robert pent up all this long. Roseen was impartial; she wouldn't judge nor would she condemn. She'd known too much of life and its experiences to be a moralist.

"The reason I didn't marry him," Flora began, slowly, quietly, "was because he had a wife already."

That was the hard bit. It came easier after that; easier to talk about her love for Robert, and his for her, and how they'd tried to forget one another over the years and never succeeded. Roseen didn't ask many questions. Once Flora had started her story, the whole thing seemed to flow out of her in a stream of words like an unblocked spring, carrying the flood of memories into the open.

She described Robert's letters; seeing each other again for the first time last year; the day spent together discussing what they must do, making their plans, dreaming of their future. She tried to make light of the fact that nothing had yet been decided between Robert and his wife, but Roseen could tell by the expression on her face that that was worrying her.

"There's something about being married that makes a man a bit of a liar," she commented when Flora had finally come to a stop. "Sounds as if your Robert's scared of telling his missus the truth just in case it upsets her. That's why he's dragging his feet so much and palming you off with excuses."

"Do you really think that's it? He's frightened of hurting Helen?"

"Well, put it this way – he's had a good three months to screw up his courage. He can't decide in which direction to jump, if you ask me."

Flora bit her lip and looked down at her hands, gripped together tightly in her lap. She hadn't realised how tense she'd become while she was talking. She still felt tense; flat and drained as well, as though the catharsis of baring herself to Roseen had purged her strength completely.

"I don't know what to do," she said after a while, in a small voice. "I don't know whether to go on waiting, and hoping . . . or do the decent thing and tell Robert it's all over between us. At least if I did that it would avoid a lot of painful scandal . . . he'd still have his family and his school career."

"Oh, don't think so much of *him* all the time!" Roseen exclaimed. "Think of yourself for a change. What is it *you* want?"

"I just – want everyone to be happy."

"Well, taking up with a married man in't the way to do it. You wouldn't be happy living with a conscience like a millstone round your neck, you know you wouldn't."

She glanced at Flora's tight, unsmiling face; and then, just a little cautiously, went on, "If this Robert wasn't in the way, d'you think you'd like to marry that other chap you mentioned – the one that lives local?"

"Who? Gerard, you mean?" Flora returned the look blankly.

"If that's his name. D'you think you might like to marry him?"

"I don't know. I really hadn't considered it."

"But you do *like* him?"

"Oh yes. He's – well, he's such easy company to be with. We get on extremely well together, as a matter of fact."

For some reason, this answer appeared to satisfy Roseen. She smiled suddenly and patted Flora's hand.

"Come on – let's get back into the house, shall we. I couldn't half fancy a nice cup of tea."

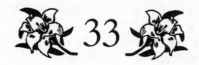

33

Dear Mr Wells

I am writing to you as a friend of Flora Hathaways without her knowing this as she doesn't know I got your address. She is very worried and unhappy on account of your friendship because she has another gentleman who likes her and would settle for him if you werent in the way. Also, he is not *married*. If you was a decent sort you would leave her alone and think of your poor wife instead, it can only bring a lot of trouble and you are stopping Flora from being realy happy with this nice *unmarried* gentleman. Remember you have to sleep with your conscense at nights.

One good turn deserved another, in Roseen's book.

Flora had been a true Samaritan to her these past few weeks, not only by taking her in and looking after her – and the physical benefits of that were already evident – but by seeing her fixed all right for money. She'd given her back her pride in herself as well, and to a woman like Roseen that counted for a great deal.

She wanted to do something positive and useful in repayment; not just a token 'thank you' but something like a proper real favour in return for all those favours Flora had done her. Experience of life, and men, prompted her action. Perhaps others might call it meddling, but as far as Roseen was concerned the means more than justified the end she hoped to achieve.

Ironically in the circumstances, it was Flora's absence from the house on hospital visiting which had presented Roseen with the opportunity to find what she wanted: Robert Wells's address. She guessed that his letters would be kept somewhere in Flora's room, either in a drawer in her bedside table or hidden away at the back of her writing bureau; and sure enough, there they were in the bureau, tied with blue ribbon, inside a plain manila folder marked in Flora's neat, small hand 'personal and private'.

The address, Roseen noted, was a box number c/o Freshwater post office on the Isle of Wight. She scribbled it down and helped herself to a sheet of notepaper, a penny stamp and an envelope before closing the bureau lid and returning unobserved to her own room.

Here she had settled herself to composing her letter.

It was posted by one of the housemaids that same afternoon; and reached Robert Wells at a critical juncture in his relationship with his family. With Helen now completely recovered from her illness, he had decided he could no longer go on prevaricating: one way or another the question of his future with Flora must be resolved. He had never been a man to lack courage, but the months spent agonising over what he must do, what was fair, what was right, had tended to sap his emotional tenacity to some extent.

The worst time had been over Christmas, trying to make it a happy one for them all and hating himself for his hypocrisy – particularly the moment when his beloved stepdaughter Meg had just unwrapped her present, something she'd especially wanted, and throwing her arms about his neck, told him he was 'the best Pa in the whole wide world'.

Would she be feeling that of him next Christmas?

Finally the pressure had become too much to bear; and one evening in the New Year, finding himself alone in the house with Helen, he'd taken the plunge and made a full and frank confession to her of his love for another woman, suggesting she give him his freedom.

Her reaction had been quite incredible. For a woman of such a placid and unemotional nature, she showed a distress which was so terrible in its intensity that it shook Robert to the very core. It was like lifting the lid of a Pandora's Box: he had never known, never in all these years even suspected, that beneath her calm exterior Helen could harbour such passionate feeling, such fiercely caring possessiveness.

She had wept and pleaded, alternately begging and reproachful, and then blazing into wounded anger that he should betray her as he had. He could scarcely believe this was the same woman he had been living with so long. She accused him of deceit, of cruelty, of taking from her the best years of her life and then spurning her for a younger woman. She demanded to know who it was so that she might make her aware of the pain and the anguish she'd caused; and when Robert wisely refused to disclose Flora's identity, she had thrown herself at his feet, imploring him not to leave her.

He was absolutely stunned by it all.

His stepchildren Meg and young Jack, when they heard, took their mother's side, of course, and added their hurt to hers. What affected him above all was that both of them, separately, went to some trouble to tell him how much as a family they loved and needed him; which, coming from his favourite Meg, was touching enough, but coming from Jack, with whom he hadn't been seeing eye to eye for some time, was food for thought indeed. It had taken the boy a lot of pluck to seek him out and speak to him as sincerely as he had, and it left upon Robert a deep and disturbing impression.

When he had first considered marriage to Helen it was her two fatherless children who had most swayed his final decision, and he'd always loved and regarded them as his own. That love still exerted a very strong pull on his heart.

What ought he to do? He wished to God he had the answer. The situation he was in at the moment, caught between the crossfire of personal wants and family loyalty, was one to strain the steadiest nerve. He wanted Flora, wanted her with every fibre of his being and always would, as long as he had life and breath within him. She didn't *need* him though; not in the same way that he was starting now to realise Helen did. A man would have to be made of stone to resist the piteous sight of his own wife lying across their bed at night and breaking her heart with grief over his faithlessness.

It lacerated his conscience to know how much he was hurting her. She was forty-two years old, at the age when a woman's looks are just beginning to fade and her femininity

314

changing: a vulnerable time of life for any woman, but especially one who feels herself unwanted and rejected, cast aside to make way for someone younger, someone more attractive and desirable.

Then, as though to add to Robert's terrible dilemma, there had arrived this letter from Wolverhampton, anonymously informing him that Flora had acquired some new admirer. It was a most peculiar missive: badly written and ungrammatical, almost spiteful in tone, with its clumsy double emphasis upon the fellow's single status and all that that implied. Who might possibly have sent it Robert had no idea: Flora had always been very circumspect about their relationship. He could only suppose it was someone who, for their own reasons, wished to see the association ended, leaving her free to choose elsewhere.

For over a fortnight he grappled with his conscience, hating himself for the disruption and heartache he was causing. He had reached a low ebb both mentally and physically, finding it difficult to concentrate on his teaching work at school because of the lack of sleep and the constant stress of his domestic situation.

Then something happened which served to tip the balance irreversibly.

He and Helen were still sharing the same room, even though sexual relations between them had virtually ceased years before. Since all this upset started, however, she had got it into her head that her coldness was in part to blame for his wanting to leave her, and more and more often now at night her pleading was taking the form of physical invitation. It was impossible for a man who had denied himself the release of intercourse not to feel some arousal. He respected Helen, he liked her, and he was bitterly sorry for the misery she was suffering; and therefore, despite the strength of his feelings for Flora, he simply couldn't bring himself to push his wife away and repulse her affection.

For whatever reason it happened – whether pity, or guilt, or the natural needs of his own body – after Robert had made love again to Helen on just that one occasion, he realised a decision had been forced upon him. Having shared physical intimacy with her, he couldn't in all conscience abandon her

315

now. No matter what cost the sacrifice, as a man who put honour above all things he must now find strength through that honour to remain with his family and keep his marriage together.

The dream was ended.

★

My darling Flora

This is without doubt the hardest letter I have ever had to write. I scarcely know where to begin, nor how to say what I must. Seeing Helen in such terrible distress has made me realise that I do not have the right to expect her to pay for my happiness at the expense of her own. She was devastated when I told her that I wanted to leave. I could not believe it. She said it would destroy her, and Meg and Jack, to lose me, that she loves me – and a great deal more besides; I cannot tell you the half of it. She has never stopped crying. The situation at home has been a nightmare these past weeks.

I feel like killing myself, except that it would resolve nothing. You know me better than anyone has ever known me, my darling, so you can understand perhaps a little of what I am suffering now that I am being forced to face the unimaginable – a future without you.

How final that sounds, and how cruel! Yet it would be unfair on both of us to pretend differently. We are not children. We know it would be impossible for us to meet ever again unless to spend the rest of our lives together, and since that has been denied us, what point is there in clinging to false hopes.

I will always love you with the deepest and most tender affection. Nothing on earth can ever take that from me. There are no words to describe the wretchedness of soul I feel at having to make this decision; but I could not possibly live with my conscience were I to do otherwise. I truly thought that Helen would not care. How wrong I was. Still waters run deep indeed.

I know how your dear heart must be breaking to read this – as mine is breaking to write it – but what choice do we have. I must be honest, Flora, and say that just as I could not bear to see you again unless it were never more to be separated from you, neither could I bear to have Helen's misery hanging like a shadow over our heads. It would be a constant blight upon our own happiness.

I love you so much. Losing the dream we shared together all these years is the worst thing which has ever happened to me. Something fundamental to my very being has been plucked out, and I shall never know now what it is to be truly self-fulfilled.

Please reply to this letter. I need to hear from you. I hope that we may continue to correspond, but of course that is your decision. Forgive me for all the pain I have caused you, my darling.

Yours, always and for ever

Robert.

He made no reference to the anonymous communication from Wolverhampton. Whether its contents were true or not, either way there was nothing to be done about the situation now. His hands were tied. If Flora had a suitor the probability was that she'd marry again some day; and in a spirit of unselfishness as well as resignation, he rather hoped she would, if only to have a husband to take care of her and her children.

It comforted him a little to think that. It was what he himself had done for Helen and Meggie and Jack, after all.

★

What astonished Flora so much upon receiving Robert's letter was that she should feel such an extraordinary surge of relief. Heartache and sadness as well, of course, and tears; but after that first reaction it was as though she had suddenly been freed of some tremendous weight which had been bowing her down for months past.

Over and over again up till now she'd kept trying to reassure herself that, once they were together, everything would be magically all right; but in her heart of hearts she'd known it was a lie – at best, a wishful dream. No matter how blissful she and Robert might have been, they would always

317

have had the stigma of divorce and the knowledge of Helen's unhappiness there in the background; and in time that knowledge would have soured their bliss and come between them as a permanent reproach.

Conscience makes cowards of us all.

Now there was no longer anything to feel guilty or ashamed about. Helen still had her husband, and the children their stepfather; Robert's career was safe; Maud Dennison could continue to hold up her head in Stockwell End society and never know how near she'd sailed to scandal; and Flora herself – ?

For years her love for Robert had existed upon memories and the stimulus of unfulfilment; but of late, all unconsciously, it had been feeding upon uneasiness and tensions and uncertainty – a diet guaranteed in time to poison it. He was right in more ways than one when he'd said that nobody should be expected to pay for another's happiness at the price of their own.

And another thing: if Flora were to be truly honest with herself, in writing that letter to him last year confessing her love and all that he'd meant to her, something in the intensity of her feelings had diminished a little, as though pouring it all out on paper had put the whole thing into perspective and somehow faded the colour from her dreams.

That was why, hard upon the heels of her heartbreak, she felt this profound relief that at last it had all been resolved, the decision taken, the onus lifted. The only thing she'd lost was something which she'd never really had, a life shared with Robert; but she still possessed first place in his heart, and always would.

Nothing was changed . . . merely rearranged. It was like the breaking of a spell. Through her tears she realised that she was finally free of the past – free to pursue the future without always looking back over her shoulder at what might have been. One of the things she'd found most disturbing in recent months had been the dichotomy of her affections – maintaining her loyalty to Robert while at the same time being drawn more and more to a realisation of her liking for Gerard Lansby. Gerard was such good fun, such enjoyable company, down to earth and *real*, someone to feel physically close to. With Robert she had only ever been able to build castles in the sky.

She wrote back after a few days, when she'd had time to adjust her emotions to the finality of the situation. It was a letter intentionally full of warmth and understanding, as one friend to another, assuring Robert of her affection and hoping that he and Helen might find a greater strength in their marriage as a positive outcome to everything.

This was a difficult period to face alone, though. She desperately needed someone to whom she could talk about her feelings, but Roseen had gone home to Raby Street and there was nobody else – certainly not her mother, back now from Worcester and complaining all the time about the inconvenience she'd been put to.

Thinking that a change of surroundings might possibly help to lift her spirits, Flora went away with the children to stay with Jessy Venables for a long weekend; but for once her friend's endlessly bright chit-chat grated upon her nerves. Instead she found she preferred to be alone in the peaceful fire-lit cosiness of the nursery, watching her darling little Imogen and her baby son play with Jessy's daughter Poppy, or else taking the three of them out for long walks in the perambulator along the wintry lanes. Her strong, deep love for her children was the bedrock of her life; and from them she drew her greatest comfort and consolation.

The following Tuesday, instead of going to the Royal Hospital as usual, she decided to ask Craddock to drive her to Raby Street.

It was a most strange experience, like journeying back into the past. Flora hadn't been to the area since before the war, and noticed at once how dingy and dilapidated it was becoming, with the smell from the nearby brewery adding its own sourness to the atmosphere.

In pleasant contrast, Roseen's house proved welcoming and cheerful. She'd obviously had someone to lend her a hand with the cleaning, and told Flora it was a friend, Annie Sutton, who'd been popping by for a couple of hours each day.

"Annie and me, we've known each other years," she explained, showing her visitor through to the back kitchen, seeming not in the least surprised to find the Dennisons'

Wolseley parked outside her door and Flora there on the step. "We've had our ups and downs, like, but when she heard I'd been in hospital she come round quick as a shot to see how I was."

She motioned with her head to a chair at one side of the fire. "Sit you down, why don't you, and I'll make us a pot of tea. The kettle's not long boiled."

Her natural manner put Flora at ease. Settling herself as invited she glanced around, noting how homely the room was with its pegged-rag rugs and its aspidistra plant and its pictures and little knick-knacks. Taking pride of place on the mantelpiece above the black-leaded range was a sepia photograph of a young man in uniform, and beside it a painted china dog, and a framed picture of some exotic kind of flowers.

"That's pretty," she said, indicating the flowers.

"Yes, your Dad took a fancy to that an' all," Roseen remarked over her shoulder. "It's tiger lilies. Our Billy won it for me at the fair one year. That's him in the photo, by the way – " She gave another nod of the head. "Take it down if you like so's you can see him better."

Flora did.

"He was a fine-looking young man, wasn't he," she commented after a few moments, reaching to put the photograph back in its place. "What a tragedy for you to lose him, just when you both had your lives before you – "

Suddenly she could keep up this social pretence no longer; and in a stumbling rush of words went on, "All that pain, that heartache . . . I can sympathise, really I can. I've just lost somebody dear myself, that's why I had to come round here this evening. Roseen – oh, Roseen, please help me."

Her outburst seemed to evoke a curious tone of satisfaction.

"It's that Robert from the Isle of Wight, I suppose."

"Yes. I've . . . had a letter from him."

Roseen carried on making the tea. "So what's he got to say for himself, then?"

Flora told her, her voice strained with tears as she spoke, knotting a lump in her throat. Although she'd come to terms with the fact that Robert had gone from her life, to speak of it upset her more than she'd thought it would.

When she'd finished, Roseen poured her a cup of tea and brought it over.

"Here, get this down you. It'll make you feel better."

Lighting a cigarette she sat herself opposite, legs crossed, leaning back in the chair. "Look at things sensibly, Flora. It hurts like hell now the whole affair's finished and done with. I know, I've felt the same myself. But you've still got your pride. You can still hold your head up high. Nobody's going to whisper behind their hand every time they see you coming in the street."

"I know, but – "

"My old Mam always used to say reach rock bottom and life can't get no worse, it can only pick up. Married men ain't that much flippin' cop, honest they ain't. They're somebody else's second-hand belongings. Give him a couple or three months to enjoy his oats and your Robert'd be treating you no different than the wife he swapped you for."

Roseen drew on her cigarette. "Love don't last. Take it from me, it don't. There's no such thing as a broken heart really, only broken hopes and promises, and bruised pride. What you need," she went on through a mouthful of smoke, watching Flora carefully, "is some other chap to take your mind off it all."

"I suppose so. I'm just . . . numb at the moment." Flora's face was a crumpled mask of misery.

"Give yourself a bit of time, see how you feel. Love's like the measles – you think you're going to die, but you don't, you get over it. Then you start forgetting how much it hurt and the next thing you know, you're asking yourself what the heck all the fuss was about. Take a tip from me, Flora – first chance you get, paint a smile on your face, put your glad rags on, and go out and enjoy yourself with that other bloke, that Gerard."

Flora fished her handkerchief from her pocket and gave her nose a good blow. Perhaps Roseen was right. What was the point of moping around wallowing in misery, reading reams of sentimental poetry, and crying herself to sleep at night over his letters. All the tears in the world weren't going to alter anything now.

She managed a small smile; and when Roseen started asking

about Gerard and about Cowpers, it was somehow comforting to get away from the subject of Robert and speak instead of something much more pleasant.

Half an hour later, after a second cup of tea, she reluctantly got up to leave.

"Call round again any time if you want another chat," Roseen said in response to her words of gratitude. "You'll always be welcome."

She showed Flora to the door and stood on the front step to watch the Wolseley off down Raby Street, lingering deliberately so that the neighbours could all see.

As the car reached the corner, Flora turned to look back and saw her still there in the spilled yellow light of the gas-lamp. For a moment, something played tricks with her imagination. She could almost believe there was a small girl with red-gold hair in corkscrew curls leaning from the upstairs window, waving.

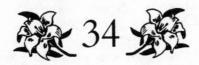

34

The unemployment situation was becoming quite serious; but things were nowhere near as bad as they were in Germany, where the value of the mark had fallen so low that the exchange rate was now 150,000 to the pound sterling and people were literally starving to death on the streets.

The Great War still cast a lengthy shadow; and that shadow lay darkest across the impoverished, the weak and the dispossessed, those whose past had been destroyed in the conflagration of carnage and who now found themselves abandoned to a future without hope and without dignity. It was against this background of German despair that dozens of minor political factions were beginning to spring up, bent upon restoring the tarnished power and glory of the Fatherland.

Occasionally the London newspapers ran a paragraph or two on the activities of the more fanatical of these groups. The name most frequently mentioned was the National Socialist German Workers' Party, a Bavarian beer-hall movement whose leader was an ex-Army corporal called Hitler. No one took much notice, however. The antics of a few young German hot-heads weren't half as interesting to read about as Oxford winning the University Boat Race, the continuing outrages in Ireland, the death of the great Sarah Bernhardt, and the mysterious 'Pharaoh's Curse' demise of Lord Carnarvon in Cairo; not to mention the more discreet coverage afforded to Dr Marie Stopes and her controversial birth control clinic.

Dr Stopes was very much closer to the hearts of British womenfolk than Herr Hitler, Lord Carnarvon or even Madame Bernhardt. At a time when medical and religious

323

prejudice against birth control was still considerable, she had courageously broken the taboos with her books, *Married Love* and *Wise Parenthood*, and after the opening of her clinic two years ago in 1921, was regarded by the more enlightened as keeper of the nation's sexual conscience.

Jessy Venables was typical of the sort of intelligent young wife who saw the advantages of limiting one's family by choice rather than by chance. In fact so great was her enthusiasm for Dr Stopes that she talked of virtually little else throughout the holiday she and Flora spent together that Easter with the children, renting a house at Tenby on the Pembroke coast. The holiday was Flora's idea: the stressful experience of ending things with Robert had left her feeling generally under the weather, and she needed these few weeks of sea air and sunshine as a tonic to revitalise her.

Jessy's constant effusiveness both amused and exasperated her in equal measure. She agreed with her friend that fewer little mouths to feed would mean less poverty, and in time fewer numbers to add to the unemployed; but she drew the line at Jessy's idea that husbands should be prosecuted if their wives bore more than three children. The poor were poor enough without making them pay for their ignorance: education was what was required, that was her opinion.

During the second week of the holiday they were joined by Winifred Unsworth, recently home from Africa on a few months' missionary leave. Winifred's presence enlivened things considerably since she was determined they should all see as much of the Pembroke peninsula as possible, and insisted on driving everyone about in a very uncomfortable old Enfield Minerva hired from the local garage. She was becoming amiably eccentric, and the children – little Poppy Venables and Flora's Imogen and baby Robert (known these days as Bobby) – utterly adored her.

She agreed not at all with Jessy on the subject of Dr Stopes, whom she considered little better than a criminal abortionist, and the evenings were passed in lively, if occasionally heated, argument, with Winifred quoting the most extraordinary passages from Scripture in defence of her beliefs. Flora enjoyed it immensely, and was sorry when their fortnight in Tenby came to an end and the holiday was over.

The only pleasant prospect in returning to Wolverhampton was that she'd promised to arrange to see Gerard Lansby as soon as she got back.

The two of them had not been out together since Christmas, when he'd taken her and the children to the pantomime at the Grand Theatre. Flora had been a little on edge on that occasion, fretting about the situation between Robert Wells and his wife; and she worried later, when Gerard failed to telephone or write, whether he'd finally grown weary of her continual brittleness.

Then at the beginning of March, to her relief, he'd called to apologise for his neglect, pleading an extra-busy lambing season; and after that, nothing more again until just a few days before she came away on holiday.

"Well, have a good time and enjoy yourself, my dear," he'd said cheerily on ringing off. "I'll wait to hear from you the minute you're back home. Don't forget!"

She didn't forget. Now that she'd been released from all promise to Robert, the initial surge of relief felt on realising the attachment was finished had grown during these intervening weeks into a permanent sense of emancipation and hope for the future, which overrode her heartache.

She was looking forward so much to being with Gerard again, and when he suggested that she might like to bring Imogen and Bobby over to Cowpers for an afternoon to see the lambs, she readily accepted. He seemed very much at ease with her children, swinging them up in his arms and clowning about to make them laugh; and Flora found her affections warming to him more and more as she watched them play so happily together.

"Have luncheon with me at the Rodney next Thursday?" Gerard proposed at parting after that visit. "Let's make it a long afternoon, shall we, just the pair of us. If the weather's fine we can walk round by the lake."

Hopes were fulfilled. Thursday proved to be one of those lovely April days of primrose sunshine; and what gave it an unexpected little touch of magic was that it happened also to be the wedding day of the young Duke of York to Lady Elizabeth Bowes-Lyon, and the narrow streets of Brewood were hung with flags and streamers by way of celebration.

"They obviously knew we were coming," Gerard joked when he saw the festoons of coloured bunting decorating the frontage of the Admiral Rodney Inn. He was in excellent spirits and kept up a flow of amusing conversation all through luncheon, making Flora rock with laughter at some of his anecdotes.

"You know, you seem a completely different person just lately," he told her. "That holiday in Tenby must have agreed with you."

"Oh, I'd say it was things in general agreeing with me," Flora said, smiling. "I feel so much happier than last year."

"Happiness suits you. It makes you beautiful."

She appreciated the compliment.

Afterwards they drove back to Cowpers to enjoy a long, leisurely stroll round the margins of the lake. It was a pictur-esque walk, especially at this time of year with the soft-green freshness of newly-opened leaves making a perfect woodland background to the stronger colours of azalea and rhododen-dron bushes along the water's edge. The air had a mildness to it which promised the warmth of summer days ahead, and from every part of the fields and woods around there echoed the sweet sounds of birdsong rising above the muted cooing of ring doves.

"This is bliss," sighed Flora, pausing to rest on a fallen trunk and raising her face, eyes closed, towards the sun. "I wish I could turn into a dryad and stay here for ever."

"I'd rather you didn't turn into anything," Gerard told her. "I much prefer you just the way you are. As for staying here for ever, though, my darling – "

He didn't say any more.

She opened her eyes again, shading them with a hand to look up at him, but the sunlight behind threw his face into shadow, preventing her from reading his expression.

"Come on." Reaching down, he pulled her gently to her feet and tucked her arm through his. "There's something special I'd like to show you."

Several hundred yards further ahead an overgrown track led off the path to the right, away from the lake, and dis-appeared into the woods. Gerard took Flora along this way, pushing aside branches and taking care that she didn't catch her legs on tendrils of bramble and briar.

As they went deeper and deeper among the trees the earth became dappled with a pattern of golden-green light reflected through the leaves, and there was a hush in the air like a listening stillness which seemed gradually to thicken and wrap itself round, drawing them into its quietness.

Just when Flora was beginning to wonder whether they'd ever find their way out again, Gerard paused and put a hand on her shoulder to point ahead.

"There it is – see? Up there through the trees."

A short way on along the track they came out into a clearing where the woodland had been cut back at some time in the past to form an open glade. After the dimness, Flora's eyes were dazzled for a moment by the sudden brilliance of sunshine; and then she caught her breath and gave a little cry of pleasure, enchanted by the beauty of the sight which lay before her. The floor of the glade was a carpet of bluish-mauve where the year's first bluebells were just unfolding into flower, and in the midst of this were the ruins of a small cottage, grown over with wild honeysuckle and dog-rose and fern. There was an atmosphere of such peace and tranquillity that it seemed almost a sacrilege to intrude.

"Once upon a time," said Gerard quietly, "when I was a very small boy, I used to believe that God lived here."

Flora turned to look up at him. His face held a rapt expression.

"We had an old woodsman who took me around with him everywhere. He swore he'd seen the fairies dancing here on Midsummer's Eve. I believed that too. When my dog died, we buried her under the hearthstone where foxes couldn't get her . . . I loved that dog. She'd been with me since I was born. And then when I was about six, I suppose, I started coming here by myself and pretending all sorts of adventures – you know the way children do, making up games and inventing things. It always seemed to be summer in those days . . ."

He stopped, and gazed round him, remembering; then after a few moments went on again, "It was this little patch of paradise that kept me sane at Ypres. *This* – more than anything else about home. When I thought I was going screaming mad with the horror of it all, the ghastly butchery, I'd conjure up my childhood here, where the world was safe and green and peaceful, and force myself to concentrate until I really believed I *was* here, and all the rest was a nightmare. That's why this place is so special to me, Flora . . . and why I wanted to show it you. It's a part of me that no one else has ever shared."

She felt a slight shiver run through her, a feeling of awe that he should entrust her with something so personal and so altogether private. She didn't know what to say, except thank you, and that sounded far too inadequate, however sincerely she meant it.

"It's true, you know." Gerard put his arm round her and gave her a little squeeze, pressing his cheek against her hair. "I've never brought anyone else here. You're the first. I knew you wouldn't spoil it by laughing at me."

"What on earth should I laugh at?"

"Oh . . . sentiment and all that. There's many people wouldn't understand. They'd think I was an idiot to attach so much affection to a tumble-down old ruin and a bit of overgrown woodland."

"There's nothing absurd about that, Gerard. We've all got our own private little worlds. When I was a child, mine was upstairs in the attics – nothing half as romantic as this, I admit, but it was *my* special place where I ceased to be an ugly duckling and became whatever I wished – depending on which of Andrew Lang's fairy books I was lost in at the time!"

The two of them exchanged smiles. There was something very intimate about sharing personal confidences like this, and it gave Flora a sudden wonderful, warm feeling of affinity with her companion, a sense of closeness which had always eluded her somehow with Robert.

"You, my dearest, were never an ugly duckling," said Gerard, giving her another squeeze. "You were soft, and shy, and very sweet. At least, *I* thought so, otherwise I wouldn't have fallen in love with you at that Dennison's Christmas party. I was twelve years old, as I remember, and thought you the nicest little girl in the room. Every time you glanced in my direction I winked back at you to try to catch your eye."

"Ah, but what a fickle admirer you proved – the devotion lasted hardly a day," she teased him.

He grinned; and then, just for a moment, his face altered and turned serious. "Even so, you were still my first love, you know, Flora . . . just as I hope you'll be my last."

He drew her against him and kissed her, his lips tasting of the fresh, clean air; then with something more like his old humour he said, "Come on – let's make a start for home before we end up like those pantomime babes in the wood. We've still got some afternoon left to enjoy. Might as well make the most of it."

Taking her by the hand, he led the way out of the glade and back along the track to the lake. By this time the April sun was starting to sink into swathes of thin, misty cloud, which had drifted in from the west, and its light was weaker now, plunging the woodlands into patches of purple shadow.

Neither of them said much. Words seemed almost superfluous. It wasn't until they reached the main path that the two began conversation again, talking about trivialities and laughing together, as people do when totally at ease in one another's company.

"Shall I tell you something – " Gerard said suddenly. They had just got as far as the bridge where they'd stopped once before, in the autumn, the last time they'd been in this direction. "I know this is going to sound a little odd, but – you seem to have woken up somehow, Flora. You've come back to life and started being your real self again. You're not going around in a dream any more."

She couldn't think quite what to answer; but in any case he saved her the need of reply, running on, "Do you recall I told you in the Rodney today that you're a different person lately? Well, it's true. It's wonderful, in fact. You must admit you've been pretty down in the dumps at times. To tell you honestly, I thought it was *me* – I thought, well, perhaps she doesn't like me all that much and she's simply humouring me for the sake of kindness. I can be very persistent, I know. If there's something I want, I can make a darn' thorough nuisance of myself trying to get it, so I don't blame you."

"Blame me for what?"

"Being fed up with me pestering you." Gerard leaned against the stone parapet and reached out to clasp her hands in his. "Bothering you all the while – turning up at the house – plaguing you on the telephone."

Flora shook her head and smiled.

"You mean that *wasn't* the reason for your long, gloomy silences?" he asked on a note of hopeful eagerness.

Instead of answering the question directly, she said, "I didn't realise I'd been such a bore. How horrid for you. I can't think why you troubled to go on seeing me." She would tell him about Robert Wells, but not yet; it was too soon and too painful.

"You know why I wanted to go on seeing you." Gerard drew her closer to him and gave her another kiss. "I've fallen in love with you all over again, Flora . . . only this time it's not for a day, or even a year, but for the rest of my life."

Startled, she glanced up into his face. It was a good face, open and humorous and honest, and for a moment her heart gave a wild skip at the look she could read there in his eyes.

"I'm not asking you to give me an answer yet, my darling," he went on quietly. "I know it's probably a bit too early. But I *do* love you, rather a lot in fact, you must believe that . . . and I'd be proud to be a father to Imogen and little Bobby. I'm prepared to wait till you're ready."

Once again, she wasn't quite sure what to say. All of a sudden she felt overwhelmed, excited, confused, almost breathless . . . it was difficult to know which sensation was the strongest. She liked Gerard so very, very much; she valued his friendship, enjoyed his company, appreciated his warm affection for her children; and now – now – she was discovering something more, that it made her extraordinarily happy to know that he loved her.

She leaned her cheek against his shoulder. It was like coming home at last.

"Dearest Gerard . . . I won't make you wait very long . . . I promise."

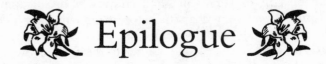 Epilogue

Roseen was bride's maid of honour at Annie Sutton's wedding. It was a bit of a poke in the eye for Aubrey Podmore, having his former mistress invited to share the nuptials, but Annie had insisted. Roseen was back to being her best pal again now and she'd share anything with her – even her old man – so they ought to let bygones be bygones.

Mr Podmore agreed, having small choice in the matter; but standing there at the altar in St George's church the thought had briefly crossed his mind that he'd rather have been marrying the bride's maid than the bride. He still carried something of a torch for Roseen, despite the way she'd acted, and at the reception after at the Criterion Hotel in Prince's Square it had taken a couple of double brandies before wedded bliss eventually caught up with him.

That reception proved an occasion to remember, what with the amount of drink everyone managed to swallow and still stay upright; the best man's speech ending in a fight between him and the bride's brother; and the mouse that somebody went and released under the fattest lady's chair, causing screaming hysterical mayhem in the place.

Roseen wouldn't have missed a minute of it, not for the world.

She had a postcard from Annie on honeymoon, showing a hand-coloured view of their Bournemouth hotel, with the cryptic message, 'Wish you was here'; and when the newly-weds were home again in Berry Street she paid a call, noting with a smirk to herself that Annie's act of being all sweetness and light had soon gone by the board now she'd got Podmore's ring safely on her finger.

That Easter, Roseen went with them both on a day's charabanc trip to Rhyl, and had enjoyed a bit of a mild flirtation with a young chap in Oxford bags who sang to her all the way back – 'Ain't We Got Fun' was her favourite just then – and asked if he could take her to the flickers the next week. She said no. It was four months since she'd had the abortion, and though her body was physically healed, somehow she couldn't bring herself to have any man touching her yet. Which was a shame, because that Freddy had seemed a very nice sort, and not half bad-looking, either.

He must have gone and taken a proper shine to her, though, since the next thing she heard, he'd been asking round the Podmores where she lived. Roseen had to give him credit for trying, at least; but still the answer was no.

By this time she was working at the old Dennison's Stores in Dudley Street, now the Home & Colonial – the very same place where she'd had her first job, thanks to Uncle George. Flora was the one who'd found her the employment, and Roseen appreciated that. It made her twice as glad that she'd done what she did, writing to that married chap on the Isle of Wight and putting a spoke in his wheel. Flora was looking a different woman these days; really blooming. Roseen liked to pay off her debts where she could.

The weeks went on towards summer. Annie kept going on at her to change her mind about walking out with Freddy. He was ever such a good catch, Annie said – he worked in Beatties' store, and his family had their own house over at Finchfield. She was daft, she was, to keep turning up her nose and saying no.

Roseen thought about it. She wished she could explain that although she did like him, the trouble was she didn't want to get too ally-pally, so what was the point. He'd soon grow fed up asking, she told Annie. In any case, she'd had enough of men for a bit. They were all after the same blinkin' thing.

Freddy Bradshaw wasn't another Maurice Lines, though; nor another Johnnie Driscoll. He was made of better stuff. Night after night after work he'd be waiting on the corner of Snow Hill in his little Austin motor-car, ready to offer a lift;

332

and night after night she refused. And that's how it went on for a while.

Then he started leaving bunches of flowers on her doorstep. He's courting you, that's what he's doing, said Annie. No one had ever courted Roseen before, not even Billy Kelly . . . well, not like this, not with bunches of flowers and little bits of poetry and notes 'from your truest admirer'. Come to that, she'd never had an admirer like this either, not one who kept his distance; the others had all been too flippin' busy breaking their necks to get her up the stairs.

It was nice to feel respected. It made her respect herself that little shade more.

Finally in June he sent her an invitation through the post to a Beatties dance at Wolverhampton Baths. A proper printed invitation, with her name *Mrs Roseen Kelly* written in copperplate; ever so posh. Annie went green when she saw it. She had to accept, of course. It would have been bad manners not to, when he'd gone to such a lot of trouble to send it.

What astonished Roseen was how much she enjoyed herself at that dance. Freddy looked really handsome in his evening suit and was very attentive and thoughtful – he'd even bought her an orchid for her corsage. Suddenly something magic was happening: she felt almost good as new. They made a lovely couple together on the dance floor, everybody said so; and at the end of the night he didn't go and spoil it all by making a nuisance of himself. All he did was kiss her hand and ask if he could take her out again.

This time she said yes.

After all, she'd got nothing to lose.

With a bit of luck she might even come out the winner for a change.